THE
LAST
ONE

THE LAST ONE

BOOK I

RACHEL HOWZELL HALL

RED TOWER
BOOKS™

Entangled Publishing, LLC
644 Shrewsbury Commons Ave., STE 181
Shrewsbury, PA 17361
rights@entangledpublishing.com

Red Tower Books is an imprint of Entangled Publishing, LLC.

Visit our website at www.entangledpublishing.com.

Edited by Liz Pelletier and Alice Jerman
Cover art and design by Bree Archer
Stock art by Kseniya Parkhimchyk/Shutterstock
Interior map design by Heidi Pettie
Interior design by Jennifer Valero
Interior formatting by Britt Marczak

Hardcover ISBN 978-1-64937-709-8
Deluxe Edition ISBN 978-1-64937-440-0
Ebook ISBN 978-1-64937-490-5

Printed in the United States of America

First Edition December 2024

10 9 8 7 6 5 4 3 2 1

RED TOWER BOOKS™

MORE FROM RACHEL HOWZELL HALL

What Never Happened
We Lie Here
These Toxic Things
And Now She's Gone
They All Fall Down
The Good Sister with James Patterson
What Fire Brings

THE LOU NORTON SERIES

City of Saviors
Trail of Echoes
Skies of Ash
Land of Shadows
A Quiet Storm

To Jill. Who knew?

The Last One is a tale of rage and magic—and the desires that set the world ablaze. The story includes elements that might not be suitable for all readers, including battle and combat, injury, death, illness, amnesia, grief, perilous situations, burning, poisoning, graphic language, racism, alcohol use, and sexual activity on the page. Imprisonment, assault, homophobia, and animal abuse are mentioned. Readers who may be sensitive to these elements, please take note, and prepare to enter the realm of Vallendor...

EAPONYS

EMPIRE OF
BRITHELLUM

SEA OF DEVOUR

MOUNT DEVOUR

CAERNO WOODS

PERIA

DUSKMOOR RIVER

HAFELD

PENEM

WEETON

CABURH

PETHORP

LINANDE

HAMOR

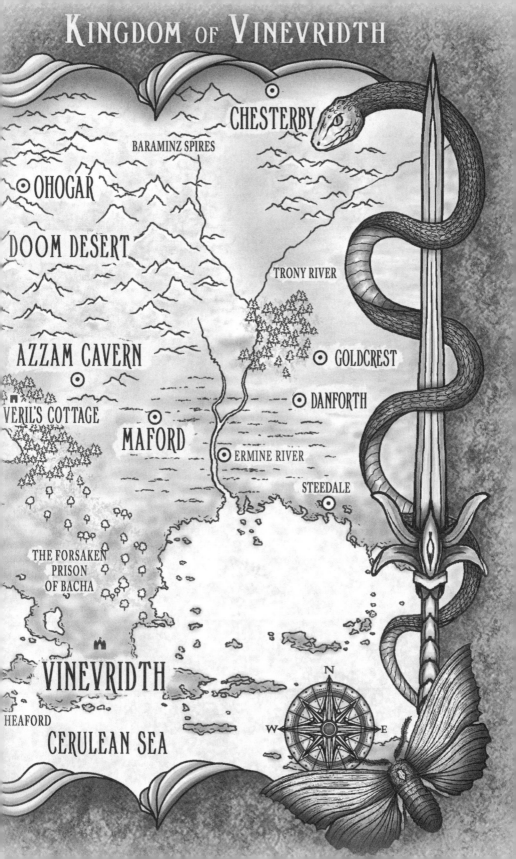

Kingdom of Vinevridth

CHESTERBY

BARAMINZ SPIRES

OHOGAR

DOOM DESERT

TRONY RIVER

AZZAM CAVERN

GOLDCREST

VERIL'S COTTAGE

DANFORTH

MAFORD

ERMINE RIVER

STEEDALE

THE FORSAKEN
PRISON
OF BACHA

VINEVRIDTH

N

HEAFORD

W   E

CERULEAN SEA

S

There are two sides to every question.

-Protagoras

PART I

WHEN A STRANGER COMES TO TOWN

In a land where stars make pearls,
A heroine awakens; her soul unfurls.
Through realms unknown, her path lies bare,
A future that she cannot share.

Hear the echoes in the breeze,
and hear the break of bending trees.
Enchanted woods and deserts grand,
In this land, she makes her stand.

Beneath the copse of leafy trees,
She fought with nerve, fell to her knees.
A warrior with a heart of gold,
with fierce ambition, with ire bold.

Hear the echoes in the breeze,
She is the one who will not please.
Tempestuous seas and mountains vast,
In this land, she stands at last.

In the maze of shadows dark,
Her mind reflects, her memories spark
The gods, they sing in realms above,
Her mother's journey, proof of love.

Through shifting sands and mountains high,
She pushed the wind and touched the sky.
A wand'rer true and heart so free,
Where dreams and truth sought to agree.

Hear the echoes in the breeze,
She is the one who will not please.
Endless meadows and steep plateaus,
In this land, she conquers foes.

As daystar sets in foreign sky,
A requiem and a lullaby.
The quilt shrinks to a cosmic strand,
Her legend hailed in this strange land.

—*An Elegy by Veril Bairnell the Sapient*

I open my eyes and choose violence.

Because I'm on my back and a woman is on top of me. Her pale hand is wrapped around my neck. She smells sickly sweet, she smells strange, and she smells foul. The whites of her large blue eyes are yellow as straw. With that smooth skin, she looks nineteen or twenty years old. Is she a thief? Is she a murderer?

Either way, she needs to get off me. So I slap at her ear with one hand and grab her fingers with the other.

"Oh!" Her eyes widen, and she successfully dodges my swipe. She tries to reel away but falls back over me instead. She gasps, and her rancid breath hits my nose.

I gag—*ugh!*—then squeeze her hand.

She doesn't wince even as I crack a bone in her smallest finger. No. She uses her free hand to dip near my neck. "Ha," she says with a grin. "Still got it."

I want to ask, *You still got what?* but my tongue droops in my mouth like a dying lily. I can't push out one word, and definitely not four.

The thief holds up a thick gold chain that sparkles in the light. A gold moth with ruby-encrusted wings dangles from that chain. The stone on the moth's thorax is the size of a robin's egg and as dark as the darkest night.

The pendant's clasp is as broken as I am, and my chest feels cold without that jeweled moth, oddly empty, like she's taken more than an amulet from me.

The thief yanks out of my hold and this time successfully scoots away. She tries to chuckle, but tears shine in her eyes as she winces and flexes her injured hand. "You didn't have to break every bone. One would've been plenty."

I open my mouth to respond—*I know you're not talking to me like that*—but the back of my head throbs, and my tongue is still stuck.

"But I'll take this necklace as an apology," the bandit says, scrambling to her feet. "Thanks." She winces again as she tries to flex her tender hand, then swings a knapsack onto her shoulder and winks at me. "Tah."

And just like that, she's gone, a flash through the grove of trees.

Did she just…? *Yeah, she did.* And…*"Tah?"*

With fire bubbling in my belly, I push up from the bed of twigs, yellowing leaves, and gray bark to follow her—but my legs flop beneath me, and I fall back into the dry rubbish.

What is happening? Why can't I stand?

My mind spins with dizziness and confusion. My feet were working fine just moments ago. I think. Because what was I doing moments ago before waking up with a thief on top of me? Uhh… I don't remember.

The rapid pulsing in my gut makes me look down to see my heaving chest protected by my favorite scarlet bandeau and—

Wait. Why the hell am I looking at my favorite bandeau?

My eyes dart to the stretch of mahogany skin across my belly and then farther down. The soil speckling my toes and ankles looks sickly gray, so stark against my brown feet, pinpoints of starlight against the velvet night sky.

I should not be seeing gray dirt. I should not be seeing my toes.

Where are my boots? Why am I so cold? Where is my cloak?

I squeeze the bridge of my aching nose.

Why do I see bare hands? Where are my gloves?

Shit.

That thief wore a bloodred leather vest, a bloodred hooded cloak, black leather gloves, and black suede boots. All of it hung off her like dead skin.

Why? Because that was *my* bloodred leather vest, that's why. And that was *my* bloodred hooded cloak, and those were *my* black leather gloves, and those were *my* suede boots that I'd finally—*finally*—broken in.

That *thief* stole my clothes. Left me wearing nothing but this bandeau and these black leather breeches.

I need my stuff, especially my amulet, and the longer I sit here, that tugging in my gut fades. Feels like something—*my pendant*—is pulling me to follow that bandit.

I try to yell, "Stop, thief!" but I can no longer see her—she ran into that copse of gray birches ahead. Words still won't work in my mouth, and trying to speak makes my head spin. But I don't need my mouth or words to catch a thief. Just my feet.

Still a bit wobbly, I push up from my nest of grass again, succeeding this time. I take a step...and then another step...and another.

Where did she go? I might not be able to see her, but I can still smell her. That distinct and unforgettable sickly sweetness means...

She's dying.

Yeah, death stinks. She didn't have any obvious injuries—besides the one I gave her—but there's something wrong with her. She looked like she hasn't eaten in several days. And her rancid breath. Some kind of sickness is eating away her insides.

That's when I notice it: a golden amber trail twisting through those ghostly trees, swirling over pink granite boulders and clouding the air. A golden amber trail that follows the thief's route through this forest.

I blink—am I seeing this stream of light because it's really there or am I seeing this stream of light because I hurt my head?

I squeeze my eyes shut, take several deep breaths, and open my eyes again.

Nothing else glows, not the trees, fallen leaves, or dirt. But that gold light remains, hovering, beckoning me to follow.

Amber must be the color of death here.

But where is "here"?

I push my fingers against my temples as though I can make another memory—*any memory*—pop into my mind. But nothing pops out. No memories left.

I don't remember roaming these woods. I don't remember the events that left me so unconscious that a bandit felt comfortable enough to steal almost every piece of clothing off my body.

I'll ponder these gaps in my memory later, hopefully with a pastry or two and a cask of rum. I guess some things, rum and cake, are more unforgettable than others. My mind pulls away from treats because I have a bigger problem right now: that cold and oddly empty sensation I felt waking up moments ago is now spreading across my chest and down to my belly.

"Cold" and "empty" are never good. "Cold" and "empty" mean danger. Even the simplest creature senses danger.

I may be near-naked, but I'm far from simple.

Yeah, I need my clothes. And my amulet.

I move faster, and my legs become steadier. Soon, I'm running, and pebbles, sharp rocks, and broken twigs stab the soles of my bare feet. Pain jolts through my heels and ankles, but I won't stop. Some walking corpse stole my stuff. And I *will* reclaim what belongs to me.

As I dart between the birches, I realize that almost every tree has holes and cracks in its bark. Thin, dying branches poke the sky, and the leaves crunch beneath my feet—more brittle brown than vibrant green, more dead than alive. The jagged rocks jabbing out of the forest floor have more hope of life than these trees.

Where am I? Such a bleak landscape should be memorable, but nothing makes me say, "Ah! Now I know!"

Rain clouds race above, their shadows darkening this dying forest. Swarms of mosquitos and hungry gnats drift through the hot, dry air and prick at me. They want a snack before the storm. Of course, I understand. Who doesn't like a delicious honeycake in heat like this? Still, these flying pests will have to catch me first.

Because I'm not stopping, not until my hands wrap around that *thief's* neck and squeeze until she takes her last breath—

Spots swirl before my eyes, and then my vision blurs, and I stumble and drop to the hard-packed earth. I'm shaky, and my stomach rolls, and I want to vomit into the piles of dry leaves. My head pounds, and I touch the back of my skull. *Oof!* Tender. A little swollen. I pull away two fingers. Blood. Not a lot, but enough. I stare at my bloody fingers and wait for this surge of sickness to pass.

What happened to me? Did someone kick me in the head? Did the bandit *kick me in the head? Was I pushed? Did I slip? Is slipping even possible in a forest this dry? And where* is *this forest? And why am I here?*

No idea, eight times.

Am I a hunter who bumped her head and lost her way? Is someone searching for me at this very moment, near tears, looking for me to round a corner or to appear on the horizon, fighting their growing fear that I've either fallen off a cliff or been eaten by a bear?

Again: no idea.

I do know this: after I retrieve my pendant, my clothes, and my broken-in boots, I will break that thief's other hand. Then I'll... I'll figure out the rest later once I'm fully clothed.

The nausea finally ebbs, and I lift my still-aching head and sniff.

Something reeks—and it's not me.

Thief!

I push myself off the ground and then push out a breath. *Go!* I race through the forest, my legs aching but stronger now.

That floating death trail still glows, but it's lightened from amber to cornsilk. And the pulsing…faint. The ghost trees thin, and the dirt trail becomes well-trod gravel. The scent of burning wood and the blossoming stench of decay tell me that I'm running in the right direction, that I'm almost there, that a thief will be at the end of this amber track, but I need to hurry.

Through the trees, I see buildings and smoke rising from chimneys. She must've run back to her town. Maybe I'll be able to slip through this village, find the thief, grab my amulet, and sneak back into the woods without being noticed.

Sounds like a good plan.

I burst from the grove and into the light.

The smell wallops me first—that sweet rot—and I push back a gag. I skid to a stop.

A noisy settlement sprawls out before me. Clusters of stone and straw-bricked houses with shingled roofs and chimney stacks lost in smoke sit along two separate gravelly footpaths. I count about twenty smaller wood cottages built behind a church, the common house, and a few shops. In the village's town square, a tall signpost has been jammed into the sandy earth. Atop the post sits a large wooden circle that has three paddles nailed across its top and three more nailed to the circle's bottom, with the middle paddle bigger and thicker than all the others. Raggedy carts filled with wares surround this signpost.

Looks like today is market day. Are most of the villagers browsing at the carts?

I creep closer, ducking along the dusty path, as inconspicuous as possible. The ground beneath my feet is more dried yellow tufts than emerald-green lawn, more burrs and foxtails than blades of grass. No water has kissed this piece of land in ages. I near what has to be a tavern—it stinks of ale, old wine, and sweat—and peek around its corner for a better view of the marketplace.

Twelve carts crammed into the town square. One cart holding bolts of fabrics, each a slightly different shade of beige. Other raggedy carts showcase bushels of sad-looking wheat, sickly vegetables, and animal hides, clucking chickens, bleating stunted sheep, and blocks of knotty lumber and charcoal. Everything lies baking beneath the daystar, the already-fading tapestries dulling and the shiny trinkets melting.

The village square buzzes with haggling voices and a lively minstrel's tune. Merchants bustle about, their hands moving quickly to arrange their meager goods into pyramids or towers. Villagers are purchasing items from these raggedy carts. They're shepherding those scrawny sheep down the road and counting wrinkled potatoes and withered turnips.

Where is the kaleidoscope of colors? The deep reds and yellows of spices? The vibrant greens and yellows of shimmering silk?

And the people here.

Swollen and thin and brittle-boned people. People with tangled hair, yellowed teeth, or no teeth, no longer handsome, no longer pretty, no longer upright. Gnarled and twisted people. Sandy-brown or dirty-blond hair that's cut short or pulled into a single ponytail, no parts on the left, no bangs in the front.

There are no reds or blues or yellows here, in ribbons, curtains, or flowers. No stars or birds or gems. The only jewelry: circular pendants with protrusions in the shape of boat paddles radiating from the edges, every pendant the same as the next. No one dares to stand out here.

But everyone glows amber.

With villagers this sick, and it looks like every villager is sick, should I be standing this close to them? Should I be breathing their air? Should I risk possibly catching their disease just to reclaim my clothes and pendant? Or should I let the bandit win for now, wait until death claims her—from the looks of this village, death *will* claim her—and then pluck my amulet from her lifeless, broken hand?

The pulsing in my gut intensifies, but that cold emptiness I've been fighting against has now reached my hip bones and the tips of my fingers. Should I stand here, succumbing to *that* instead of whatever sickness is making this village glow?

None of these choices bring me joy.

The decision is made for me when I spot her. *Thief!* She's talking to the merchant selling dull-colored fabrics and holding up one of my gloves! The merchant rubs my precious glove between his grimy fingers.

No, no, no. She's not selling my stuff.

I take a deep breath and hold it as though holding my breath will keep me safe. I take ten cautious steps, and then I lose that breath, exhaling loud enough for some villagers to hear.

And now, those villagers turn around and gape as they look up at me. Their faces show strain and stress, every eye following as I slip past.

So much for inconspicuous.

"Sweet cheese," a man shouts, gawking at me. "She's almost naked."

Two young women gasp and back away.

"What is it?" a young man wonders with tears of fear in his eyes.

"Have you ever seen a girl that tall?" an old woman puzzles.

"Her hair," a young man whispers. "It's so…so…"

"She's one of them."

"They're on their way."

"Supreme will protect us."

"Father Knete! Find Father Knete!"

"What nerve," they're all tutting.

Yeah, well…I woke up like this. In bare feet, I've chased a thief and found this village, all while being tall and naked.

What nerve?

I'm *all* nerve.

A tawny-skinned woman with long, coiled hair stands out in this field of faces. She wears a blue-and-green shawl, and she sparkles. Her glow is not amber-colored, though. No, her light reminds me of the nightstar's silvery halo.

Seated on a stool before her, a red-faced woman weaves a straw basket. She doesn't see or sense me staring at her.

There she is—*Thief!*—cradling her injured hand as she leaves the merchant to greet a copper-haired girl wearing a sage-green dress too dramatic for this doomed village. Another burst of color, that red hair and green frock. The two young women walk arm in arm, and other than the basket weavers, they're the only people who haven't noticed my arrival.

Above me, the skies turn slate as the clouds from outside this town catch up like they're following me. These clouds make the villagers look up to the sky in wonder. I glare at those clouds, hoping that the rain waits until I've completed my task and returned to…to…wherever I call home.

I slip from cart to cart, creeping toward the two women, skulking past stands of shriveled carrots and carts of hideous skirts and smocks. Hiding behind a cart painted with circles and paddles and filled with jewel-colored vials, I watch as the bandit marches up to another merchant, holding up my glove for his inspection.

This merchant tries to tug my glove onto his filthy hand.

No, no, no, absolutely not!

Furious, I pop up and accidentally knock over a display of vials, which break and spill liquids that smell of mint and fish.

The vendor selling these now-broken vials is a frog-faced man with boils on his neck. He shakes his plump fist at me and yells, "Cabbagehead!"

Cabbagehead? *Try harder, sir.* I roll my eyes and ignore his curse. I have no time for him today. I go back to following the thief.

"...just *lying* there," the bandit says to her green-frocked friend, my poor glove still in her grasp, "in the middle of the forest, wearing this killer outfit. So, I said to myself, 'Olivia, you will *kick* yourself for leaving all that haul on this poor girl's corpse, especially since these clothes will bring us closer to leaving this stupid town.' Obviously, she wasn't dead, so stop worrying about that. I didn't cause her to pass out, so stop worrying about *that*. She *did* hurt me, practically crushed my hand. My pinkie feels better, thank Supreme. But look at this!"

The bandit pauses long enough to grab some of the leather of my vest, gathering it beneath her breasts. "I can either take it all in, since she was bigger and taller than me, *or* I can make an entirely new outfit using all the fabric from the cloak. We could sell it for a hundred geld. *Two* hundred geld."

"I wish you wouldn't do things like that," Copperhair murmurs. "Yes, these items will fetch a fine price, but it's like you're a grave robber."

"I told you," the thief says, her confidence flagging, "she wasn't dead. I promise you."

Copperhair sighs. "It *is* a nice vest. And the cloak—I absolutely love the color."

Hearing these two talk about my possessions makes my vision shard, and I now see countless bragging thieves walking arm in arm with countless copper-haired girls. I make a choice and pounce, shoving the clearest bragging thief.

Copperhair shouts, "Olivia!"

Olivia shrieks as she flies across the square and lands with a bang against a crate of rolled rugs. She groans and writhes in pain with her eyes squeezed into slits.

In two steps, I reach her, straddle her on the dirt, and wrap my hands around her neck.

Her jaundiced blue eyes sparkle, bright with fear and surprise. She coughs, and her life-beat thumps wildly against my palms as her pulse slows.

"Hello," I say, "it's me again."

Words! I finally have words. Gripping my hands around her neck has somehow loosened the strangled cords in my throat, and now, words slip between my lips like honey and smoke.

Copperhair has words, too, loud words, and she screams, "Help! Someone, stop her!" as she pounds my back.

I ignore the redhead and continue to squeeze her friend's neck. I may not know who I am or how I got here, but I *do* know that I will be made whole once my boots are back on my feet and my pendant is hanging again around my neck.

But as I squeeze, something, maybe a memory, flitters in my mind. Someone, somewhere told me that I am too quick to act, too quick to judge, too impatient to make the best decisions, that I need to consider the consequences more carefully.

Okay. Fine. I'll work on my personal growth *after* I handle this fucking thief.

Because at this very moment? I'm living my dream. "How does it feel, huh?" I sneer at the bandit, all my senses shaken and stirred. "How does it feel to wake up with a stranger's hands wrapped around *your* neck? How does it feel to be—?"

"Stop!" a man shouts.

"Never," I snap, my eyes still on my prize.

"You will cease this immediately," he demands, his voice raspy and gruff.

"No, I won't," I say, my teeth gritted even as Olivia tries to smack away my arms.

"Stop," the gruff-voiced man repeats, "or I'll—"

"Or you'll what?" I challenge, still grinning, though, at the criminal now caught between some rocks and my hard hands.

What's the worst this stranger can do to me?

Something cold and hard presses against my cheek.

Ah.

That.

I don't know who I am or how I got here, but I *do* remember weapons of war.

They're sharp. They're pointy. They're dangerous.

And I don't have one.

Yet.

2

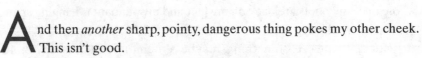

And then *another* sharp, pointy, dangerous thing pokes my other cheek. This isn't good.

Villagers crowd around us, everyone glowing amber.

Life isn't going so well for them, either.

Will any of us be left standing at the end of this day?

Some villagers close their eyes and pray:

"Strike down this creature, Supreme."

"Banish it from our presence, in Your name…"

Cold sweat creeps across my forehead.

Strike down? They're praying for my death!

"Sweep this pestilence from this earth."

"Protect us from this vile one."

I just want my things. Why can't I just have my things? My stomach roils again, and that surge of sickness I'd experienced earlier makes me close my eyes.

"You move again, and you die," the gruff-voiced man warns. "Now. Slowly. Take your hands off her." But his voice doesn't sound as solid as his swords.

Still, I'm not interested in dying today. I growl at the girl trapped beneath me, then slowly release my grip around her neck, leaving behind two scarlet bands on her pale skin.

The man sheaths one of his swords, yanks me by my elbow to my feet, and spins me around to face him. He shudders as he looks up at me, then shrinks back until he squares his shoulders, remembering that *he's* the one with dual blades.

The faces of the traders manning the closest carts are twisted in fear and shock. They move in front of their trade, arms folded, to protect their potatoes and pottery from being destroyed or stolen in the commotion. Other traders are closing up shop altogether, shaking their heads and glaring at me for causing a disturbance.

"Those eyes!" a tinkly-voiced woman behind him exclaims. "Do you see her eyes? They're gold, like a cat's." She tugs at his filthy tunic and cries, "You're the guard, Johny! Do something! Stop her!"

Stop me? From doing what? He's the one holding a weapon on me.

Johny sheathes his second blade, tightens his grip around my arm, then pridefully lifts his lantern jaw. "We don't like mudscrapers in this town."

Mudscraper? I'm no mudscraper.

If anyone looks like they've been scraping mud, it's this man, with his goofy rusted helmet and shabby, stained smock.

Be better than them, Johny. You can do it! I need you to be better!

"That Gorga attacked Olivia for no good reason!" Copperhair yells as she tries to pull Olivia to her feet.

I snort, then say, "Oh, I have a *very* good reason."

Olivia falls back on her rear, out of breath. She manages to croak, "She assaulted me!"

"Don't look at her eyes," that tinkly-voiced woman insists. "You'll be cursed if you look at her eyes!"

Everyone ignores Tinkly Voice's warning as they gape at me.

Coil-haired Nightstar Sparkle, who'd stood by the basket weaver, now comes to stand beside me. She's stooped, older, as I see her this close. She quickly sweeps her hand over my ear. *"You can't be here,"* she whispers. But she isn't whispering—she hasn't even opened her mouth.

What new trick is this, and why can I hear...?

As she gathers the shawl around her thin shoulders, the woman's voice buzzes in my head. *"You don't belong here."*

My jaw goes slack. How can I hear her?

"This is a gift," she says—no, she *thinks. "Don't expect any others from me."*

My shock quickly converts to ire, and I now glare at her.

First of all, I didn't ask her for any gifts, especially to hear the thoughts of others.

And second: *"No shit I don't belong here."*

I mean...these people are praying for my *death.*

The woman gives me the smallest headshake. *"I know."*

I shudder. She heard me?

Her lips become a tight line. *"Yes, I heard you. Now, listen: leave as soon as you can."*

I lift my eyebrows. *"How am I supposed to do that?"*

Above us, the sky turns heavy and those puffy white clouds roll back to let charcoal ones roll in. Around me, some villagers and traders gape at the sky as an excited hush settles over a town that hasn't seen rain in ages.

"I *said*, what's your name?" Johny the guard shouts, shaking me by my arm. "Don't make me ask you again."

My mind spins at his question but stays blank. I can't even suggest one possibility. My mind stops spinning, leaving me with the soft noise of empty space.

Not good.

Still, I lift my chin and stick out my chest. "You may call me... Call me..." Sweat now beads along my forehead, and my mind starts wheeling around my head again. "My name is..."

Cassandra? Rose? Marget?

None of those sound right. None of those *feel* right.

Why do I know these names but I can't remember my own?

Johny squeezes my arm.

Yeow! My knees buckle.

"And where are your clothes?" His beady eyes linger on my thin bandeau and the curves beneath it. His gaze sits like a boulder on my chest.

I nod toward the thief named Olivia. "*She* has my clothes. She *stole* my clothes."

Here I'd hoped that Johny would be better than them. By the way his leer claws at my skin, though, I see that he's worse.

I yearn to scratch out his eyes. And I will. Sooner rather than later. First, I need my stuff.

"Arrest that mudscraper!" a woman wearing a dirty bonnet shrieks. "Arrest her for attempted murder! For indecency!"

The air turns even thicker as the clouds push down and the villagers press closer around me. I'm overwhelmed by the pungent scent of a hundred bodies, their sweat and fear mingling with the smells of sheep, dust, and rotting vegetables. Market days are supposed to smell of spices, fruits, and freshly baked bread. Not shit and sheep.

The villagers continue to babble.

"Nothing good ever happens when strangers come here."

"She's cursed by Supreme. Just look at her!"

"Them circles on her bandeau! Witchcraft."

"Can you see the drawings of elk and whirly things on her pants?"

Some think their thoughts while others whisper to one another and to the skies like they're wishing upon a star. So many judgments against me, in fear of me, a witch and now a sorceress, and their words collide in my head and burst my heart. All of it hurts and threatens to rip me apart. All this glowing amber light makes my eyelids twitch, and this noise makes recalling my name impossible, and I want to close my eyes for relief and to remember. But there's no time or space for that.

I don't belong here? No shit.

Once they quit whispering and take a breath, once they let me explain, they'll understand. They'll say, "Oh, well, that's reasonable," and then they'll turn to Olivia and say, "Stop being an ass. Return her things at once." And then Olivia will give me every item that she stole. Then I'll leave their grubby little village, fully dressed, and I'll never come back.

Johny shakes me by the arm. "You wanna act tough in my town? We'll see how tough you are."

I desperately lock eyes with Nightstar Sparkle, the only person in this village who might be on my side. But she merely tilts her head and watches. *"They do not understand, child. They are dying and desperate. They will see you dead, too, if you continue this path."* Her thoughts stand as bright and apart from the others as the daystar.

"That's why they're glowing amber, isn't it?" I ask, directing my thought to her.

The woman gives a small nod.

"Come on, stop dawdling." Johny yanks me away from the market and pulls me down a dirt path that becomes rockier with each step. Out of the corner of my eye, I see Copperhair using the tail of a cloak, *my* cloak, to dry tears from the bandit's pink cheeks.

Obviously, I didn't choke Olivia enough—she's still standing here, breathing.

Why isn't Nightstar Sparkle speaking up for me? She knows that I've done nothing wrong. Why was she kind only to abandon me now? I'd rather have her speak on my behalf than give me the "gift" of hearing the thoughts of dunderheads.

With some of the villagers following us, Johny pulls me to a squalid bungalow that thrums with death glow. A bronze oared circle is nailed above the door of this windowless hut, and the soil around it is thick with brown and putrid green clots. Fat, happy flies bumble around the iron door. By the smell of it, there's plenty here for *them* to eat.

Many people have died in this rancid shack. Many people are *still* dying in this rancid shack, and though I can't see them through the open doorway, I see their amber silhouettes crammed together like this guard's teeth. I can't hear their thoughts, though. Perhaps that's because the people jailed within these rotting timber walls are barely alive.

"This one's well-fed," a villager remarks. "She'll last a nice long time in the clink." Then she spits at me and thrusts a totem of that symbolic circle in front of my face.

"No sores on her skin, either," Dirty Bonnet adds, clutching a smaller totem but reluctant to hold it out. Amber glows brightest around this woman. The sore on her top lip weeps with pus and feeds the other poisons streaming in her blood. She *needs* to worry about her failing heart instead of tormenting me.

"That'll change in the clink," Spitter says.

They laugh.

Where is Nightstar Sparkle? I search for her in the crowd. She's gone.

Panic rises in my chest. This is worse than cold-emptiness. I *know* cold-emptiness. But this feeling is terrifying. I know of panic, but I've never panicked. Until now. Between the ire of these villagers and my inability to remember one damned thing, I'm...overwhelmed.

"Is it safe to keep this one locked up with the other prisoners?" an older man with rotten teeth asks. "If she's a wraith, she might suck the life out of them in there."

"But wraiths don't look like that," Spitter says. "Wraiths got that crinkly skin and them pointy fingers. They don't touch the ground, neither. This one, though. Look at her. Stompin' around on them big feet she got."

"So, what *is* she?" the man asks.

I try to take deep breaths, but no deep breaths come. I want to scream, "I'm no one, I'm nothing, just let me go," but I need to breathe to scream. I can't breathe, I can't scream, and I can't think because I'm panicking because I can't breathe. *Overwhelmed.*

"She's Gorga," Dirty Bonnet says.

Gorga? That verbal slap stops my mind's spiraling.

"Gorga aren't real no more."

"Maybe she's Jundum. They've cursed this town before. Brought in the Miasma."

Jundum? Mias—what? What are these people *talking* about? This is outrageous. This is preposterous. But this detour into the absurd offers me something to grasp. What ridiculous notions of who and what I am will I hear now? I may not know much about myself, but I do know that I'm not a fucking troll or a Gorga.

Spitter says, "She's one of the Vile."

Dirty Bonnet sucks her teeth. "But aren't the Vile the most beautiful of them all? She's not beautiful."

"Not at all," Johny says.

I can't believe these horrible people are saying such horrible things. I can't believe these horrible people with their rotten teeth and dirty hair, their bleeding sores and warty noses are calling *me* vile. A small part of me wants to laugh, but most of me wants to weep.

Their noise and their smell make my knees weak, and not one person in the crowd says, "Maybe we're being too hasty," or "I think we should hear her out," or any word that would make them stand apart from their hive.

I wobble in Johny's hold. His hands burn my skin, and his touch twists something deeper, something untouchable down in my core. Despite the almost overwhelming stink of this jail, I want to lean against its closest wall just to remain upright. Just to find balance before figuring out my next steps, figuring out a way to escape this monster's grip.

But Johny won't let me go, and so I have no place to rest except against *him*.

I grit my jaw. *No. Never.* I'd rather sink here, right outside this prison, and let all of the crap from every village in this realm ooze over me until I've drowned and awakened in the presence of their beloved Supreme.

Far-off thunder rumbles across the hills, and the breeze picks up to become wind, distracting the crowd. Those clouds that followed me to this village at last open, and rain drifts like shredded veils from the sky and softens the hard air. Soon, raindrops pebble on top of the villagers' amber glow. The water hits me, too, and I feel heavier, weaker.

The crowd gapes at the weeping clouds. Spitter cries, "Hurry! Get the buckets!"

The now-muddied pathways clear as villagers run to houses and return outdoors to set pails on the gravel paths, on the dried grass, and beneath the eaves of every building. *Clink-clink-clink.* Fading colors darken because of the falling water. Tree leaves swell as the parched earth sucks up raindrops the moment they hit the dirt.

The traveling merchants shift nervously before their carts. *A naked wraith and now rain?* They find tarps and canvas to cover their wares, then return to gawking at me.

Johny's grip never loosens around my arm, despite the commotion. Not a single drop of drought-quenching rain distracts him from his job. He whistles, then shouts, "Narder! Got another one for you."

"You can't arrest me," I spit. "I've done nothing wrong."

A man with a rusted key tied to his waistcoat clomps through the rain toward us. His thick eyebrows slash down, and his eyes scratch like talons across my skin. His long, pockmarked face needs soap and water. Flies swarm around him like pets.

"Johny!" he booms. "What do we have here?" His voice rattles with phlegm and evil.

"A new plaything for you," the guard says. "Isn't she a sight? This one's goin' around town, scaring people, and bein' a real nuisance. We can hold her here in the clink for now."

"Why are you punishing *me*?" I point to the bandit and Copperhair, who are now gaping at the wet sky. "*She's* the thief! Arrest her!"

Johny tightens his grip around my arm even more, and I wince.

"This isn't right," I protest.

No one backs me up.

My heart drops to my stomach—if I go into this building, I know I'll never come out again. At least not as the me I'm supposed to be. But there's nothing more I can do beyond shout, "Let me go!" and thrash against the guard as I try to break out of his hold.

Johny's hold, though, is too tight and too sure.

Fury and fear surge in my chest once Narder grabs hold of my other arm. My legs sag in strength, and though I'm fighting to hold my ground, my bare feet slip in the new mud. I want to wail out of anger, out of frustration and bewilderment, but I refuse to shed a single tear even as the two men drag me closer to my doom.

"Oh yeah," Narder the jailer says. "She's definitely a feisty one."

"And I'm gonna tear her apart," he thinks.

"You touch me," I snap, "and I'll—"

"And you'll what?" Johny squeezes my arm until I squeal. To Narder, he says, "She's mouthy, too. I know you like 'em with a bit of fire."

Okay, so I'll slay Johny first, and then I'll slay Narder, but only after I slay—

"Stop!" a woman shouts.

Only after I slay *her*.

The thief—Olivia—charges down the muddy path, her expression panicked but petulant. Somehow, she's quickly changed her clothes and is now wearing a black brocaded cloak and a blue dress with a waist cinched just below her breasts. That isn't my cloak across her shoulders. What did she do with my vest and pendant? Those black boots on her feet belong to me. And those hot-pink handprints around her pale neck? Those belong to me, too. A stuffed leather satchel hangs off Copperhair's shoulder. Did they hide my things in that bag?

"This is none of your business, Olivia," Narder growls.

"I wish to drop the charges." Olivia's eyes look wild in the rain, and she's gained a shitload of composure and authority since we shared space moments ago. Now, with her shoulders back and chin high, she glares at the men standing before her. "Didn't you hear me? I'd like for you to stand down, please."

The guard and jailer look at each other, then throw their heads back and laugh.

"She's talking like she's the queen," Johny says, snickering.

"Stand down, please," Narder mocks, his voice high.

The crowd laughs. The death-glows that had been glaring around their bodies and around the guard and jailer have nearly faded, thanks to the rain.

"This isn't a joke," Olivia sniffs. "Release this young woman immediately. Please."

"Under whose authority?" the guard sneers, all humor gone. "Oh. That's right. You have none, you simpleminded liar. You're not fooling me again. Not after that last time."

Olivia flushes as she shakes her head. "This is all one big misunderstanding. She thought I'd stolen something of hers, which I hadn't, of course."

"Empty your pockets," I demand. "Empty that bag! She's hiding my amulet."

The guard yanks me. "Quiet."

Olivia throws me an annoyed glance, and I hear her thoughts more clearly than I hear my own: *Sweet Supreme, lady. Just shut up and let me handle this.*

To Olivia, the guard says, "You know the drill. Empty your pockets. *Now.*"

Olivia pulls out one of the cloak's pockets. Empty. "Satisfied?"

"Lemme see the other one," the guard demands.

Olivia hesitates, grumbles, "Fine, whatever," then pulls my pendant from the cloak's second pocket. Her cheeks and ears grow hot pink.

"I told you! That's mine!" I lunge for my necklace, but the guard jerks me back.

Icy-blue lightning sizzles across the sky, turning those dark clouds lilac. In the distance, villagers whoop and throw down more buckets. *Clink-clink-clink.*

Maybe my captors will be struck by a bolt or two.

Johny laughs as he taps at my pendant. "All this commotion over *this* piece of trash? This necklace looks like something my granny would wear."

The jailer joins in the laughter.

Even Olivia cracks a smile.

"Stop," I plead, near tears. "Just give me what's mine and I'll go." My legs weaken even more, and I go limp and slip out of Johny's hold, sinking to my knees. Feels like lightning is crackling across my scalp. At least the rain brings some relief.

Olivia observes me with concern before turning to the guard. "Let's make a deal, just like before. You let this woman go, and I'll sell the pendant in Pethorp and split the geld with you. With everything happening right now because of the drought, I know you need geld. And you know that *I* need geld—"

"It's not yours to sell," I yell from the mud. "You can't sell it. I won't let you."

"Shut yer trap." The guard tosses the pendant to Olivia, then kicks my arm, sending me facedown in the wet earth. And just like that, I *am* a mudscraper.

"Stop," Olivia begs. "You're hurting her."

Narder scoffs. "She's Dashmala. They don't feel no pain." He kicks me in the side. "See? She didn't feel that."

I definitely felt that. Heat sizzles into my bones and burns my breath away. The hurt in my ribs radiates in every direction—from my smallest toes all the way to my teeth. Defiant, I push myself and sit back on my heels to glare at the guards.

"Never seen no Dashmala warriors anywhere in Maford or in Pethorp," Narder says. "Looks like she's dying, full of disease. She looks *dry*. You know, like how dirt turns hard right before it stops growin' carrots and tatos? Same thing with this one. I know hard dirt when I see it, and trust me. This girl's hard dirt."

Olivia's expression flashes quickly from alarm to anger. "That's clearly not true. She's *not* hard dirt! Look at her!" She pushes Narder away from me. "Please stop."

With his palms up, Narder backs off, chuckling at Olivia's efforts. "Can you believe that one?" the jailer asks the guard.

"Okay, you'll release her now?" Olivia slips my necklace back into her cloak pocket. "On my honor, she won't give you any more problems. You must believe me."

"Believe you?" Johny says, his eyes wide. "Your *honor*?" He flicks his hand at her. "You're nineteen years old. You don't have no honor. And those bronze cups you sold me last week never did hold water."

Olivia shakes her head. "This is different, though—"

Johny runs his tongue over his fleshy lips as he regards Olivia. "Did you hear me? I'm not taking part in your little rackets no more. So why don't you go play with your needles and threads before I arrest you for disturbin' the peace."

"Yeah," Narder says, "you don't got no say around here."

"But *I* do," a deep voice rumbles from the crowd.

3

The man who just spoke is broad-shouldered and two heads taller than the tallest man in the crowd. His walnut-brown hair is swept back from his forehead. The crowd parts as he strides toward us, his head held high. The whites of his blue eyes aren't jaundiced like the others'.

He is a gift, a wonderful distraction, a respite for my eyes in this shit-colored town.

I blink at him, forgetting for a second that I'm incredibly pissed off, in pain, and on my knees in the mud. Because, *sweet honey in the rock*, if this is the man who's gonna save me, I'd let Johny capture me all over again. Not really. But still…

Gorgeous comes to a halt beside Olivia and rests his fists on his hips. He hasn't escaped this town's grunge. There's a soiled bandage wrapped around his large right hand, and grime dirties the nail beds of his left. If he lived somewhere other than here, he'd be a dashing knight or a powerful sorcerer. Too bad he's a no one stuck in a shit-colored town. He gives Olivia a hard look, and then he turns to stare at me with his brow furrowed in concern.

"What's going on here?" Gorgeous asks Olivia.

"Jadon, it's all a misunderstanding," she says.

"Just another mess your thievin' sister made," Narder sneers. "Okay, Jadon. What wisdom will you impart to us lesser creatures today?"

I lift an eyebrow. *Well, Jadon?*

Frowning, Jadon rubs a hand along the day-old growth of beard on his square jaw. I can hear his thoughts directed at his sister. *"Again with the drama, Olivia? Why do you keep doing this?"* Then his eyes return to mine. *"Poor woman,"* he thinks. *"Poor, beautiful woman."* He clears his throat and points at Narder and then points at me. "Help her up, Narder," he commands.

Narder grumbles as he reluctantly yanks me to my feet.

Jadon pivots to Olivia. "What did you do to her?"

"Nothing," Olivia says. "I didn't hurt her. Really, this has all been a terrible misunderstanding and it's gone too far now."

"Then tell me about this misunderstanding," Jadon says, giving me the "I'm here, so you're okay" nod. His eyes skip over me to make sure that's true. His gaze lingers on my hips, and one thought breaks past all his other thoughts. *"Sweet Supreme. Even with mud everywhere..."*

In any other situation, I would've wholeheartedly agreed with his assessment and cracked, *"Right? I am* stunning. Thank you for noticing." But I'm covered in dirt and chicken feathers, and Narder's meaty hand is still wrapped around my arm. If Jadon wants a personal tour of my secret garden, he needs to first fix his sister's mess. And then he needs to find me soap and clean water. Also, a few pastries, a cask of rum, and all my stolen belongings.

"I'm trying to explain, but no one is listening to me," Olivia grumbles. "It's really quite simple. See: this poor lady thought I had something of hers, and so we fought, and, well, I tried to run, but she fell on top of me, since it's so slippery around here with this sudden shower, and isn't it great that we're finally getting some rain?"

"Okay, okay," Narder says, rolling his eyes.

"Olivia," Jadon warns.

"It's all a mistake," Olivia continues. "Really, it is. So I—I mean, *Jadon*—would like to drop the charges."

Awed, I tilt my head. "You are nonsense."

"If you only knew." Jadon's glimmering eyes catch mine before focusing on his sister. He's a few years older than Olivia, maybe twenty-three or twenty-four, but with the gray circles beneath his eyes, it looks like he hasn't slept *ever.* How many "misunderstandings" a day does Olivia have that require his diplomacy?

"I'm sorry for this," Olivia says to Johny and Narder. "Aren't we just trying to survive? Aren't we all just keeping our heads above water? Making a wave when we can?"

More nonsense.

"Olivia, you're being ridiculous again." Jadon pushes out a breath, then turns to Johny and Narder. "Even though Olivia is...*Olivia*, she's right. The crops aren't feeding the village. No one can afford anything, even food. I mean, really. Look at how pitiful this market is." He gestures toward the sad collection of wagons set up in the town circle with the vendors still watching us.

On cue, a wheel on a wood cart breaks, sending withered turnips and wrinkled potatoes rolling into the mud.

Jadon shakes his head and looks back at Narder and Johny. "Everyone's exhausted, which means tempers are running high. But let's just take a breath and apologize—"

"Apologize?" I interrupt. "She stole my belongings." I don't care how handsome he is, he's not convincing me that I'm wrong nor will I allow him to calm us all down without fixing the problem.

"Fine." Olivia takes a deep breath, then slowly releases it, just like her brother did. "I apologize…Forest…Girl. I didn't mean for you to suffer."

"I still need my belongings," I say, holding firm.

"What about Freyney's cart and those broken vials?" Narder asks Jadon, ignoring me.

Oh. Yeah. That. I did knock over a few things before vaulting into the air and landing on top of a thief.

"And what about the public disturbance she's caused?" Johny asks. "Everybody—especially you—should be celebrating. Cuz we finally captured one of theirs! And you couldn't have missed that she's standing here naked."

Jadon makes a strangled noise in his throat, and by the way his mouth tenses, he already knows he's about to stumble over every word he wants to say. So, he just says, "Hmm."

Yeah, he noticed.

"We need those medicines," Narder continues. "Are you willing to pay for that?"

"*Pay?*" Jadon barks, able to speak now. "Absolutely not! I don't have money to pay Freyney, of all people."

"Then she'll work off her debts," Narder says.

"*What?*" I shout. "I'm the one who's owed a debt—a debt of my belongings."

"Where's she supposed to stay while she's working off her debts?" the jailer growls, ignoring me again. "There's no place for her to lodge. Not for her kind, at least." He pauses, then holds up a filthy finger. "*Hey!* I got an idea! She can stay in my lovely penal accommodations here." He leers at me. "*Or* she can choose to roost in my cottage."

"Bed's big enough for two," Johny says, elbowing him, "now that Marget's dead."

I shiver as I glare at both men. "I'd rather sleep with dead Marget."

Olivia flings out her arms. "She'll board with us."

Jadon and I both startle. He says, "No, she won't," at the same time I say, "No, I won't."

"There's room in our barn," Olivia says, nodding. "Good. Lovely. It's settled." She eyes Jadon, then turns back to me, beaming. *"It's settled,"* I hear her think. *"Now please shut up."*

The guard points at Jadon. "You'll make sure she pays Freyney all that he's owed? If I'm just eyeballin'…twelve geld will make it right."

"Twelve?" Olivia repeats, not taking her own advice and shutting up. "Aestard killed his father last week and had to pay only three geld."

"His father was a blasphemous jackass and deserved to have his neck slit," Johny spits. "Anyway, six geld for Freyney and six geld for the town disturbance. She's disrupted market day, and now the wanderweavers may get the wrong idea—that we tolerate thieving, mudscraping Dashmala, that our people run around naked, tipping over carts and causing havoc. And if they stop comin' here, we won't get any fresh veg or *good* wine or anything else we need to survive. Six geld to Freyney, six geld to me. Don't make me increase it to seven apiece."

"But why is her price so high?" Olivia asks.

"Olivia," Jadon snaps.

Johny bends until he's face-to-face with the thief. "It's the price she owes. And if she runs off, it's gonna be the price *you* owe, and she'll bring all of 'em back here, so I suggest keeping an eye on her. Otherwise, Narder and I will come looking for you to pay up."

"We still haven't addressed the fact that she took my belongings," I snarl. "When are you going to fine *her* twelve geld—?"

Johny spins toward me, one of his swords held high.

I duck and prepare to be struck.

"Don't." Jadon doesn't shout, but the guard jumps back and immediately freezes as though Jadon had.

My heart pounds in my head. I can't feel anything else because I'm numb.

"Put your sword down, Johny," Jadon says, a glint in his eye. "Now, tell me, one reasonable man to another. How is she supposed to earn twelve geld when no one in this village has enough money to buy food?" He turns to the jailer. "Narder, any ideas?"

"Don't know," Narder says. "But if you can't figure it out quick, she goes to jail."

My breath catches. "But I didn't do anything."

"Your handprints are *still* around Olivia's neck," the guard says.

The thief nudges Jadon, who has now closed his eyes and is pressing the bridge of his nose. His lips are an angry white slash against his face, and the muscles in his jaw tense.

I know simmering anger when I see it, and this man is simmering.

Olivia nudges Jadon harder. *"Sweet Supreme,"* she's thinking, *"say it so we can go."*

Jadon's eyes pop open, and he growls, "Stop," at his sister.

My heart races from the threat of Johny's sword and the fear that Jadon's about to say, "She's on her own," and that I'll be dragged to the house of poor dead Marget against my will.

Jadon continues to simmer, and he keeps squeezing the bridge of his nose. But his eyes catch mine, and his face relaxes. *"I can't let them hurt her again."* That's what he's thinking. He makes an assured nod and says, "Fine. We'll figure something out."

And I allow myself to breathe.

Narder pulls me so close that I can see the pores on his face and the purple veins that travel across his nose. "You will pay off your debt," he says to me. Then he whirls to Olivia and Jadon. "She skips town, you're paying the geld. If I were you, I'd hold that ugly piece of jewelry as bond until she makes it right."

I gasp. "That's not—"

Johny whirls back to me, his scowl deeper than before. "Maybe I'll take it. Melt it down and make me a spoon and some nails with it. You want that instead?"

I give the guard the smallest headshake. My eyes sting with tears as I imagine my pendant melting over some blacksmith's fire.

Johny leans in even closer and jabs his finger at my chest. "You will attend the next Assent and ask Supreme for forgiveness. And when you've done that, I want you outta my town. We don't want your kind here. Go back to those savages and butchers who sent you here to kill us and tell 'em we're protected by Supreme."

He pauses, then adds, "And if you don't stop glaring at me with them wicked eyes, I'll chop your head off."

Wicked eyes. Fine. Sure. Whatever. I agree with Narder on one point and one point alone: I want out of this town, and as quickly as possible.

"Go!" The guard pushes me away from him.

Jadon and Olivia catch me before I scrape the mud again.

Fire speeds from my elbows to my lungs. I wobble out of their hold and try to exhale as that fiery pressure wanes. At least I'm free from Johny's touch. A small victory. But now my possessions will be held hostage by two strangers. A bigger defeat.

Together, we watch Johny tromp back toward the crowded village square as Narder turns his attention back to that putrid prison.

The small audience disperses, hesitant to return to their scrawny sheep and carts of withered potatoes. The minstrel restarts his wandering and sings off-key to the strums of his out-of-tune lute. The sound of rain and geld patter against the tables. Everyone's trying to find calm so that market day can carry on. The threat—me—has been handled. For now.

I once again scan the crowd, hoping to find Nightstar Sparkle, but she's gone. So gone that I wonder if she ever existed.

Jadon points at his sister, teeth clenched. "I'm tired of cleaning up your messes."

"I've heard it before," Olivia trills and starts walking.

A lock of Jadon's thick hair falls over his forehead. He's coming undone. He runs a hand over his head to push it back and attempts to shoot me a quick glance. His breath stutters, I know it does, because his skin flushes and he forgets to finish yelling at his sister.

I raise an eyebrow and smirk. He's having a hard time unsticking his eyes from mine.

Yeah, I'm sticky.

He stops trying to look away and chooses instead to walk backward, settling in, never breaking eye contact with me.

Oh. Shit. He's calling my bluff. This time, I blink first. Heat blooms under my skin as I nervously flick mud off my arms. I sneak another peek. He's still looking at me, and my face grows hotter still.

"Don't look away," he thinks. *"Don't look away. She's still looking, yes!"*

My heart jerks in an uneven stutter as our gazes hold.

Apparently satisfied, he turns back to Olivia, his scowl more relaxed than before, and I can finally draw a complete breath.

"You're gonna get *both* our heads chopped off one day," he tells his sister. "Now put out some buckets to catch the rain before it stops." Without uttering another word to me, he strides toward the edge of the village.

Face still warm, my lips quirk into an almost smile. *Look at him.* All weary and worried, and above it all, all sass and ass. You *go*, Jadon.

Olivia rolls her eyes, then yells after him. "It's too late for buckets, Jay. The rain's already stopping." To me, she says, "I really *am* sorry. We needed money. If you can't tell, we're not exactly thriving in this place. Just a suggestion: maybe you shouldn't fall asleep in the forest next time?"

Her tone is almost kind, but her words still make me bristle. "Just a suggestion," I snap. "Maybe *you* should try not to steal things that don't belong to you. You're gonna take from the wrong *mudscraper* next time, and you'll suffer a fate worse than handprints left on your neck."

Olivia raises her hands. "Got it. Understood. Never again."

I hold her sincere gaze for a moment, then nod. "So, now what?" I swipe at my muddy pants, then glare at the thief standing before me. "Where am I? What town is this?"

Olivia sheds her wet cloak and drapes it across her arm. She waggles her eyebrows and grins. "Welcome to market days in Maford, Forest Girl. You're gonna hate it here."

4

Olivia runs to catch up with her brother. "Jadon, stop."

Despite the cramping around my ribs, I forge ahead after them, recoiling as I walk barefoot on slimy dirt and sharp pebbles. I wish I had my clothes, or even just my boots.

The rest of Maford unfolds before me. I may not remember where I came from, but I know that I've never seen a village like this. Maford couldn't have always looked and smelled this rank. Right? Straw- and timber-built shops lean into one another like bitter old men and gossiping hags. Peeling paint and warped wood tell tales of neglect and misfortune. Over there sits a tavern that stinks of stale ale, and beyond it, a schoolhouse with hay poking out of its two windows like spiky innards. The rain has brought out a new odor—damp stone combined with decaying wood—and it lingers above the stench of death.

These villagers may not be able to fix every shop and home, but they could certainly clean up sheep shit and maybe even stow trash in one dedicated space. If it rains hard enough, maybe floodwaters can knock everything down so that they can start over.

One can hope.

One can also hope that I'll be long gone before this place is wiped off the map.

Olivia is still trying to calm Jadon. "Relax, brother. It's not that big of a deal."

Jadon's head snaps her way, his worry lines etched even deeper into his forehead. "Any time you say that, it means it's definitely that big of a deal."

Olivia stomps ahead of us.

For several moments, Jadon and I walk in silence, side by side. I'm uncomfortably aware of this man, so dichotomous to these pitiful surroundings.

"Charming town you have here," I say finally, wearing a sarcastic smile.

His gaze, so moody and sullen, meets mine and instantly changes. A muscle in his jaw flexes. Any minute now he will burst into flame. And honestly, I might join him. But then his hand finds his hair again and he exhales. So maybe no flames after all.

I lift my chin and try not to laugh. I've got him all worked up and confused, and we've only just met. I don't plan on staying in this town longer than necessary, but maybe we'll have a good time before I leave. "That was a joke," I say. "I think a cemetery placed in a swamp is more charming than Maford. And you…"

He finally cracks a smile, and his eyes spark. "Not charming enough for you?"

"Can you both button your breeches, please?" Olivia snaps, waiting for us.

Without another word, he marches ahead, his sister hot on his heels.

As much as I want to enjoy watching him stomp away, though…

Geld. I need it. My amulet. I want it. This place. I hate it.

Just *thinking* about working for anyone in this town makes me boil. How long will it take to do what I must before I can leave? Maybe I can take my shit without anyone knowing and slip into the night like a phantom. Let the true culprit in all of this, Olivia, figure out how to pay off that twelve geld.

I follow the siblings to a grove of blue firs near the edge of town. I hear Olivia saying, "…couldn't let her stay there."

We're heading toward a stone house with a thatched roof and a dying flower bed. Another stout dwelling squats beside it, smaller than the house and covered with soot. The yard is also covered with soot, and black dust has settled on every surface, including the small circle-with-paddles nailed above the barn doors.

"Jadon," Olivia continues, her voice prickly, "are you even listening to me? We may be poor right now, but we're not despicable. You know what unspeakable things Narder does to some of his prisoners. Were we supposed to just let her *rot* in that place?"

Jadon shoots his sister a glare, then looks back at me. "I don't want you rotting anywhere. Please don't think that. It's just…complicated." He nods at Olivia. "And she knows it." His shoulders rise and fall as he takes a deep breath. "I'll get blankets." He heads to the nicer cottage.

Wide-eyed, I ask, "What unspeakable things does Narder do to prisoners?"

Olivia grimaces. "Didn't I just use the word 'unspeakable'?"

I hear her thoughts, though, and those things Narder does to some of his prisoners are so unthinkable that I shiver in horror. Those poor souls locked in that horrendous jail. "Why won't someone stop him?"

"We've tried, but everyone's scared of him. You saw how no one spoke up. How no one stopped him from grabbing you like that. Jadon's come close to killing Johny a few times, but he doesn't want me in danger if something happens to him.

"*And*," she continues, "Narder arranges for the wanderweavers to include us on their market routes. They're a traveling market, basically, and they bring us food and goods, and we sell things in return. Sometimes, I sell a few of my dresses. My brother's a blacksmith. From spoons to swords, Jadon Ealdrehrt crafts the finest tools on this side of Aldon Lake, but since no one's around to help him at the forge, he can't take time off to go purchase supplies at another village. We'd starve and freeze to death if it wasn't for the wanderweavers, so—and it pains me to say this—Narder has to stay."

The wanderweavers. A thought flares in my mind. Maybe that's it. Maybe I was traveling with them, and bandits were robbing my group, and I tried to escape, but one bandit caught up to me, and we fought, and he hit me on the head, I blacked out, and he left me for dead.

My skin flushes, and I look back to the village square and those traveling merchants plying their wares. Maybe that's why my clothes are fancier and brightly colored. Because I roam from one town to the next with a caravan of wanderweavers. But if I'm one of those merchants, someone would've recognized me. I *do* stand out. Someone would've fought for me and demanded my freedom. They would've pooled their geld and paid my bond.

That didn't happen, though. The wanderweavers looked at me like the villagers had: a giant near-naked stranger chasing a tiny, sickly villager from cart to cart.

No, these merchants can't be my companions. I need to leave as soon as possible. Maybe I *will* slip out tonight… I point at the gloves on Olivia's hands and the boots on her feet. "I'm taking back my things. Every single item. If that means more handprints around someone's neck, then so be it."

Olivia curtsies, then says, "Of course."

"Do you mean 'Of course' as in 'You'll get your clothes back'? Or do you mean 'Of course you want your things because everything you had on was really nice'?"

I can't determine her intent. How honest can she be wearing someone else's boots?

Olivia tousles her hair. "I mean of course we'll return your things after you've earned the twelve geld. I know: It's awful how all of this turned out, but the law is the law, and we can't afford to have you running off. However!" Smiling, she holds up a finger before I can protest. "I'll let you borrow some of my clothes in the meantime. They're almost as fancy as yours."

Hearing the thoughts of others—this gift of mine courtesy of the woman with the silver glow—would be a glorious trick if there was also a bullshit-truth-telling crystal built in. Guess I can't have everything.

"And I'll even wash your clothes before I hand them back," Olivia offers. "Can't have you walking around in muddy leather, can we? I must admit—I felt pretty audacious wearing all your things. This weird energy was rushing through me, like I could lift a house and eat thirty chickens, and I felt my scalp tingling like my hair was being stretched, and I don't think I would've been able to stand in front of Johny and Narder demanding your freedom if your cloak and vest and moth charm hadn't made me feel *invincible*."

Her neck blazes red as she meets my gaze. "Is that how it feels to be you? Invincible?"

I blink at her, fists balling at my sides. "I wouldn't know, since I don't have my cloak and vest and moth charm at the moment." Deep down, though, I *do* know. If that cloak was just a cloak, I wouldn't be standing here right now. If that pendant was just some random piece of jewelry, I wouldn't have risked being assaulted by two despotic shitbags. An ordinary pair of boots wouldn't pull at me the way these boots are pulling at me right now.

Olivia only says, "Hmm," and points past me. "That's the barn. You can stay there." She isn't pointing to the nicer cottage with the cute yellow window curtains.

I cough and choke out, *"There?"*

There is where sharp, pointy, dangerous things hang from hooks, dangle from stands, and rest near an open firepit. *There* is where an anvil lives, looking heavier than all of creation and blacker than the space between the realms. *There* is where all things smell burned and sulfurous, wood-smoked and dirty. There's a waterwheel behind the barn, but it doesn't turn—there is no water. It's as useless and broken as the rest of this place.

Olivia follows my gaze. "You'll sleep in the loft over the forge. Jadon won't be too much of a bother. He's usually more polite than he's acting at the moment. But he also gets cranky when he's frustrated or hungry or breathing, so please excuse his bad manners. We were raised better than that. Well, *I* was raised better than that."

I ignore her, since she's still wearing boots that she stole from me as I was passed out in the woods, and is that something her parents would be proud of? But I don't ask any of this. Instead, I focus on one of those wooden circle-with-paddles above the doors of the shack I'll be occupying. "Tell me, what is that?"

She turns to see what I'm looking at and scrunches her eyebrows. "Seriously?"

I blink at her. *Well, what is it?*

"It's a colure."

"What does it signify?"

"The three sculls up top represent man in his three states: baby, adult, old. The two sculls beneath represent animals and nature. Dogs, bears, mountains, lakes. The circle in the middle is the emperor, supposedly. And the big scull at the base, holding everything up, is Supreme. Naturally." She pauses, takes a breath, then continues. "You've heard the fable. Excuse me, I mean, the very true account of the realm's very beginnings, yes?"

I shake my head. "No."

Confused, she squints at me. "Where the heck are you from, then? Everyone everywhere has heard the story." When I don't respond, she shrugs. "Well, according to Emperor Wake…" She dramatically clears her throat. "In the beginning of the world, Syrus Wake was born, the first child of the original man and woman. And because he is the long-living, immortal firstborn of the first race, he is to be worshipped."

She glances at me, clearly enjoying her role of storyteller. "Not only that, he claims that the entire realm of Vallendor is his birthright, and so he has declared that, as emperor, he is the center of the colure and that his empire of Brithellum—which is north of here—is the holiest place in the entire realm. All those who disagree, including the kings and queens of the still-free provinces across Vallendor, are usurpers, and they must be defeated and the people converted."

Olivia pauses, brushes some stray hairs from her forehead, then adds, "Not one ruler believes this, by the way. Maford falls under the reign of the Vinevridth province, ruled by King Exley, and he refuses to bend the knee. Most people here in Maford don't believe the emperor is really Supreme, but there are a few who do, and they're powerful. Father Knete, he's a true believer, as is the mayor. I'm sure there are other spies around."

She flicks her hand at the colure. "You see these everywhere so that Maford can exist in peace so that if—*when*—Wake's men come, they might not be as violent."

"So you're surrendering to Wake before he even arrives?" I ask, frowning.

I can't imagine refusing to fight for what I believe in, and giving up before the fight even begins. How pitiful is that?

"We're just a hundred or so people," Olivia says, looking slightly embarrassed. "Very hungry and sick people. We can't defend ourselves from an army as big as Wake's. He's unmatched in might."

I narrow my eyes. "So believe in me or die?"

"Yes."

"And he thinks that divine power works like that? That someone's fear of dying is better than someone choosing to believe?"

She snorts. "You're asking questions like you're brand new to Vallendor."

My face flushes. I don't remember any of this, so, yeah, in a sense, I am brand new. "I just wanna know what kind of town I'm in."

"Ah," she says, squinting at me. "Any more questions?"

"Before Wake declared himself the center of the colure," I say, "what did the colure represent?"

Olivia shakes her head. "The colure didn't represent anything if you chose not to believe. People did their own thing. Prayed to whoever they wanted to pray to." She moves closer to me and whispers, "Some people who shall go unnamed still have other talismans up. Blue eyes, carved pieces of ivory, small paintings, other gods. You know, the goddess of rain and the god of bountiful crops and all that. Those charms don't work, either. Probably because people hide them in their attics or the granary. They'd be called primitives and heathens, children of the Vile. The Vile One is the ultimate evil being who wants to destroy all of what Supreme has created."

I ask, "How do you know about paintings and icons and all that if they're being hidden?"

"Because I make dresses," she says with a shrug. "I visit people in their homes. Since I'm handy with a needle and thread, they ask me to also repair rugs and curtains. A few times, I've stitched up a gash on someone's leg. In those kinds of situations, though, people forget to hide their altars.

And to be perfectly honest, what others believe is none of my business."

I rub my chin, thinking, then point to the colure above the barn door. "So, do you and your brother think that's bullshit or...?"

Olivia arches an eyebrow. "Of course, we believe that the emperor is Supreme." She holds my gaze and thinks, *"What if she's a spy from Brithellum?"*

"You don't have to worry about me," I say to assuage her suspicion. "I obviously don't know the first thing about Wake. Don't care much for what I've heard."

Olivia clears her throat, and her eyes drift behind me. "Brother, you're back. Are you still angry?"

Jadon joins us holding a stack of quilts. "I'm exhausted, Olivia. This could've gone worse than it did. What would've happened to her if I was in Pethorp?"

"Thank you for your concern," I say, my throat tightening at his sincere worry, "and for coming to my aid. I do appreciate it."

"Yeah, of course," he says, meeting my gaze. "It was the right thing to do. I would've done it for..." He looks away. He doesn't say "anyone" because he knows that's not true. I don't even have to read his mind to know that he's trying not to think about me the way I know he wants to think about me.

Whatever he needs to do to walk straight and focus.

"Let's get you settled." He beckons me to follow him into the barn.

I can't help but appreciate how his arms, shoulders, and back flex as he climbs the ladder to the loft with those clean, soft quilts.

"None of this would've happened," he says from up high, "if you just resisted the urge to be a criminal, Olivia."

"I'm not a criminal," she sniffs. "There are perfectly good reasons for swiping. Feeding your family, for instance."

Jadon climbs back down the ladder and stands over his sister. "Did you or did you not swipe her clothes and pendant?"

Olivia tilts her head as she pulls the amulet from her pocket to examine it. "You say 'swipe,' I say repurpose and reuse." When neither Jadon nor I react, she scowls at me. "I thought you were *dead*! Why were you out in the woods anyway?"

I open my mouth to retort, but for the first time, I don't have anything to say. Uneasy, I make a fist and bounce it against my lips.

"What's wrong?" Jadon asks, stepping toward me.

Revealing the truth will render me vulnerable, but they'll figure it out eventually. I take a breath and stare at one of the soot-covered, knotty-wooded poles that support the barn loft before confessing, "I don't remember anything before waking up with Olivia *swiping* my belongings." Saying this feels like I'm overreacting and wrongly accusing Olivia of doing something horrible. But she stole from me. I have nothing to be ashamed of.

"When you say, 'anything,'" Jadon says, "does that include where you're from?"

"Yes." Desperation bordering on panic tightens my throat. "Not my name. Not my town. Not one thing."

Jadon gapes at me.

Olivia gasps. "Maybe you were dropped here by a giant eagle who caught you for dinner or—" She gasps again. "Maybe you're a hunter and you were hiding in a blind and a falling star hit you and knocked you out of a tree. Or maybe you were in a gigantic explosion, like a volcano eruption."

"A falling star?" Jadon asks incredulously. "A volcano? There aren't any volcanoes in this part of Vallendor."

I want to laugh, but something stays my humor. Maybe the Olivia-concocted giant eagle bullshit theory could also be part possibility. A hunter in a blind. Now, *that* scenario feels right. Maybe not a volcano, but something explosive had to have launched me across the forest.

"Or…" Olivia grins and then snorts. "Maybe you were flitting about in the heavens, napping on your perfect little cloud, and then, out of nowhere, that falling star hit you and sent you tumbling down, down, down until you landed here."

Falling star. Something about *that* tugs at the back of my mind.

"Don't be ridiculous," Jadon says. "That sounds—"

I hold up my hand to stop him. "Why do you say a falling star?"

"Because," Olivia says, "I saw this bright light streaking down from the sky, and I ran into the woods to see what it was, and I found you."

Jadon gapes at his sister. "You're not serious. People don't fall from the sky."

I hold up my hand again. "Did I fall far? Was there fire or smoke? How long between when you saw that bright light streaking down and when you found me?"

Olivia shrugs. "I don't know. Not long?"

"If Olivia really saw something," Jadon says, "it really could have been a falling star, like she said."

I say, "Hmm," unable to say *no* outright.

Because there's something to this story. I feel it. Like a burr on my sock. Like a fly buzzing in my ear. The more I think about it, the quicker my heart beats. Are there mountains around here? Geysers? Anything that I would have fallen from? A giant eagle? A tornado possibly? Falling. Hitting my head from the force.

A gust of wind could've carried me from wherever I was and lost some of its power and dropped me in the woods. There were clouds and rain in a town that hadn't seen wet weather in a long time. "Was there wind?" I ask. "From which direction did I fall? Straight or slanted?"

"I don't know." Olivia throws her hands up with a frustrated huff. "All I know is, I saw a burst of light and found you sprawled out there, beneath the trees. You weren't moving, you weren't breathing, but you had on that fierce leather vest and that absolutely ferocious cloak, and it was like… like…someone pushed you off the fancy-nancy cart and left you there to die. Then I saw that necklace!"

Olivia pulls the pendant and chain out of her pocket and strokes the black stone in the moth's thorax.

My fingers itch to yank it from her thieving hands, but my yanking could result in some private time with Narder. So I hold—for now.

"All these jewels caught the light, and Jadon—" She spins to her brother, who's staring at my amulet with his brow furrowed. "We're *really* not in a position to just leave treasure sitting there on the ground!"

"It wasn't sitting on the ground," I retort. "It was dangling from my *neck*."

"And I thought you were dead!" She massages her temples as though she has a right to have a headache. "I thought that I could sell all of it for food, for iron, for something, *anything*." When Jadon says nothing, she adds, sheepishly, "I would have come back to bury you."

"We can solve this right now," I snap. "Give me my stuff back and I'll leave."

Jadon heaves a resigned sigh. "I apologize. I'm sorry you're in this position but…"

"But *what*?" I prompt, impatient.

"We can't." His eyes soften. "You heard Johny. He threatened all of us." And he thinks: *"And that's bullshit, too. I hate every second of this conversation."*

"And why are you in a rush anyway?" he asks aloud. "If you don't know who you are, how do you know where you're supposed to go?"

"Maybe having my possessions will open something up in my mind?" I say, pressing my forehead to staunch the ache emerging behind my eyes. "Like how certain smells make you remember things? The aroma of cakes baking reminding you of childhood? Or how hearing a certain song makes you cry? I don't know. Just let me hold them so that I can see if that works."

"We can't," he says. "I wish I could. And I wish I knew how you could've fallen from the sky, but I'll help you figure it out as much as I can, which may not be much." Jadon offers a miserable smile, then studies his sister. "You didn't have to do this. We wouldn't be here—she wouldn't be here—if you'd just…"

"So what's changed?" Olivia asks, truly perplexed. "You've never asked me before where I've found things. You're just happy to have the money."

"Oh, I worry about the way you acquire coin," Jadon corrects, "but I also know convincing you to stop would take more breath than I can draw."

I roll my eyes. "Young people these days."

He folds his arms. "I blame the parents. Back in my day, we kept our hands to ourselves."

"Very true," I say.

"What?" Olivia spits. "Neither of you are that much older than me."

I cock an eyebrow. "You don't know how old I am. *I* don't know how old I am." But after the day I'm having, feels like I've been alive since the beginning of time.

We're saved from any more discussion when a dog with a mottled black coat and icy-blue eyes scampers into the barn.

"Milo!" Olivia stuffs the amulet back in her pocket, scoops up the dog, and waggles his paw at me. "Forest Girl, meet—"

The toothless dog growls, barks, and lunges at me.

I hop back. "You know what, Milo? You need to relax."

"Milo!" Olivia says. "Bad dog!"

The dog whines, then nestles his face in the crook of Olivia's arm.

My eyes narrow. "Don't worry about feeding me. I'll just eat *him*."

Olivia chokes. "Huh?"

The dog whimpers.

I wave my hand dismissively. "Changed my mind. He's probably full of worms anyway. Last thing I need right now is some weird disease that makes me grow a tail." I look over my shoulder at my bottom. "Don't wanna mess up perfection, know what I mean?"

Olivia looks at her own rear and snickers. "Not at all."

"Let me take him back to Gery next door," Jadon says, sneaking a peek at my perfection. Don't even have to hear his thoughts to know he agrees. *Perfection, indeed.* For a hot second, he meets my gaze, and my pulse goes *boom.*

This time, I *do* throw him a grin. *Caught you looking.* I'm *this close* to turning completely around so that he can fully appreciate me—because I'm *that* helpful.

Before I can perform this charitable act, however, Jadon plucks the dog from his sister's arms. Milo licks his face and then snarls at me one last time.

"Fine," I say to him, "you don't have worms."

Milo barks, then wags his tail.

I scratch the top of his head. "Who's a good boy? *You're* a good boy, aren't you?"

Once I have my clothes, I will leave this death village, and I might just invite Milo to travel with me. And maybe I'll ask Jadon to join me, too, at least some of the way.

Olivia pulls her short hair into a messy bun and taps my shoulder. "Are you hungry?" She ambles out of the barn and toward the nicer dwelling, the one with the curtains the color of the daystar. "You're in for a treat," she says. "I made potato-and-leek soup."

On cue, my stomach growls. "I'll eat anything."

5

But I'm not eating anything before I find soap, water, and something decent to wear. I won't spend another minute looking like I've been dragged across all of Maford in the rain. I've remained in this village long enough for the daystar to slip across the sky and drift down to the horizon in the west. Which means that the Ealdrehrt cottage sits at the southern edge of town. Good to know if I try to escape.

While Jadon returns Milo to Gery, Olivia hands me a bar of soap, a washcloth, a large brown tunic, a pair of dark boots, and a blue dress. "You'll need to fit in more if you want to avoid Narder's attention. Not wandering around naked will help."

"You think?" I ask, a smile playing at the edge of my mouth.

"You can sleep in the tunic," Olivia says. "It's Jadon's old shirt, so it's a little big but more comfortable than wearing just your muddy breeches and bandeau. And tomorrow, you can wear the dress. It'll be a little short on you, but once you've bathed, we can see where it falls so that I can adjust or find you something else sooner rather than later."

She leads me to the other side of the barn, entering a dark nook with a barrel of water hidden behind a wooden divider. "For a little privacy. You can wash up back here, okay?"

After Olivia wanders away, I peel off my breeches and bandeau and set them on the closest bale of hay. The cold water makes me shiver, and the soap smells like licorice and vinegar, but the washcloth helps scrub the mud away along with some of my anger and frustration.

Clean now, I tug the short-sleeved peacock-blue dress over my head. Its hem is lined with yellow felt circles and diamonds. The dress is tight around my chest and hips, and I wince—sore from the jailer's kick to my ribs—but there's give in the sleeves. The blue material scratches against my skin, but I'll survive. As Olivia predicted, the hem skims the middle of my calves and hits the cuffs of my borrowed boots.

Olivia returns to the nook, and her gaze immediately snaps to my dirty clothes.

I know what she's thinking without even listening.

"I could try them on, just to see—"

"Don't even think about it." I throw her a scowl that tells her, *promises* her, that my hands will wrap around her neck again if she even *touches* my last two possessions.

She slips her hands into the pockets of her skirt. "I was just admiring the circles on your lovely scarlet bandeau. And those elks on your leather breeches? Absolutely fabulous." She then angles her head as she peers at me in the dress. "Not perfect, but it'll have to do. No one here in Maford is as tall as you. Except Jadon."

I turn this way and that, looking at the pattern on the cloth as she pulls strings and fastens buttons. "What do the circles and diamonds signify?"

"Huh?"

"Strength? Wisdom? Holiness?"

She blinks at me. "I think they're pretty."

I wait a beat, then say, "You just put shapes on your clothes because they're pretty?"

"Umm... Yeah?" Olivia plucks the seams on my shoulder and sleeve. "I'm guessing that circles and diamonds mean something wherever you're from."

I stare at the elks on my breeches and nod, wishing I knew more about their meaning. But I *do* know they mean something.

"Good clue," Olivia says, tapping her chin. "You can't be from Pethorp. They see even less meaning in things than we do. Or maybe—" She gasps. "Chesterby! It's far, far north of here, high up in the mountains past Baraminz Spires. We got word not too long ago that Chesterby was totally destroyed by an earthshake, and that a fire spread across the mountains, and that people from Chesterby and the small towns around it were displaced."

Chesterby. My body shivers just thinking the name.

"You know what else?" Olivia leans in, lowering her voice to a harsh whisper as if she's sharing choice gossip. "They say that a lot of strange animals folks had never seen before lost their homes in the woods and started wandering south looking for new forests." She straightens, and her face brightens with excitement. "Maybe you were trying to escape the fires and a giant eagle that used to roost in those trees spotted you, thought you were food, picked you up, flew around looking for a place to eat, and accidentally dropped you." She places her hands on her hips, obviously proud of this story.

I want to smirk at the image of a giant eagle, but I can't shake off the sensation of falling. It wouldn't explain the great light in the sky, though. But still... *Chesterby.* The name pricks like needles in the back of my brain. I cock my head. "I think you're onto something. And those people saw meanings in shapes?"

Olivia shrugs. "No clue, but I think I'm onto something, too." She smiles and pats herself on the back. "Good job, Olivia. So now, we just need to find someone who can tell us what elks mean and if the people who lived in the northern mountains believe that circles hold a mystery. Or we can find someone who's been to Chesterby."

"Is there anyone in Maford who can do that?"

She laughs. "Nope. All the sages left this town ages ago. Jadon may have an idea. We'll ask him over dinner."

My muscles ease now that I have a few, very real possibilities.

Olivia tugs at the hem of my borrowed dress. "Jadon and I will be leaving Maford very soon and settling in Vinevridth next. There's no sickness in the kingdom city. And there's more food. Cleaner water. He'll start another forge, and I'll open a shop—I'll have you know that you're wearing an original design. Soon, I'll be known throughout the kingdom for my dresses, and I'll dress all the fancy royals in O.E.C. originals—that's Olivia Ealdrehrt Creation."

I trace a finger over the tight, even stitches on the sleeve cuff. "I'm sure you will." Really, the needlework in this dress is impressive. Customers would probably even sit through her winding monologues to wear dresses this well-made.

"I'll clothe regular people, too," Olivia continues, her expression soft and dreamy, "but the rich... They'll be able to introduce me to merchants who sell silks as soft as butter. And they'll commission gowns decorated with the finest jewels in the realm. You know, the wealthy have so much stuff they don't need, they practically toss their jewels out with their bathwater. So why not use them to fancy up a gown? Wouldn't that be amazing?"

She circles me and clucks her tongue. "Maybe you wouldn't be surprised by what the wealthy do. Maybe you already know about that kind of life. Because maybe you're from one of those fancy places and not some mountain town like Chesterby. Maybe even a different empire. Like

Brithellum—I can see you there with your great taste in clothes and…"
She clicks her teeth and bites her upper lip before saying, "Okay, don't
take this the wrong way."

I steel myself for whatever offensive thing she's about to say.

"But…what *are* you?" She studies me, eyes narrowed. "Half human
and half what?"

My belly fills with prickly heat, and the breath from my nostrils singes
my top lip. My words flow like slow lava across my tongue. "What kind of
question is *that*?"

"Because," Olivia continues, oblivious to my anger, "your eyes are this
really weird gold. And then your hair. What color *is* that? Seriously, it just
looks *impossible*." Olivia must not sense the danger she's in, because she
reaches out to touch my impossible hair.

I swat her hand.

She hisses with pain. "*Damn!* Why'd you hit me?"

"Don't *ever* do that," I say, finger in her face.

Wide-eyed, she nods, then goes back to observing me with a probing
gaze.

But I take a breath and ask myself the same question. I can hear the
thoughts of people, and I somehow survived a fall from the sky. Maybe
that *does* mean I'm more than human.

"Or maybe…" Olivia fluffs out the skirt of the blue dress and yanks
away another loose string. "Johny kept calling you 'Dashmala,' but you
don't have those bone things on the sides of your face. Maybe you're a
mage-in-training. You look like you're around my age. You're what, twenty?
Twenty-one? Definitely too young to be a full-on sorceress."

It's a good suggestion, and probably closer to the truth than me being
inhuman in some way. Because if I were more than human, why am I here?
Why is my body so weak? That woman with the silvery glow saw something
in me and gifted me with hearing the thoughts of others. I doubt she'd give
that ability to just anyone. Maybe *she* knows what the elks mean.

I need to find her.

"It's a good suggestion," I say, "me being a mage."

Olivia's skin flushes, and she jams her lips together. "If you are," she
whispers, "you can't tell *anyone*. Don't suggest it. Don't even *say* the word
'magic' or 'mage' or anything that would suggest such an idea. You're safer
being a barbarian than a mage. The mayor and Father Knete forced all the
magic-makers out of Maford, never to be seen again, including the sage

who could've told you about the elks and circles. I'm being very serious right now. Please don't say anything. You're already in trouble."

Pulse racing, I nod and say, "Okay." I take off the blue dress and pass it to Olivia to make her adjustments. Then I pull on Jadon's old tunic.

As I follow Olivia to the front of the barn, I cast my eyes toward the rest of drought-choked Maford where the sky has forgotten how to cry—at least until I arrived. Perhaps I should forgive this place. Thirst can turn men into monsters, with every act of kindness received with hostility, scrutinized for the dagger hidden beneath the thoughtfulness.

Are the towns beyond this place just as dry, just as angry?

Olivia dashes into the cottage to finish preparing dinner just as Jadon returns to the barn from Gery's with a new bale of hay. Seeing me again, he double takes and says, "Oh. Hey." His eyes linger on his brown tunic now on my body.

I blush and hold out my arms. "Hope you don't mind. Olivia loaned it to me—"

"No," he says, shaking his head. "I don't mind at all. Looks better on you anyway." He smiles and continues tidying up the space.

Right as I find a clean bale of hay to sit on, I catch my reflection in a cracked mirror placed near the barn door. The world spins, and my mind pops. *There I am!* My hair is a cloud of mulberry-sapphire-blue and cinnamon-hued curls. No wonder Olivia's fascinated.

My reflection in the mirror blurs for a moment, and my brain hums. I blink, concentrating on my image as it gradually comes back into focus along with a hard truth.

"My name is Kai." My voice sounds distant in my still-fuzzy brain.

Jadon meets my eyes in the mirror, and my breath catches at his intense stare and rigid posture.

Olivia strides into the barn carrying a pot, looking from me to Jadon and back again. "What?"

"*Kai,*" Jadon says, shoulders relaxing. He smiles. "That's pretty."

Olivia grins and places the pot on Jadon's worktable. "You remembered your name?"

I nod, still studying my reflection.

She runs over and hugs me. "That's wonderful! Aren't you happy?"

Near tears and shaking, I let out a long breath and fan my face. "I am." Knees weak, I sink onto the bale of hay and clutch my elbows. Remembering something as simple as my name has sapped all my energy.

"Kai: that's a little strange for this part of the world," Olivia says to Jadon. "Don't you think?"

Jadon nods. "What about your family's surname? Kai...*what*?"

I level my shoulders and force myself to will the shakes away. "My surname?" I start to speak—the answer is right there, on the edge of my memory, and I can almost touch it, but there's blank space there and thick quiet. I shake my head. "*Kai* have-no-idea."

Olivia snorts.

Jadon says, "Ha."

"Would that name come from Chesterby?" I ask.

Jadon frowns. "Chesterby?"

Olivia nods. "We think maybe that's where she's from." Then she offers her theory about the destroyed town, the eagle, the symbols on my clothing. And now, my name.

Jadon says, "Hmm. They kept to themselves in Chesterby. Didn't want outsiders coming in. They had a lot of old customs, I hear, and a different belief system. Now we just need to find someone who knows more about all that."

"But first," Olivia says, "we'll celebrate over bowls of soup!"

We aren't eating dinner in the house. Instead, Olivia and I sit on the cleanest of the smelly bales of hay in the barn's doorway, balancing bowls of soup on our knees while Jadon huddles over his bowl at the workbench.

The food looks rank and the surroundings ranker.

The wood of the barn creaks and groans. Not a pleasant sound. A slight breeze brings with it the stench of a dying river and ailing horses. From the farm next door, a woman coughs. She sounds really sick, and her coughs are deep and wet, like she can't breathe. A man from the same farm joins her with his own cough. His cough doesn't sound as dangerous as hers, though he's not too far behind. Annoyed with the newest sounds and smells of Maford, I shift my gaze from the colure above the door to the soot-covered ground and then down to my bowl, filled with a pasty white substance that I'm supposed to eat. *Oh, sacred paddle-circle thing.*

Protect me from this place and from this meal.

The coughing next door starts up again and makes this goopy soup look even nastier.

"Why are we eating out here?" I ask. "Wouldn't it be easier for you, Olivia, if we ate inside? That way, you wouldn't have to go back and forth, carrying a heavy soup pot and bowls."

The siblings exchange a look before their gazes lower. There's silence until Olivia clears her throat. "It's just more refreshing outdoors."

"And there's a sickness going around town," Jadon says. "Something called Miasma. That's what you're hearing next door at the Gerys' farm."

"I'm not sick," I say.

"But we may be." Olivia doesn't look up from her bowl of soup. "We just may not be in the 'hacking up a lung' phase yet."

"It's *very* contagious," Jadon adds.

Olivia offers a sad sigh. "Very contagious."

"You don't want to risk it," Jadon continues, "especially if you plan to leave Maford after paying your fine. You don't know how your body would react to it."

"If Miasma's so bad," I ask, my eyebrow cocked, "then why haven't you left?"

Jadon smirks. "I don't know where you're from—"

"She doesn't, either," Olivia adds.

"But it takes geld to pick up and relocate." He dips his spoon into his soup and takes a bite.

All of this may be true, but none of these factors are their current concern.

"We can't let her in the house." That's what they're thinking. I don't want to be in their dirty little house anyway. My stomach twists. I'm not sure that I *haven't* caught the disease. Since washing up and pulling on Jadon's shirt, I feel slower, constricted, and there's this weird pressure against my chest. A feeling beyond the cold emptiness that I've experienced since waking up in the forest. This newest sensation, I thought, was exhaustion. Chasing Olivia through the woods. Strangling Olivia in the square. Being shoved, pushed, kicked, cursed, and spat upon by some of Maford's finest people. Maybe it's more than that? Maybe it's Miasma?

I focus on my bowl of soup, lifting the spoon to my mouth, and… My skin prickles with a memory. Sitting at a dinner table, a blue-and-white tureen of steaming potato-leek soup before me. Singing? I'm smiling as a hand dips a large spoon into the tureen and ladles more soup into my almost-empty bowl. The hand, brown and slender, a woman's hand, squeezes my shoulder. My mother's hand?

Leeks are supposed to be delicious green vegetables—my memory of smiling as I consumed another helping of that soup tells me so. But in this soup, they're far from delicious and have the consistency of slime falling from a cow's mouth. Olivia doesn't seem to care. The sound of her soup-slurping is worse than the barn's creaking or Gery and his wife's hacking.

"I don't think I've ever had leeks that tasted like *this* before," I say, attempting small talk. I poke my spoon at a brownish-gray lump also in my bowl. "And what is *this*?"

Olivia bites into her own chunk of *this*. "Lamb."

"Oh!" I pry a piece away with my spoon and pop it in my mouth. Almost immediately, my mouth rebukes this funky, fatty piece of meat. I gag and spit out the meat, which tumbles to the dirt. My cheeks burn with embarrassment, and I choke out, "I apologize. That was rude."

Jadon grimaces as he chews a bite. "Not a lot of grass for the sheep to eat, so it's a little gamey."

A *little* gamey? And I'm a little tall and a little brown.

"I'm not a good cook," Olivia says, her eyes sad, her cheeks pink, "but I do try to make the best of what we have. Which isn't a lot."

"It's very generous of you to feed me," I say, my tongue slick. "This soup is certainly..." I clear my throat to keep from gagging. "Unforgettable."

Jadon snickers as he pushes his spoon around his bowl.

I won't insult my host further by mentioning what I'm now remembering, what my palate is demanding: texture and seasoning. Salt and pepper, carrots, rosemary. Something, anything that crunches. *Be gracious. There's always something to compliment.* I remember hearing those instructions. I remember someone tugging my braid. The owner of that slender brown hand?

I'm trying hard to be gracious and complimentary—*this soup is unforgettable*. And that's the truth. I'm a guest here. No, I'm a *prisoner* here. Trapped in this village, my clothes and amulet held hostage. The sooner I get them, the sooner I can leave Maford and its Miasma and find someone who knows more about Chesterby's past.

"So." I set the bowl of soup aside. "How do I earn twelve geld?"

"First thing in the morning," Jadon says, "we'll put you to work."

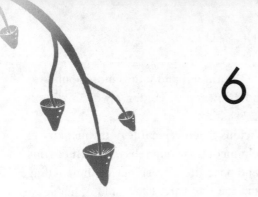

6

T he nightstar hangs low in the sky, casting her light across the tall grass
that hides us. The blades bend with a breeze now sweeping over us.

Jadon's fingers graze my cheek, brush away strands of my long, curly
hair that have fallen across my face. His touch is fire. I can barely move
even with just his fingers on my skin.

"Come with me," I whisper. "We're made for each other."

Will he leave everything behind for me?

Jadon's brow furrows. "I *do* want to come with you."

"But?"

"But..." He lies on his back, his eyes to the stars. "I can't. No matter
how much I want to. Unless..."

I don't speak and hold my breath, listening to the distant rustle of
leaves, the soft murmurs of night creatures, his heartbeat, mine. The entire
realm holds its breath with me, waiting for his answer.

Unless...?

Jadon turns back to me. "I can't," he whispers. "No matter how much
I want to, how much I want you."

A single teardrop trails across the bridge of my nose and plops on his
hand. "I have you now, though, yes? You and I and no one else? Until the
start of tomorrow?"

He smiles, and his "Yes" is just a puff of air from his lips to mine, and
I want more.

"Hey," he whispers.

"Hey," I whisper and lean in.

He leans in closer.

An explosion rips through the silence, and the nightstar is swallowed
by fire. The earth splits open between us and a great beast—a wolf or a
bear or a man—climbs out of that fracture, teeth bared, talons bloody.
The creature roars but then it disappears as thick gray smoke billows
from the fires burning above the earth and from the faults breaking the

earth apart.

Ashes swirl and sting my eyes.

"Kai!" Jadon shouts.

"Where are you?" I shout back, crawling through the meadow, lost in the smoky dark.

"Follow the sound of my voice," he shouts, sounding farther away.

I can only hear iron striking iron. Swords? Is Jadon fighting that creature? I hear screaming now. More striking. Roaring. The noise, this fight, sounds closer...closer... Screaming. Who's screaming? *Bam! Bam! Bam!* Is that a sword? Is that Jadon—?

Roars cut through the explosions.

My eyes feel like they're burning, and I close them.

Screaming. *It's me.* I'm screaming. My cheek burns. I scream louder and touch that burning cheek. My fingers come away wet. Blood on my fingertips. I'm bleeding and now the flames lick at my bare feet and I scream and the creature bursts through the gray smoke and it swipes its claw across my face and—

My eyes pop open, and I bolt upright, gasping for breath. My throat feels raw. Jadon's brown tunic sticks to my sweaty skin.

The world smells of smoke and sheep.

"Finally!" Olivia is sitting cross-legged behind me. "I thought you'd never wake up."

"What's wrong?" I blink back at her and then send my eyes darting around the...

Where am I? I'm sitting on quilts with yellow straw all around me. The small slot window shows only dingy blue sky. I'm high up.

Bam! Bam! Hiss!

Ah. Yes. I'm in the loft above the forge, not stuck in my dream with all those explosions of earth and sea of flames. But my memory of those explosions, the sea of flames and billowing smoke, the creature attacking me, losing Jadon, everything from my dream... It feels so real even as I sit here in a decrepit barn, fully awake, heart still pounding loud enough for the entire village of Maford to hear. And the other part of the dream, the part with Jadon… My skin heats at the memory of his touch, of the way he looked at me like I meant everything, the way he turned away and told me that he couldn't come with me.

Bam! Bam! Hiss!

I scowl and rub my face with both hands. "Why is it so loud?" I massage my aching biceps and twist my head to loosen the muscles in my neck.

"Forges usually are," Olivia says. "And it's loud because Jadon's working. Dawn was four hours ago, and you're sleeping like you're a duchess with a rich husband and servants when you've got geld to earn back today."

Bam! Bam! Hiss!

I peek over the edge of the loft.

Jadon's wielding a thickheaded hammer across a soft, red-hot shaft of metal. The air trembles from the violence, and I'm transfixed.

"I've been thinking," Olivia says.

I ignore her, still focused on her brother. My dream is sharp and fresh in my mind—

"Are you listening to me?" Olivia barks. "I said you can go next door to Farmer Gery's and help him out, since his wife is too ill to work. Milk his cow. Also, muck the stalls for the horses. He may need you to shear the sheep. Don't go inside their house, though."

"Miasma," I say, nodding, eyes on the muscles twining and flexing beneath Jadon's shirt as he lifts the hammer again. Sparks fly from the glowing metal as he strikes.

"Exactly," Olivia says. "Stay out in the open. Then, after the farming chores, visit the candlemaker across from the school and retrieve the new candlesticks that will be lit in the church's candelabras. I'm supposed to go, but since you're here, you can. I think Father Knete will also need you to polish those candelabras and polish the altar and the pews."

I say, "Umhmm," as Jadon wipes sweat from his brow with a sleeve and adjusts his grip on the hammer.

He pauses before striking the metal again. Does he sense me watching? He looks over his shoulder and then up to the loft, and our eyes lock. He does. "Hey," he says, smiling.

Just like he said it in the dream, except we were resting beside each other, closer, much closer. And now, my cheeks burn and I open my mouth to say—

"Be sure to wipe off the sheep shit before you step into the church," Olivia says.

I grimace at her over my shoulder. "What?"

She scowls. "Didn't you hear me?"

I turn back to look down at Jadon as a frizzy-haired brunette with a toothy grin enters the barn's double doors. She's holding a broken meat cleaver and bats her eyes at him. "I know you just fixed it last week—"

I roll my eyes and sigh, settling back into the straw. "Yes, I heard you. Sheep shit. Got it."

Olivia rubs her neck, and I notice my left-behind handprints have faded. The whites of her eyes are no longer jaundiced. She looks healthier today than she did yesterday. "The moment I opened my eyes this morning, I remembered where I'd seen a name like yours."

I perk up. "Yeah?"

She smiles at me and crawls over to the corner of the loft and lifts a bale of hay. "In here." She pulls out a book, but it's not an ordinary book. The cover is encrusted with jewel-colored glass. Square red garnets edge the book, as well as circles of mother-of-pearl, tiny squares of green glass, and flecks of yellow topaz. Thick jeweled lines segment the cover into four quadrants. An angel sits in the top left corner, and an eagle sits in the right. A boy holding a sword takes up the lower left corner, and a girl holding a hammer takes up the lower right. Each figure is embossed, and the soft leather looks buttery, as though hundreds of hands have stroked this hide before it found its way to a sooty forge in Maford.

"It's breathtaking," I whisper. "But what does this have to do with my name?"

"This isn't just one story," Olivia says, "but a bunch of stories. About knights and ladies and dragons. There's one story about a pretty girl named Larissa and a strong, handsome boy named Hammond, and they've been banished from the kingdom of Cahyrst and sent to sail across Devour. That's a sea far, far away from here. They have these adventures based on the Wheel of Fortune. Trust, war, peace, love, power, death. You know, *fate*.

"Hammond and Larissa learn that the king wants them dead, and the death warrant is hidden in Hammond's knapsack. They need to find this safe place called the Mount of Outer Places, but there are monsters on the road and magnificent beasts that they must fight while also avoiding all the king's men. They both find love, but then those loves are smashed by either fiery rocks falling from the sky or melted and drowned in the Sea of Devour. That's my favorite one."

"So, these are cheerful tales, then," I say.

"Absolutely. See?" She pushes the book toward me and points to something on the page.

I scan the words and find the name. *Kaivara.* I gasp like I've been punched in the gut. My heart rolls with thunders. *Kaivara. Kai. My name.* I scan the story:

In the mythic land of Toskin, a deity named Kaivara holds dominion over the villages closest to the treacherous sea named Devour. Even though her countenance hides behind a glaring silver glow, she can still survey the lands before her. The parched, cracked earth. The bare trees. The scattered bones of animals. In one hand, Kaivara holds fire, and in the other hand, she holds a cloud filled with rain. Amber glows everywhere her gaze touches, especially around the multitude of people on their knees, looking up to her, their hands clenched in prayer.

"Lady Kaivara," the cleric pleads. "Please bless us."

But Kaivara turns her back to them, for they have disobeyed her every command. Though they claim that they have changed their ways, she knows they haven't.

I continue reading until the end, and that's when I gasp. I look up to Olivia with wide eyes. "She kills them."

"Does this story sound familiar?" Olivia asks. "Maybe your mother read it to you?"

A shaft of sunlight slices through the loft's small window and shines across my knee. "I don't know this tale."

"Well, I've always hated it," Olivia says, "and I hate that goddess. She's just so cruel."

Neck prickling, I raise my eyes from the page. "Does this town, Toskin, exist?"

Olivia shakes her head. "But the Sea of Devour does. There are towns scattered around it. But then, beyond those towns, walls of sharp gray rock build, one atop the other, higher and higher still, never crumbling, only growing. Heaps of gray rocks taller than the tallest tree, but there are no trees, there are no crags or paths to climb and ascend— the mountain refuses to be scaled by man or beast. And if there *is* a top, the mountain refuses to let any eye glimpse past thick white clouds that never part."

My mind aches trying to imagine a mountain so bold yet elusive, so formidable yet incurious, a mountain that *refuses* to be summited. My skin turns clammy with dread—nothing should be that powerful, that... *impossible.*

"Maybe I was named after this goddess." I shift on the uncomfortable hay bale and lift the book into my lap. "And maybe one of the towns around this sea is my home." I slide my finger down the last page to the illustration of an amber-glowing heap of dead villagers baking under the relentless daystar. The prickles on the back of my neck sharpen. "Why would my parents have named me after someone so cruel, though?"

There must be more to this goddess than this story.

Olivia takes the book from my hands, then shoves it back beneath the bale of hay.

"Why are you hiding it over there?" I ask, squinting at her.

Her face colors red as a blister.

I grimace. "Must you steal every shiny thing in Maford?"

"This didn't come from Maford," she sniffs.

"Oh, pardon me. You would never steal from this pigsty of a town, would you? Olivia Ealdrehrt steals only from *fancy-nancy* places with *incredible* hauls. Is that how you'd say it?"

Color splotching her face, Olivia looks like she's about to argue, but the rage disappears, and she peeks over the edge of the loft at the forge before saying, "Don't ever mention that I have this book, okay? It doesn't exist, understand?"

I stare at her.

She holds my gaze with her own.

"Olivia," Jadon calls from below. "Kai really should get started."

Olivia shouts, "We're coming down now," without losing eye contact with me.

I whisper, "Does he know you have this?"

"He does." Olivia continues to stare at me, eyes solemn and steady.

This is not her normal demeanor. Finally, I blink. "Okay, I won't say anything."

She exhales and tosses me a grateful smile. "Get changed and come on down."

As I pull off the tunic and drag the peacock-blue dress over my head, I think about the story in that jeweled book. Who is Kaivara? Did my parents worship her and take the smaller version of her name for me? Or did they name me "Kai" because they saw something in me that reminded them of her? Also: Where is this sea called Devour? Is it anywhere near Chesterby? How long would it take me to get there? And if I go there, will I find my family?

J adon has sent the frizzy-haired woman away, and he's examining the broken cleaver.

Olivia and I join him at his worktable. "Good morning again, Jadon," I say, smiling.

Jadon turns to me, and his mood instantly brightens. "Good morning again, Kai. Wow. That dress looks great on you."

And now, I'm grinning like a dewy-eyed fawn. Ridiculous.

Olivia wriggles her nose. "It's a little tight around the bust—"

Jadon's gaze drops to my bust.

I stand perfectly still and arch an eyebrow in challenge, my pulse racing. "Looks okay to me," he says.

I snort. "Just okay?"

"How about…" He scans me as if analyzing a sculpture, then searches the sky for a word, eyes narrowed, his finger tapping his chin. "Celestial? Or elysian?"

"I'm thinking supernal," I say with a nod.

"I'll accept that answer," he says. Heat arcs between us like it has since we met.

"Are you two done?" Olivia snarks. "Or shall I come back for the baby shower?"

Jadon rolls his eyes and hangs the meat cleaver on a nail over the worktable. "Sorry about all the noise, Kai. I hope I didn't wake you with all that banging."

"Not at all." My face and neck warm as I remember my dream and resist the urge to fidget. "Olivia was just sharing a story with me about a deity named 'Kaivara.'"

His eyebrows lift. "I've heard that name before. From Dashmala nomads around Devour."

My heart jumps. "Really?"

"When were you at the Sea of Devour?" Olivia asks her brother.

He brushes her comment away with a flip of his hand and says to me, "You know what? They sew and stitch circles in their clothes. Brand it on their horses' rumps. And they carry these totems of their goddess, 'Kaivara.' That would make sense if that's where you're from—if you're one of those people."

"Not Chesterby after all?" I say.

"Maybe, maybe not." He grabs short strips of iron from a bucket.

"While I'm earning twelve geld," I say, "I'll figure out a way to get back to Devour. Maybe I can find a sage in the next town over who'd know about Chesterby and Kaivara." For the first time since landing here, I feel a solid sense of identity, direction, purpose.

In my mind's eye, I see... Rays from the daystar shining across fields of stone. I see... A colorless sea, bleached shells and stones covering its banks. I see... Shining jewel-colored lights racing across the sky and disappearing into the clouds...

Bam!

I startle, knocked from my vision and pulled back into the Ealdrehrts' forge.

Jadon has resumed work. "Sorry. Needed to get back to it before it turned cold." He lifts the hammer again and strikes a glowing orange, mean-looking rod of steel between the vise.

My hands shake, and I step back. This banging sounds close to that steel in my dream, after the earth split apart.

"What are you making now?" Hopefully, Jadon doesn't notice my voice wavering. "A pike? A lance?" Good. Back to sounding assured and solid.

Jadon blinks at me. "Spoons."

For some reason, this towering, well-muscled man creating spoons out of fire and ore seems off. "Ah. Useful." I rub my sweaty hands on my skirt. Perhaps it's the memory or the violence from my dream, but my skin feels tight and itchy and my breathing hitches in my chest and I'm ready to leave this part of the barn. "Work," I say. "Gery's farm next door first, yes?"

"Yep." Jadon shoots me a smile. "You'll earn twelve geld in no time. And then you'll be free of Maford and free of us."

I nod and follow Olivia out of the barn.

Being free of Jadon?

Hmm.

For some reason, that thought chills my heart.

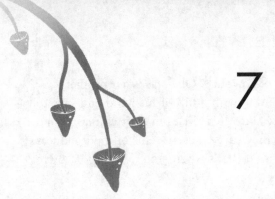

7

A fter a breakfast of brown bread, cheese, and boiled potatoes, I walk to Gery's, ready to earn twelve geld doing farm work.

When I arrive, Gery, a bone-thin man with a hound dog face and strong hands, stands on the other side of his barn with a soiled handkerchief held to his mouth. Between coughing fits, he nods to the cow. "Her name's Molly." He points to the milking pail and then a bag of oats for his horses.

"When you're done with all that." He gestures toward a pile of newly shorn sheep wool. "Bag that up for the market." Once he assigns me these tasks, Gery shuffles back to his house and to his wife, who's still too ill to leave her bed.

I dump oats in the trough for the horses. "Enjoy, lovelies," I say.

That was easy.

There's a stool near the door, and I set it on the right side of the cow. "I have no idea how to do this," I tell Molly, stroking her bangs. "You're gonna have to take the lead."

Molly blinks her big black cow eyes at me and snuffles. If I didn't know any better, I'd think she was laughing at me.

I perch on the stool and rub my hands together to warm them. Reaching for the udder, I whisper, "I know we just met, darling, and I'm sorry about this. Just don't kick me, okay?"

Her tail flicks, and she snuffles again—this time, a sigh.

I want a cow. Maybe I already *have* a cow and maybe I already have my own farm back where I'm from. Maybe I was charged with tending the livestock in our group.

And now for my last farm chore: bagging newly shorn wool into burlap sacks. The wool makes my hands itch. I liked tending to Molly much better.

Before I leave, Farmer Gery makes me turn out the pockets of my skirt. "I hear your kind likes to steal." He tosses me my pay from the other side of the barn.

I catch it in my swollen hand.

One geld.

Are you fucking kidding me?

The daystar burns high in the sky by the time I leave Gery's. The baking hard, dirt-packed roads haven't softened even after the water from yesterday's rain. In such bright light, Maford looks faded, like a memory disappearing moment by moment. The market is gone this morning—the wanderweavers must have packed up overnight and moved on to the next village.

The few townspeople out in this heat give me space, their hands trembling and their eyes filled with fear, preferring to take the long way around instead of walking beside me.

I search the sparse crowds for the tawny-skinned woman with the silver glow. She's the only person, other than Jadon, who has talked to me with decency. I haven't asked Jadon or Olivia about her, remembering Olivia's warning about those who may use magic. She was so frightened, I didn't want her to even think about another person using magic in town.

Still, I hope to see that woman again. Maybe she knows about Chesterby and Devour, the nomads who worship Kaivara, and people with hair the colors of mulberry and cinnamon.

"You there!" a man shouts. "Blue-dress stranger!" He stands in the shop doorway a few doors down, glowing amber like everyone else. He beckons me over. "You the one who has to pay a fine?"

I look across the way. There's the school. This must be the candle shop. Still, I hesitate before saying, "Yes sir. I'm supposed to help you today."

"Fine," he mutters. "Follow me."

I pause in my step, angry heat blooming on the back of my neck. *Eleven geld*, I remind myself. After taking a deep breath, I follow the man into a shop filled with candles and beeswax. But we don't pause here. No, he leads me down a dark corridor and back out to a slowly dying garden of violets and goldenrod, foxglove and lavender.

Before the drought, this garden with all its color would've dropped me to my knees. Now, though, my gasp is not that of delight but regret. The garden and its five straw baskets buzz with fat bees that bumble from withering blossom to dead blossom.

In natural light, I see that the candlemaker's an older man, and his face is misshapen and pink. "Bee stings," he mutters, catching me staring. "Gotta admit: it's nice to have someone else for these maggots to gape at."

I surprise myself with a laugh. "Glad to be of service."

"You are as lovely as they say," he offers, his head bowed.

I stare at him. "Lovely as *who* says?" I've heard not one nice word outside of the Ealdrehrts' cottage directed my way, spoken or thought. Is he just being agreeable?

His smile falters, his blush deepens, and he clears his throat. "Well, this is where all the magic happens." He pauses, looking even more flustered. "Not magic-magic, I mean—"

I raise my hand and smile. "No need to explain. I understand your meaning."

"Ever do any of this before?" he asks. "Beekeeping? Candle-making?"

No clue. So I shake my head. "But I'm eager to learn."

"I've been Maford's candlemaker all my life. My gardens used to spread all the way back there." He points to the tree line of the forest. "But creatures kept knocking over the hives and stealing the honey. So I built this fence." Tall wooden planks have been erected around the backyard. Iron spikes travel across the top of the barriers.

I shiver, thinking about the kind of creatures that would need to be kept out with spikes. "How can I help you today?" I ask. "Olivia told me—"

He flicks his hand. "I don't care what Olivia says. I need you to help me dunk wicks into the melted beeswax. I'll offer you two geld every four candles. You do the math."

Twelve candles for six geld.

"Doesn't seem like a lot of candles," I say, shrugging. "Beware: I've never done this."

He sets up two stools on either side of a campfire. A big metal pot sits atop hot stones over the fire.

I sit on one of the stools while he fusses with the hives. "You're lucky to work with these bees," I say. "I *love* honey. There's no better taste in the realm." Not a recalled memory—just common sense.

"This isn't about the honey." He reaches beneath one of the hives. "This is what I need." He lifts the wax sheet he just harvested and trundles over to a small table with wood plates. "What's your name, young one?"

I dip my head out of respect. "Kai, sir. And you are?"

"Jamart." He presses the wax sheet beneath the wood plates. Honey drips from the plates and into a tub beneath the stand. He then takes the pressed wax and washes it in another tub until it's as gold as the honey.

"Wax." He holds up the clean flat sheet. "*That's* the treasure, Kai. Wax makes candles. Everybody needs candles. In their houses, in their churches, in their stores. Healers like Freyney need it for medicines. Coating the throat and covering sores. The rich folk with important business to do. They mix it up with resin and make seals to close their fancy documents."

He scratches at a fresh, red sting on his neck. "I should be one of those rich folk, to tell you the truth. But my bees are dying. There's no water. Bad air. Dying flowers. This town, it's killing the bees." He pushes out a breath, then says, "Let's get to it, then, while we can."

Candle-making is quiet work. Jamart doesn't speak as we suspend the dripping wicks from sticks across buckets.

"Any family?" I ask. "It's so quiet here. Other than the bees, of course."

"No," he says. "Wife's passed. My daughter, Lively... She's gone. Not dead. Just... She got in some trouble and... She's in the jail down the way."

"I'm sorry to hear that." A pit opens in my stomach as I remember the conditions of that horrible place. No one deserves to be imprisoned there, no matter what they did. "May I ask what happened?"

He stares at the bubbling wax. "She took down the colure that used to hang on my front door."

Olivia's fear at the mention of magic and her warnings echo in my mind.

"That's horrible," I whisper. "The leaders of this town should be driven out."

"Don't say that," Jamart says quickly, eyes nervously skipping around the garden. "We're all doing the best we can."

I can't agree with him, but I understand his need to change the subject. I don't want my words bringing even more trouble to him or his family.

The buzzing grows louder as more bees dip in and out of the hives and bumble from foxglove to lavender.

"I think every bee in Maford is here," I say, grinning, trying to lighten the mood.

Jamart laughs. "Of course they are! They want to meet our guest."

I blush and wave my hand in small circles. "Hello, hive. Such an honor to meet the makers of my favorite thing in this realm and the next." I cast my gaze around the garden that used to be so abundant and vibrant. "You don't worry that your neighbors or bandits may take the hives and wax and everything else?"

The candlemaker studies his workshop, his cheer diminishing. "I think about it almost every day."

I peer at the bubbling cauldron, the drying candles, the golden sheets of wax. "This may not mean much, but I wish you protection and peace, Jamart. This is a lovely place of respite, at least for me, which sounds a little selfish but..." I sweep my hand—*this town is horrible.* "I wish to come back to your shop so I hope that it will never be harmed or looted."

Jamart's eyes glisten with tears. "Thank you," he whispers. "I've forgotten natural kindness, and your blessing reminds me that it still exists. Your presence brings me hope."

I force myself to smile. "I'm just here, sir. Making candles. Enjoying your company."

"It is in your nature to be kind," he says.

"Sure," I say, chuckling, "but I'm just..." I shrug, confused. I haven't gone out of my way to be cheerful, to be respectful. I am who I am. But I'm glad Jamart sees beyond my hair and my height, what I am or where I'm from.

"You're just being yourself." He smiles as he takes another wax plate from the last hive.

I suppose I am, and now, I have more information about who I am. I'm kind, cheerful, someone who brings peace to someone like Jamart. I like that. And I like him, and I want to know more about him. As we work, I can't help but dip in and out of his head, a butterfly fluttering the fields. His thoughts are simple: *"bees, wax, candles..."*

And then his thoughts turn to...

"Oh Guardian, gentle Lady of the Verdant Realm, hear the humble plea of Thy devoted servant seeking the grace of Your divine touch. Coax life from the earth and cast Thy benevolent gaze upon my humble hives. Let their honey flow like liquid sunlight radiating the warmth of Your divine favor."

What a lovely prayer from such an uncomplicated man.

A thought strikes me like a spark in the dark, but I wait for him to finish his prayer to this Guardian, this gentle Lady of the Verdant Realm.

"I have an idea," I say. "What if you add flower petals to the melted wax? That way, there's scent, like lavender, for example, as the candles burn?"

His eyes light up, and he hustles over to his garden. A moment later, he brings back sprigs of lavender, crushing them before dropping them into the cauldron of wax. "If this works—"

"It *will* work. If not, there's no risk in trying."

He takes a whiff of the lavender warming in the pot. "People may even pay a little bit more for these. If it works—"

"Stop saying 'if,'" I say, laughing. "Not only will your candles smell nice, but they'll be beautiful to behold. Your customers won't know how you've done it. They'll call you genius."

"And I will give all the glory to you," he says.

"Just give me a free candle." I lower a wick into the melted wax. "Soon, word will spread that the candlemaker in Maford has breathed new life into candles. You'll make a lot of geld."

"You answered my prayers." His mouth tightens, and his lips quiver. Tears brighten in his eyes but never fall.

I help him make these new candles, smiling as the aroma of lavender wafts around us. I'm sad once we've finished. My time with Jamart is over, and I must move on to my next task.

"I should go," I say. "I'm to stop by the church to polish candelabras and pews."

"*You?*" he asks, eyebrows scrunched.

"Me," I say. "I'm happy to report that my time here has been the most pleasant since arriving in Maford."

Jamart's smile is as bright as his honey as he leads me back down the corridor, stopping in the sitting room. "Almost forgot," he says, holding up a finger. "Please give me a moment." He rushes to the pantry.

I wander the dim space. Something in the corner of the room catches my eye. It's hard to see at first, but as I slip closer, I find that it's an altar: a wood carving of a woman's face, her arms full of blooms, her hair abundant and represented by squiggly grooves cut into the wood. Fresh flowers from the garden have been arranged around the icon as well as burning fat candles.

This is one of the altars Olivia mentioned.

A fullness, something like frothy milk or new cream, swells from my feet to my head. Such care has been taken with creating and tending this shrine. Unlike the displays of colures nailed, worn, and thrust upon others like knives, I feel devotion rippling through Jamart's display. After hearing his prayer, I sense sincerity in his belief and in his love for this deity. Delight flutters through me, a moth slipping from one light to the next.

"For you," Jamart says, back by my side. Head bowed, he hands me a small pouch.

Inside: a jar of golden honey, a block of yellow beeswax, and eight geld.

Rattled, I shake my head and offer back two geld. "This is too much. I can't possibly—"

"No, I won't hear of it." He leads me to the front door. "Thank you, kind lady. You've blessed me today. The wax and the blooms—I would never have thought of that." The irritation from the bee stings on his neck and face has waned some. His skin appears less inflamed, his glow a flickering, lightening amber. Good company and quiet can be healing, I'm sure. My own stings from Maford's citizens have healed some, too.

I leave Jamart's home, my cheeks strained from my smile. Maybe, in my old age, I will also make scented candles from my own beehives. A girl can dream, can't she?

After speaking with Jamart, I can't bring myself to go to the church. Instead, I find myself standing before the jailhouse. The amber glow of the building has dimmed. There's one fewer soul than yesterday. I pray that it wasn't Lively.

The heat of rage and the iciness of helplessness mix in my gut, and I don't know how I should be feeling right now. I don't know which emotion has brought these tears now stinging my eyes. My heart burns in my chest as I imagine my last hours alive in a rancid pit that stinks of death and despair. I tremble as I imagine a young woman with Jamart's nose, Lively, being dragged to this cesspool by the same men who pushed me around yesterday and hinted at the extra violence they'd take against me. All because she dared to believe in something or someone other than Emperor Supreme? This is justice? Reverence? This is who their god is? Violent? Depraved? And they dared call *me* vile? Are they—Narder and Johny— not the vile ones?

No one else stands near the fetid structure, offering prayers or companionship. Not even Narder stalks around the hut. For now, these prisoners are forgotten.

I tiptoe over to the rancid shack, fighting the urge to vomit, fixing my eyes everywhere else but the limestone-flecked shit clumping around the cracked foundation. I edge as close as possible without fouling my borrowed boots and whisper, "Hello?" to the wall.

"Who's there?" a man's coarse voice rasps.

"You don't know me," I whisper. "Is Narder nearby?"

"He's at the tavern," he whispers. "He drinks there all day and comes back in a worse temper than when he left."

"Are you the only one alive in there?" I ask.

"No." A young woman.

"I'm here, too." An older man, weaker-voiced.

"Is Lively there?" I ask.

A gasp from the woman. "That's me."

"I just met your father. He's very kind." I close my eyes to fight nausea, to calm the ugly headache blooming behind my ears. "You others. What did you do to be jailed?"

"I stole," the coarse-voiced man says. "Though it was only food to feed my parents. We had nothing and I was desperate and it was just sitting at the altar in the chapel. It's not like Supreme is here to actually eat it, and I don't think He'd want His faithful servants to starve. That's what I thought. But I was wrong. I am to serve my sentence before He will forgive me."

My headache grows and spreads past my eyes.

"My niece and I," the old man says, "we drank wine."

I wait to hear more. When the man doesn't continue, I say, "And?"

"And," the old man says, "we didn't offer the first taste to Supreme. But we wanted to make sure that it tasted right, with the drought and all. We couldn't offer Father Knete and Mayor Raffolk rancid wine."

I frown. "*They're* drinking the wine? Not Supreme?"

Silence.

"And are they eating the food you all leave?" Anger prickles over my skin like stings from Jamart's bees.

More silence.

"So, that's it?" I ask. "Food and wine will be the reasons you die here? And you, Lively, because you removed something from your own door?"

No response from the prisoners. The young woman starts to cry.

Sensing danger, my neck and ears tingle. "Who passed yesterday?" I ask, my eyes skirting the doors and windows of the cottages and shops behind me.

"My son," the older man says, barely containing his sob. "He was a good man—"

"...before I chop your head and hands off!"

Narder!

I peek around the corner of the jail.

The jailer is shoving a red-faced man up the road, heading in this direction. Both men are drunk and stumbling over their own feet. But only one man has the key to the clink and the authority to do what he wants to whomever he wants.

"Help us," the young man whispers. "We will never leave this place."

"No one ever does," the old man adds. "Not alive, at least."

Not from this jail. Not from this town.

"I will." My voice catches, and tears slip down my cheeks. One drops and splatters in the dirt. I don't know these people, but my heart feels like I do. "I'll figure it out. No one else will die in here. I promise." I close my eyes and touch the wall.

But what sort of promise can I make? I'm also a captive in this town. How can I free others when I can't even free myself? I don't know. But I can't leave them. I *won't*. As I hurry away from the structure before Narder comes, I make a vow: Whatever I do, it will have to be more than just leaving a single teardrop.

8

Black smoke pours from the forge's doors. Jadon, now wearing a long leather smock, is still working, and he grimaces as he bends a hot orange steel rod now clamped in a vise. The veins in his arms and hands push against his skin.

Fuck. After working so hard mucking, milking, and dipping, he is a welcome sight. My pulse races everywhere, from my throat to my feet.

"Kai! Just in time." He smiles, his teeth bright against the soot.

I blink and snap out of my trance. "Huh?"

"I want to hear how your day went," he says, "but first could you do me a favor? Could you collect wood for the forge? I need to start stacking up to make charcoal."

"Sure." I grab an empty pail and a hatchet near a bin of thick, dark nails. "Is this free labor or am I receiving a wage?" I ask, smiling.

He pauses and holds my gaze. "How much do you want?"

I tilt my head and arch an eyebrow. "How much do you have?"

His gaze lingers and a slow smile eases to his lips, and I smolder like his forge.

"Jadon." I nod to the metal clamped in the vise. "Your rod's getting hard."

He blinks, then looks down to see that the steel rod has lost its glow. "Shit."

I laugh and back away from him. "Any kind of wood or…?"

"Oak, beech, no pine," he says, loosening the vise. "Appreciate it."

I head toward the back barn doors, a smile on my face. I don't even have to look back to know that he's watching me…and that his rod is still hard.

In this forest, pine and birch trees abound, but there are more oak tree stumps than oak tree trunks. My throat grows tight as I gaze out at this ghost forest. I scan the ground, searching for wood that won't require me to cut down a living tree.

Two red cardinals perch on one of those stumps. The red birds chirp and flutter their wings at me, and I say, "Makes me sad, too." I dip my head. "But it's nice to meet you lovelies, nonetheless."

I grab fallen branches from the ground and start a pile.

The cardinals keep chirping.

Such pretty birds. How is it their feathers are still so shiny in this wretched town?

Once I've gathered a decent amount, I grab the hatchet and start chopping branches in half, using a stump as a chopping block. I grin at the cardinals. "Impressed? You two remind me of something. I've seen birds like you before. Don't know where, though."

I chop and stack, and the birds chirp and hop. "This is a lot of work," I whisper to them. "I don't think I've done this before. My hands are too soft for this kind of—"

My body freezes in place. *What's that?*

I sniff. Snuffed-out candles. Night-blooming jasmine crushed underfoot. The scent is not native to Maford. It's far too pleasant for Maford. I scan the woods, seeing only those ghostly birch trees and the death-glows of four-legged creatures.

There! Her! That old woman with the silver sparkle and the long, coiled hair—the one who gifted me the ability to hear thoughts. Nightstar Sparkle carries a golden pail as she walks through the woods. She doesn't look as stooped as she was back in the village and has ditched the shawl for a creamy white robe. Once she sees me, she heads in my direction, her face shining like diamonds and light.

The closer she comes, the more my heart swells and the more my chest squeezes. Finally, the pressure releases once I shed a single teardrop that tumbles down my cheek.

I quickly glance behind to ensure we're away from Maford's magic-hating men.

Nightstar Sparkle looks different than yesterday, but somehow, she looks the same. Her face isn't blurry, but neither is it clear. She's *magnificent*, and it's like I'm staring at four faces at the same time, each face wearing a different expression. There's the glow and softness of joy. The flaring nostrils and flinty eyes of anger. There's the trembling chin and wet, dull eyes of sorrow, and the popped eyebrow and open stare of awe.

Am I the only person in Maford who has seen these four faces?

Who's seen that she's more than human?

"Who am I speaking with right now?" I whisper, dropping the hatchet onto my stack of wood, sending several sticks tumbling.

She reaches out and touches my cheek. Her touch tingles, and my skin tingles, ultra-alive now. "I'm the only friend you have in this realm." She gazes at me like a mother studying her child.

I'm trying hard not to cry out of confusion, relief, and hope. "What is your name?" I ask, voice quavering.

"Search your thoughts, Kai," she whispers.

I shake my head. "But I don't—"

"Shh," she whispers.

I close my eyes, and my nose fills with the scents of cherry blossoms and woodsmoke. I meet her gaze. "Sybel." I startle at this realization. Where did this memory come from? Was it her touch alone? Did it bring to the surface something I knew within my heart? The palms of my hands are clammy, but my mind feels brighter, faster. How is it possible that I'm just standing here when I feel like I'm doing more? I'm remembering.

"Lift your head, child," Sybel says, her fingers raising my chin. "Your journey is not over. No, it's only begun."

"But how did it begin?" I ask, my whisper burning with urgency. "How did I reach that forest where I opened my eyes? Where was I before that? Did I fall from the sky? Am I from the nomads at Devour?"

Silver hands pushing me forward—and the sky...

Sybel shakes her head. "That 'how' doesn't matter right now. The questions you should be asking are, 'Where do I go next? Who must I become to get there?'" She holds out a hand, and now the face she wears is the one of flared nostrils. "And most importantly: 'How will I make amends for my failures?'"

I take a step back as heat rises behind my eyelids. "*Failures?* Surely, you don't mean me knocking over Freyney's cart—"

"Shh," she says again and claps once, hard, and the sound bounces around the woods. "Listen, for once in your life—"

My stomach lurches at her abrupt change of tone. "How do you know that I don't listen?"

She flashes a cold smile. "Because you aren't listening at this very moment."

I bite the inside of my cheek to contain my rising anger and confusion.

"If you continue to reverse everything that I've done for this place," Sybel says, "that I've done for you—"

"Done for me?" I take another step back, shaking my head.

"Hey, Kai," Jadon calls.

I startle, whirling toward him.

Still wearing his long leather smock, Jadon strides in my direction with a crooked grin. "I need wood *today*. You take the scenic route?"

I look back, but Sybel has disappeared.

9

Jadon grows serious when he sees my expression. "Who were you talking to?" His eyes skip around the tree line.

"The old woman," I say, looking back to the forest, heart still racing.

"Which old woman? Maford's full of old women." His words sound light, but his lips become white slashes. "Did she threaten you? Did she hurt you?"

"No. Just…" I gape at him, stumped, then take a quick peek at the forest again.

Where did she go? And why did she snap at me? She smiled at me yesterday and called me "child" and touched my ears so that I could hear the thoughts of others. Peeved—that was her mood now. And *if you continue to reverse everything that I've done*? What does that even mean? And *failures*? What have I failed at? I've been in Maford for a day now, and I've already earned more than half of the twelve geld I need, and I haven't misbehaved. Well, strangling Olivia wasn't the *best* behavior, but I had reasons. Is that what she's talking about? Unless…

Ice spreads across my stomach. What does Sybel know about me that I've forgotten? Is Jamart wrong? Is kindness *not* in my nature? Am I more a strangler than a comforter? Have I misused my hands before? Has Sybel witnessed me do bad things and is exhausted by my behavior and that's why she said I don't listen and I need to make amends?

I pinch the bridge of my nose to contain the frustrated tears building behind my eyes. *Everything that I've done for you.* Why did she scold me when she knows I'm lost? Who must I become to get *where*? Who the fuck am I *now*?

"Well, if anyone bothers you," Jadon says, tightening the bandage around his hand with his teeth, "just tell me. I'll handle them."

"I can handle myself, thank you," I say, prickling.

"I didn't mean—"

I hold up my hands in apology. "I know." My gaze wanders back to the trees and those stumps. "This place is exhausting." I poke the pitiful lengths of wood with my foot. "If I'm being honest, you are *all* awful."

Jadon clears his throat and pokes the inside of his cheek with his tongue.

Ugh. I did it again. "I didn't mean *you*. I meant collectively. You've been so accommodating, and I do appreciate your kindness." My head is now killing me, and I just want to lie down.

"Sounds like you and Jamart hit it off," he says with a lifted eyebrow.

I blanch. "How do you know we got along?"

"Small town. Word travels fast. Especially when someone who's known to be grumpy is seen grinning from ear to ear after spending time with a lovely young lady."

"I have that effect on some people." Despite a flush of warmth at his flattery, my voice sounds weary and flat. "And in this town, I have that effect on only one person."

He squints into the sky. "Oh, there's more than one person."

I sigh, unable to conjure a witty comeback. I'm in no mood for banter, even with Jadon. That confrontation with Sybel has left me feeling hollow and ungrounded.

Jadon nods at the pouch from Jamart tied to my sash. "A gift?"

"Yep." I tap the small bag. "Some men know how to treat a lady."

He shoves his hands into his pockets. "Really? What could he have possibly given you?"

I lift my chin. "Eight geld for starters. Am I giving the geld to you to pay off my debt? If you don't mind, I'd prefer that. I don't wanna be near Freyney or Narder again."

Jadon studies me. "I'll handle it." He steps closer. "What's going on? You're troubled."

I pick up the hatchet and focus on chopping more branches in half.

"You can talk to me," he says. "I wanna help. I don't make candles, but I think spoons are also great, and if you want to learn how to make one—"

I snort and laugh, resting the hatchet on the stump I'm using as a block. "Spoons?"

He waggles his eyebrows. "Forks, if you wanna live dangerously."

For a moment, our eyes lock and I'm tempted. I want to talk to him. I want him to comfort me. I want to reach out and stroke his cheek, kiss his injured hand, call him "lovely," and take a nap right here with him beside me. I want him to say my name again, and I want to tell him about growing up in some part of Vallendor far from here and the name of my favorite horse and what I like to do after a long workday. But I know none of these things, *still*, and after talking with Sybel, I don't know if I *want* to know.

The sting of tears again. "I'm…" Exhausted. Frustrated. Woeful.

Jadon hesitates before quickly setting a comforting hand on my arm and just as quickly withdrawing it. "Hey, it's okay to be sad. To be disappointed. I know it must be hard to not remember your past life. But you'll remember, I promise."

A defeated sigh escapes my lips. No one can promise such a thing. Not even this man with his comforting voice and sincere expression. I place several pieces of wood in the bucket.

"When I told you that I'd help you figure it out, I meant it, okay?" He offers me a soft smile tinged with sadness. "Think of it this way: not knowing your past may be better than having an awful one. I know there could be countless reasons that keep you from remembering—and to be frank, you may want to forget what happened before yesterday. I guess…"

He chews his bottom lip, thinking. "I guess I don't want you to despair. Maybe this is a chance to start over, make new memories. Do things differently this time. Take a chance or hold back. Go left instead of right."

How will I make amends for my failures?

Maybe that's all Sybel meant—this is my new start, a new beginning.

"That's an interesting way of looking at it." I push out a breath and shake it off, shoving several more pieces of wood into the bucket, then straightening. "I know you mean well, but… You have no idea how untethered I am. You don't want me to despair, but I'm well into despair, and my new start hasn't been as promising as you just made it sound."

"Maford," he says.

"Maford," I say, nodding.

"Sorry." He flushes. "You're right. I have no idea what you're feeling."

"You don't." *I* don't even know what I'm feeling.

I pick up the hatchet, place another branch on the block, hack it into two pieces, and drop them in the bucket. "Has Maford always been this way?"

"Blame bad fortune—that's made many of us suspicious, and obviously no one like you lives here. Shit. I didn't mean…" He pushes his hand through his hair. "That came out wrong. I meant to say: if Farmer Gery showed up in Brithellum in his dusty clothes and chicken feathers, he'd stick out, too. And who likes sticking out?"

"Some of us can't help it."

"And I'm grateful," he says, touching his heart. "You are unlike anyone I've ever met *anywhere*. Not just Maford. I feel…" He searches the horizon for that emotion, and I hold my breath. "I feel like we came from the same cabbage patch or something." Then he looks at me as though I'm the last star in the sky before dawn, the last sip of clean water ever. And the world around us stands utterly still.

My muscles loosen, and my heartbeat slows, and Jadon Ealdrehrt has become Jamart's garden but with beautiful eyes, a tender smile, and a kind heart. If I *must* start over again… But I can't start over *here*. I need to move on and discover who I am, where I'm from, and what I've done that Sybel's had to fix. I won't discover that in Maford. Leaving this place doesn't make me sad. Who I'll have to leave behind? *That* makes me sad. And I remember my dream, asking him to come with me, and I remember his answer.

No.

And just like that, the moment's gone.

I blink and remember that I'm holding a hatchet. "So I have…" I gesture to the bucket of wood.

"I'll get that." He reaches for the handle with his injured hand. Both of his shirtsleeves are rolled up, and before now, I couldn't see the angry red welts and burns scarring his arms. Some scars are old, but some are so new that I wince from the heat of their viciousness.

"Is that all from the forge?" I nod at his injuries, and he drops his hands to his sides, bucket forgotten.

Some of these burns look intentional. Like brands.

"They can't all come from making spoons, right?" I ask. "Those slashes. From swords? What happened?"

Our gazes collide, and in that moment, I know this man. Even though I don't know who I am or where I'm from, I do know that the violence on his arm is evil with intention, a marking that serves as a reminder to the bearer and to someone standing so close they can feel its cruelty. Love leaves no mark like this. Love doesn't burn against skin like this. At least, I hope it doesn't.

"Who wounded you?" I whisper, setting the hatchet back on the stump.

He tries to smile and busies himself unrolling his sleeves to cover the marks. "I'm okay, Kai. These are old. They look worse than they feel."

I swallow to loosen the tightness in my throat, fighting the urge again to reach out to him and to offer comfort. My core bends toward him, urging me to slip my arms around his waist and place my cheek against his. The intense need to remove his suffering sweeps through my heart in a painful wave, overwhelming me, disorienting me, because I don't know *what this is*. Desire? Care? Both?

Jadon senses something, too, and he steps toward me like he knows what I want.

And I move closer like this is my calling, not to *fix* him but to…

The moment the warmth of his body drifts to meet mine, we both tremble.

Somewhere in a cottage nearby, a man coughs. Another man coughs. Deep. Phlegmy.

Jadon takes a deep breath and steps away from me. After a moment, his jaw hardens, and he reaches for the bucket. "We should finish this up before the day ends."

"Don't worry," I say, moving it out of his reach. "Even though you say you're not, I know that you're still hurt. I'll carry the bucket."

"No, I'm okay," he insists.

I tilt my head and study his tense features. Why won't he let me help him? "Jadon, you wanted me to get wood. If *you* could get it, then why send *me*?"

"It's fine, Kai. I do everything around here anyway."

A smile warbles on my lips, half amused, half serious as I pick up the bucket by the handle. "Do you think asking for help makes you weak?"

His jaw tightens. *Yes.* "I know what I need." He places his hands to the outside of mine on the handle.

I side-eye him. "*Do* you?"

He flushes. *No.* His eyes drift to a point over my shoulder. "You can let go now."

"You can *also* let go." My cheeks burn. "Surrender. You may enjoy it. I won't tell."

His gaze, hot and poisoned, snaps to mine. "I'm not joking, Kai."

What just happened? What made him change like that so quickly?

We stand there, both holding the bucket handle but standing miles apart, eyes locked in a sudden and silent battle of wills. And even though I don't know much, I do know that we look foolish. Since I'm no fool…

"You don't want my help? Then…" I release the handle, and the bucket drops and lands on his foot, wood bouncing out.

Jadon winces, mutters, "Shit," and kicks the bucket as though this is all the bucket's fault. Then he jolts in pain and grabs at his foot.

Impressed, I lift my eyebrows as I watch the pail's trajectory into the forest. "Did that make you feel better? Hurting yourself to prove something to me?"

He peers at me, his eyes now a foggy blue, then swipes his face with his bandages. "My hand's not *that* messed up."

"Okay," I say, shrugging. "How messed up is it, then?"

"Long story."

I cross my arms. "I'm not doing anything else right now."

He shoves his hands beneath his armpits. "I got distracted making a mace. That's it."

I squint at that hand. His fingers don't look swollen, and the redness peeking from beneath that bandage isn't blood. It looks more like…ink? "And that's why you're wearing a bandage?"

He nods and releases a breath.

I try to hear his thoughts, but my parlor trick isn't working. Did Sybel un-gift me? Was she upset with the way I was using my gift? Is that why she was short with me?

I smile and pitch my head sideways. "Now, was that so difficult? Don't you feel better?"

He drops his head, then puts his fists on his hips. "Kai, that…was not intended. I'm sorry. Everything's different with you, and I'm not used to someone really showing concern. Who won't use my weakness for their gain. I apologize. Okay?"

I consider him for a moment, sense his exhausted sincerity, and nod.

"I came out here to give you this." He pulls an object wrapped in thick burlap from his apron pocket. He offers me the bundle. "Hope this makes things better for you."

"What is it?" I unwrap the burlap, only to find layers of cotton swaddling his gift.

"Wanted to make sure it was safe," he says, his face reddening.

I unwrap the first layer of cotton and unwrap another layer, and then another layer and…

"My pendant!" Lightness sweeps over me, and I let out an "eek." My smile is so big, it spills over into my heart. Even my headache eases and my eyes hurt less. "Thank you, Jadon, for protecting it with all the…" I motion to the burlap and cotton in the grass. "You have no idea how important this is to me."

I hold up the amulet. The dark stone floats in the middle of the moth's thorax. Like it's waiting. I'm one step closer to understanding who I am.

"And Olivia promises to clean your vest and cloak before returning them," he says. "Everything should be dry by tomorrow. We don't want you to feel like a prisoner here, but I'd appreciate it if you finish paying off the rest of what you owe."

"Sure." I fasten the pendant around my neck. The clasp is loose, thanks to Olivia snatching it from me, but I'm just happy to have it back. My throat opens, and my breathing deepens, and something rumbles in my gut, like I've been born again, and the amulet becomes a part of me, just as much as my heart and my eyes.

Vision crisper, I see that the daystar will soon kiss the horizon and that the sky has turned rose-colored with evening light. Lungs stronger, I inhale air scented with jasmine and woodsmoke, and for a moment, Maford has rejuvenated, its glow no longer that of death.

Jadon stares at me, color rising in his cheeks again, but not because he's angry, embarrassed, or uncontrolled.

Because he wants me? Because he wants to protect me? Both?

"Kai…" His body heat wraps around me like a blanket.

"That's my name." I touch his arm, skimming my fingers down to his bandaged hand.

He wraps his finger around mine, and I place my free hand atop—

The sky flashes bright white.

I suck air through clenched teeth.

Before we can drop hands, a powerful force yanks my hair from behind. Before I can free myself, I fall down…down…down… And it feels like… like…

Like I've done this before.

10

pen your eyes.

My breath comes quick and shallow. I'm panting like a dog, my head swimming and my pulse thundering in my ears.

Wake up.

Stars smudge the black sky. Then Jadon's and Olivia's faces block that star-smudged sky. But Olivia isn't looking at me. Her gaze lingers on my neck.

The amulet has hypnotized her.

"Olivia," I whisper. "Stop."

She blinks, pulled from her dream. "Thank Supreme, she's alive." Clear-eyed, she sits back on her haunches.

"You scared us," Jadon says, scooting away from me.

I sit up. To my left, there's a stump with a hatchet on it. Lengths of cut wood lie scattered about. My forehead feels tight, my scalp stretched, my stomach sour. "What happened?"

Jadon grimaces. "You fainted."

Olivia smirks. "Jay has that effect on women—I was hoping you were immune."

Jadon makes a face at her.

Olivia's eyes flick back to my pendant.

I cover it with my hand to break the spell before it even starts. The gems vibrate beneath my fingers, and I remember:

Walking to the forest for wood. Spotting that woman, Sybel, holding a golden bucket. Talking to Jadon about his hand. The amulet. My mind filling with white light as we touched.

"Was it the pendant?" I tap the moth. "After you handed it to me?"

"But why would you react to something that's yours?" Olivia asks.

"Maybe because she's been without it for too long?" Jadon says pointedly to his sister.

"That's ridiculous." Olivia snorts. "It's not like it's medicine."

"Says who?" I snap. "You don't know *what* it is and what it does. To me. *For* me." Hell, I don't even know that myself.

Olivia shrinks back.

I press my fingers harder against the stones, trying to make sense of it. The moment Jadon handed the amulet over, I felt so protected, closer to *being* my name and not just remembering it. Why would this pendant hurt me?

A woman's scream pierces the air.

A horse neighs. Men shout.

I twist toward the sound.

Twenty men on horseback, wearing copper-painted mail and plate armor over blue tunics, gallop toward the dilapidated oak gates of the village. All of them, even the steeds, glow with blue light. Healthy. Fed. Strong.

"Who are they?" I push off the ground, ignoring the intensifying vibrations against my chest from the moth pendant as I stand.

"Emperor Wake's men," Jadon says grimly. "From Brithellum."

Just yesterday, Olivia told me that the emperor's men would find Maford. She also told me that the colures would protect them. But these soldiers don't care to ask who the villagers worship. They charge right into town, torches burning, fiercely shouting, "For Brithellum," as they spread throughout the village.

Olivia presses a trembling hand to her chest. "They're gonna kill us. They're gonna kill us." She says this over and over again, her eyes getting bigger, her breaths getting shallower.

"Olivia," I say, surprised by my calm, "take it easy. Slow down. Breathe."

Behind us, villagers scream as they dart from cottage to cottage, seeking hiding places.

The soldiers dismount and draw swords. The lead soldier, a tall, muscular man with bulldog eyes and a turnip-shaped nose, turns to the growing crowd of villagers. "By order of Emperor Syrus Wake, the Manifestation of Supreme, Lord of Vallendor and All Realms, the Divine and Most Holy, the town of Maford is now a part of the blessed kingdom of Brithellum. Either bend the knee, declaring your fidelity to Supreme and turning away from the false King Exley, or…die."

The villagers gape at one another. Two step away from the others and drop to their knees.

Fucking cowards.

A soldier marches over to the two men, yanks them to their feet, and pushes them away from the others. Bulldog sneers at the remaining standing villagers and shouts, "Are there no more?"

"This is our town," a man yells. "We already have the colures up. We already pray—"

Bulldog knocks the man's head back with the pommel of his sword.

"How dare you!" a townsman shouts as the villager crumples to the rocky dirt.

"I'll ask one more time," Bulldog warns. "Are there any others who are ready to declare their fealty to Supreme?"

For all my hatred of Mafordians, I feel horror at the callous quickness with which the Brithellum soldier killed that villager.

"What should we do?" Olivia whispers to Jadon.

Jadon spins to his sister. "Hide. *Now*." He looks at me. "Go with Livvy!"

"No," I say. "I don't run. We have to defend ourselves." The roots of my hair tingle, and my shoulder blades itch. My amulet pulses, and my entire body screams, *Fight! Fight! Fight!*

"You have to hide, Kai," Olivia says, big eyes bigger. "They won't hesitate to gut you."

"I fear no man," I say, standing, feeling strength in my legs again. I squeeze my amulet for reassurance. Just then, in my mind's eye, I see myself with bloody hands, my face to the sky, the emperor's men at my feet. "We can't run. We have to fight."

"You just fainted," Jadon says. "And even if you didn't just faint, you can't fight."

"The *fuck* I can't," I snap. "And I feel fine. You can't tell me what to do."

A guttural scream from the center of town draws our attention. Another soldier has struck a pathetic Mafordian as more soldiers fan through the town square, kicking in doors and cutting down anyone who defends their home.

"Olivia, go hide," Jadon says. "Kai, please go with her. Make sure she's safe. I'm begging you. I'll take care of the soldiers."

Tears stream down Olivia's face. "But they'll see you and—"

A villager with an ax dashes past us. "Ealdrehrt, we need you!"

Other men hurry into the village square with their basic weapons and old breastplates to protect their chests.

Jadon shouts, "I'm coming!" He looks back at us. "Please hide."

Olivia grabs my dress.

I look in the direction of doors cracking and villagers shrieking, then to Jadon and his sister. "Fine," I say, "but I'm not hiding. I'm protecting—"

"Fine," Jadon replies. *"Go!"*

Olivia and I join a group of women and children hiding in a nearby barn. The inside smells of oily smoke and wet wool as weak light slips through the spaces between the barn's wooden slats. A few scrawny chickens scratch at the dirt while puffy-coated sheep crowd at the water trough. Sharp, pointy, dangerous things hang from pegs and knobs, threatening to butcher every creature that bleeds—including those of us walking upright.

Some women rock and pray, their eyes squeezed shut. Other women hold small colures to their lips. The rest stare at me, and I feel their heated glares even in this stuffy hot air.

"Violent witch."

"Barbarian bitch."

"Vile."

"Her fault the soldiers are here."

"She'll be the death of us all."

I wish that I could counter these clucking, gossipy hens with the truth, but I don't *know* the truth. *Am* I a witch? *Am* I a brute? Vile? My instinct is to fight for these people, and yet I know in my heart that they don't deserve one drop of my spilled blood.

How will I make amends for my failures? Have I failed to defend someone in the past? Did I hide? Abandon them to their fate because I didn't like them? Am I a coward? Is that what Sybel's referring to?

Or does she think that I should first seek a more diplomatic solution before choosing violence? *Let's sit down and break bread together. Be reasonable. Now, how can we arrive at a decision that makes us all happy?*

But soldiers like the men outside this barn don't compromise or offer reasonable solutions. They don't care about anyone's happiness other than the emperor's. They fight. And you meet fight with might. Unless that's wrong, too.

Ugh.

One young woman giggles, interrupting my thoughts, and says, "You see her dress, Ma? She looks so ridiculous."

"Don't look at her." It's the hag who spat at me as Johny dragged me to that jail. "I can't believe Olivia brought that disgusting Jundum with her."

Ice fills my veins, and I blurt, "Call me 'disgusting' again, and my Jundum ass will turn you into a toad."

Shocked, the hag holds her stomach. "She's threatening me!"

"*Shh!* The soldiers will hear you," Olivia whispers. "And remember what I told you about magic!"

"That was a bluff. I don't know how to turn her into a toad," I murmur.

Outside the barn, a man screams. It's the kind of desperate shriek that chills your bones. We all go still. Near tears, someone whispers, "Who was that?"

All around the barn, the women forget about me, quaking with fear as they peer through the slats to watch soldiers fight their loved ones or kick down cottage doors.

"How did they find us?"

"Why won't they spare us?"

"The sign of Supreme is everywhere."

"Quiet down. You're talking too loud."

"You see Oric and Tomas on their fucking knees?"

"Hypocrites."

"I hear the last town the emperor took? No one survived. The soldiers killed everybody."

The sounds of battle and death crash all around this barn.

Olivia stands at a wall, unmoving, unblinking, staring out between the slats to follow the action. Her specter-energy spooks the chickens clucking at her heels.

"He'll be fine, Olivia," I whisper, hand on the small of her back. "Take a breath. You're gonna pass out."

Even in the darkness, I see her large eyes peep at me, unbelieving and yet still hopeful. Then she looks back through the slats, but at least she's now breathing.

My amulet pulses against my chest, surprising me with its intense vibrations. There are pinpricks of light in the dark stone of the moth's thorax. As though it's guiding me, I move over to the barn's low door used by goats and sheep to get a good view of the fighting. Through the torchlight, I watch villagers doing their best with homemade or dulled weapons and mismatched armor. Jadon's wearing mail and plate, shinier and stronger-looking than his ragtag fighters, easily wielding a gray-bladed broadsword with much more skill and ease than the others. My hands itch to join him.

"Jadon Ealdrehrt was born a god," another woman coos, peering through the slats. "You see how he moves? How he charges forward? No one else fights like that. A god living among men. If anyone can defeat Emperor Wake's troops, it's him."

"Better be careful talking that way," an older woman says. "Father Knete's gonna hear all your lusting and worshipping, and he'll have you tossed in jail with Jamart's girl."

"And gods don't live in towns like Maford, girl," another old woman adds. "Gods are born in beautiful castles. Jadon Ealdrehrt only makes weapons; that's why he knows how to use them. He's a peasant just like us."

Olivia scowls at them, mutters, "He's *nothing* like you," and returns to watching the fighting beyond the slats.

I understand the Jadon worship, especially watching him fight. He's something special.

If only the other Maford men could fight as well. Even if their weapons weren't rudimentary, they'd still be no match for the highly trained, better-fed soldiers. Soon, the cries of villagers are cut short by the slash and gash of heavy metal.

I tiptoe closer to the low barn door, still watching Jadon through the slats.

He swings his weapon like it weighs less than a thought, and the blade slides into a soldier's gut like a minnow slips through water.

I may not know who I am or where I'm from, but I *do* know this: I *love* a good fight.

Another soldier pushes Jadon from behind, knocking that gray-bladed sword out of his hands and into the bloody dirt. But that doesn't stop him.

Jadon grabs the man who pushed him from behind and pulls him into a clench, bringing him close. Hands gripping the man's head, Jadon bends the soldier over, and *bam!* Strikes the man's face with his knee.

Beautiful! Even over the screams and shouts, over the clash of metal against man, I hear the soldier's nose break, and I smell the new blood now spurting from his shattered face.

Where did Jadon learn to fight like this? Certainly not in the dying burg of Maford.

Two soldiers rush toward Jadon, their swords ready.

Jadon, still without a weapon, slips as he tries to retrieve his sword.

Shit.

He's in trouble.

I can't just watch this happen. But I'm also without a sword. I scan the barn and find...*that*! I grab the garden hoe from its place in a dusty corner. The vibration from my pendant quickens, as though it's affirming my choice of weapon. "Hold this." I untie my pouch from the peacock-blue dress's sash and hand it to Olivia.

"Where are you going?" Olivia whispers, clutching Jamart's gift to her chest.

"Out there," I whisper. "Jadon's in trouble. He needs my help."

I creep out the door and over to a bale of hay closest to the action, gripping my hoe like I've named it.

Jadon dodges one of the soldiers, spinning to avoid another blow when he sees me rush toward them, hoe high. *"What the hell is she doing?"*

And for a moment, the soldiers, and even Jadon, gape at me. The two soldiers laugh at my pitiful choice of weapon, but their humor is cut short once I swing that hoe and slam it into the taller man's neck.

"Laugh again," I say to the dead man.

"Kai, this is no place for you! Get back inside!" Jadon yells.

The surviving soldier shouts to the sky and charges toward me.

"Are you gonna talk, Jadon, or are we gonna fight?" I swing the hoe in time for the blade to hit its mark—the soldier's nose—and the impact from the strike makes the handle vibrate.

The soldier collapses before Jadon.

Jadon's eyebrows rise. "Guess we're fighting."

I shimmy my shoulders. "Look at me handling a weapon that isn't even supposed to *be* a weapon. And you're welcome."

He frowns. *"For?"*

"For saving your life." I run past him, then yell back, "Don't worry about me. I was born to do this."

Those words—*I was born to do this*—burn like acid in my throat. I didn't come out of my mother's womb knowing how to take a hoe and make it a deadly weapon; I know this much is true. Yet here I am, wielding a hoe like it's as natural as breathing.

The remaining soldiers have spotted what we've done and rush toward

Jadon and me all in one wave.

Jadon and I glance at each other one last time before we're submerged in chaos. I give him a wolf's smile. "Ready?"

"Show me what you got." He winks at me before he charges into the fray.

11

A cting fast, I swing the hoe again, this time with enough force to wedge the blade into a soldier's forehead. I grip the handle tighter and kick the now-dead man's chest, freeing my weapon for more work. In the pandemonium, I spot Narder the jailer, spiked iron ball in hand, hiding behind a stack of crates, his expression a mix of fear and distress. The coward sees me marching toward him, and he doesn't know whether to sneer or shriek. He makes his choice, squaring his shoulders. "You should've picked my bed."

"And you should've run the moment you saw me," I spit, my breath hot.

Narder swings his spiked ball at me.

I duck.

He grabs at my dress.

I stomp on his foot.

He yelps, but his cry is lost in the noise of fighting.

I swing my garden hoe.

But he knocks me off-balance, and I miss him with my swing.

I scramble away from him and find my footing.

He swings the flail again.

I dodge, but the ball catches the sleeve of my dress. Heat crackles up my arm, and the spikes gouge long lines into my skin. I grab a wood shield from the ground and swing it just as Narder whips his flail at me. The ball embeds into the wood, cracking it.

Narder yanks, trying to free his weapon, not paying attention to the hoe's blade in my other hand. My weapon finds its mark, right in his throat. Blood spurts from the wound, and he howls, falling to the ground, clutching at his neck.

Before I turn back to the chaos behind me, I spot a ring of giant keys hanging from Narder's belt as he thrashes on the ground. "I'll take these," I say, grabbing them. "*Tah*, bitch."

He doesn't respond as life drains from his panicked eyes.

I straighten, catching my breath. Where am I? Where's the jail? Over there. Way over there.

Shit.

I leap over dead villagers and injured soldiers, booting a soldier charging at me with his sword lifted. I weave past horses rearing back and kicking high. I stumble in the bloody mud, and the key ring flies out of my hand but I catch it with my other. As I regain my balance, my borrowed dress snags on the tip of a dead man's sword. The taffeta rips as I yank it free. I wince—*shit*—and then lunge toward the jail as though it is a safe harbor.

Where's the entrance?

On the other side.

Fuck.

Breathing hard, I push my back against the wall, trying to stay hidden from soldiers and villagers while wearing a shredded bright-blue dress.

"Hey!" Two soldiers spot me at the same time and sprint toward me from different directions. Both men raise their weapons. I duck right as they swing and slice each other's ear and chin.

Careful now to stay out of sight, I make my way around the corners of the clink.

There's the door! I hurry forward, hands shaking, and I try one key after the next on the cumbersome key ring. Why did Narder have half a dozen keys? I push and wiggle and twist, one key after another, but none fit. I wipe my sweaty fingers on the front of the dress. Only two keys left. I growl, suck in a deep breath, and try the second to last key on the ring. It takes several tries to slip that key into the lock, but finally, a *click* and a *clack* and I push the door open and peer into the jail.

The prisoners—one, two…four of them—blink up through the darkness.

"I'm getting you out of here." I step over the waste and trash piled everywhere, charging deeper into the single cell. I help the weakest to their feet and lead them out of the stagnant death trap. They're all filthy and ragged, and in this dim light of night, I can't tell which prisoner is Jamart's daughter. Unsteady on their weak legs, the group stays close, one gripping the other as one clutches me. I feel their collective panic as they glimpse the frightful battle surrounding us.

Under the cover of darkness, to the dissonant harmony of bloodcurdling screams and the frantic clash of weapons, I lead the prisoners to Jamart's shop, which blessedly still stands amid the wreckage. In fact, it looks stronger than it did this afternoon.

Jamart is hiding just inside the door. Once he spies me, he tumbles out of his house and greets his daughter with tears and hugs. To me he says, "You've blessed me again."

There's no time for blessings. I point at the candlemaker, Lively, and the other prisoners. "Go. Find hiding places. Stay out of sight of the soldiers."

And pray a good prayer to Jamart's Lady of the Verdant Realm.

Keep them safe is my own prayer as I return to retrieve my hoe from beside Narder's body. I scoff at the jailer's empty eyes—his death gives more good to the world than he ever gave to it alive. Unspeakable things led him here, to this eventuality, and ending him felt good. Even better than taking care of these soldiers, especially since the soldiers haven't made this fight personal.

I scan the violence around me and find Jadon battling two soldiers at once. I race over, ducking horses and swords again, sliding and weaving my way over to him. I swing at the back of one of the soldiers hitting him, striking the warrior in the neck.

Jadon swings at the other soldier, bashing that warrior in the face.

Both men collapse in front of us. But more soldiers take their places, popping up like mushrooms after a storm.

"Where have you been?" Jadon shouts over the fray, the gray-bladed sword back in his hands. "You get scared?"

"Of course not." I knock one soldier back and stomp his head. "I just had to take out the trash."

To my left, a soldier leaves a house carrying a wooden chest. Is it not bad enough they have to kill these people? They're stealing from them, too? "Hey," I shout, running over to the thief. "Is that yours?"

He scowls and growls, "Fuck you, you mudscraping—"

"That's a no." I kick the side of his thigh, and the chest falls out of his arms.

He's now free, though, to pull the sword from his scabbard.

I give him no time to swing or insult me again. He's already dead from a hoe to his head.

Across the village square, the site of yesterday's market day, I spy another soldier looting a cart of pitiful carrots and potatoes. "Stop that!" I shout, marching toward him.

He pulls out his sword even as fear flashes across his face.

"Yeah, you *should* be scared." I swing the hoe's splintered pole.

The soldier ducks my charge and jabs his sword at my hip.

I hop back, but the tip of his weapon still rips my skirt. *Damn it!*

The soldier inches forward, cocky now that he's actually made contact. His breath comes loud and fast.

The hoe's handle has softened, squishy and wet now with blood and bone. The blade wobbles at the end of the stick, one swing away from flying off completely.

With a fierce cry, the soldier lunges.

I jab using the blade for the last time. The metal wedge falls off, leaving behind a splintered end. Perfect. I spear the jagged wood into the soldier's mouth and up through his nose. Down he goes. And then there's silence. Except for the booming of my heart. And the groans of dying men. And the clucking of manic chickens. The ground oozes, slick with blood. The emperor's men lie dead and defeated around us, their armor and swords glinting dully in the torchlight.

Before I can knead any tension from my shoulders, something shifts in the darkness toward the edge of the village. And then, out of a bank of smoke, *he* steps forward. A titan of a soldier protected by a mine's worth of iron.

Jadon whispers, "Shit."

I gawk at the behemoth headed our way. "What the hell is he? Not human."

"Otaan," Jadon says.

"How do you know?"

"His mouth."

Long canine teeth. Severe underbite. No lips. His forehead and his bald scalp bristle with pointy spikes. And he's completely covered in blood.

"Cannibals, Kai, that's what they are. Wake's soldiers always travel with one, as insurance against loss. He's been eating dead villagers." A swatch of blue tunic is caught in his teeth. Jadon glances over at me. "And a few of his fallen fellow soldiers."

With my eyes still fixed on the giant, I wrest away a sword from the clutches of the closest dead soldier. The handle is slick with blood, and there is no time to clean it. I tighten my grip as best I can and ask Jadon, "Can he die?"

"Probably?" Jadon pushes out a breath. "Ready?"

My amulet heats, and my muscles tense.

The titan closes the distance between us, bringing with him the smells of fire, rotten meat, and the musk of all humanity. The Otaan looks at me, and his eyebrows lift. *"You."* There's a spark of recognition in the giant's eyes that I can't place. He snarls at me, and his hatred rolls toward me in waves. Whoever he is, he's no friend of mine.

"Remember why we fight," Jadon says, almost to himself.

To keep Jadon and Olivia alive. To reverse the wrongs I've done but can't recall. To succeed instead of failing at something I don't even remember.

The mountain of a man charges toward us, clumsy in his armor, a bear in a teakettle.

Jadon and I rush to meet him, a battle cry erupting from the depths of our souls, perfectly entwined. I swing first, and the giant's great sword clashes with mine. It sounds like thunder, and the vibrations traveling up my arms make the sword wobble in my hand.

The giant notices my momentary confoundment and slaps me away from him.

My feet leave the ground, and I fly back until I hit an overturned wagon.

Oomph! All the air leaves my body, and sharp pain zips up my spine.

The Otaan lurches toward me. "You let them come," he growls, his voice as heavy and jagged as stone.

What? Through watery eyes, I see Jadon swing his sword, and the blade bounces off the behemoth's breastplate. I let *who* come?

The giant blocks another swing, then backhands Jadon just as he slapped me, sending him crashing into the remains of a chicken coop.

The Otaan rushes over to him the moment he hits the ground, swinging his sword at Jadon. The blade whooshes as it misses Jadon's head by a hair.

I see a weakness: the titan's breastplate has no back. He's too big for a full suit of armor. His undertunic has ripped, and round bony knots the size of crabapples run from the top of his bare spine to the end of his lower back. His skin looks as tough and leathery as a lizard's.

But that is exposed skin—even if it's tough. And if he breathes, he bleeds.

Jadon has recovered, and he swings and blocks desperately, though the giant shows no sign of fatigue.

Just hold him off a little longer, I think at Jadon as I creep toward the

Otaan. I focus on that band of exposed skin, on the smooth spaces between those balls of bone along his spine.

Jadon's attention flashes at me, as though he, too, can read my thoughts. He nods and renews his attack, keeping the Otaan distracted.

Closer... The sound of metal, the heat of striking blades, the growl of a monster. *Closer...* Strain and fatigue slow Jadon's motion. He catches my eye again. *"There. Go, Kai! Now!"*

I close the distance, sword ready and—

The Otaan howls as my blade finds its mark in the center of his spine.

Jadon whirls away from the startled warrior and jams his own blade in the space above mine. Together, we push in our swords. Jadon's blade jammed near the titan's head, my sword in his lower back.

"They destroy us," the Otaan screams as he falls to his knees. "You let them!"

The sound of the giant's agony hurts my heart, and I shout, "Surrender!"

The Otaan growls, "I curse your name—"

I jam my sword in the base of his skull.

Jadon kicks him, and the giant tips forward and into the bloody soil.

Unable to remove the blade, I stumble back, bloodied and exhausted.

Jadon, bent over and breathing hard, keeps his eye on the giant just in case he's not as dead as he seems.

But he *is* as dead as he seems.

I crouch, my body weak now that all stores of adrenaline have been spent. Every injury from the fight is now making itself known, including the cuts down my arm from Narder's flail.

They destroy us.

You let them.

Who is "them"? Who is "us"?

I curse your name.

Who did the Otaan think I was?

And was he right?

Eventually, Jadon stoops before the fallen Otaan and wrests away the giant's great sword. He staggers over to me and presents the weapon. Even though it's covered in gore and mud, the blade's engravings twinkle in the torchlight.

I peer at the markings running along the blade and make out a repeated image of a beast resembling a wolf or lion, encircled with stars linking the circles together. Letters unfamiliar to me have been inscribed on the cross-guard.

"It's yours," Jadon says, his voice hoarse.

I stand, taking this gift. The sword is heavy but...*not* heavy. A rush of icy-warm power sluices through me. Clearly, I know my way around weapons—both those forged for the purpose of battle and those crafted to till land. I'm a soldier. That's undeniable now. Maybe this is why I'm here. To protect this village. To protect people like Jadon.

But if I *am* a soldier, where is my army? Now, though, I mutter, "Wow." Even in torchlight, I can clearly see the mess in the town square, including dead soldiers and dead villagers. But there are survivors. A handful of people are leaving the shelter of their cottages and barns. They find each other in the darkness, hold each other tight, peck foreheads with teary kisses.

"Maford lives to see another day," I say, finding Jamart's shop in the dim light. Still standing. Unblemished.

Jadon grins. "Thanks to you. That was *incredible!*" He tilts his head back and howls, "Yes!" to the sky.

"I know I'm good, but how about you?" Awed, I shove him and say, "I saw how you slipped your blade under that guy's breastplate—"

"But you using *that*?" He points to the fallen blade of the hoe, his mouth widening. "That was fucking wild—"

My smile dies as my eyes shift from Jadon to the scene behind him.

Jadon, seeing my expression change, turns around.

Some of the surviving men in the village have fallen to their knees. Some women are draped over the bodies of their dead. Parts of soldiers not consumed by the Otaan are scattered across the dirt road. Women clutch their injured sons to their breasts or drape their husbands' arms around their necks, and together, they stumble through the streets and back to their homes. The first wail pierces the night. And then another wail. And then prayers and curses.

I squeeze the handle of the Otaan's great sword as sadness squeezes out my triumph.

They destroy us.

You let them.

Some protector.

12

"**D**rink." A woman, her eyes swollen from smoke and tears, drapes a quilt over my shoulders and thrusts one of two pitchers of water into my hands. "You must be thirsty." She offers Jadon the second pitcher. "Bless you," she says to me. "And you as well, Ealdrehrt."

As I drink, I take it all in. Broken carts. Overturned bins... The villagers who haven't left with their wounded loved ones pick over the destruction. "Where do you even begin to set this upright again?" I wonder.

Jadon drinks from the pitcher, then pours water over the back of his neck. "There will probably be a meeting with the surviving town leaders. Figure out priorities. Where to get supplies needed for repair. Where to bury all the bodies."

Near the jail, Johny crouches over Narder's body. The guard shakes his head, then squeezes the bridge of his nose. His shoulders shudder. He's weeping. As he cries, a man wearing a brown vest and matching breeches comes around the corner of the jail and stands behind the guard. He didn't fight. There's no blood on his clothes, in his hair, on his face. He looks worried but refreshed, as though he just awoke from a nap and had the most horrific dream.

I nudge Jadon and whisper, "Who is that? The fancy one standing behind Johny."

Jadon finds the two men. "Mayor Raffolk." He cocks an eyebrow. No additional comment is needed.

Does Johny know that the emperor's men didn't kill Narder? Does he know that I did?

The guard lifts his head and scans the wreckage until he finds me. He points at me, and the mayor turns to see who he's pointing to.

Yeah. He knows.

My attention is pulled away by more villagers. My chest swells to hear their voices, to see their tear-stained faces, and to feel the warmth of their gratitude cutting through the chill of death enveloping me. An older man totters over and offers me a basket of bread and cheese. "It's not much," he says, "but most of my pantry was ransacked."

"Thank you, sir." I bow my head. "I appreciate your generosity."

Raffolk and Johny might hate me, but there are plenty in Maford who don't.

Jadon plucks a roll from the basket and says, "I'm gonna look around. Find Olivia."

Ah. I forgot about Olivia.

I watch Jadon wander off, gnawing bread, squeezing the shoulders of the grateful villagers he passes. Piles of goods continue to grow around me: wine and veg, a basket of fabrics, a few candles, and a small pot of honey.

A warm wave of pride washes across my bones. I am their champion. Protect and battle? That's what I do. And my work here more than covers my fine of twelve geld.

My spine feels straighter, my mind clearer, my limbs stronger. It's as if I've grown three heads taller and three bodies wider. I'm not even breathing heavily, but damn am I hungry. For food. For drink. For Jadon. I scan the square and find him talking with a group of villagers who have stopped him again. He points this way and that, and the villagers nod in agreement. I imagine him with me instead, nestled high in the loft. With my gifted jars of honey. That warmth in my bones now flares to heat.

"You're alive!" Olivia barrels toward me and skids to a stop before trampling over the pile of offerings. "What's all this?"

"Meet the new Queen of Maford," I tell her, palming the jar of honey. "Your townsfolk love me and have chosen to show just how much they appreciate me with gifts of bread, honey, cheese, fabric, and other bric-a-brac."

Olivia's eyebrows lift. "I think you should slow down your celebration."

Still surrounded by villagers, Jadon frowns, and concern clouds his expression. Raffolk and Freyney have joined his group, anger plain on their faces.

"What's wrong?" I ask, but I already hear the familiar hisses of angry thoughts.

"She brought this upon us."

"We should've killed her when we could."

"We need to do it now."

Shit.

My heart crumbles. So much for my newfound love from the townsfolk.

I slip the jar of honey into my pocket. At least this is mine.

"You have something to say?" Jadon shouts at the angry crowd.

"I do," Johny says. The energy of his fury crackles like storm clouds. "Now that we've killed Wake's men, we're gonna be even *bigger* targets. More soldiers will return, and who knows what they'll do to us. And that mudscraping whore—" He glares over at me.

"Oh?" I rise and step over the offerings to join Jadon. Indignation buzzes like a hornet's nest in my ears, and I take a calming breath.

"Be careful, Kai," Olivia whispers.

"Always."

I reach the mob and level my gaze on the angry villagers. "Anything you wanna say about me, say it to my face."

"Leave her alone," Olivia shouts behind me. "She saved us. Show some gratitude!"

I lift my hand to her and turn back to Johny. "If you were all dead beside this heap of bodies," I ask with reason and patience, "would that have been your preferred outcome?"

No patience left, Jadon glares at the guard and then at the group. "You're all talk. Playing knight with your dull blades and slow swings. But when it's time to actually fight, what did you do?" He throws the borrowed sword he used to the ground and mutters, "You let the two of us fight your battles. Now that it's over, you wanna nitpick how we did it? Ungrateful pricks." He turns on his heel and marches back toward his forge without another word.

"What about Narder, *prick*?" Johny shouts. "This bitch killed him."

"She needs to atone for his death," another man shouts.

Unrepentant, I fold my arms. "Anything else?"

"Narder was our last connection to the wanderweavers." Freyney spits.

"They'll never come here now!" another man adds.

"We'll all starve."

There's no arguing that point. They may have been cowards when the soldiers invaded Maford, but that will change. Under the cover of night, weak men always find the courage to do their worst. All the honey, candles, and loaves of bread in the realm won't keep them from driving my head and Jadon's down on pikes.

These surviving Mafordians are making it difficult for me to be their protector right now, and if they continue this course, I may choose to never fight for them again. Yes, this mudscraping whore killed Narder, and she feels absolutely unapologetic about driving a blade through his neck. Because she also killed half of the men wearing copper armor.

The emperor *will* send more men. He has to. And when they come, Johny and his band of malcontents won't be among the Mafordians I'll protect.

This ain't over. Far from. And next time, they'll find themselves fighting alone. Unprotected.

A new day in Maford, and I wake in the loft to the golden light of a bright morning. Peering out the little loft window, I see how that light shines upon the copper mail of the last soldiers needing to be buried. That same golden light reveals the true destruction from the battle the night before. Shattered windows. Trampled and dying flower beds. Broken and twisted colures. The reek of new blood and the waste of dead men. Most of the village has fallen over like a barrel of wine, and its people are now soaked and drowning in the flood.

But some of this golden glow doesn't originate from the daystar. Another kind of amber light had pulsed throughout Maford before soldiers stormed past its gates. Death was always coming for this village—some just met their ends quicker, with steel instead of disease.

An old man wearing a stocking cap pushes a wheelbarrow carrying a bag of limestone. Milo, his tail tucked, minces his way across the village square, a temporary grave for the fallen.

I slept as well as I could, even though Jadon's forge has been firing white-hot since the early hours. Every dead soldier's sword has been cast into the fire, and they now glow as they melt into useless pools of iron. Jadon's worked without stop, crafting new weapons from these old ones. Preparing for the inevitable next attack.

Olivia climbs up to the loft, bringing me wet towels, a clean white tunic, and brown suede breeches. She sighs at the spoiled peacock-blue dress and whispers, "Oh well."

"She was a beautiful frock," I say.

Olivia tries to chuckle but can only say, "Yeah."

By the time I change my clothes, Olivia has brought breakfast out to the forge. She hurries through her potatoes, her eyes popping wide once she finishes. She whispers, "*Shit. My book!*" She races to the hayloft, leaving me to wash the dishes in a bucket of water and to take them back to the cottage alone, without a chaperone.

And the cottage… I couldn't see the fullness of its destruction last night, but now, standing before it, I see how bad it is.

The yellow curtains hang limply across the shattered window. The front door has been kicked in, no longer capable of blocking my entry. The hinges squeak with the wind.

Olivia's still at the barn, searching the straw for her fancy, probably stolen, book, and Jadon's at the forge, repairing swords. Neither of them can stop me from stepping across the cottage's threshold. And so, I do.

This cottage, even in its best state, is far from impressive. Really: is *this* what Jadon and Olivia wanted to hide from me, the reason why they didn't invite me in? I knew that it couldn't be because they're poor and embarrassed by it. I never believed that excuse about me catching Miasma from them—they're both healthy.

The books have been pushed to the parlor floor, which itself is crowded with broken tokens and baubles. Not one thing has been left upright or unspoiled. Every place my eye lands, there is a monument of destruction left behind by angry men.

I set the breakfast plates on the pantry table and wander back to the parlor. The room is cluttered with overturned furniture: two armchairs, a spinning wheel, a stool, and a rocking chair. The rug shines bright with shards of glass and pottery. The only untouched piece of furniture is the tall, two-doored wardrobe that almost touches the ceiling.

Nothing special. Nothing fancy. I thought the sitting room would have hosted golden thrones because of their insistence that I not enter. For a second, I wonder if any of those broken pots were stolen. If the lavender sprigs were plucked without permission. If the cutting shears were lifted from a tailor's shop.

Olivia *is* a thief, after all.

Maybe they thought I'd steal their knickknacks, thingamabobs, and shriveled potatoes? Did they fear I was a thief just like Olivia, and that I'd do to them as she's done to others? Yet Gery had the nerve to make *me* turn out my pockets after I mucked and milked my way around his barn.

I hear the crunch of bootsteps headed my way. *Shit.* If it's Jadon, he'll see that I'm standing in prohibited space. What will he say? Will he be upset that I entered his home without explicit permission?

"Hey." Jadon rounds the corner, carrying wood boards, nails, and a hammer.

I let out the breath I was holding to say, "Hey."

He drops all the supplies into a noisy pile. "You're like water, you know that?"

I cock my head. "Pardon?"

"You slip in wherever you please," he says. "Nothing can stop you from entering any space, big or small."

I swallow. "I needed to bring in the breakfast dishes. I'm not interested in taking your things, if that's what you're worried about."

"Kai," he says, shaking his head, "we fought side by side last night. Don't you trust me by now? Anyway, that wasn't the reason we didn't want you coming in."

"What was the reason, then?"

"Exactly what I said. *Miasma*. No one knows how it's passed. If it's in the air or if it's in the water or the food. If it's in the air, we didn't want a third person who may have had it in close quarters. Olivia and I have escaped with good health because we've been very careful, and we'd just met you."

"Ah." Whatever. There are now bigger things to worry about.

Jadon grabs the hammer from the pile to start repairs. He lifts a massive board. "Nothing to say?" he asks, squinting back at me.

I tilt my head. "Huh?"

"About, you know, my massive wood or…?" He grins. "Something else to make me laugh and enjoy a moment before dealing with everything?"

I blink at him, excitement flooding through me like hot water. "What a big hammer you have."

"Nope." He shakes his head. "You're faking it."

"I'm not. Bang something hard for me." I pause, my skin tingling. "Make me jump."

"That's better." He sets the board against the doorjamb.

"I'm astounded by all your wood," I say, lowering my gaze…lower… lower… There.

"Okay, I get it," he says, then sticks nails in his mouth.

I fight the urge to giggle. "Do you need me to hold your wood?"

"That's enough, Kai." He chuckles as he drives the first nail into the plank.

"Harder, Jadon," I say, breathless. "Hit it like you mean it."

"You know what?" He shakes his head, trying not to smile. "Are you gonna just stand there and watch, or are you gonna—?"

"Guide your hand?" Legs trembling and body buzzing, I pick my way over the broken plates and splintered beams.

"If you want," he says, biting his lower lip. "And then we can do it together." He peers at me with his smoky blue eyes. "We'll hit it like we mean it."

My tongue pokes my cheek. "I don't think I've ever been this excited about woodwork."

"Kai," Jadon says, his deep voice rumbling all through my body, "you have no idea how excited I am."

My eyes flit from his face, down his torso, and lower still, where they linger on the best wood in Maford. "Oh, I think I do."

He drops the hammer and looks at me with a glint in his eye. "So you've noticed."

I stare at him, my breaths shallow. "Umhmm." The heat of my anticipation smolders against his.

He holds my gaze, drinking me in, and takes a step toward me.

An achy shiver ticks the base of my spine. If he touched me right now, I'd fucking—

"Good morning?" A man's voice comes from outside.

"Damn, and we were almost there," I say, dizzy, carefully prying my eyes from Jadon's to land on the intruder. "Good morning." I still burn from Jadon's attention.

Farmer Gery takes off his field hat and wipes his sweaty forehead with the sleeve of his shirt. He peeks up at Jadon. "My missus, Zinnia. She's not feelin' well. Much worse since yesterday, and the soldiers, they hurt her. I don't know what to do, and I know you're not a healer, but you're plenty smart. Freyney's busy with the other wounded. Can you look in on her?"

Jadon says, "Sure, but I need to fix a few cracked beams before this part of the cottage collapses. Hopefully, it shouldn't take too long."

"Okay," Gery says, but he's not okay.

"I can come over and look," I say. "I'm not a healer, but I can stay with her as you tend to other tasks around the farm."

Farmer Gery blinks at me, eyes my pendant with distrust, then shifts his gaze to Jadon. "That will be appreciated," he says, dipping his head in thanks.

I follow the farmer next door to his barn. I stutter in my step, though, as I remember Olivia's warning before I started my chores to earn geld. *Don't go inside their house.* And I recall Jadon's concern about not knowing how Miasma is spread.

Shit.

"A soldier pushed her out the bed," Gery says, oblivious to my hesitation. "He was trying to steal some jewelry she was wearing. A butterfly ring I gave her on our wedding day. She fell, and when I picked her up, she felt *broken.* Freyney refuses to help—he says she's not a priority." A teardrop slides down his cheek. "I brought her outside for some fresh air—she has Miasma. I'm sure you heard."

I nod, breathing a sigh of relief now that I no longer have to enter their home. We reach the garden behind the barn, and that's where a pale Zinnia Gery rests on a featherbed.

Her cheeks are sunken, and her bones poke at her sallow skin. Her death glow is more straw-colored than all the hay on this farm. She's barely conscious and merely murmurs at the sight of her husband.

"I'm gonna show her," Gery says to his wife, pulling back her nightshirt. He points to the bruise on her hip. "This came due to the fall."

I peer at the purple discoloration that nearly blends into the grayness of her skin. "I'm going to touch you," I tell Zinnia. "I'll try not to hurt you." Then I feel her hip bone, lightly press her ribs, her arms, and her back.

"Her bones *are* brittle," I say, "but I feel no broken ones. She didn't wince from my pressing. There's no swelling." She looks as though she's sinking inward even as I crouch here beside her. My own limbs feel heavy, but that isn't sickness. That is sorrow. "She's bruised from the soldier's assault, but she isn't broken. This sudden decline is from…"

"Miasma." Farmer Gery nods.

Zinnia mutters something and tries to sit up in the bed.

I touch her chest to keep her still. "Don't. Please."

She groans, then settles back onto the featherbed.

I look down at the woman with great sadness. "I wish I knew how to heal. If I did, I'd certainly help Zinnia recover."

Her amber glow is brightening. Won't be long now.

I lift her hand and kiss her knuckles, not sure how contagious this Miasma sickness is but now not caring at all. "I wish you both peace," I whisper.

Zinnia's eyes close. Her hand goes limp. Her heartbeat slows.

I stay beside her as Gery tends to the horses and to Molly. Anytime Zinnia stirs, I whisper, "I'm right here," until she slips back into the space between life and death. I trace the stones of my pendant and feel its pulse beneath my fingertips.

The work of putting Maford back together again echoes all around me. Hammering and sawing. Chopping. Shouting. My mind wanders as I sit here, and snippets of poems and songs appear in my thoughts.

With healing hands, she gently weaves...
...for the souls she grieves...
...mourns with a heavy heart...
...dawn approaches.

Are these prayers from my homeland? Something to be recited above a sickbed? I say them aloud as reassurance for Zinnia that I'm still here, as a way to force the rest of this poem from the dim spaces in my mind.

...dawn approaches.

Zinnia opens her eyes, and a faint smile tugs at her lips. "Thank you," she whispers, the words barely audible before sleep claims her once more.

Farmer Gery slips back into the garden and offers me a meat pie.

I thank him. I'm hungry. I don't recognize the taste of the meat, but it's not foul.

The farmer completes a few more tasks and finishes by putting out fresh water for Milo.

Zinnia's breathing is peaceful and unlabored when he returns to her side, and her amber glow wavers, as if death is struggling to keep a foothold.

"I don't know how to thank you," he says. "But I have these." He holds out a bundle wrapped with cloth. "More meat pies for later."

I thank him and make my way back to the cottage. Jadon's finished hanging the door, and now he's fixing the fence. He smiles when he sees me, but then his cheer fades at my expression. "That bad?"

"That bad. She's not broken. Bruised, certainly. The soldier stole her butterfly ring that Gery gave her on their wedding day. But that's not why she's weak. It's Miasma."

He watches me sit on the only patch of grass in the yard. "She's one of the first to get Miasma. She's held on for a while now."

My heart swells sharply, and I flick away a tear rolling down my cheek.

He tugs at the bandage on his hand, then comes to sit across from me.

"Sorry, Kai. Did she pass?"

I shake my head. "Not yet. She continues to hold on, and I don't know if that's a good thing or…" I shrug and offer him a weak smile. "But that's not my decision, is it?" At least she was peaceful when I left. I lift the bundle. "Gery gave me meat pies for my time. They're pretty good. Want one?"

He takes one and bites into it. "It's good." He chews for a moment. "I'll tell the men doing all the burying to look for the ring in a soldier's pocket."

I think about those men doing all that burying.

We should've killed her when we could.

Still, I nod my thanks, and we finish our pies in silence.

Which of us will they bury next?

13

"**O**h shit. Not now." Finished with his pie, Jadon stands and frowns at something happening behind me.

I turn to see an older man wearing a long black tunic and a soft black hat. His steps are like ghosts, because I didn't hear his approach. I pull myself up and stand beside Jadon.

"Father Knete," Jadon says, his hands now folded.

The man's hazel eyes, deep-set and knowing, bore into mine. His smile is soft and compassionate. "You must be our newest hero." His voice is smooth as soap.

I squint my eyes. "I wouldn't say 'hero.'" Even though I'd said something similar just last night. I've seen enough darkness now to not revel in the violence.

The minister places his hand over his heart. "Well, you've earned a number of admirers. I had to come meet this 'Lady Kai' myself. I was expecting you yesterday. Olivia mentioned that you'd be polishing the silver and the pews because you needed to earn geld."

Shit. Forgot about that.

Jadon clears his throat and says, "Kai." To the minister: "It's been a long day. Now isn't a good time." He moves toward the threshold of the cottage.

"Give me a minute," I say.

Jadon holds my gaze. There's a question in his look.

"I'm fine," I assure him, then turn back to Knete.

Eventually, the repaired door to the cottage closes.

"So much has happened," I say to Knete. "The emperor's invasion, for one. And I figured, since I helped with everything last night, my debt would be forgiven."

"I don't know about *that*," the minister says. "But we're having Assent this evening, which has now turned into a special service for the dead. I saw Olivia in town this afternoon, and she promised me that you'd show up after you failed to show yesterday."

My stomach twists. I really don't want to go, and I really don't think I should *have* to go, especially since this man is partially responsible for Jamart's daughter being jailed. But I also don't want to get Olivia in trouble. She did arrange this job. "I can help now."

His eyes light up. "Wonderful. Let's walk over to the church together, then."

The air buzzes with the sounds of work and renovation. The villagers are leading the orphaned horses to their new homes. Poor horses, who will no longer have good oats to eat. Some men roll the dead soldiers onto wheelbarrows, two at a time. The ground is soft beneath my feet. Not from rain but from blood.

"How are you finding Maford?" Father Knete asks. "Aside from the violence last night?" He pauses, then adds, "Though I'm sure where you're from you're probably used to it."

What? I jam my lips together as my mind searches for the most diplomatic answer. "Maford is an interesting place."

"What province are you from?" he asks.

"Oh," I say. "Here and there. I'm just trying to figure out where to go next."

True.

"You have no family?"

My chest tightens. "I do have family."

"And did they not want to join you in Maford?" he asks. "Or have you abandoned your Dashmala ways? Brutality and raiding and heresy? Are you now ready to be transformed?"

"I didn't actually choose to be here. Circumstances led me here." I rub the space above my eyebrow. "Circumstances that resulted in my need to earn twelve geld. As for transformation, I'm fine just the way I am. Respectfully speaking."

Father Knete, his hands clasped behind his back, says, "Hmm."

"Last night," I say, "I fought for a town that's been so unkind to me, with the exception of a few people. And yet some are still scared of me or angry with me—"

"You murdered an important leader of this town," he says sternly. "Their reaction isn't arbitrary. The only reason you're not locked in that jail is because you have Ealdrehrt on your side. But I know and Supreme knows what you did. How many soldiers you slaughtered."

I snort. "Are you referring to the soldiers who killed more villagers than I did?"

He says, "Mmm. May I ask? Your pendant. It's interesting. What does it signify?"

No idea, but he can't know that. "The typical things moths symbolize."

"Transformation," he says. "Death. We don't subscribe to such symbolism, nor do we wear charms and totems like yours in our village."

"Just the one totem," I say, nodding. "The colures. They're everywhere. On shops, on carts, hanging around people's necks. I've been told that the paddles and the circles symbolize your belief system."

Too bad they didn't stop the emperor's men from killing the villagers. But that doesn't matter to Knete. He's already loyal to the emperor. He went untouched in the battle.

He chuckles. "I understand your meaning. I'll admit that the colure does symbolize our relationship with Supreme."

We stop before steps leading up to a tall stone building with colored glass windows and a large colure nailed over the entry. The open doors offer quiet, cool respite and sweet-smelling air.

"Shall I ask Supreme for forgiveness on your behalf?" the minister asks. "If you are to stay in this town, if you are to walk into this holy place, this consecrated ground, you must be free from iniquity."

I start to say, "Pardon?" but he's already extended a hand over my head.

Eyes closed, he says, "Divine, guide this lost soul. May she put down her anger to follow in Your way. Let her move from self and on to You. Open her mind. Open her heart. Keep her from her murderous inclinations to do Your will and Your work. Forgive her for her transgressions against Your servants and let her join You in the great reformation of this realm and its people. In Your name and in the name of our emperor..." He opens his eyes and smiles.

I scowl and push down the urge to knock his hand away from my head. He knows nothing, and his hand is good only for blocking me from the setting daystar's glare. Heat rises off my prickling scalp, and my fingertips burn. I take a breath and then another to stop the buzzing in my ears. His prayer is useless. No clarity unfurls before me. Just the same hollow echo inside my skull. My heart clenches more than it did before his prayer.

Bile creeps up my throat. Something about this man, about his prayer, his talk of transgression. My heart and my gut are not at peace with any of this. The voice in my head whispers, *You know the truth. You know all that he's saying is not truth.* I don't need to know my history to know this voice is right.

"Patience, child," the minister says, as though he can read my mind. "Prayer is not an instant salve, but you wouldn't know that, would you? The blessings you seek must be earned, starting with acknowledging that it was not you but Supreme who granted your so-called victory over the emperor's men."

"So-called?" A spark of defiance ignites within me. "No disrespect, Father Knete, but it was Jadon Ealdrehrt and I who bled those soldiers, who saved this town. That is called 'victory.'" We hold each other's gaze—I will not retreat from this belief.

His eyes burn, and his breathing is hot. He's holding back his ire. "You are troubled, child. Because you are a visitor here and a newcomer to this province, I will hold my tongue. There are still some parts of Vallendor that have not heard the truth and are filled with primitives who believe in false gods. You come from one of these places."

I lift an eyebrow. "And you know this...*how*?"

He levels his shoulders. "You were brought to us for a reason. I will do my best to show you truth. I haven't had to teach a beginner like you in a very long time." He smiles. "I look forward to the challenge. You will soon discover how wrong you and your people have been. And Supreme will welcome you, all of you, with open arms."

I say nothing.

"I have something for you." The man searches the pockets of his robe. "You can't see yourself right now, but if you could, you'd see the pain and anguish you are experiencing— Ah. Here it is." He pulls out a small, rolled piece of paper, and though he smiles, his eyes remain flat. "This is what your heart is telling me. When you are ready to speak, Supreme will hear." He holds out the scroll.

I hesitate but take it anyway.

"I no longer need your assistance in the sanctuary," he says. "You are confused, child, and if it is Supreme's will, your aid will come." He thinks, *"And your aid will never come, child of the Vile,"* before heading up the steps, leaving me there, alone, in the coming dark.

Olivia and Jadon are in deep conversation when I enter the cottage. They fall silent. Olivia's cheeks color, and she pops up from her seat, plucking an unfinished dress hanging beside the lavender bundles.

I toss her a smile and drop into the chair she just abandoned. "I haven't seen *you* all day. You will not believe the conversation I had with your…" I squint at her. "Something wrong?"

Jadon tries to smile. "What makes you think something's wrong? We're just sitting."

Olivia averts her eyes and paws through her sewing basket.

I shrug and say, "Okay. I brought back a souvenir." I hold up the prayer scroll. "Did you tell Olivia I accompanied the minister on a walk to the church?"

"What did you two talk about?" Jadon sounds hesitant.

"Many things," I say, "including his belief that I'm a lost child of the Dashmala and that Supreme was the one who defeated Wake's men, not us. Oh, and that I'm a child of the Vile."

"The Vile?" Olivia snaps, glaring. "That's ridiculous."

"I'm sorry," Jadon says, expression darkening.

"And he gave me this." I toss up the prayer scroll and catch it. "For when I'm ready to accept the truth."

Olivia sucks her teeth. "I have, like, fifteen of those prayer scrolls."

"If you collect twenty," Jadon says, "you win a ticket to heaven."

I groan and pull off my boots. "I'm exhausted."

Jadon stands and says, "Same. But my day's not over. As much as I want to stay and complain about Father Knete, I can't."

I waggle my eyebrows and twirl the prayer scroll with my fingers. "A pre-Assent date?"

"Meeting at the mayor's house down the road," he says. "Town leaders will be making big decisions about what to do if Wake's men return… *When* Wake's men return."

"Wait!" I reach into my pouch and grab the geld I earned yesterday. "It's not twelve, but again: I fought for this town last night. That has to count for something." I hand Jadon my fine. "Please consult with the leaders about if I'm now free to reclaim my belongings and leave."

Jadon pockets the coins and nods, a little stiffly. "I will. Just know that you don't have to leave, like, immediately." Then he and Olivia exchange looks. "I won't be long." He leaves the cottage without a goodbye.

"Did something happen?" I ask, anxious. "Did Zinnia pass?"

"What?" Olivia snaps, irritated. "No. She's still alive."

Her thoughts, though, speed through her mind. *"Why can't this be simple? Why can't I just exist? When will this be over?"*

When will *what* be over? My living here? I sit up in the chair. "If Jadon comes back with good news, that I can leave, I'll take my things and head out first thing in the morning. Then you can go back to your lives before you found me passed out in the forest."

She stares at me with exhausted eyes, then gazes into her sewing basket. "You're the least of our worries."

Before I can ask her what that could possibly mean, someone raps on the pantry door.

Olivia shouts, "Come in, Phily!"

The girl I recognize as Copperhair rushes into the sitting room. Her eyes roll wild in her head with fear like a stallion's. Her sage-colored dress gleams in the gloom.

"Sweetie!" Copperhair runs into her friend's arms for a hug.

"Philia! You're back!" Olivia plants kisses all around her face and lips, turns her this way and that to search for injuries. "I'm so glad you and your uncle went to Pethorp yesterday."

"We heard about what happened," the young woman says. "I wanted to come back home last night, but Uncle Darrick said it was too dangerous. I didn't sleep at all because I was so worried about—" She finally sees me seated in the armchair. She gasps, startled. "What are *you* doing here?" Her frightened eyes find Olivia's.

"Minding my business while looking bloody fabulous," I say, smiling. "Did you hear that I also looked bloody fabulous during yesterday's invasion?"

Philia scowls, then turns back to Olivia.

But Olivia's arms are crossed. "She's right, Philia. She and Jadon saved us. Your house is still standing because of her. You should be grateful."

Philia stares at her friend as though she's waiting for the punchline to this joke. But Olivia's mouth is set firm. She's not joking. Philia turns to me and clears her throat. "Thank you for fighting." Her cheeks turn bright red.

"You're welcome, Philia." I give her a wide smile. "I'm Kai—"

"*You're* Kai?" Phily's eyes widen in surprise.

"What is it?" Olivia asks.

"It's just—" The redhead looks flustered as her eyes bounce between Olivia and me. "Just now, on the road outside of Pethorp, we saw Helman. He said that there's a woman and two men on the road, and that they looked peculiar, like no one he's ever seen. He says they're wearing fancy clothes and that there are bright-red cardinals flitting around their heads."

Cardinals? Yesterday afternoon, I saw two red birds in the woods.

"He said a bandit tried to rob these travelers," Philia continues, "but one of the strange men lifted the bandit right off his feet, held him high into the sky, and then slung him into a tree, and every bone in the bandit's body broke into a million little pieces!"

Olivia frowns, her eyes big. *"What?"*

Philia nods. "Helman says that they're on their way to Maford *right now*. They're coming here." Wide-eyed, she turns to me. "And Kai, they said they're looking for *you*."

14

Philia sneaks back out the pantry door.

"Be careful," Olivia whispers. Even after Philia disappears into the night, Olivia stays at the door, watching until Copperhair's long gone.

The air in the cottage has turned hot and muggy. Or maybe it's just me.

When she returns, Olivia glares with hard, slitted eyes. "Who are those travelers? And why are they looking for you?"

My heart pounds wildly in my chest. My stomach churns with nausea. "Open a window."

Olivia lifts the sash of the parlor window.

My mouth waters, and a flush creeps over my skin and swirls beneath my amulet. As cooler air drifts into the room, I pace in front of the fireplace.

Olivia runs her fingers through her short hair. "What did you do before coming to Maford, Kai? Tell me."

"Will you shut up?" I shout at her. "I'm trying to think."

"I don't believe you," she accuses.

"That I'm trying to think?"

"You nearly choked me to death just two days ago," Olivia says. "Maybe you strangled somebody else the day before. You certainly know how to kill—you made that obvious last night."

I clutch my stomach. "To protect *your* town, not mine." I glare at her, my nerves sizzling and popping. "I may not remember my origin story, and right now, I wish that I could. But I don't hang out with people who hurl other people through the air. I am not that person."

Make amends.

Failure.

They destroy us.

You let them.

Sybel's words and the Otaan giant's accusations race around my mind as my underarms prickle with sweat and my pacing quickens. "And as far as me strangling you? *You stole from me.* Am I not supposed to respond?

Am I supposed to ignore that?"

"Why can't you remember?" she demands. "Are you willfully forgetting? What's your family name? Where did you live before coming here? Where were you going two days ago before you arrived in our forest? Tell me that, and I'll tell you how you should respond."

My mouth pops open, then closes. I square my shoulders, then say, "I don't have to tell you *anything*. And what I was doing, where I was going? That's also none of your—"

"People of Maford," a woman's voice calls outside, chilly yet commanding.

Her voice raises the hairs on my neck.

Olivia stumbles over to the window. "Something's happening at the chapel." Olivia looks back at me with wide eyes. "I think it's the lady Philia told us about."

"Let's go, then." I head to the door.

Olivia grabs my hand. "What if she plans to do to you what she did to that bandit?"

I push out a breath. "What do you suggest I do?"

"Let's just…" Olivia shakes her head. "Let's just sneak out and listen to what she says. If you still want to confront her, then at least you know what to expect. You'll have the advantage."

A moment later, we creep out the pantry door and slip over to hide behind a discarded pile of stone and planks of thick wood, some pocked with rusty nails, some blackened from fire or mildew. From our hiding spot, we can see the three strangers standing before the chapel.

The air smells of night-blooming jasmine and snuffed-out candles.

My heart races like I've run up a mountain twice. Why am I panicking? I was the picture of calm and competence during last night's fighting. Now, though? I can't catch my breath. What's different? I survey the strange men flanking the bottom of the chapel's steps. They're each as tall as three Maford men, one standing on another's shoulders. They wear platinum breastplates without tunics, and long red ribbons wrap around their bare arms. Their skin is as white as the hair billowing like waves from their heads. The lower halves of their faces hide behind gray kerchiefs. They scan the square with gray eyes, ready to pounce if they find anything threatening.

I don't know them.

At the top of the steps is the woman Phily spoke of. White-haired with rich light-brown skin and narrow eyes, she wears a cloak of swirling golds and blues. She's not as tall as the guards but still taller than the average Maford man. She looks to be somewhere in her twenties and holds an ivory walking stick that looks like it's made of clouds and snow, just like her long, thick hair.

I don't know her, either. Nothing about them—their faces, their armor, their snow-white hair—looks familiar. So how do they know me?

Women and older men have gathered around the chapel steps. Their faces, bright with awe, quiver with fear. At their feet: the last few swords and daggers that survived the fight against Emperor Wake's battalion. Were they planning to fight these strangers? Silence now drops like a heavy quilt over the town, but their thoughts and prayers sound like shouts.

"Supreme protect us."

"Where's Johny?"

"Where's Father Knete?"

"We need Ealdrehrt!"

Jadon mentioned that the town leaders were meeting at the mayor's house.

Where is the mayor's house? They must still be there.

These villagers look as ill as I feel. Their muscles are rigid, and many clutch their stomachs as beads of sweat roll down their faces.

"You may call me Elyn," the woman begins. Her voice is hard things and soft, granite and silk, lava and fresh snow, wise, warrior. She paces, twirling that cane as she surveys the crowd. "I'm looking for a young woman named Kai. She's about my height, hair the color of plums and chestnuts, hair that's way out to here." She holds her hands far away from her head. "She's strong-willed. Smart. Unforgettable."

"Plums and chestnuts?" Philia holds her hands out from her head. "No. We haven't seen anyone like that."

"Shut up, Phily," Olivia thinks. *"Don't try to be clever."*

Elyn's gold eyes brighten, and her white hair darkens to gray, but that agitation dies; her eyes soften again, and her hair reverts to the color of snow. She stares at the redhead.

Philia drops to her knees, clutches her gut, and her skin pales.

"There's no need to be foolishly obtuse," Elyn says. "Of *course*, she could've changed her hair. Kai is extremely versatile. Her style tends to befit her *situation*."

I am? Does it? I glance down at my borrowed tunic and breeches. Nothing special. I don't stand out anymore. Which befits my situation: the need to blend in. *Oh.*

"Enchanting little town you used to have," the woman says, eyes skipping to the splintered carts, the mounds of limestone, the pools of congealing blood. "*Someone* was angry."

When no one says anything, she saunters down the steps. "Oh dear. There's no food here." Elyn plucks a withered potato from an overturned produce cart and *tsks*. "Hardworking people like you deserve more than *this* shriveled-up thing." She twists the potato in the air, and that shriveled-up thing becomes a fat thing, a potato big enough to feed two people.

She tosses the potato to Philia, who catches it. "Are you tired of potatoes? *Philia*, yes?"

Olivia thinks, *"Oh shit, oh shit, how does she know her name?"*

With a damp face and tear-filled eyes, Philia whispers, "Yes, ma'am."

"Do you ever go to bed with your stomach growling, Philia?" Elyn asks.

A glittering teardrop slips down Philia's bright-pink cheek. "Yes, ma'am."

Elyn smiles. "Oh, I'm too young to be a 'ma'am,' but I appreciate good manners." Then, with a wave of her hand, Elyn summons an entire cartful of fat carrots, onions, cabbages, peapods and potatoes, all big enough to feed three families for a week.

The villagers gasp, and some reach with tentative hands out to the vegetables.

"Not so fast," Elyn booms, her voice paralyzing the villagers. "I need your help with something before you can enjoy the food." She paces before the villagers, a commander facing her pitiful army. "Have you seen this before?" She flicks her hand, and now she's holding a necklace heavy with a ruby-and-gold-jeweled moth.

Olivia and I both take a breath.

The onyx stone in the moth's thorax swirls with all the colors ever created. This amulet resembles the one hanging from my neck. But Elyn's pendant is an illusion.

"Well?" Elyn asks.

An old man who presented me with twisted carrots as his thanks for saving the village peers up at the amulet, then shakes his head. "We're not a rich village. Just farmers. Treasures like the one you're holding? If someone owned *that*, they wouldn't be living *here*. Not anymore."

Elyn says, "Okay," and flicks her hand again. The pendant's gone. She furrows her brow, clearly frustrated. Even with all her power, Elyn can't sense me. Her lips become a hard line, and the freckles across the bridge of her nose darken. She's beautiful, and she's plump. With that cape, with that flawless skin, she's obviously rich. She's also wearing an amulet around her neck: six small rubies on a swirling rose-gold vine surrounding a dove, a glossy black stone in its center.

Maybe she's Emperor Wake's daughter. Only a royal could afford an amulet with—

Wait! My amulet also boasts jewels. Maybe I've run away from Brithellum after all, deserting my position at the court and leaving behind my important and wealthy family. Maybe I *did* attack someone before I met Olivia, and maybe Elyn is Justice Incarnate, searching for me, a fugitive, to mete out punishment.

"I'd appreciate any help you can offer," Elyn says in her honeyed voice. "No detail is unimportant. Everything matters in this task. Kai may have forgotten, but we made an agreement, and she broke her half of that agreement. So much is at stake right now. Life and death, I must say, though that sounds *incredibly* dramatic." She turns to Philia. "With that in mind, one last time. Any tidbits to share?"

Is that desperation I hear?

Philia closes her eyes, and she shakes her head.

Elyn tilts her head. "Really: Kai and I... We're old friends. We go back, *way* back, and I'd simply *love* to catch up with her and talk out our differences. Do each other's hair, ha." Another small smile at Philia before she looks back at the carrot farmer. "Have you thought of anything yet? Anything at all, old man?"

He shakes his head.

Looking at this group of villagers, I recognize most of them as the ones praising my name and showering me and Jadon with gifts. I see a few malcontents, but by the way they're shaking, they're now too scared to speak.

"You might think you're protecting her." Elyn's gaze stays on Philia's bowed head. "She is a danger to you." Then she looks at the group. "She's a danger to Maford. She's violent, selfish." She narrows her eyes. "Trust me when I tell you that she'll turn on you just like she's turned on her family, on me."

Carrot Farmer shakes his head. "She's been our savior. Our champion."

"No she hasn't. She's the Vile," another farmer says, finally working up the courage to speak. He then spits to the ground. "She's trash."

"Really?" Elyn asks, smiling at him. *"Trash?"*

Why is she suddenly smiling?

The farmer collapses. No light—not amber or blue—glows around his body. He's dead.

"What just happened?" Olivia whispers. "Why is Old Milton on the ground? Didn't he tell her what she wanted to know?"

I shake my head. He didn't, though. He insulted me.

Maybe Elyn didn't like him referring to me as trash? On that, Elyn and I agree.

"Take this seriously." The stranger pushes a breath through clenched teeth. "If you don't help me find her, she will bring *each* of you death. She's already brought you so much violence."

A woman is now crying as she gazes down at Old Milton.

A blast of thunder booms from the skies above.

"So, you've been no help," Elyn says. "You've wasted my time. I don't appreciate that." She fakes a gasp, then looks to the sky. "Oh, look. More guests."

A howl as vicious as thunder and deeper than the bellows of the stormiest sea shakes the town square. In the sky, I can see the outline of the creature that made that deafening roar, only by its vibrant blue glow and its belly filled with flame.

The villagers scream, huddling together for protection.

"So," Elyn says, her voice heavier, "if you decide that you've seen my old friend, just call my name and I'll come running."

My skin feels like it's being poked by millions of knitting needles, and the tendons of my neck tighten. I want to scream, but I can't scream. Not yet.

Another blast from the sky, this one bursting with flame. A fireball strikes the steeple of the chapel. When the smoke clears, Elyn and her sentinels are gone, no longer holding court in the village square.

Townspeople scream and scatter as another fireball strikes the chapel.

"C'mon," I tell Olivia, scrambling out from the rubble.

People dart from the square to their homes. The closest buildings to the chapel, though, are already burning.

"Where is Father Knete!"

"Run!"

"The chapel's on fire. We have to put out the fire!"

People duck and shove, cry and stumble as a giant creature—*is that a fly?* —swoops and shoots burning breath into the village. Smoke billows to the sky as flames lick across the rooftops and consume the remaining carts of vegetables.

"Kai!" That's Jadon.

I grab Olivia by the arm and race to find him. Thankfully, he's wearing his steel-and-leather breastplate again and carrying two swords.

"Where have you been?" I shout.

"Raffolk was scared shitless, and he forced us to stay to protect him. I left anyway and ran to get my armor and—" He peers at my hands. "Where's the sword from the Otaan soldier?"

"At the cottage," I say.

"Use this for now." He tosses me his second sword, one with a silver blade and a golden-leather handle.

Another roar from the creature still circling the smoky sky, and that roar sounds like scores of beasts and infinite boulders slamming into a canyon. Its bellow vibrates across my face and shoulders, pinches my skin, and constricts my lungs.

The jail catches fire. Most of the timber cottages are burning, too. The flying beast dips lower to the ground.

I duck, and now I can better see this creature. Shit. I gasp, and my blood runs cold with recognition.

Cursufly.

But the creatures I remember were the size of deer. The cursufly now hovering over the burning church is bigger than any deer. It's larger than a cottage. Its six scaled legs are thick as birch tree trunks. Its vulture-like feathers are as long as cottage doors. White lights glow where eyes should be. Long, lank hair falls from its head like a crone's. Flames shoot from its mouth, and the stench of sulfur gurgles like an everlasting spring in its belly.

Smaller cursuflies swoop through town, fire bursting from their mouths also.

I'm prepared to fight but not sure how. These things fly. Jadon and I do not. And now, I remember something horrifying about cursuflies. They feed on human flesh. We may not be able to reach them in the air, but if these creatures are here to feed, then they must come down to where the food is. And that's what I shout to Jadon. "That's the only chance we have."

He looks ill at the suggestion, his complexion gray, but nods.

So, we wait, legs spread apart, swords held back, willing the giant flies to come closer...

One creature hovers before me and studies me with its white eyes. Before it unlocks its jaws, I thrust my sword into its heart, then hop back as green blood bursts and spills onto the dirt.

One cursufly down. Countless to go.

Other villagers have taken up their weapons and are hacking and swinging their swords, their brooms and rakes, whenever the beasts get too close. They're not killing them, though, since they're unable to reach them to strike a fatal blow. We're losing this fight.

I look over to Jadon, and as tall as he is, he can't reach flies that dart out of the way before his sword can make—

A smaller cursufly hurtles toward me, its head down like a ram.

I turn to face it, tripping over some dropped potatoes, and my sword tumbles to the ground. With nothing but my hands, I swat blindly at the creature before it bites me. Wind from my slap sends the cursufly slamming into the side of the burning jail. I gape at the fiery fly. How could a swat do something a sword couldn't?

Barking pulls me back into the now.

Milo! The poor dog is trembling beneath a cart, hiding from a cursufly.

Another cursufly swoops at me from the right.

I raise my hand to see if swatting it works again.

The beast is thrown backward, stopping only when it crashes into the burning tavern.

But I didn't even touch the creature. That realization puts a hitch in my step.

Milo barks as the cursufly bumps the cart, trying to overturn it.

I run faster, stopping only to grab my sword. At least this beast is low enough to slash with my sword. Hands burning, I grip the handle tighter. *What the…?* The fingertips of my free left hand are glowing coral, red, and blue, and they're hot, so hot that I wince and flick them for relief. This time, I see blue air burst from my glowing fingertips, and immediately, the cursufly racing beside me goes flying into a burning shop.

Did that just happen?

I sprint to the cart protecting Milo, and this time, I intentionally flick my hand at the cursufly threatening the Gerys' dog. Blue air gusts from my fingers. The fly goes *whoosh.* The cart flips. Milo scurries over to me. My mouth hangs open because *what the fuck?* Have I always been able to wind whip and only now have rediscovered it? Or is this a new power? I drop the useless sword and scoop up the dog in my right hand. Does my right hand push wind, too?

Another fly homes in on Milo and me.

I switch the dog to my left hand and thrust with my right. I send the creature flying into the darkness. Left hand out—another fly gone. Right hand out—a cart lifts high in the air and knocks a fly to the ground. I laugh. "Milo, do you see this?"

The dog barks and licks my face.

There's a fly over there, chasing the old carrot farmer.

I push my hand. Blue air crackles. Cursufly gone. *Oops.* Too much wind—I've also knocked down the farmer. But he gets up and gapes at me. *I'm just as amazed as you are, old man.*

Every time I flick my hand, wind bursts from my fingers, causing the cursuflies near me to lose all control, landing in heaps, never moving again.

Where's Jadon?

My gaze skips around, from fire to fire, from one collapsing cottage to the still-burning chapel. Milo hops out of my arms and races through the smoke to...

Zinnia Gery! She's standing on two feet. She's not dead and strong enough to catch Milo bounding into her arms. Her amber glow has softened. How is that possible?

I can't help but gawk at her as she and Milo rush back to their barn, which is miraculously still standing. I spin around, trying to find Jadon again, but all I see is the ground around me flickering with dying amber light of fallen villagers, and villagers with no light at all.

A single cursufly screams above me. I see fire bubbling in its cauldron-like belly as it lets loose a fall of fire. In the light, I see Jadon, still on his feet, still fighting. He swings his sword and dodges the fly's ball of fire.

As the cursufly blasts another fireball and then another, Jadon rolls and ducks, but he's running out of room. The fire is spreading and encircling him.

I race over to Jadon before he's trapped in a ring of fire. I skid to a stop and thrust both of my hands at the beast. Blue wind swirls from my fingers, lifting the massive creature higher into the air. Higher. I keep my hands up, and the fly hangs there, its legs twitching, completely helpless in the space it should own.

Huh. So I can also control this wind? Let's see what else I can do with it.

I hammer down my hands.

The creature slams into the ground and craters the earth.

Jadon barrels toward it, his blade ready.

The giant cursufly, now amber, writhes in its new grave, and that fire in its belly fades.

Jadon plunges his sword into the belly's hotspot, and his blade quivers and turns fiery orange, burning up to the hilt, making the pommel glow like hot coal. He jerks back—his leather gloves are smoking.

"Are you okay?" I shout, running toward him. "Where's Olivia?"

"Don't know," he pants. "What did you just do?"

Before I can speak, though, something behind him catches my eye. "What is that?"

"Is there another one?" he asks. "I'm so tired of fighting."

But there is no new enemy to fight. A group of ragged villagers, including Olivia, are staring at the chapel, which is still engulfed in flames.

Jadon and I edge closer to the group.

They're staring at the doors of the chapel, which aren't singed or even covered in ashes. On these impossibly white doors, someone's used red paint—or blood—to leave a message:

WE WILL HELP YOU REBUILD

WE WILL GIVE YOU RICHES

GIVE US KAI

15

Those bloodred letters are singed in my mind. Even if I close my eyes, and I keep closing my eyes, the words remain. But I can't bring myself to move away from the chapel or away from the small group of surviving villagers. Together, we watch the building burn as the doors remain standing.

Olivia watches with one arm around Phily, who hasn't stopped shaking. With her free hand, she takes mine and looks up to me. "What does she want?"

I shake my head. I take back my tender hands and hide them beneath my armpits. Moments ago, I was awed by my new ability, shooting wind, a confirmation that I'm someone special, despite the minister's words. But now my ability feels sinister. Are there other mortals who can hurl wind? Is that why Elyn is looking for me? Did I misuse my power in the past? Does *she* want to use my power?

Jadon hasn't stopped staring at those chapel doors. He looks back at me over his shoulder. No, he's not looking at *me*. He's looking at my hands.

I imagine the same questions are going through his mind. *What kind of monstrosity am I? What have I brought to this town?*

A few of the surviving townsfolk, including Freyney, Dirty Bonnet, and Johny, think the same thoughts as they scowl at me.

"She's the cause of this."

"I should've spoken up."

"I told all of you she was a threat."

"We have nothing."

Right now, as their town burns, they don't care if a day ago, I defended Maford. They don't care that I defeated the cursuflies. None of that matters. Their town has been destroyed.

It's not the smoke that's choking me. It's not the fire that burns my skin. It's the collective glare of those who have survived. It's their simmering hate now boiling over and ready to cook me and feed me to the fires that surround us.

"I need to leave," I say, my voice low. "I need to get my things from the cottage and go."

Jadon eyes me. He knows I'm right. "I'll walk you back." He starts toward the cottage.

"They're not that angry," Olivia says, running ahead of us. But she can't hear their thoughts.

"Supreme is displeased."

"Where is that piece of shit who ruined my home?"

"The white-haired one will be our salvation."

I jog beside Jadon to the cottage. I can't stop smelling the scent of night-blooming jasmine, heavier than all the burning flesh. If Elyn will burn Maford down—because *she* did that, not me—what would she do to me? She's extreme and dangerous, and I'm not going anywhere near her until I learn the truth about myself. Until I know what she wants and how to handle her.

But before I know any of that, I need to leave this town lest the survivors call her back...or before one of them kills me.

"I'll go with you a ways," Jadon says. "Just to watch your back until you're far enough."

My heart won't let me admit how much I want him to join me in my journey. How much I *need* him. But the memory of my dream of him and me in the forest remains.

Come with me.

No.

"Those flying things," Olivia says. "I've read about them in my book, and I've heard stories. I didn't think they were *real*. Did you, Jay? Were you as freaked out as I was?"

"Olivia," Jadon snaps. "Turn around. Pay attention where you're walking."

We're running now, and the roar of the fire diminishes the closer we get to the cottage.

I don't have the breath to say it, but yes, the cursuflies scared me, especially since I knew what they were but couldn't remember *why* I knew what they were. And then there was my ability to send wind. That scared me even more, and I can't remember how I acquired that power, or if I've always had it.

Neither Jadon nor Olivia mention that they noticed the wind from my hands sweeping those creatures into burning buildings and slamming them to the ground. I'm sure Jadon saw it. Did he also see that crackling blue air rolling out of my fingertips?

Olivia flies through the front door of the cottage.

"I think your decision to leave is the right one," Jadon says as we hurry up the walkway. "That's what the village council decided tonight."

I don't wanna be here as much as they don't want me, so…*bye*.

Once we're inside, Jadon shouts, "Livvy, bring Kai's clothes."

"Okay," she shouts from the back rooms.

Jadon rushes to the pantry. "We don't have much, but…" He looks back at me. "Oh."

"She needs to hurry." I've already taken off the soiled tunic—I can't stand these strange clothes touching me any longer. My amulet swings from my neck as I pull off my boots so that I can change back into my pants. I'm back to wearing a bandeau and breeches.

"You need a bag for a few supplies." Jadon disappears deeper into the pantry.

"Hurry," I say, pacing.

Vibrations from the hardwood floor judder beneath my feet and zing up my legs. The palms of my hands tingle as those vibrations work themselves up and across my cheeks. Something's coming.

Olivia returns from the back rooms. Empty-handed. She looks me up and down and takes in my state of undress. "Again?"

My heart flares. "Where are my things?"

"In the loft. I washed them. Everything's drying. Why are you naked again?"

"Because you were supposed to be bringing me my shit," I yell.

Jadon dashes back into the sitting room, a leather satchel, his sword, and another sword in hand. "Kai, I'm giving you a sword, and I've put in a few potatoes and…" He looks from me to Olivia. "What's happening?"

The vibrations beneath the floor are gaining strength. Olivia doesn't notice, but Jadon does, and he's now staring at the floor.

Yes, something's coming. All of me coils inward, preparing for the worst.

"Where are her clothes?" Jadon asks, eyes still on the floor.

"In the barn," Olivia answers.

He looks up, annoyed. "What? Why?"

But before she can answer, the floor in the parlor explodes, sending wood splinters and shards into the walls and ceiling. The angry smells of hot earth and dead things roil the air and clash with the scents of night-blooming jasmine, sweat, and lavender.

Three creatures with skin as smooth and flaky as the trunks of birches burst out of that hole in the floor. Each of their heads is shaped like a ram's, with four horns swirling from the tops of their skulls. Except for mouths and jagged teeth, their faces have no features. No eyes. No hair. No ears. Their long arms end in sharpened talons that resemble twisted tree roots.

Olivia shrieks, then runs back into the pantry.

Jadon whispers, "Kai?" He backs away from the creatures and drops the satchel. "Catch." Without taking his eyes off the beasts before us, he tosses me the second sword.

I catch the long sword and sink back into my crouch in the space between the pantry and sitting room, painfully aware that I'm not wearing a shirt or boots.

Olivia shakes her head in disbelief. "What are they?"

Jadon whispers, "Sunabi." He launches ahead and swings his sword at a sunabi's neck.

The blade breaks like brittle bark, and a shattered piece nicks the scoop between my collarbones.

"Shit," I say, wincing.

"You okay?" Jadon holds off the snarling sunabi with the broken stub of his sword.

I nod and say, "Yeah." I squeeze my eyes shut to push against the pain. A trickle of warm blood drips from the cut and soaks into my bandeau. Wounded already, and I haven't even started to fight. The cut burns in its small space, but my body feels heavy. All of me tingles. I take a step back.

The sunabi step forward, the talons on their feet clicking against the hardwood floor. One sunabi advances in front of the others, its breathing noisy, its scissor teeth bared.

I take another step back.

Jadon moves to flank them. "Is this the plan?" he asks, his shattered sword ready.

"Sure?" I say, short-winded.

These creatures could tear the three of us apart in seconds. But they hesitate. We stand there, these creatures and I. They turn their heads away from Jadon and in my direction. If they had eyes, they'd be staring at me right now. One sunabi snarls, its claws digging into the wood floor as it steps forward. The sunabi's hot breath burns my skin, but I have no fear. No, I'm filled with sorrow, cold and hollow. This creature, this *otherworldly*, does not belong in this realm.

Neither do I. Not in Maford, anyway.

I grip my sword tight, my focus on the otherworldly before me. "Please," I say to the creature, "just leave this place."

"Kai, we need to kill them," Jadon says, his voice hard.

Maybe it knows the word "kill," because the sunabi lunges at me.

I shout, "No," and thrust out my left hand.

The creature slams back into the wall and sinks to the ground.

The second sunabi pounces.

I throw my left hand again.

The creature hurtles back, knocking over one of the armchairs.

Like before, my hands burn, and like before, my fingertips glow coral, red, and blue.

The first sunabi writhes on the floor after hitting that invisible wall and thrashes its wounded body into the cupboard, bringing down with it the remaining unbroken plates and cups. It lies there then, motionless among broken shards of glass and clay.

Jadon jabs hard at the third sunabi, but the blade bounces off the creature's skin. Annoyed, the sunabi springs at Jadon.

I scream, *"No,"* again, drop my sword, and throw out both hands.

The sunabi flies backward and smashes into Olivia's spinning wheel. Like the first creature, it lies there, unmoving.

My hands glow even brighter. My amulet radiates like the daystar, its glow so bright that Jadon hides his face in his shoulder. I tiptoe closer to the last surviving sunabi, collapsed near the rocking chair. Its breathing sounds ragged and wet. My amulet's glow softens as I control my panting breath. I tiptoe closer to the sunabi.

Jadon also inches closer until he's standing over it.

The sunabi's face glows green, and its skin crinkles around the edges of its mouth. Air pushes between the creature's razor-sharp teeth as green blood pools beneath its body.

"Who sent you?" Jadon demands, crouching now. "Was it Elyn?"

"Danar... Ruh-ruh..." The sunabi coughs up green blood.

"Who?" I murmur, moving closer to the creature.

The sunabi whispers, and the sound bristles against my ear.

Jadon stands, then steps back, his gaze lingering on the creature.

"What?" I ask it, tears burning my throat. I can't understand what the sunabi is saying nor can I understand why I recognize the language of this creature.

"De-vour," the beast rasps, its words almost liquid. "Here...now."

"*What's* here now?" I'm almost kneeling beside the fallen beast. I want to touch it, heal it, pull it away from its doom. Talk to it now that I can understand.

"Be..." the sunabi rasps.

"Be...*what*?" I ask.

"Be...*ware*." The sunabi shivers, and its breath rattles until...

No no no.

Dead. But...

Beware?

Of *what*?

16

Once again, I stand over destruction.

Broken furniture, broken sword, discarded sword, and three dead sunabi.

She is a danger to you.

Elyn said that, and she's right. Maford, and now Jadon and Olivia's cottage.

My breath hitches in my chest as those words swell larger, larger, until they are the only words I hear. Elyn claimed that I turned on her, turned on my family. The sunabi said, "Devour." If I'm from that region and my people live in one of those villages around the sea, just as Jadon suggested, what happens if I go there? What will happen? Will I receive the same greeting that Elyn would have given me?

Jadon and Olivia are standing near the front door, silent. She's gaping at the dead sunabi. *"Is this for real? Am I looking at sunabi? Who is she?"* He's staring at me. *"This didn't happen, this couldn't have happened."*

In the congealing pool of sunabi blood, six shrinking ivory horns the length of a child's hand shimmer against the green-stained floor.

I crawl over and pluck one of the horns from the drying blood.

Olivia is curious enough to slink closer.

I offer her a horn, and I offer Jadon a horn. I take two.

"What am I supposed to do with this?" Olivia asks, rolling the horn between her fingers.

"Keep it for good luck," Jadon says, then turns to me. "Your hands. Wind or something shoots from them. How?"

Olivia pales with fear. "Magic?"

"I don't know if that's the right word," I say, "but I can't call it anything else." I meet Olivia's eyes. "You told me that magic has been banished from the towns. And so far, I've met no one else who can do what I can. And now, I'm thinking." I dip into silence, letting my creaking brain do its job. "If mages have been pushed to the ends of the realm, and people who look like me, who named me after its deity, are in Devour, maybe that's where I need to go."

She'll turn on you just like she's turned on her family, on me. Elyn said that tonight.

Make amends. Sybel told me that days ago.

I slowly stand. "I need to go to the Sea of Devour."

"You're not serious, are you?" Jadon asks. "That's really, *really* far. You don't know how dangerous it is—or even how to get there—"

"No, I don't." I straighten my shoulders. "But the sage you mentioned, the one who was kicked out of Maford. He'd know. Where would this sage be? Or any other sages? I need to talk to someone with a deep understanding of Vallendor and its peoples."

"Outside of Pethorp," Jadon says. "But I don't know for sure."

"I'll find him," I say with a nod.

"My book!" Olivia gasps. "It might help you. It had that story about Kaivara. It might have something else. I'll go get it!" She turns to leave.

"And my clothes," I shout after her. "I don't care if they're damp, if they're dirty, I need them. Understand?"

Olivia nods, then darts out of the pantry door.

"How do I get to Pethorp?" I ask.

Jadon crosses the room and opens the wardrobe doors. He grabs two tunics, tosses me the white one, keeps the black one. "It's west of here. We can make it in two days." He pulls off his filthy shirt. His chest is hard, defined by fighting and forging. Pearly scars crisscross his ribs, like sutures keeping him whole. His belt buckle hangs low, his hip bones exposed and... and...

My pulse bangs from my temples to my toes, tiny explosions everywhere. "You're coming with me?" I ask, dizzy now as he slips the clean tunic over his head.

"I told you I would." He pauses, and our gazes lock. "I told you I'd help you find yourself, Kai, and I meant it."

Come with me.

No.

I exhale, my heart swelling with relief, with hope, with *want.* "Glad to hear that."

Jadon continues to stare, and I stare right back. Then his brow furrows and he tilts his head, studying my left shoulder.

"What?" I peek over my shoulder but see nothing.

He reaches toward me but stops before his fingers touch my skin, which vibrates now beneath his hovering hand. "You have a tattoo."

"I do? What does it look like?"

He bends to study the marking more, and his breath warms my skin.

My knees weaken, his warmth so delicious that I close my eyes to enjoy it.

"Crimson ink," he whispers. "A circle filled in. A smaller circle connected to it by a tendril? And something else." He leans in even more.

My knees are almost pulp now—he's so close to me. "What?" I whisper, my neck tingling. My arms drop, perfectly still, no longer hiding my bandeau from his gaze.

"Letters," he whispers. "Or symbols? I don't know what they are. There's another, but it's hidden mostly beneath your chest wrap. You'd have to move it down some if you want me to see all of it."

I reach back to unclasp my bandeau. "Is it ugly?" I ask, my head lolling to the right.

"On you?" His breath teases my shoulder. "I don't think anything would look ugly on you."

My heartbeat quickens, my limbs too heavy to move.

Then he says, "Do you know what it means?" His breath licks the nape of my neck.

I shudder and shake my head. "No." Eyes closed, I imagine his hand coaxing me back…back…until I'm firm against him, immovable. I draw in a shaking breath, and just as I prepare to drop my bandeau to let him see everything, he takes a step back and then another step back.

"What's wrong?" I ask, confusion replacing heat.

"The sunabi—" He's looking down at the corpses on the floor.

Desire no longer floods my veins because, across the sitting room, the sunabi have begun to shrivel. I pull on Jadon's white tunic and wander over to the drying pools of sunabi blood. Cold, damp air pushes up from the hole the creatures dug to breach the parlor floor. I crouch and swipe a finger through the clotted green goop.

With a rush, a vision flashes behind my eyes. A white sunabi, its birch-branch skin luminescent, bares its jagged teeth, glares at me even without eyes. A lake behind it, its glassy surface still and glowing a malignant green. *Devour.* It must be. I look beyond that glowing sunabi and see waves of sunabi and waves of cursuflies. I spin around, and behind me, rising in a red ash sky, high in the clouds, are mountains of silver rock. I turn back, wanting to rush forward and begin my assault of the attacking otherworldly, but smoky tendrils drifting from that mountain hold me back.

"What is it?" Jadon whispers from behind me.

"I'm remembering something," I say, staring at my soiled fingers, "but I can't quite describe it out loud. I don't think it would make sense." It seemed unreal, but my trembling is not.

"I'll listen when you're ready," Jadon says. "I'll always listen. Know that."

I nod, pulling my attention from the blood on my finger to his sincere gaze, and my trembling fades.

"How's that cut?" He touches his own collarbone.

I look down at the wound made by that shard of steel. "It doesn't hurt that much."

"You sure?" He stares at the bloody mark, then takes a step toward me.

My muscles tighten and heat—my body remembers. *Come closer.* I want him near. I want his touch. I want his comfort. I want more.

He doesn't come closer, but he doesn't move away, either, as the air between us sizzles.

As if on cue, Olivia hurries back into the cottage, Philia in tow. "If I'm coming with you," she says, "Phily needs to come, too."

"I didn't know you were coming," I say, pulling my gaze from Jadon's face.

"Of course I am." Olivia produces her precious book from where it was hidden beneath her shirt. "You'll need this. It could give us some clues about what's happening. And I don't go anywhere without it." She dashes to the back rooms.

"Are you sure about coming?" I ask Philia. "We're heading west, toward Pethorp. And we'll be moving fast. It won't be easy."

The young woman's lip quivers. "I-I have no one now. My brothers and my mother—" A strangled noise comes from her throat, and she whispers, "They're dead now. And my uncle…" She clamps her lips, shrugs, and shakes her head.

I pause, then touch my heart. "I'm sorry. Really, I am."

Copperhair nods, relief in her relaxing facial muscles. "I know it wasn't all your fault," she says. "That woman, Elyn—she was terrifying. I don't blame you for hiding from her."

"Take this and let's go." Jadon hands me a sword and the bag he's prepared for me. He slings his knapsack over his shoulders as well as a sack full of other weaponry.

"I've never in my life seen things like that before," Olivia calls from the bedroom as she finishes packing. "But she flicked them away like fleas, Phily." She returns to the sitting room with two bags filled with who-knows-what and puffs of tulle. She tosses me a bag.

My clothes! My still-muddy clothes that she said she'd wash.

She catches me looking and says, "There was a lot of mud. They probably need to be washed two more times." She blushes. "Looks like Jadon's given you another shirt to wear. So, I'll clean your clothes once we get to Pethorp. But you have them now. Happy?"

"We need to leave now!" Jadon shouts from the pantry door. "Right now."

Olivia surveys the destroyed sitting room and near-empty pantry. Her eyes glisten with tears, but her posture remains proud, almost regal. "Goodbye, little cottage. Thank you for protecting us." With that, she and Philia brush past me, disappearing into the night with Jadon.

I take in the cottage as I pull on another pair of borrowed breeches. The room smells sour, like turned stew and animal hides. But the odor isn't causing the worry gnawing at my stomach.

It's too many things. That woman. Those sunabi. Their warnings.

But I'm not planning to be captured—by Elyn, by birch-skinned creatures, by whatever it is that now waits for me in that dark night. I might not know much, but I know *that.*

"I need to check on Jamart before I leave Maford."

"Why?" my three companions ask, scowls on their faces.

"Kai." Jadon shifts his bag of gear on his shoulder. "We can't go back. I'm trying to get you out of here."

"Jamart's one of the few people here who treated me like a person instead of an outcast," I say. "I have to say goodbye. Any more questions?"

Silence for a moment—embarrassment for all three—until Jadon says, "Meet us at Gery's barn. We'll grab some horses and go from there." He points at me with concern in his eyes. "Stay in the shadows. Don't get caught."

I set off back to the town square. The fire still lights up the night, and the smoke makes the dark sky white. Survivors either try to douse the flames or comb through houses and shops in search of the living. Some wrap bandages around their injuries while others drink wine and water straight from casks and barrels. The white wooden doors of the chapel still stand, that bloody message—GIVE US KAI—bright as the flames around it.

I'm relieved to find Jamart alive. The candlemaker sits on his porch, his head in his hands and tears streaking down his dirty face. The candles in his shop have survived, but now their wicks flicker with flame. The air around him smells of beeswax and lilac.

"This town," Jamart says, weeping. "What has happened to this town?"

Jamart and I sat back in that garden not long ago, dipping wicks into wax. Not long ago, this Mafordian treated me with respect and kindness. While the straw-basket beehives have survived, no bees dart in and out of those holes. Melting wax and honey pool in the dirt. This place of quiet respite is now destroyed.

"Lady Kai," Jamart says between sobs when he sees me, "it's all gone." He drops his head, and his tears darken the ashen ground.

"But your house and shop," I say, looking at the still-standing structure behind him. "It hasn't burned down. Your candles may have melted some, but—"

"Who is around to buy anything?" he says. "I don't know who's still alive, but I know plenty are dead."

"Your daughter?" I ask.

He nods and swipes his eyes. "She's here. At least I got my girl back." He meets my eyes. "Thank you for rescuing her, but now..."

I tilt my head. "Now, what?"

He swipes at his mouth. "Every time they look at her, they'll see Narder dead, all because she was spared." He tries to smile. "Guess that's why they say be careful what you pray for."

I step away from him, disappointed that he's disappointed.

"I am grateful for your blessing," he says. "I am." His glazed eyes take in the destruction, and he whispers, "I am." He keeps his gaze on the town.

A breeze whispers across my cheeks. "I need to go," I say, dropping to my knees to meet his eyes. "I'm sorry for your loss but I'm happy that you lived. Would you rather have what so many are dealing with right now? No home? No family? Sickness?"

He bites his lips, his eyebrows crumple, and he whispers, "I don't know." He pauses, then says, "I don't know what to believe. Who to believe in. I thought you…you…" His gaze dips, and he wrings his hands. "But I think, I think I believe the white-haired one."

I stare at him—for ages, it seems. The muscles around my face feel like they're all twitching, and I touch my cheek as a comfort. I will no longer find any here. I step away from Jamart, back, back, back until he's lost in the smoke and I can no longer see him. Grief swells in my throat, and it cinches the sobs threatening to overwhelm me.

Holding my breath, I hurry back toward Gery's barn. Just as I reach the edge of town, where the woods border the road to the barn, I slow my step, shivering, but not from the chill in the air. Something isn't right. The reek of decay and rot wafts around me, a worse odor than cow manure and anxious sheep. I take a few steps before stopping again. That *smell*. It's drawing closer. Like it's following me. I whip around.

"Lucky me." Johny the guard sidles out of the shadows of the trees. He's been injured in the skirmish, and the wounds on his neck and bared stomach glisten with pus and poison.

"What do you want?" My voice is steady, but I touch my amulet for reassurance. My itching shoulder blades and burning fingers alert me. I'm ready.

Johny grins. "Just enjoying the night out with some friends."

That's when a colossus of a man tromps beside him. He already smells dead, like mud and rancid meat. The knots on his thick arms are not all muscle. No, his body is revolting against him, making little boils that might explode.

"My favorite prisoner," Johny says, coming closer now. "Maford's own troublemaking mudscraper. Coming here, destroying our town, killing our people. Life was perfect before you came and fucked it all up."

"I'd like some private time with her before the end," another man says.

But not the giant standing with Johny. No, another monster lurks behind me.

I smell him. A pigsty smells better.

"I've been thinking, girl," Johny says. "You burned down this town, and now you got a bunch of fines to work off. This time, you can work off your offenses in a different kind of way."

Fingertips buzzing and pulse hammering, I take a step back.

"What's your hurry, Gorga sweetie?" Pigsty creeps toward me.

My blood fizzes, and my breath leaves my chest. I hold up my hands, ready to blast wind again. "I'm not in the mood to do anything else with you tonight."

"That's too bad. Cuz I am." Johny's gaze turns from regular angry to leering angry.

The three men close in on me, their stench heavy on the wind that's kicked up around us.

I keep my hands raised.

The trees of the forest behind us tremble, and the high grass rustles. Johny grabs for me.

I hop back and slam into his accomplice.

The wind now shrieks around us, bringing with it sounds from the forest. Hissing. And a heartbeat. *Sss-ba-bum… Sss-ba-bum…*

Johny's accomplice clamps a hand on my shoulder, but my attention is directed at the thing inching through the forest.

Do these men hear what I hear? Do they see what I see?

They must not, because they continue in their assault. Boil Man digs his fingers into my shoulder while Johny grabs for the fabric of my borrowed shirt. I throw my elbow into Boil Man's gut, still watching what they cannot see: slithery amber slipping out of the forest, out of the woods, closer to us, closer, through the grasses, swaying, waiting, *hungry.*

"I'm pleading with you," I say, breathing heavy now, "please go home."

The creature in the grass slips closer still. Its giant head rises above the high grass. Its eyes are dark and deep, and suddenly, my fear is replaced by something else.

Knowing.

My jaw drops.

"What are *you* staring at?" Pigsty jeers.

"See for yourself." Wrenching away, I drop to the dirt just as the giant snake, taller and wider than any tree, lunges at the three men. I roll out of their way and take a moment to behold the otherworldly creature before me.

Black bands, red bands, white scales; a head as big as a boulder; a tongue longer than the longest creek. And though this snake may be a giant, its scales look dull and ashen, and its belly doesn't bulge with food.

"I'm hungry, so hungry." The snake's voice sounds hoarse, weak.

"Here's dinner, then," I say to the creature, not sure if I'm hearing what I'm hearing or imagining what a snake would say. "Go ahead. Enjoy."

The snake snaps its jaw around the head of Boil Man.

The third man, Pigsty, squeaks and squeals and stumbles as he runs back to town.

"Coward!" Johny calls after him and pulls his dual blades from their sheaths. He glares at the snake. "C'mon, you fucker."

Bad idea. But Johny doesn't know a bad idea from a hole in the ground, and he thrusts one blade at a spot near the snake's neck.

The blade hits its mark, and the snake hisses and thrashes.

"Not so tough, are you?" Johny taunts.

My blood begins to bubble again, in anger this time. I push myself to stand as the injured snake recoils in pain from the wound on its neck.

Johny lunges forward to thrust his dagger in the snake a second time.

I shriek, "No," and my blood flares. I throw out my hands, and—

Whoosh! Like with the sunabi, Johny flies into the sky.

He screams, eyes wide with terror, as he dangles in the air.

Yes!

I creep over to the snake, drawn to see its injury up close. "Oh no. You poor thing." I reach to touch it with my free hand, and the wound heats under my fingers. The snake closes the transparent lids over its eyes, then opens them again.

"Please," Johny shrieks from up high. "Lemme go. I won't hurt you. I swear it."

The snake twists around, recovered now from its injury. The beast stares eye to eye with Johny, nudging the guard's grimy legs with its snout.

"Is it true that you and Narder hurt the people in your custody?" I ask, still holding out the hand locking him in place.

"It meant nothing," he says. "Just a little fun. No one got hurt. I swear it."

I slam Johny into the ground. "No one got hurt?" I slowly circle him as he squirms in the dirt. "Well, then, I'll take that into consideration. When my friend here swallows you whole, you won't feel a thing. It won't hurt. I swear it." I snort, then say, "Finish him," yielding to the snake and watching as it wraps its mouth around Johny's head. The snake closes its eyes as it gulps and gulps, working toward the guard's torso.

Why isn't this otherworldly attacking me like the sunabi and cursuflies did? Other than its size, though, nothing else seems *off* with this snake. Perhaps it's because I've offered it a meal. Assuaged its hunger.

"I'm leaving now," I tell my serpent friend. "Thank you for coming to my aid. Help yourself to all of this." I gesture to the rotting town. "Except for the candlemaker, his kin, the Gerys, and the little dog, Milo. Don't make yourself sick on it, though."

I remember those who do right by me—and those who did me wrong.

The snake's eyes glow in the darkness, winking in thanks. *"You are a blessing, Lady."*

Now where have I heard that before?

PART II

THROUGH THE FIRE

In the shadows, there dangers breed,
Enigmas stand in urgent need.
Beneath the realm's cold, watchful gaze,
Serpents follow through thickest haze.

Hear the haunting notes this night,
A haunting note, this dreadful plight.
Through the darkness, a whispered prayer.
In this realm, they tread with care.

Across the woods and murky streams,
She navigates soft elusive dreams.
Visions ride the sighing breeze
As danger prowls through ancient trees.

Hear the haunting this night,
A haunting note, this dreadful plight.
Doors stay fastened, no working key,
No return, gods do decree.

The shadows dance—the shadows sway
This legend fights, caught in the fray.
A silken web, this danger tight,
Her fate entwines with coming night.

Through darkest caves and forests wide,
She battles fears from every side.
The realms, they know her valiant heart,
She is danger, a poisoned dart.

Hear the haunting notes this night,
A haunting note, this dreadful plight.
Foes chase shadows, vault over walls.
Down dark roads and down dark halls.

As music fades, a light remains,
A spark of hope shoots through her veins.
This wicked night, she finds her way—
But hope eludes her, truth stays gray.

—An Elegy by Veril Bairnell the Sapient

17

Leaving Maford behind is a gift, not a loss, and I allow hope to rise unchecked for the first time since I landed in this dismal place. Battling fire-breathing flies, razor-toothed creatures, three monstrous men, and a giant snake has kept me shallow-breathed. But I believe that one day soon — and maybe with the man riding beside me — I'll be able to breathe deeply without having to scream, fight, or curse.

I shift in the saddle of one of the three horses given to us by Zinnia Gery. "So, Jadon, anything exciting happening in your life?"

He barks a laugh, a sound sweeter than the hypnotic clomp of horse hooves. He turns to me with a straight face and says, "Same ol', same ol'."

"That's what I figured." I watch the fog race above us as we ride toward a range of purple mountains so far away, they may not exist. "Nothing exciting ever happens to me."

He huffs another laugh. I like the sound of it. I like *him*. We ride together in silence as behind us Olivia and Philia whisper and giggle from atop the horse they share. The farther we move away from Maford, the fresher the air becomes, the denser the fog. The grass in this section of the plains reaches the horses' knees, and I let my fingers drift across the wildflowers that I ride past. There are no glows of other creatures around us. Just the colors of the horses and my companions, wavering blues and yellows that make a softer shade of green. The nightstar has moved across the sky, but dawn is still far-off. We all sag in our saddles, exhausted and hungry, sore from riding for hours.

I glance at Jadon again. The fog and quiet have softened the hard angles of his face, the stress that's been cutting into his features since we met. Right now, he looks his age, younger, less troubled by the chaos around him. He wears tranquil well. I wait a beat, wondering if the questions I'm about to ask will be too personal. Then again, he's seen my naked back, and I wanted him to see my luscious front. Just thinking about that moment in the cottage blisters my cheeks and shortens my breaths.

If that's not the "we're at that stage of our almost-immediate friendship," then I don't know what would be.

"Ask your question, Kai," he says as his careful gaze skips across the plains.

I tighten my grip on the reins. How did he know?

My stomach twists into knots as I give him a sidelong glance—no reaction from him. "Why aren't you nestled beside a pretty wife nursing your pretty baby girl in your perfect cottage with two horses in the stable and fruit trees on your incredibly fertile plot of land?"

His laugh sounds wistful, and he studies me the way I study him. "Are you telling me that I'm not just dreaming all of this while sleeping beside my pretty wife?"

I nudge his calf with my foot. "Sorry. You're not dreaming." That simple nudge has made fire spread up my leg.

With color rising in his face, Jadon hooks his foot around mine. He says, "Hmm," and pulls away his gaze—and his boot.

After a moment of silence, he says, "Well…" His smile tightens as he inhales and slowly exhales. "I want those things, and I thought I'd have at least the fruit trees and two-horses part of your storyline of my life, but… Fate decided for me."

Something about his voice makes me tremble. I'm so close to falling. So close.

"Fate," I say, "not Supreme?"

He squints into the distance. "Same thing, right?"

I lift my eyebrows and shrug. Embers now flicker inside my chest, threatening to engulf my heart.

His face flashes from sorrow to indifference, and he whispers, "Same thing."

We ride on, silent.

"I kind of like this right now." His attention shifts to my lips. "Not necessarily fighting for my life—"

"But not making spoons, either?" My eyes also shift to his lips. I will not be the same at the end of this ride.

"I guess what I mean is," he says, chuckling, "I like adventure. And I like adventuring *with* someone. I want a pretty wife with a grove of fruit trees in the backyard, but I also want a life with someone who's smart, who desires to travel and see how other people live in other parts of the realm. She's good with a sword when needed, and good with…*other* things as needed."

"You want a lot," I say, patting my horse's neck with a shaky hand.

"But I'm willing to compromise," he says, his left boot brushing against mine. "Except for one thing. Nonnegotiable."

"And what's that?"

He bites his lip and smiles. "She must absolutely adore me and think I'm the most handsome creature in all of Vallendor. I want her to sigh every time I walk into a room."

I want to sigh right *now*, but I don't. If I reached for his hand and kissed his fingertips, what would he do? "I don't think that's too much to ask."

He nods, but his smile dissolves. "And you?"

"I don't know what I wanted before…but I have a pretty good idea of what I want now."

He glances at me, holding my gaze for a moment, before staring ahead again. "Oh yeah?"

"Yeah," I say. "I hope once I find out who I am, she wants the same things I want now."

"I hope so, too." He sighs and says, "They're quiet back there."

We turn to look back at the girls. Philia still holds the reins, but her head bobs as if she's about to doze off. Behind her, Olivia is absently twisting a lock of Philia's hair around her finger. She whispers in the redhead's ear. Philia nods and asks, "Can we stop soon?"

"We will but not here," Jadon says. "I'm looking for a spot that offers a better vantage point. The grass is too high, and the fog is too heavy."

"Just hold on a little longer," I say, scanning the path before us.

Nothing glows yellow or blue.

"It must be hard for you right now," Jadon says, eyes on the plains. "Not remembering something as simple as the way you want to love someone."

His insight is an ambush—I didn't expect it at all, and now, a lump forms deep in my throat. "Yeah." I suck in my cheeks. And fold all those wonderings into the larger ones, like, *Who am I, Why am I here,* and *How is it that I'm able to push wind from my hands.*

Am I a good person or not…?

"I've been thinking about this," Jadon says, his eyes turning into slits, "and I've come up with a new theory. I think you're a gifted mage and warrior. You can wield a sword, a garden hoe, and wind—that's an incredible feat for anyone except you. I think you hated your village. It was too small, in thought and in size, and so you struck out on your own. Though you're gifted, you're still young and you don't know enough to master your gifts.

"I think one of your spells backfired. Olivia said you fell from the sky. Maybe that was your magic backfiring, and whatever spell you cast sent you soaring to the sky, and you fell back, and your descent looked like a starburst to her. You landed in that forest, and it was a rough landing, and the force may not have broken you into little pieces, as it would've anyone else, but it did drive every memory you've ever collected into the great nowhere. That means you can't remember who you are or where you came from. And you can't remember your magic, although now, slowly, very slowly, it's all coming back to you.

"I also think... When you *finally* remember everything, you won't spend another minute here. This time, you'll forget Maford, Olivia, and slimy leeks—"

"And you?" I brave a glance at the man riding beside me.

He keeps his eyes on the horizon. "If you're lucky, even me."

We ride in silence for a while until I say, "That story needs a happier ending."

His lips slant, ready to warble into a smile. "I'll work on it some more."

Jadon pulls his horse to a stop. He sits up, rigid. "Shit. Do you see that?" He leans forward, squinting into the foggy distance.

I follow his gaze, barely making out what he sees, but I see enough to make my heart pound. "Oh no," I whisper, clutching the reins tighter to steady my trembling hands.

An abandoned campsite. A large flag flaps in the wind, familiar symbols embroidered into its fabric. But there are no soft orange glows from any campfires. No soldiers sleeping with bundled tunics serving as pillows. Has the army moved on to invade the next town and force people to their knees?

I know this flag—those leopards are unforgettable.

Emperor Wake's men.

"What now?" Philia whispers behind us.

"We can't turn back," I say.

Jadon whispers, "We won't turn back."

With dread pooling in our stomachs, Jadon and I exchange a worried glance.

All we can do is pray that we make it to the other side...alive.

18

We ride on, and my heart pounds with uncertainty as the landscape around us changes. The silence is interrupted by the rustle of cloth snapping in the breeze and the crackle of dead and brittle things beneath our horses' hooves. We near the source of that flapping—it's the flag in the middle of the burned-out campfire, and now, the fog lifts and the wild grasses lose their height, becoming matted and clumped, as though some great beast made its nest here.

No, it's worse than a great beast.

Parts of this meadow have been scorched black, and as we look down from our horses, we see they are stepping over broken blades, broken bones, and abandoned pieces of armor—a greave over there, a pauldron over there, breastplates and gauntlets everywhere. The air still holds the acrid stench of fighting and death. This smell is too weighted, too coarse, and my nose burns. There's the flag that we saw, one corner tangled around the branches of a burned tree and another corner end tied around the neck of a dead man shorn apart by arrows and axes.

There's another trampled flag of the emperor over there, stomped to its death and left in that muddy grave. Over there, a trampled flag of a kingdom with a sigil of a golden griffin, soaring pine trees, and green hexagons. There's a decomposing hand with a thick-banded ring still on its finger and clutching both Wake's flag and this mystery kingdom's flag.

That makes me sit upright in my saddle.

The horses snuffle and shake their heads and lose the rhythm of their trots. They, too, sense the phantoms of this battle, of the warriors who died in this meadow.

"What happened here?" I ask.

"Wake," Jadon whispers.

"The flag with the griffin," I say, my chest tightening. "Whose flag…?"

Jadon frowns but doesn't speak.

"Whose flag, Jadon?" I ask, dread gripping me.

"I've seen it around Pethorp," Jadon says, "flown by one of King Exley's battalions who serve as protectors of the town."

"Does that mean…? Should we…?" I swallow, then push out, "Has Wake hit Pethorp? Are we walking into a trap? Not Miasma but the emperor's men?"

Jadon runs his hand over his mouth, shaking his head. "We'll know soon enough."

"What's the point of this carnage?" My eyes pinch with angry tears. "Who even won this battle? What's the fucking point?"

"Other than Wake quenching his insatiable thirst for power and his insatiable desire to be exalted as the greatest ruler in history?" Jadon asks.

"Yeah. Other than that."

"Power," Jadon says. "Emperor Wake seeks unity and peace." As we ride through this graveyard, Jadon tells me that Wake believes that uniting all the provinces under one ruler, and absorbing any culture or belief that would create division and conflict, will bring about an age of peace and prosperity. As Supreme Manifest, Wake considers this campaign his divine right.

"His successful reign will fulfill an ancient prophecy," Jadon continues. "One ruler uniting the realm, shepherding all of Vallendor away from impending doom and closer to a world of peace."

"What kind of impending doom?" I ask.

Jadon shrugs. "The collapse of Vallendor."

My cheeks burn hot as I think about those charred trees and scorched bones across the fields behind us. "Wake's strategy to bring about peace and save the realm is…threatening people? Burning them alive if they don't surrender?"

"Whatever works, right?" Jadon says.

Several paces behind us, Olivia coughs and asks, "Are we there yet?"

"Nope," Jadon says. "Not for a—"

Above us, veiled by the haze of smoke and ashes, a bird's song pierces the crackles of dying fire. *Cheer-cheer-cheer.*

Jadon glances my way, his eyes narrowed with cautious curiosity. I cast a brief look to the sky above. We ride on in silence, both of us pretending that we never heard that cardinal's song.

"Are Pethorpians also believers in 'the emperor is Supreme Manifest'?" I ask, stomach churning.

"Not yet," Jadon says, "that is, unless that abandoned flag back there has changed things. If not, Pethorp remains a part of the kingdom of Vinevridth, under King Exley's rule."

"Which means, then," I say, "Wake's men were on their way to Pethorp but were stopped by that battalion back there on that battlefield."

Olivia lifts her chin and says, "Told you we should've — "

"Don't," Jadon warns, hard eyes on his sister. "And we can't assume that Pethorp lost the skirmish. The flag in that hand could mean nothing more than that. A flag in a hand."

We ride silently for a moment, until Philia says, "Kai, Pethorp had lovely colures even before someone decided that colures now mean that you believe Emperor Wake is Supreme Manifest. When my father was alive, he did the glasswork for the colure over their chapel door, the colure over the mayor's front door, and a few inside, and in the town square. And not one colure was meant to symbolize Wake as Supreme Manifest."

"Phily, don't make Pethorp better than it is," Olivia grumbles, then winces as she shifts in the saddle. "Their beliefs aren't too far from being icky. They believe that if you have more, you are closer to Supreme. They believe that the better you dress, the prettier you are, the richer you are, that you're closer and more devoted to Supreme. That you will receive the biggest blessing."

"Maybe they're right," Philia says, reaching one arm across her body to stretch. "Maford's been in a drought for years. No one can even make babies anymore. And now, the emperor's about to take the town for himself. That's not a town that's been blessed."

"If Wake completes his invasion of Maford," I say, "does that mean, then, that Maford's women will go back to popping out babies? All because Wake is supposedly shepherding all of Vallendor away from impending doom?"

Jadon nods. "At least, that's how it's supposed to work. I don't think diamond-encrusted colures can prevent the inevitable."

My mood sours, made worse by my aching back. "And what is the inevitable?"

"People will die from Miasma," Jadon says. "Wake doesn't care about them dying. More dead means fewer people to rebel against him."

"And no one can stop him?" I ask, my eyes skipping to the sky.

Up there, a flash of red pulses through the gray...

I think.

"No one can stop him." Jadon tips his head side to side to loosen his neck muscles. "King Exley's armies have made successful stands against Wake's men partly because ages ago, Exley's father had mages, alchemists, and woodsmen work together to make the forests a maze. Wake's men risk walking in circles for the rest of their lives, especially since King Exley has started to call back some of these mages for himself." He falls silent now and stares at me.

My eyes widen. "All the magic makers were pushed to the edges of the realm, yes?"

Jadon nods. "They were."

"But Exley is calling them back to fight under his flag."

"Yeah," Jadon says. "That's the latest wanderweavers gossip I heard at market days."

"Is that what you're thinking?" I straighten in my saddle. "That I was on my way to Vinevridth to help with defense—"

"And while you were on your way," Jadon says, "you were practicing a trick and you messed up."

I bristle at the "messed up" part, but I nod anyway. "And I left my family to help King Exley, possibly leaving my own town vulnerable and open to Wake's invasion."

She'll turn on you...

The cardinal makes no sound as it escapes the twilight, soaring higher, higher into the boundless sky. Higher still, until it is just a flicker of red before vanishing altogether.

If my companions witnessed this bird's arrogant display, none of them speak of it. Their silence grants me the quiet I need to realize this:

I will never again move unseen through Vallendor Realm.

19

The sky lightens from indigo to violet, the light of the new day being coaxed from the shadows. My tunic sticks to my sweaty skin, and I pluck at its neckline to cool down. Olivia and Philia share a sleeping bag— both snoring so heavily they may not wake up until next week. Jadon isn't resting where I saw him last. He has moved to sit on a moss-covered log about twenty paces away. He strikes a lonely figure, sitting there, and something inside me tugs.

Lonely. Alone. Just like me. We can be alone together.

I groan, my muscles stiff and sore, then grab two honeycakes from his food bag. I push my borrowed blanket off my legs, and cold air brings immediate relief.

High above the poplar grove, clouds shaped like blowfish drift across the face of the nightstar. This meadow with its crickets and mosquitos is nothing like Maford. There's green, soft grass here. The trees have leaves, and their bark is free of knots and holes. Fresh water must be close—it's saturating the earth enough to grow these wildflowers and form this mist. Gophers can dig through earth supple enough for tunnels.

Jadon perches, cross-legged, on that log. His head is bowed as his gaze shifts between his hands and those far-off purple mountains.

He makes me forget that my back aches. I whisper, "Hey."

"Hey." His voice is soft thunder in this predawn quiet.

I sit at the other end of the log. "Couldn't sleep?"

He peeps over at me, and his eyes shine like the last blinks of candlelight. "You heard that cardinal, didn't you?"

I chew the inside of my cheek. "I was hoping that I was imagining it. But then I saw it."

"You didn't say anything," he says.

"You didn't, either."

He shakes his head, then says, "This isn't the way it was supposed to go."

"For you." I place one of the honeycakes in the center of the log. "I don't even know what your 'this' is, but it can be applied to anything that's happened since I landed here." My mind swims as I nibble my snack. "Talk about an unforgettable experience."

"Yep." Jadon reaches between us for his cake. "You'll never forget how I made you feel warm and fuzzy inside."

"Really?" I ask, already warm and fuzzy inside.

"I see it on your face." His grin is playful and cocky. "You can't *wait* to have memories of me."

"I've been exposed," I say, the back of my hand pressed against my forehead. "And every time I have a memory of you, I'm gonna write a sonnet, and one of those sonnets will be a recollection of that time we sat together on a log in the middle of wherever we are. People will cry at the tender urgency of my poetry."

He chuckles, then sighs. "Oh, Kai."

I blush, then say, "Oh, Jadon." I take a nibble of honeycake, letting the sweetness roll over my tongue before sneaking another glance at Jadon. What would it be like to kiss this man? Would his kisses be slow and deliberate? Urgent and wonderfully chaotic? Does he even *like* kissing? The times I've caught him studying my lips make me think… Yes, he does.

We pick away at pieces of cake, but mine no longer tastes as sweet—I want a new favorite thing.

A star shoots across the sky, a lavender snake across the unknown. Jadon closes his eyes. I close mine.

"What are you wishing?" His voice is deep and rich.

I keep my eyes closed, tipsy from his attention. "I'm wishing that my mind would hurry up and work again so that I can start reconciling the old version of me with the version that gets the warm fuzzies and thinks of writing long poems about someone sitting a reach away from me."

"And I wish that I could remember if I've dreamed of having nights like this with him." I open my eyes and stare straight ahead.

I want to ask about his wish, but then again, maybe I don't. I just hope it involves me.

Jadon pokes his tongue at his cheek. "What if the old you hated nights like this with someone like me?" His gaze flits to the sky, then back to me, back to my lips. "What if you were already in love before waking up in Maford? What if someone's waiting for you?"

"What if," I counter, "no one loves me back at home and no one's waiting?" My eyes sting with tears. Fuck.

"What is your heart telling you?" he asks.

My throat tightens, and I whisper, "It's telling me, 'No, there's no one waiting for me.'"

His eyebrows crumple. "That's sad, Kai. Why not?"

I shrug, but that's a lie. *She'll turn on you just like she's turned on her family.* I blink rapidly, my heart twisting. "Wouldn't a heart remember that kind of love? Wouldn't it be like walking? Wouldn't it be unforgettable?"

He says nothing and returns his gaze to the sky. "This is fucked up."

"You told me something," I say, leveling my head, pushing away sorrow. "I don't remember if it was today or yesterday, but you said, 'Not knowing your past may be better than having an awful one.'" I shift to face him. "That was a very wise thought."

"I'm a very wise man," he says, his smile crooked. That smile pins me to this log like a moth in a cherished collection of one.

I eat pieces of honeycake to tamp down my urge to close the distance between us. "I know why *I'm* sad right now, but why are you? And I'm not talking about Maford burning down. Your past—what happened for you to be so...melancholy?"

Jadon startles, and his spine straightens. "I'm not..." He bites the inside of his cheek, then nods, accepting the word. "Been thinking about my family, about my father. He resented me. Felt that I was...*thrust* upon him. That kind of rejection would make anyone melancholy, right? He eventually found me useful, but..."

He peers at the sky, but I can tell that he doesn't really see it. "My tutor, General Stery, made me feel worthy of love. He's the one who taught me to fight, and after fighting beside him in a few skirmishes, I got good at it."

I scoff, admiration now overtaking desire. "I've seen you fight, Jadon. You're more than *good* at it."

He tries to smile. "General Stery convinced me that I'd make a great knight and a wise and brilliant tactician. I'd command armies one day. Take his place and even be renowned."

"How did you end up back in dusty little Maford, running a forge in the back of town?"

"Well..." Jadon swallows, then his lips twitch downward. "General Stery died, and his replacement felt threatened by me. He had my father's ear and told him that I wasn't loyal enough to be a knight or to lead a battalion. That made my father find even less value in me. My mother wanted to step in, but she hadn't stepped in all this time, so why start now? It was bad before, but with General Stery gone, I had no safe place—emotionally, at least—so..."

"You left the battlefield and returned to the crappy burg of Maford."

"More or less."

My heart wobbles as I hug my knees to my chest. "The entire realm could love you, but it doesn't matter if one person you love—your father— has rejected you."

He thinks about it and admits to the sky, "Yeah."

I bump my chin against my knees a few times, then say, "Hey."

Jadon says, "Hmm?" He's sitting so still.

I lay my warm cheek across my knees to gaze at this man who steals my breath. "Don't let his rejection make you become someone you weren't supposed to become. You're a better warrior than they *say* you are, and you are more cherished and respected than you think.

"Scorch his world by simply believing you are worthy of being loved by a person who will love you always. Your father may be the daystar, but the nightstar creates the tides of the seas that sustain life. The nightstar provides light in the darkness, relief from unbearable heat; it slows the realm and allows life to flourish.

"Let him enjoy his time as the daystar. Hot and dangerous causes forests to catch fire and waters to dry up. Be the nightstar, Jadon." I point up to it now as care and concern twist through me. "Beautiful, right?"

But he doesn't turn away from me to look at the celestial body hanging above us. "Beautiful. Absolutely."

We sit there, unmoving, as the veil between us lifts. Our eyes fix on each other, and even though our bodies haven't moved, some part of us reaches across to touch and wonder.

Cheer-cheer-cheer.

Elyn's sentinel has returned.

I'm the first to look away—but I will not look for that taunting cardinal. No, I bite into my cake, closing my eyes not to enjoy the taste but to staunch the dueling swells of longing and loathing.

"One moment," Jadon thinks. *"Can we just have* one *moment?"*

After a moment, I swallow and open my eyes to find Jadon studying me, defiance in his soft gaze.

"I worried about you back in Maford," he says, picking at a loose string unraveling from his bandage. "I feared you'd get seriously hurt fighting those soldiers and then the otherworldly."

The embers from earlier warm deep in my body. He's sitting way over there. And I'm sitting way over here. What are we gonna do about that?

"And I worried about you," I reply.

We hold each other's gaze for a moment, then look up to the sky together.

No cardinal.

Even covered with soot, ash, and the blood of others, Jadon is so... *beautiful.* Yes, his hard jaw and lovely eyes. Yes, his thick hair and strong arms. But there's his courage. His honesty and loyalty. His wisdom and ability to listen. All of this adds to a beauty that is so...*otherworldly.*

"You'll discover your truth, Kai," he says gently. "I know you will."

Way up high, those stars continue to race across the realm. Way up high, other worlds are being born—or at least I hope so. There *must* be, there *has* to be, a place better than this.

20

The sky continues to lighten, becoming a palette of pale pinks and blues, fiery red dulled by the cover of fog. Soon it will be time to leave this camp behind and resume our journey.

"Question," I say, running my fingers over the log's rough surface. "I've asked Olivia to explain this, but I'd like your insight now. The town you lived in is called Maford. And the kingdom is...?"

"Seriously?"

"Ha. That's what Olivia said."

Jadon looks at me with amused eyes. "Maford is in the kingdom of Vinevridth."

"In the realm of...?"

"Vallendor."

"And beyond Vallendor?"

"Some call it 'heaven.'"

"Some? What do *you* call it?"

"I have no opinion."

Doubt that.

"What are the names of other realms beyond Vallendor?" I ask.

Jadon shakes his head. "According to the emperor and therefore more than half of the provinces, there *are* no other realms, Kai. At least none that matter to regular people. Clerics have always told stories about destroyed worlds to keep children from stealing sweets. The realm of Ithlon, for example. The old tales say that Ithlon was destroyed by the gods. But Emperor Wake refutes that and says that there is no proof of such a place and that the people telling those tales are just trying to subvert him. And 'gods'? Anyone looking to believe or even acknowledge gods is beaten and burned."

"And what do *you* believe?"

"That there is one Supreme who couldn't care less about any of us."

I watch the sky. "You think Supreme made Vallendor and created beings, then said, 'You're on your own, good luck, pray to me'?"

He sucks in his cheeks. "I have no opinion."

"Do you think Supreme created other beings beyond those living in Vallendor Realm?"

"Why are we discussing this?" he snaps.

"Because something is happening here," I say. "Something that neither of us understand. I'm just trying to hear other perspectives. Work on my *self-growth*."

Because no matter how hard he tries to convince me that I'm a mage from a neighboring town or a pariah kicked out of my community of magic-makers, I know there's more to me than that. Sybel's warnings and Elyn's anger don't make sense if I was just someone's lost daughter or a wandering mage. I know my abilities—thought-reading, communing with animals, seeing the glows of death, flicking air with my hand, all of it—are bigger than anything a mage can do.

"What about beings that rank somewhere between the Most High and... *you*?" I ask.

"Like angels or gods?"

I tug on my amulet. "Not quite immortal but long-living. Not all-powerful but stronger than a regular being."

He shakes his head. "I don't know if those beings have a name. And if there *are* beings like the ones you describe, they're messy and selfish and, like Supreme, probably care even *less* about people. Why should they? Humans, especially, can offer nothing to someone who can bend time and manipulate objects or whatever."

I pick at the bark on the log. "But you believe they exist?"

"I do, but I also believe that everyone does what they want. Including Supreme and these nameless demigods."

"Do you think these nameless demigods are actually children of the Vile?"

He shakes his head. "But who says that they're children of Supreme? What if they simply existed? What if they simply enjoyed being powerful and almost immortal? Perfect in every way but delightfully..."

"Delightfully...?"

"Shameless. Pleasantly unrepentant. Deliciously transgressive."

I lift my eyebrows. "Whew."

He chuckles and shrugs. "Don't listen to me, Kai. I know nothing. You want spoons, I'm your guy. If you want a sage who ponders the realms and the beings who inhabit them, you should've crashed in the forest and ran into town naked before I became the guy who made fucking spoons."

"Don't do that," I snap, annoyed.

He tosses me a look. "Don't do *what*?"

"Don't diminish yourself like that. I'm going to chalk up your grumpiness to you being tired and hungry, in need of a stiff drink and a massage. But it needs to stop at dawn. You're more than the guy who makes fucking spoons. People look up to you. Or *looked* up to you.

"The ladies of Maford, the ones who were hiding with Olivia and me in the barn when the emperor's men stormed into town? You should've heard them go on about how glorious you are. A few of them even called you a god among men. They would've run naked through town if that landed you in their bed."

"Why?" he asks.

"Because of the way you moved out there with your big sword and your bigger—"

"No," he says, "why do you think that there's *more* out there?"

I chew on his question, then straddle the log to face him. "Don't know, but let's look at the evidence." I hold up my hands. "This wind power had to come from somewhere, and I haven't seen anyone except me chuck wind to knock big-ass flies out of the sky."

"I told you, though," Jadon says, "magic exists throughout Vallendor. Sorcerers, mages, healers. Just because no one in Maford shared your skill doesn't mean that others in the realm don't. Elyn, for example."

"Elyn is no simple sorcerer. You weren't there. You didn't see her. If you did…" I shake my head, awed. "She is something else. *I* am something else."

"Don't let Emperor Wake ever hear you say that," Jadon says. "He'll jail you, charge you with heresy, blasphemy, anything that ends in *Y*, and then he'll hang you on the public gallows. Now that Wake has told them that they are an extension of his own power and that of his church, mayors of the towns he's conquered have started punishing people the same way."

My scalp crawls as I picture Jamart and his daughter hanging side by side. "Olivia told me she's seen altars that were hidden in homes around Maford."

He nods. "Jamart was a member of one of those cults—Wake sympathizers' word, not mine. He and his family—the people you freed from jail—worshipped…" Jadon presses his fingers against his forehead, trying to remember. "The Lady…the Lady…"

"Of the Verdant Realm," I complete.

"Yeah, Lady of the Verdant Realm. I think it was Cecie, Freyney's wife, who'd gone to buy wax from Jamart's shop, and she spotted an altar in their sitting room."

The woman's face carved in wood. Flowers. Candles.

I remember Jamart's expression on that afternoon I inspired him to make a new kind of candle. I recall how he looked at me with that light in his eyes. He glowed as though he knew he was in the company of...of a...

A chill zips up my spine. No. That's not... I'm not...

Blasphemy, Father Knete would scold.

Anxiety swarms in my chest, and my nerves pull, tangled and tight.

"Cecie rushed over to the chapel," Jadon is saying, "and when Jamart's daughter took the colure down from the door, that was beyond the pale, so they arrested her instead, and the rest is history. They didn't arrest Jamart because he's the only one in Maford who can make candles. He's also the only one who isn't scared of bees." Jadon folds his arms, satisfied. "Guess he didn't tell you that he was a heretic, right?"

I look over at him. It sounded like a joke, but he's frowning as though my friendship with the candlemaker makes him ill. "Your reaction suggests that you're jealous," I say.

"Worried."

"That...?"

"That people will mistake your kindness for affinity. I don't want them coming for you."

I stretch until my backbone clicks. "Let them come for me and mine, and I'll burn down their houses, too. They will perish, guaranteed, without forethought."

Jadon studies me and chuckles. "What the fuck was in those honeycakes?"

I lift my face to the sky again and let cool, moist air sweep over me. "Yeah, I got honeycake courage."

"You do."

"You like it?"

"I'm lightheaded."

I laugh. "Faint and prove it."

"Keep threatening to destroy whole towns and I'll do more than faint."

Delightfully shameless. Pleasantly unrepentant. Deliciously transgressive.

"I care for you," he says. "That's why I'm saying this. I don't want you to get hurt."

I close my eyes again, buzzy and lightheaded, hesitant to let this moment go. I'm happy that he isn't a zealot. Don't know what I'd do if he were. Relieved, I rise from the log and stretch my sore back, readying for another day of riding—

What was that? Out of the corner of my eye, I *think* I saw a flash of white slipping through the copse of poplars. My heart bangs once, and I go rigid. Maybe I imagined it.

No, I didn't imagine...

The wolf is real. Long and lean, its fur whiter than any snow, its glow a hard blue, like it will never die. The beast's silver eyes glimmer, and its lips curl to reveal sharp teeth. Even this far away, I smell its fur: wet dog and pine needles.

The beast stands there, on the other end of the dell, staring at me.

I keep my focus on the wolf as I whisper, "Jadon."

He smiles and says, "Kai?" Seeing my expression, his face hardens. "What? What's wrong?"

I hold a finger to my mouth, "Shh," and nod to the forest at his back.

Right at the perimeter of that poplar forest, the white wolf stands, an odd brightness amid those columns of slender gray trees. The last pulses from the nightstar shine slices of pearly light to illuminate him.

21

"Wake the girls and ready the horses while I cover," Jadon says, standing and drawing his sword. "We need to leave before the rest of the pack comes."

"We're not fighting?" I ask.

"Not unless we have to."

Both Olivia and Philia grouse about being awakened, until they see the white wolf on the other side of the meadow. Both shriek.

The wolf snarls and lopes in our direction.

Hearing that snarl makes our three horses jerk their reins from my hold and bolt, racing east across the meadow and back toward Maford. Pissed, I slap my hand against my thigh, then shout, "Go!" pulling Olivia and Philia to their feet and leading them into the woods.

We all agreed before nightfall to sleep in our clothes for this very reason—to be ready for the worst. Fortunately, both girls kept their shoes on, too. "Go!" I shout again. There's no time to grab our satchels—I can practically feel the wolf's breath on my back as we tear through the dark undergrowth. Burs and thistles scrape against our skin while branches tangle in our hair.

Jadon brings up the rear, his hand ready on his weapon.

The land tilts as we run uphill through the woods, and the dark, slippery path of the poplars' glossy triangular leaves keep us tripping and twisting our ankles. I'm running hard and fast, and sweat bubbles in my hair and across my top lip.

"Faster!" I yell to the girls. My leg muscles cramp after hopping and scooting over gnarled this and ducking and crawling beneath spiraled that.

"We have to go faster!" I urge.

Olivia's and Philia's faces show strain and exhaustion. With a glance backward, I read the same on Jadon's face. But we can't stop—this wolf certainly hasn't.

We quicken our pace, slipping now on wet granite and slick roots. But

I learn to anticipate these obstacles, and now I no longer slip, not anymore, and I call "jump" and "duck" and "scoot" to the young women behind me. It works until the forest turns from the orderly rows of poplars to tangled willows that soar impossibly high over us.

The foliage is so thick, I can't see where the path ends until we're nearly on top of it. We skid to a stop and nearly tumble into the bank of a stream. I throw my hands out to catch Olivia and Philia before they fall into the dazzling silver-blue water that cuts through the earth before us. I try to catch my breath from the running, and I heave lungfuls of thick, swampy air.

"Where are we?" Olivia asks, stumbling behind me, Philia clutching her hand.

"The wolf's not following us," Jadon says, catching up but still looking over his shoulder to watch the woods. "Feels like this place is hidden, protected."

I feel it, too, this muffled sense of magic creating a bubble of peace around us. It makes my skin prickle, though. We don't know where we are and whose circle of protection we've wandered into. What little I've seen of magic tells me that not every mage is a friend. I shiver as I scan our surroundings for clues. The air shimmers with color and light, and the sky is too vivid—the wildflowers and grass too perfect. This is a meadow glimpsed in a painting. Not real. Fear clutches my heart like a vise, and I turn a circle to confirm we're alone. What if this place belongs to Elyn? What if it is her magic I feel? What if that wolf was another creature sent by her and it has successfully chased me right into her trap?

"We need to keep moving," I say, now deeply uncomfortable and vulnerable standing in this space. "Let's—"

A distant howl from the woods. The wolf, and it's still on our trail.

We hurry along the creek until we reach a gleaming dell clear of giant trees and gnarled roots—without those obstacles, a wolf can lope here, speed up to catch its quarry. The air smells of soft, green grass and sweet clover. If there wasn't a wolf chasing us, I'd think this place would host only happy times. Families spreading picnic blankets, lovers holding hands and kissing, babies learning to walk.

But a growl disrupts this vision—and that growl sounds much closer this time. I spin in a circle, my eyes skirting across the forest to the perimeter of the clearing.

There.

A flash of white muzzle, a wink of a whiter tail.

"Oh no," Olivia murmurs.

"Girls, stay behind us." Jadon pushes out a breath, flexing his hand around the sword's handle. His eyes meet mine. "Ready?"

"Do I have a choice?" I also flex my hands, wind power the only weapon I brought with me and still learning to control it. And now that I'm in danger again, I pray that it works. Muscles bunching and pulse pounding, I clench my fists, prepared to conjure wind.

Jadon and I stand with the girls between us. Another growl—this one deeper and meaner—rumbles from behind us. We spin to face it.

A lesser growl rolls from the shadows at the other edge of the wood.

Three distinct growls.

The original predator has brought friends.

Olivia whimpers. Philia scans the ground, probably searching for something sharp and stabby.

Then we see their eyes: three pairs, silver and sharp, floating in the dark shadows of the forest. And then we smell the sickeningly sweet perfume of decaying meat. The stench of death.

My breath bounces like balls of fire in my chest. But I don't move, I don't cower.

Let them come.

The first wolf steps out of the gloom and into the dell. Its bared fangs are so long and so sharp that they could tear me apart on the first chomp. The wolf's thick coat is brilliant white, and I squint to avoid being blinded by its glare. The beast swaggers, moving like it already knows the ending to our story.

On our right side, a second wolf, bigger and brighter than the first, stalks into the clearing. Another lopes behind him, wearing a lazy smile.

"Breathe, Kai, breathe," I tell myself, breathless. I lick my lips and taste the salt of my sweat. I try to reach inside me, invoke the buzz of wind power generating through my arms. I even touch my amulet, urging it to come alive, but nothing happens. What did I do before to make the wind? My fingers aren't burning like they did right before fighting the sunabi and cursuflies.

Not good.

I clench and unclench my fists, willing the heat to come. *Please, please, please.* My fingers remain cold. Begging doesn't work. Not a great time for my new power to abandon me.

At least Jadon has his sword. Good old steel. Always ready.

The pack stands around the dell, but they don't come any closer. They bark and yip, speaking wolf to one another.

I widen my stance and focus on the beast closest to me. A blue lightning bolt zigzags down his snout.

I don't know which wolf Jadon's chosen, but I feel the tension wafting from him.

"They don't stand a chance." That's what he's thinking. *"None of you will win this fight. I've killed stronger things—and I'll kill these things, too."*

This time, I'm glad I'm listening to his thoughts, and I let his confidence drown out the fearful thoughts of the young women between us.

"I'm gonna die."

"Will it hurt?"

"I don't wanna die."

I straighten my shoulders and lift my chin. I didn't fall from the sky and run naked through a town to be defeated by a pack of wolves. Like Jadon, I've killed stronger things: cursuflies, sunabi, and Narder the jailer. I refuse to be defeated by a pack of *dogs*. They should've chased another group of people because they're about to get their asses kicked. I pump my fingers again, trying to generate the wind my hands hold. Nothing happens.

Shit-shit-shit.

"Don't do this, boys," I whisper now to the wolves. "We're leaving this forest, okay? If you wanna walk out of here alive, you should back away right now."

Olivia's thoughts skitter through mine. *"Why the fuck is she talking to them? Kill them!"*

The creature with the blue zigzag stares at me with gleaming silver eyes, then looks at his two watchful brothers. There's agreement there, and he approaches me, slow, intentional. One of his brothers heads to our right and the other to our left.

As he nears, his scent of sweet decay fills my nose. His nostrils flare, too—he smells me. Sweat, soot, and honeycakes.

"Stop waiting," I growl, beckoning him to come for me. "Let's do it."

As if he understands me, Zigzag stops pacing and lowers his snout to the ground. A growl grows in his throat. Then he leaps.

Olivia shrieks and drops into a tight ball. Philia drops and grabs a handful of rocks.

I sidestep, bend my leg, pull up my knee, and kick the creature's thigh.

Caught off guard by the attack, the wolf lands with a thump, shakes its head, then looks back at me, teeth bared.

"Surprise," I say, smiling. "I'm that bitch." I plant my feet even firmer this time.

Zigzag paces and recalibrates.

"You all right?" Jadon asks over his shoulder. He's pacing, too, keeping his eyes on the other two stone-still wolves.

"Sure am," I say, eyes locked on Zigzag.

The wolf sinks low to the ground.

I sink even lower.

Zigzag bounds forward.

I roll to my left.

Zigzag pivots and swipes his paw.

I shriek as his claws scrape my leg, tearing through my leather breeches and scouring flesh. Blood—*my blood*—twinkles against my skin like those falling stars, the cool air making the scrape sting even more. Pain—so much pain rages inside me that I gag.

"Kai, come closer," Jadon says, alarm in his voice.

"No." I can't. The girls are closer to him than to me. I need to draw Zigzag farther away. I press my hand against the wound. I'm confident the cut is not so deep that I'll die from blood loss. But I *am* having trouble putting weight on the leg.

Zigzag yips, celebrating my pain.

Another wolf takes this moment to ram into Jadon, hitting him right in the gut and launching him into the air. The wolf simply watches as he thumps hard on the ground.

Jadon rises, then groans as he spits out dirt, grass, and pine needles. He touches his forehead and, without even looking at his fingers, winces as blood seeps from the new gash in his skin. He's standing, though.

I try to catch his eyes to make sure he's okay.

"Kai, watch out!" Olivia yells.

But Zigzag's paw has already slapped at my forehead, bringing me back to the fight.

I roll away from the wolf before he swipes again. My leg—and now the left side of my face—burst with pain.

Zigzag growls and slaps at me a third time.

And I roll away again. A bead of blood plops from my brow onto my eyelashes, and now I'm seeing red.

My hands burn, but that's not because they're ready to whip wind. They burn because I'm using them to roll, to push up and roll some more. *Please come. Now, sweet wind. Please come.* Anger more than fear starts to bubble deep inside me.

The third wolf howls, tired of watching his breakfast roll around in the meadow. By the way my limbs are tiring, though, his breakfast won't be fighting much longer.

Jadon, sword in hand, grapples with the second wolf.

A rock hits the side of Zigzag's head, and both the beast and I turn to see Philia and Olivia throwing stones. The wolf snarls in their direction, giving me enough time to grab a jagged stick from the dirt. This twig feels small and insignificant in my hand, and *I* feel as small and insignificant as the twig.

I am just a mosquito—a woman with no flag, no power, no sword, no armor.

Zigzag lifts his head and howls to the nightstar.

The other wolves lift their heads and throw their howls to the nightstar, too. Are they reveling in this hunt?

I squeeze my eyes shut and open them again, dread's icy fingers scraping my spine.

No. Something else is happening. Something far more terrible than howls. The wolves' hair is turning grayer and redder.

"Kai," Jadon murmurs, "do you see this?"

The wolves' front legs have become muscled arms. Their torsos lengthen as they rear back onto two legs, and then the wolves...*stand on two feet.*

22

"What is happening?" Olivia whispers.

"Burnu," I mutter, the name pushing through my fuzzy memory. I drop the twig. My breath becomes a brick in my belly.

"But what *are* they?" Philia wonders.

"Something worse than a wolf," Jadon says. His eyes flicker to his sword, and the muscles in his jaw flex. Even *he* doesn't think his sword stands a chance against these creatures.

The wolves, still mid-transformation, roar. But this is no wolf roar. This roar is fire and thunder.

Olivia whimpers, and her fear cracks something open in me. A burning fuzziness fills my blood, and warmth radiates from my chest and through my arms and down my legs. My amulet pulses in time with my heart, and that dark stone comes alive with soft light.

I have no memories of it but know without a doubt that I've met beasts like this before. I've *slain* beasts like this before. And I can do it again.

My amulet pulses as fog rises and swirls across the glen like glossy white ribbons.

"Phily, Olivia," Jadon whispers, "Kai and I will fight. When I say so, run to the first tree you see and climb as high as possible."

"Climb?" Olivia repeats. "But wolves—"

"Can't climb trees," Philia says.

"But those aren't wolves," Olivia snaps, "not anymore."

She's right, but the only hope for survival is for us to defeat the burnu, and that will be impossible with two girls underfoot.

A quick glance reveals that all three creatures are in the last stages of transformation. We're out of time.

"The safest place is up," I say, jerking my chin in the direction of the trees behind us.

"We'll keep them from coming close to you," Jadon shouts. "Now *go.*"

Olivia and Philia race back to the poplars right as the three fully transformed creatures rise to their full, impossible height and roar.

My amulet beats, and a buzz fizzes through my body until my fingertips tingle. Heat rushes through all ten digits like wildfire. The wind is ready. But why now? What's changed? Is it because *they* changed from wolves to…*this*? Burnu? Otherworldly?

I make eye contact with Zigzag, still marked by that blue lightning bolt on his snout even in his new form. "Let's see what you're made of."

The burnu to our left pounces.

Before Zigzag can attack me, I lift my arm. The powerful punch of wind bursts from me, driving the burnu back. He crashes against a tree, rolling and recovering too quickly. I can't build up any more force, not so fast, and he's already on me. I scrabble over the rocky forest floor until I find another stick, a thicker stick. With a wrenching howl, I strike and twist the stick hard enough to drive it deep into his eye. Warm, bright-green liquid erupts over my hand. But that doesn't kill him. I release the bloody weapon and grab another stick from the grassy ground.

Jadon makes quick work of another burnu with his sword, jabbing it into the creature's eye. More spurts of warm green blood. That burnu's definitely not having breakfast this morning…at least not in *this* realm.

With only one working eye, Zigzag's head dips and stays low as he watches his fellow burnu fall. But his attention quickly turns to the beta burnu, who's still lurching from Jadon's strike. Zigzag barks at him, and the beta growls in response.

The beta lunges, and Jadon spins to face him, wielding his sword in a clean arc.

Green blood explodes from the beast.

The second burnu charges at Jadon, but I don't turn to watch. No, I've got my eyes and hands trained on Zigzag, who hasn't let a twig in his face stop him. My fingers fluctuate from hot to cold. *No!* I can't wait for whatever's happening with my hands to either stop or start, so I grab three more sticks and a jagged rock from the grass, tuck them into my ripped breeches. In the light of the rising daystar, I can see every hair on Zigzag's coat and the fine gray bristles on his snout.

"Why are you here?" I murmur to Zigzag, readying myself, feet apart. "Who sent you?"

Zigzag responds with a growl that ends in one word. *"Destroyer."*

What does that mean?

He snarls, *"Die!"*

A growl starts in my belly, twists up my throat, and then thunders like an erupting volcano. My amulet is hot against my chest, alive. *"Make me."*

The burnu rushes at me and—

Howls of pain. The creature is suddenly wrapped in a purple light, a spectral lasso that wasn't thrown by me.

I leap backward in surprise and watch as the mysterious lasso tightens, digging into the beast's fur, past his skin, until all of the burnu glows lavender. But that light does more than glow. That light *grows.* And grows, and grows, pushing and expanding the burnu from inside until…

The creature explodes; pieces of burnu fly everywhere.

Then that purple light dissolves, and two burnu lie still among chunks of the third. The glen slips into a nervous quiet—interrupted only by my ragged breaths and pounding heart. But I don't dare move. Is it over? How is it over?

Slowly, I face Jadon.

He's breathing heavily, wearing a similar expression of surprise. "Was that you?" he asks. "That light?"

"No. I… No." Awed, I stare at the space where I first saw that violet light. I want to say more, but I can only say, "No," again.

"Then…" Jadon swallows, fighting through his shock. "What was it?"

I tear my eyes away from the sky and peer at the trees. "There's something back there," I say. "We felt it at the river's edge, remember?"

"Maybe? You're better at sensing those vibes than me." Jadon kneels beside the two intact burnu corpses, and his eyes roam across their bodies, across their pools of blood. "Yeah. *Something* stopped that burnu, and it wasn't us. There's more than just burnu here."

He makes a quick scan of the forest, then positions himself before the dead beta. With both hands, he pries open the burnu's jaws until there's a sickening, wet crack of bone and muscle. The eyeteeth twinkle in the morning light. Jadon grabs one of those canines and wiggles it back and forth.

As he works, I notice the bandage that protected Jadon's hand is gone. It must have fallen off during the fighting. But there's no bloody wound there. Just a tattoo with an intricate design that I can't make out.

"What's that?" I ask, nodding at his hand.

"What's what?" He doesn't stop pushing around the burnu's tooth to look down at his hand. "Nothing." The tooth pops out, and he says, "Success." He tosses me the trophy, even though it hadn't been my power to end this beast.

I catch the tooth, then watch as he tugs his sleeve down to shield his marked hand.

"We shouldn't linger." He pulls out the second tooth easier than the first. He drops his trophy into his breech's slitted pocket, then turns to the poplar grove and shouts, "Phily! Olivia! Come down—it's safe!"

I take a step toward Jadon, but I sink to one knee. The adrenaline from combat is draining from me, and now, pain in my leg and forehead runs free across my body. I try to stand, but a potent combination of exhaustion, fear, and bone-breaking pain pushes and punches me. I stagger over to a tree trunk, completely unable to hold myself up.

"Shit, Kai." Jadon bounds across the fallen burnu to reach me. His eyes search for my injuries, pausing at my banged-up hands, my scraped forehead, and the worst injury of all: my ripped, bloody leg. His eyebrows rise, and he mutters, "Shit," again. "Why didn't you tell me you were hurt?"

"I didn't think it was this bad." My words are slurred and soft. My vision swims, and two Jadons gape at me, their four eyes filled with concern.

"We need to look for help," he says. "You'll die out here."

"We need to get back to camp," Olivia whispers.

Just the idea of walking back to camp makes me sink against the tree.

"We'll go back once we get her someplace safe," Jadon says.

Philia says, "But we might have something in our packs to—"

I wince as pain fragments explode from my leg up to my hip.

"She needs something more than whatever's in our bags," Jadon says, voice strained.

Through a gap in the trees, I see a slope that ends with white smoke rising in the daybreak.

"There." I point toward it.

"Where there's smoke," Jadon says, "there's fire."

And where there's fire, there's a house filled with people.

"Let's get you some help," Jadon says. "Can you walk at all?"

I close my eyes, my lashes now tacky with tears and burnu gore. I rub my temples and try to convince my body that *we're fine, we're okay, we can make it to the white smoke. We're fine, we're okay, we can make it to the white smoke.* I keep thinking that, over and over until I'm standing and limping through the grove of trees. The undergrowth quickly swallows us, and between the fire in my leg and the pain ripping through my head, I can only trundle, trip, run, start, stop, and—

"Jadon?" I've lost track of him. Maybe he's fallen back to check on the girls. "Where did you—?"

And then I hit a wall and cry out as I crash back onto the ground. I try to sit up on my elbows to see what I hit and I see that it's not a wall at all. And *I* didn't hit it.

No, an old man has just plowed into me. He's gray-haired and silver-bearded, with smooth, parchment-pale skin. His eyes are bright lavender, and in his long hands he clutches a dark wooden staff topped by an iron snake eating its tail. There are cutouts through the snake's metal body, and all of it pulses with the same lavender glow that killed the burnu.

I can't take my eyes off that illuminated ouroboros.

"Oh goodness," the man says.

"Kai?" Jadon calls somewhere behind me.

But I don't turn around. I can't. My eyes are caught in this old man's lavender gaze.

Then those lavender eyes drop down to my amulet, and they widen. He takes a quick breath, then says, "You're here."

23

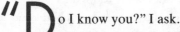

"**D**o I know you?" I ask.

"Kai?" Jadon calls. "Where are you—?" He breaks from the trees, sword at the ready, and comes to a stop behind me.

Seeing Jadon, the stranger recoils and backs away. He mutters, "I must," and then, "Oh dear." Without another word, he turns and runs back into the forest.

"Hey!" I shout after him, but he doesn't stop.

"Who was that?" Olivia asks as she and Philia catch up.

Jadon slips his sword into its sheath and helps me up from the ground. "What happened?"

But I can't answer him, not that I know anyway. Right now, my brain is fuzzy and wavers like a mirage. That man's eyes, that vibrant color of lilacs, are unlocking a memory. But only flashes—nothing recognizable or substantial. Biting back the pain from my injuries, I stagger through the woods, trying my best to keep up with the stranger. He is many, *many* years older than me, yet I'm struggling to catch up. How is he running so fast?

I direct my focus to the distant violet glow emanating from the ouroboros on the old man's staff.

That staff, that snake, it symbolizes…

A name snaps into my mind, and I stumble, bracing myself on a tree to break my fall. *Renrian.* The order of enchanters. I take off again, leaves crunching beneath my feet as I pick up speed. I've met a Renrian before. I know I have. As I run, I coax the memory from my mind's shadows.

A banquet table…and golden cups of wine…applause and…shouts… glistening lavender eyes and air that shimmered and…goodness. Kindness. I don't remember much else, but I do recall that Renrians like parties. Renrians are also wise and kind, and obviously good in a fight. The old man clearly helped us defeat the burnu and didn't turn his staff on Jadon and me. He's seen my injuries, and I'm hoping, since Renrians are good, wise, and kind, he'll assist in some way. Bandages. Soap. Rum, maybe.

"Kai, wait up!" Jadon shouts.

I look over my shoulder but don't stop my stride—I may not be able to start again, not with this bright-white pain shooting through my body.

Jadon runs behind me, his giant sword ready, the blade sharp and sticky with dead burnu. Farther back, the girls follow, twigs snapping under their frantic footfalls.

I trip over a log and fall into the dirt. Tangled tree roots and vines snag my clothes and yank my hair. Jadon scuttles from behind and helps me free myself from their grasp. With his help, I stand and sway, but the forest now tilts and swings, and hot spasms of fire convulse up and down the left side of my body.

"Kai." Jadon's voice sounds far away. "Hold on to me!"

I blink but see only reds and blacks, then smoke, reds and blacks. I grasp his arm with my hot hands, my core hotter. "I'm okay," I say. "I'm okay," but I dare not let him go.

We stagger through the forest, and sometimes my feet touch ground, sometimes my body feels light.

"Almost there." Jadon's arms around my waist are steel buckles keeping me from collapsing. His hands feel like balms and fire. His lips singe my forehead.

The forest is a jumble of sticks and branches, rocks and trees. Though my head swims, I know that we're staggering up and out of the woods. The cold, loose air tells me that we've stepped into a clearing. There, ahead of me, a cottage perches on a small bluff, and a column of smoke puffs from its chimney. The house is cloaked in a sea of mist, droopy branches, and the dark leaves of weeping willows. No light escapes from behind its shuttered windows—but there *is* the cobalt glow of an old man shining through the walls.

"He's in there," I whisper.

"Hiding?" Philia's out of breath, and her voice is strained and shrill. "Didn't he see you were injured? You need help."

We lurch up the flagstone walkway, and Jadon bangs on the solid oak door with the side of his fist. "We know you're in there," Jadon yells. "Either you open the door right now, or I'll—"

The door swings wide, and light spills out. "Or you'll what?" the old man growls, snapping back the bell-shaped sleeves of his robe.

"Please, let us in," I say, gasping as pain overwhelms me.

The old man hesitates, and his unsettled gaze shifts from my contorted face to the girls huddled behind us to Jadon's giant sword.

"She's injured," Jadon says. "We need help. We won't ask for more than she requires."

"Help me," I beg. "Please?"

The Renrian squints at Jadon, then steps back to open the door wider. "For her."

Jadon helps me cross the threshold into the cottage.

I look back at the Renrian, placing a hand over my pounding heart. "Thank you…" The words barely make it past my lips as the world goes black.

"Kai, can you hear me?" Jadon's voice sounds fuzzy and far away. I open my eyes to find him seated next to me on the floor where I'm propped up on a sea of brocaded pillows. I shift on the pillows and hiss a breath as pain radiates from my injured leg—now wrapped tightly with bright-white gauze—and tendrils throughout my body.

The old man studies me from across the room. Behind him, a kettle bubbles over a fire blazing bright in the stone hearth. Shadows of the flame flicker across the dark ceiling beams. In the pantry, steel cookware with silver-tacked leather handles gleam as bright as the glass and ceramic dishware on the shelves. Jadon's sword leans against the front door.

"Where are the girls?" I croak.

"Camping outside," Jadon says, concern furrowing his brow as he leans closer. Despite the shadows of the cabin, the warm blue of his eyes twinkles. "How do you feel?"

How do I feel? I feel like I've touched the rim of death. If it weren't for him—

He's why I'm here. Those were Jadon's hands holding me and guiding me through the woods. Those were his arms clenched around me, keeping me from falling. Those soft eyes, assuring me that he's got me. Remembering all that makes heat flood through me. Heat that I welcome, heat that doesn't hurt.

Even with that cut on his cheek, Jadon still looks as though he rode a star to join us mere mortals in a cottage. Me? I feel and taste like a pit of dirty water skimmed with furry mold after a storm of skunks and bears drowned in its depths.

No matter. I lift a heavy arm to touch Jadon's face in gratitude. "You saved me," I say, my words thick and syrupy.

"Actually, *I* saved you," the Renrian interrupts.

Jadon clears his throat and stands. The air chills without him close.

"Sir, we're very grateful," Jadon says. "Even if you did run from us."

"Do you mean I overreacted?" the Renrian asks, placing his hand over his heart in mock disbelief. "Do you mean that I, an old man, should have stood there and allowed you, a young man, a much bigger man, wielding a great sword that was already dripping with gore and violence, to attack me? Are you saying that I shouldn't have run from *that*?"

I shift my gaze from the old man's face to the ouroboros staff set against a workbench. "We didn't expect to find anything good out in those woods," I say. "Please understand that we'd just survived a burnu attack. We're grateful for your help back at the dell, too."

The old man respectfully nods his head and says, "Of course." He then lifts a silver brow at Jadon. "See how easy it is to have good manners?"

"We're trying to reach Pethorp," Jadon says, his cheeks red. "Are we close?"

The old man waggles his hand. "Closer than you are farther."

Jadon grumbles, but I can only laugh. This is familiar and so welcome after the days I've had. "You are Renrian, yes?" I ask, my voice as coarse as gravel.

Our host nods again. "Since the day I was born."

"My memory is somewhat foggy." I carefully shift to a more upright position, shoving several pillows behind me. "Please forgive me if I'm incorrect, but Renrians are shothis, yes?"

"I've met Renrians before," Jadon cuts in, "but I don't know that term—"

"*Shothi?*" The old man's tone is one of outrage. "Respectfully, Renrians are no mere *sages*. While we are scholars who know countless spells because we've read about them, we do more than *read* about anything. We create spells, potions, and tonics because we are *alchemists*, too. My potions and tonics do more than paralyze limbs or grow hair," the Renrian continues, "though they do that, too. My brews and elixirs change people and objects from blah to bold. A *shothi*," he scoffs. "*Really.*"

His violet eyes glow bright as he gestures to his staff leaning against the wall. "Warruin, my staff, has changed the course of history. Why... Do you not recall the Battle of Riddy Vale, during the Great War? The Dashmala warriors were closing in on that vale of men inhabited mostly by women, children, and the aged? There were a few healthy soldiers left, but nowhere near the numbers needed to defeat the Dashmala."

Jadon opens his mouth to speak but changes his mind once I give him the slightest shake of my head. We can't afford to offend our long-winded host, not with my grave injuries. The old man wants to talk? Let him talk. And then let him offer food and water and continue to treat my injuries while he blathers on about battles and wars.

The old man lifts his hands and stares out across the room as if witnessing the battle. "And there I was, with countless defenseless people around me, and I lifted Warruin, and I held her out over the vale, and I made that valley resemble a fiery chasm of rock and lava."

He sweeps a hand over that fiery valley he's envisioning. "And as the Dashmala—who, to this day, hate me—as they reached the outskirts of Riddy Vale, they saw desolation, the end of the world." The old man juts his chin and points to himself. "That chasm appeared due to a simple spell and the tilt of my head. I alter the looks of things and the behavior of things, making them more powerful than what they truly are. They become *enchanted*. Because I do *that*, too." He smirks. "A *shothi*. Dearest, I am *all the things*."

I dip my head. "Okay."

His ivory cheeks brighten, his shoulders sag, and his chest deflates. "That's all you can say after hearing my epic tale of cunning and ingenuity?"

I pause, then say, "You are *all the things* and more."

He smiles, lifts his chin. "Thank you."

"Tell me your name." I try to focus on him, but he's blurry and his blue light is far too bright. Everything in this sitting room is far too bright.

He bows. "Veril Bairnell the Sapient. And now, what do they call you?"

"Nothing special. Just Kai." I point at Jadon. "And he's—"

"He's already told me," Veril says. "While you were passed out. And such a boring name at that."

Jadon fake-smiles and gives an annoyed *I'm standing right here* wave.

Veril considers him, grunts, then returns his attention to me. "You say that you're suffering from memory lapses, but how do you know of shothis, Just Kai?"

I run my fingers over the soft edge of a pillow at my side. "To clarify—

'just' is not a part of my name. I'm Kai, and I know that term because…
I… I remember sitting in an outdoor classroom next to a boy with eyes
like yours. His name was…" I stare at the flames in the hearth, searching
my brain, then sigh. "I don't remember, but he taught me 'shothi' and
'examia'—"

"Truth," he translates, nodding.

"And 'dawstering'—"

"Daughter."

"I think his parents worked for my parents… Or maybe his parents
were my teachers?" My mind muddles, and I squeeze my eyes shut to stave
off the coming wave of nausea. "Forgive me—I haven't been myself lately."
I slump back on the pillows.

Jadon kneels beside me again. "We appreciate your help with her leg
and for allowing us to stay until we can be on our way. We're a long way
from home."

"Some of us more than others." Veril scrutinizes the bandage wrapped
around my leg. "Oh dear. At it again. I didn't think you had any blood left,
Just Kai."

I push out a breath. "This wasn't my best battle." I try to sit myself
up again on my elbows, but my body rebels, and I lose the battle against
nausea and fogginess. I want to vomit.

"So, can you help her more?" Jadon asks. "I mean, beyond the
bandages?"

"Of course I can," Veril says, shuffling to a small alcove off the sitting
room. "I must gather a few more things first. If you'll excuse me."

I turn on my side and study the room to distract myself from the pain.

Over there, drying herbs and dry-aging ducks hang from string and
nails. Living plants, some with flowers, grow on vines. Rows of jars filled
with green things, slimy things, and prickly things sit over there, there, and
there. There is not one crumb, not one fallen leaf on the bright wood floors.
The lamps burn bright and steady. Wood crackles in the hearth, and the
room isn't too hot, nor is it too cold. All of it is orderly. Too orderly.

The sitting room shimmers with flecks of silver as though this space
doesn't really exist, as though this space is a mirage…which it may be. He
is Renrian, after all. Enchantments—that's just one of *all the things* his
order does; he's told us so much already.

"How can I help?" Jadon asks, sitting cross-legged beside me.

"Make everything stop hurting." Tears burn my eyes, and my side pulses.

"We'll fix you back up," he says.

A teardrop rolls across the bridge of my nose. "Thank you for not leaving me behind."

He catches my teardrop on his knuckle. "I'll never leave you behind, Kai. We've got places to go, right? People to find."

"Amends to make," I whisper.

He catches another teardrop. "I'll do anything to make you whole, to keep you safe."

"Promise?" My skin warms from his touch, and his touch is all I want right now.

His eyes soften. "Promise."

My cheeks grow hot.

"Here we are!" Veril announces, tottering back into the room. "Hope I'm not interrupting anything!"

Startled, Jadon sits back, and just like that, the air around me turns chilly again.

Veril sets an armful of clean cloth, several small bottles and jars, and a big bowl of soapy water on the table.

"Would you help me expose the wound again, young man?" he asks. "We'll start with the leg and work our way up, just like before."

Jadon meets my eyes. "Kai?"

I nod. "Go ahead."

Jadon's touch is soft and careful as he tears away the rest of the tattered pants leg, then peels back the gauze above my ankle. He pulls his hands away in horror and whispers, "Fuck, Kai."

I shudder at the exposed injury. "Oh no."

Long, jagged claw marks stretch across the length of my thigh. No longer smooth, the skin is inflamed and swollen, hot to the touch. Fresh blood seeps from the deep, raw gashes. No matter how much I want to look away, I can't. Heart hammering, I draw a ragged breath. The metallic scent of blood mixes with the smell of brewing infection. While I'm satisfied I've survived this attack, I shudder knowing that despite my new powers...

If he breathes, he bleeds. That's what I knew about the Otaan back in Maford. And if it bleeds, then it can die. *I* can die.

Jadon makes room for Veril to work. Scraping a hand through his hair, he retreats to the fireplace, that deep, broody scowl back on his face.

"They certainly took a few good swipes," Veril says, his expression grim.

"One of them died with a little bit of me caught beneath his nails, that's for sure." I try to smile bravely, but the smile slips as the pain flares hot and sharp.

"Oh, he got more than a little bit," Veril says with a wink. "But worry not, dearest. It may take a moment, but we'll get you patched up. Then we'll sit down to a good meal, and you can share the adventures that led you to fight burnu in the dell."

"Whatever you need me to do," Jadon says, pacing now, "please let me know."

Veril looks over to Jadon and nods. "First things first...*again*." He reaches behind him and turns back to me holding a cup and a flask. "Rum, the most proficient medicine of all."

As I drink, the good kind of heat spreads across my chest. I hold the cup out to Jadon. "You need medicine, too."

He laughs, then returns to crouch beside me. He drains the cup, and color blooms in his face. "That makes me want to cry."

Veril says, "The best rum in all of Vallendor."

Jadon returns to the fireplace, averting his gaze as Veril dabs my skin with wet rags.

"Progress," Veril says. "When I cleaned your leg the first time, I used eight rags. Now, only three." He selects a pearled vial from the many spread around him and pulls away cotton from the bigger puff. "You've told me how you know about shothi, but tell me about you."

"What do you want to know?" I grit my teeth even before he applies the soaked cotton to the top of the gashes.

"Your amulet caught my eye back in the woods," Veril says. "This sounds dramatic, but it was *alive*. Glowing. Beautiful. I've seen—" He pauses, his gaze on my neck.

"What's wrong?" I reach for my amulet and then move my fingers over my collarbone. I don't feel the chain, and I don't feel the pendant. "Oh, no."

Jadon glances at us over his shoulder. "What's wrong?"

"Where did it go?" My heartbeat bursts through the rum cloud and hammers wildly again. I sit up, patting my tunic, checking the floor around me. "It's gone. My amulet is gone!"

Is this why I've been so weak? Is this why I can hardly stand the pain from these wounds? Is my amulet as protective as I'm making it out to be?

"When did you last have it?" Jadon asks, shuffling the pillows to look underneath.

I close my eyes and remember the pendant glowing as we fought the burnu. After we bumped into each other, I remember Veril staring at it. After that…I don't remember it at all.

"You chased me through the forest," Veril says.

I whisper, "Yes," then look to Jadon in desperation. "And I fell, and the trees and roots grabbed for me, and I didn't check to see that my amulet was still on. It must've fallen out between the dell and your cottage." The clasp was weakened when Olivia yanked the pendant from my neck. But I didn't expect it to fail.

I could wring her neck. *Again.*

Breathe. Breathe. Breathe. I press my warm cheeks to tamp down my rising panic.

Jadon is searching near the front door and beneath the table.

"Did you see it fall?" I ask him.

"No." Jadon shakes his head. "I didn't."

"But I need to find it! I need to go—" I yelp as I try to rise from my nest in the pillows.

Jadon hurries over and places his hand on my shoulder to keep me from standing. "Kai, you can't go back out there. You're *hurt*, and those woods are treacherous."

I try to rise again, but my leg screams with pain, forcing surrender. The pain rolls back like the surf, leaving welcomed numbness, then surges forward again, meaner this time, and I groan. Again, the wave pulls back—I feel nothing, and then rolls forward—I feel everything.

My spirit sags. I've lost my amulet again. I'm left with nothing to connect me to my past. How could I have been so careless?

"Wherever it is, it will still be there in the morning." Veril offers a reassuring smile. "You'll have to wait anyway until I bind these wounds. I don't know if you noticed, dearest, but your leg is split open."

My throat chokes with tears and disappointment, and I nod.

"I'll go out and search," Jadon offers, his eyes bright with urgency.

"Are you sure?" I ask.

"What did I tell you moments ago, Kai?" He traces the edge of my face with a finger.

I'll do anything to make you whole.

My body has swung back into numbness, and I can't feel his touch. But I can imagine. "Thank you," I whisper, my imagination making me breathless. A teardrop filled with relief and gratitude rolls down my cheek.

Jadon catches it on his knuckle, just as he's caught the others, and smiles. That smile is like the dawn. That smile is hope renewed. He holds my gaze for a heartbeat more, then nods to Veril and grabs his sword from its place near the door. Sliding the weapon into his back scabbard, he pauses for a moment. Our gazes meet again, and I feel his promise as if he's said it aloud. *I'll do anything to make you whole.* He opens the door, levels his shoulders, pushes out a breath, and heads into the fading darkness without another word.

24

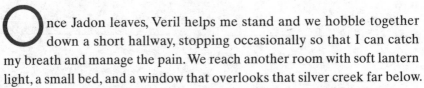

O nce Jadon leaves, Veril helps me stand and we hobble together down a short hallway, stopping occasionally so that I can catch my breath and manage the pain. We reach another room with soft lantern light, a small bed, and a window that overlooks that silver creek far below.

"You'll recover here, dearest." The old man settles me onto the bed, pulls off my boots, and says, "Let's get you out of these rags." He uses shears to cut away the torn pants and cuts the back of my tunic up the middle.

I pull off my shirt and gingerly remove my pants.

Veril leaves the room and returns quickly with a basin of fresh water.

I prop a pillow against the headboard and sit back. "Really, thank you for your kind hospitality."

"Oh, you don't have to thank me." He shuffles over to a large wood trunk and opens the lid. "Now tell me about your companion. Are you two...*together*?"

"When you say 'together'...?"

"Betrothed, dearest." Veril pulls a blanket out of the chest. "Or simply... enjoying the benefits of such?"

I bark out a laugh and wince. Even that simple movement causes pain to shoot up my leg. "Far from the first and far from the second, to be honest."

He lifts an eyebrow. "Does the man not *see* you?"

"He does, but it's complicated," I say. "He's kind. He's brave. He's a pleasure to behold."

Veril snorts. "You can do better." He rolls up the blanket and arranges it beneath my leg, providing slight relief from the incessant throbbing.

I place a finger to my lips. "Let me guess. You have a nephew over in Pethorp you want me to meet."

Veril chortles and returns to the chest for a bar of soap, a sponge, a large towel, and a clean linen robe the color of flames. "Call if you need me," he says, tottering from the room.

The water that Veril left is cool against my skin. The soap smells of fresh lemon and mint. The sponge is clean and fluffy. I look over my shoulder to see if I can glimpse the marking there. No luck. I try to glimpse the marking beneath my left breast. I spot only a shape that could be a box.

Once I'm cleaned up and wrapped in the robe, Veril rolls in a chair with wheels. "You may join me up front if you wish—that's where I'll be preparing more poultices for your injuries as well as breakfast."

Whatever he's cooking smells incredible. "I'd like to come up front with you, please." I wiggle to the edge of the bed.

After he rolls me to the worktable, he shuffles to the hearth. There, a kettle bubbles into the fire. He plucks a leaf from a plant twisting around the cupboard and tears it over the brew. "How did you come to acquire such a special pendant, if I may ask?"

"I don't remember how I acquired it," I say, frowning, "but it's always been mine. You're not suggesting that I *stole* it, are you?"

"I'm *suggesting* that amulets like the one you wore are extremely rare. I haven't seen one in person in ages. And yet here you are, wearing one. Or you *were* until…"

"It's mine," I say. "It was made for me even though I don't…" I twist my hands in my lap, clamp my lips, and square my shoulders. "Recent events have caused me to forget some things." *Some?* "Some memories are missing."

"If you hit your head fighting burnu," Veril says, chuckling, "you should be happy that your memory is the only part of you that's missing."

Will I have to admit to everyone I meet that a big part of me is missing? That I can no longer recall what I was doing prior to a few mere dawns ago? That I no longer remember my surname or the shape of my mother's face? Something about this kindly Renrian makes me want to trust him, and I know I will eventually open up to him. For now, though…

"What do you know about amulets like mine?"

Veril stares into his bubbling pot. "I know that they are special and hold powerful magic that is inaccessible even to me…and to most. Its wearer— any wearer—will be endowed with whatever qualities are attributed to it, but only the true owner can access its full capabilities."

"So it wouldn't be *totally* useless to someone…?"

Like Olivia. Or Philia. Or even Jadon.

"Not *totally* useful, but not completely *useless.* Definitely not safe to wear for anyone other than its owner. That's because amulets are blessed pieces. There are repercussions for blocking another's blessing, yes?" He peers back at me. "No, it's never wise to wear the items not made for you... except for that linen robe. You look lovely—better than I ever did. That shade of tangerine makes you look healthier than you are."

I tap my hair, mocking my trampled beauty. "And if someone finds my pendant and wears it?"

"If they wear it for a prolonged time, it will be the last thing they'll wear. *Ever.*"

"Well, I've certainly survived wearing it so far."

Though this is some fucked-up surviving.

The Renrian brings a stool to sit before me with a brush and jar of oil that smells of rosemary and eucalyptus. With great care, starting at the top of my thigh, he removes the gauze to expose the violent gash. "Sometimes," he says, slathering the thick concoction over my bare leg, "the best thing to do when healing is nothing at all. You'll need to be still for a few days, dearest. Let the medicines work."

He brushes my leg with oil and then rolls the gauze back over the wound. "Now be still as I look at..." He pushes the tangerine-colored robe aside and peels away more gauze to peer at the wound on my hip. "That is the ugliest thing these walls have ever seen." He straightens, then dips his brush into the salve. "You're lucky to be sitting upright in this chair, Just Kai."

I wince as the oil seeps into my skin.

He works in silence for a moment, then says, "Tell me. What brought you to the dreary hamlet of Maford? And what brought you here to these woods? How in all the realms did you end up requiring my services after a fight with burnu?"

I may be hurting, but that doesn't mean I can't laugh, and so I do. "That's a long story."

"We have plenty of time," he says.

True. So, I tell him everything—from Olivia stealing my necklace and Wake's men invading the village, from Sybel scolding me, Elyn and her threats and otherworldly creatures, to our flight from Maford. Through my entire tale, Veril listens with interest, not scoffing or doubting. Occasionally he nods but never interrupts or interjects.

"I worry that Elyn is hunting me, even now," I say. "The burnu in the wood—do you think maybe she sent them?"

"She very well might have." Veril's tone is strangely light.

"And you aren't worried—?"

"I'm a Renrian, dearest." He spreads his arms out and smiles. "My cottage is protected and enchanted. No one will find you here unless I let them. And I won't let them."

"Even against someone who commands otherworldly?"

He points to his staff, Warruin. "She is fully capable of hiding you from roaming mercenaries, dearest—even one who knows a spell or two. You'll have enough time to recover before you confront her, but we're not at that point yet, are we? Until you are, I will shift the elements around my cottage to make it difficult to detect."

I sag with relief, and the turmoil in my stomach eases. "You can do that?"

"I performed grander tricks in my younger days." Before he sits on the stool beside me, he stretches, and his bones *click-click-click*. "Years ago, I performed one of my best illusions for King Exley: walking through the wall that surrounds the castle. That afternoon, he and his courtiers arrived, and musicians played, and it was all so very dramatic."

"Let me guess," I say. "You used shadow and light."

He lifts his chin. "*Well*, dearest. I *did* walk through the wall. You see, Kai. *That* part of the wall had crumbled away due to age and earthshake. The king's head mason, a dear friend of mine, had asked weeks before that I enchant that part of the wall while he recovered from a sprained back. After I hid the gap, only he knew that part of the wall had crumbled away.

"So, for the performance, I simply chose the spot where there was no wall. I tricked the king and never told my mason friend how I did it—I would've opened myself to extortion, maybe even death, because people, even dear friends, can turn on you. And that is why you should—"

"Never tell someone your entire plan," I say. "They may use it against you."

"And that, Just Kai, is the point." He bows his head.

"Thank you." I smile gratefully at him. "Since you know all the things, as you say, there's something I'm in need of." I chew on my bottom lip, preparing for disappointment. "Do you have a spell to help me remember more about myself?"

"Of course I do. And I also have something to help you forget—but that's just a bottle of wine as old as my father."

I laugh. "Let me remember a little more first before we open that."

Veril stands. "I must warn you, Just Kai, I have a memory elixir, but no one has ever tried it. It may work. It may not. If it doesn't, then we'll have to prepare another, which means foraging for the materials needed to brew it. But before I administer the existing elixir, you must eat. Never drink magic on an empty stomach."

25

Veril stirs a large pot hanging over the hot coals of his hearth, and the smell of meat, vegetables, and spices fills the room. "I apologize. I haven't prepared typical breakfast foods. I do have eggs and potatoes, a small slab of bacon, crabapples, but that may take a moment—"

"No, this is fine," I say, my mouth watering. "I don't stand on ceremony when it comes to food, especially if someone's prepared a meal as wonderful as this." *This.* Generous chunks of beef, radishes, potatoes, and carrots in a sauce flecked with herbs. Fresh-baked bread with split tops. "And is that butter?" I ask, agog, pointing to the miniature cast-iron pot.

Veril tosses me a self-satisfied smile. "It certainly is. Smells heavenly. Wouldn't you agree?" Veril fills a bowl, then plucks a slice of thick bread from the table and hands both to me.

I eagerly accept the bowl, inhaling deeply to savor the rich steam rising from the stew's surface. "Why are you here, in the middle of nowhere?"

He hands me a spoon. "City life is loud and dirty. How can anyone abide it? *Ugh.* I must find my herbs in the forest, so here I stay."

The stew has body—the peas aren't completely mashed. "I taste onions, and I taste sugar, and I taste oil." My taste buds tingle because I also taste pepper and saffron. "You have no idea how much I've missed pepper! And *saffron*?"

"How do you know it's saffron?" he asks.

"My village must have used it."

"Hmm." He taps his finger against his chin. "If you know that spice, then yes, they did. Most Vallendorians have never tasted saffron. It is *very* expensive—worth more than gold. Peria, in particular, on the southern side of Devour, the deadliest sea in Vallendor, grows the most saffron in Vallendor. Fields of saffron crocus as far as the eye can see, beautiful purple flowers with those beautiful crimson threads. If you can identify saffron, dearest, then I'd say that Peria is your home."

Peria. "Hmm. I don't remember it."

"Mages settled there after being expelled from the Holy Kingdom of Dorwinthe," Veril says. "They took their totems of Kaivara and seeds of saffron crocus with them and settled in Peria, thriving there for ages. Each mage dedicated the totality of their powers to create a barrier of protection. But that barrier is losing its fortitude—there are some younger mages who have deserted Peria for adventure or to serve Wake. Cracks in the barrier mean the barrier will not hold, which means…"

He sighs. "Well, we know what it means. Let us all hope, though, Peria pulls back from its destruction. Some of the best magic has come from that part of the realm—and definitely the best saffron."

If you can identify saffron, dearest, then I'd say that Peria is your home. I tear off a piece of bread. *Peria…on the southern side of Devour, the deadliest sea in Vallendor.* I dip a hunk of bread into the stew. Well, then, that's where I'll head after healing.

Spirit lifted, I close my eyes as the combined foods melt in my mouth. "This is beyond delicious."

Veril steeples his hands and presses them to his lips. "Well, thank you. I work very hard to make something out of nothing. That is an unspoken power of the Renrian, a passive skill, one would say." He dips the ladle into a smaller pot hanging over the glowing orange logs and pours liquid into a mug. "It just so happens that the leaves in this tea are known for clearing one's mind, Just Kai. And if it's not enough, then there are stronger tea leaves in one of these jars. So tell me: What else have you forgotten?"

I laugh and take the mug. "How much time do you have?"

"No, dearest…" He doesn't laugh. "How much time do *you* have?"

26

Veril's memory tea smells like berries and cinnamon bark.

"Does this tea do anything else?" I rub the sides of the mug. "Will it make me stronger? Open my mind enough so that I can see the future?"

He sips from his own mug. "It's not a strength serum, dearest, nor does it foster clairvoyance. It's just something I created to nudge forward what's already there. And it tastes lovely." Veril plops into a chair by the window. "Usually, I enjoy a cup of tea with little cakes made with apricot jam and cocoa, but I didn't bake last night. I didn't plan to have guests."

I sip my tea and grimace—I just burned my tongue. And now it tastes different than it smells: melon and pepper instead of rum and acorns. "What were you doing out at that dell?"

The old man says, "Searching for plants that only bloom hours before dawn. The burnu attack interrupted my foraging. I heard the growling and peeked through to see that you were in a bit of trouble. I don't fear them—as you can see, Warruin and I made quick work of one."

I nod. "There's something else I've been thinking about," I say. "When you said, 'You're here,' after we bumped into each other, what did you mean by that?"

He takes a while to answer as he brings the delicate cup to his mouth. "I *meant*: No one's crossed that meadow in a very long time, and the last people who tried didn't survive. They were the emperor's scouts—no tears were shed on their behalf. But I saw that you weren't wearing the sigil of that awful man and so I decided to help. Even still, I was shocked that you were alive."

I sense his explanation is not complete. He's not lying but he's not forthcoming, either. I swirl the tea in my cup and watch bits of the leaves circle. It would be helpful to read this old man's thoughts, but my mind wanders through haze as I try. Is he purposefully blocking me out?

"Yes, I am," he says.

I startle. "Huh?"

His eyes glisten above the rim of the mug. "I *am* purposefully blocking you from hearing my thoughts. For us Renrians, our thoughts are our last refuge. Over hundreds of years, we've honed the ability to block intrusion into our minds, and now, only Supreme can poke around." He taps his temple. "Don't worry—despite this one trick, I haven't listened in on your thoughts. However, if you ask me what it is you want to know, I just might tell you."

"Okay. If nothing in the woods scares you because of your trusty staff, then why did you run from us?" I ask. "Truthfully."

"'*Us*'? I wasn't running from *you*. I wasn't expecting to see anyone in that part of the forest—I hadn't since those scouts. You caught me off guard, and so I reacted in a more extreme manner than I customarily would have. I wasn't in the best state of mind, understand. There were *many* beings in that forest I wished not to be around."

"Beings. Like…?"

Veril's lavender eyes brighten and then settle into brown. "Like sunabi. And burnu."

"And?"

There is a pause before he answers, "Your companion."

Oh. "Because he was wielding his sword? He didn't mean to frighten you."

He tugs an earlobe. "I'm aware you haven't known him for long."

"And?"

"He's willfully doing all of this for a stranger?"

Heat climbs up my neck, and I say, "Sometimes, life comes at you fast." I pause, then add, "And here I am, under your roof, accepting your kindness and generosity, when I've known you for less time than I've known my companion."

"I'd say you and I are different than you and he." He sits back in his chair. "And just as you did with me moments ago, dearest, you should slow down and ask more questions of *him*."

Now, my scalp prickles with countless pins. "It's not like I'm blindly following him, Veril. I'm not following him at all. And I *have* asked questions, and he's answered them." The prickles move down my neck to my shoulder blades. "And he's been open and honest with me. For the questions he can't answer, we will seek out a sage who can." Before he interjects, I say, "Jadon's helped me all this time. He's protected me, and he didn't have to. He's out there, in the woods, right now, searching for my amulet. He's been nothing but kind."

He relaxes back in his chair. "Mmm."

Nostrils flaring, I narrow my gaze. "Say what you're thinking or stop batting me with your paws."

The Renrian blinks at me with shiny lavender eyes. "I haven't seen it in a long time, so I may be wrong."

"Wrong about…?"

He lifts the mug to his lips and says, before he drinks, "Ask Ealdrehrt about the marking on his hand."

I open my mouth to say, "So what? I've got markings, too," but I remember how Jadon had wrapped his inking with gauze, hiding it from me. Even though he'd scrutinized my own markings, up close and wonderfully personal, he didn't offer insight about his own. My clammy hands slip on the handle of my cup.

"Would you like more tea?" Veril asks innocently, as though he hasn't just kicked a hole in the circle of trust I've built around Jadon and me.

I shake my head. "No thank you." Chin cocked, I force nonchalance. "What does his marking mean?"

"Like I said," Veril says, "I can't be sure. It's been a while, but markings like those demonstrate kinships or loyalties."

"Loyalties," I say. "To whom?"

"That's not a question you should be asking *me*," he says, eyebrow high. "I'm not the one with a tattoo on my hand."

Do my markings mean the same? Who am I loyal to? Despite the tea, no memory has been nudged to the front of my brain.

A wedge-shaped shadow swoops past the darkened windows of the cottage.

My heart pounds, and I sit up straight. "What was…?"

"Something wrong, dearest?" Veril glances over his shoulder at the windows.

"I…think…" I want to rush over to see for myself but my injuries keep me seated.

"Did you see something?" the Renrian asks, shuffling to the window.

"A shadow," I say, lowering my gaze to my lap, my cheeks flushed with embarrassment.

Veril chuckles. "I'm afraid shadows in the forest are ever-present no matter how enchanted they are."

The tea in my cup is now cold.

Veril pulls a white bamboo fife from his sleeve. "Tell me more about this Elyn."

I tell him about Elyn's snow-and-clouds cane and the red ribbons that wrapped around her guards' arms. Their astounding height. Her sleight of hand with potatoes. The apocalypse that followed her departure. The bloodred message she left on those chapel doors.

Veril runs his fingers over the holes of the fife. "Sounds like Elyn and her guards are Executioners."

The teacup nearly slips from my grip as I bolt upright in my wheeled chair. *"Executioners?"* I bark, eyes big. "As in…'those who kill'?"

"Correct." Then he plays a single low note on his fife. "Executioners are a very staunch order who serve Supreme in their own way. They have specific jobs, one of which is to accompany throughout the realms high mages who are charged with finding fugitives from justice."

My pulse pops. *"Fugitives?* What would their crime be?"

Veril shrugs. "For this order to be involved, it would be somehow directly disobeying the will of Supreme—and I'm not referring to Syrus Wake. I mean *true* Supreme."

"So she's here to *kill* me?" Sweat bursts across my skin. "I've been marked for execution?" I swallow, but my throat has gone dry. Elyn's words echo in my ears. *She is a danger to you.* I've done something wrong, and now she's here to avenge it.

"They have other jobs as well," Veril says, no doubt reading the look of panic in my eyes. "When one realm falters, it is the Executioners who clean up the mess. They're not too different from vultures who clean up carcasses."

"Is Vallendor faltering?" I ask, my scalp crawling with invisible spiders.

Veril holds the fife to his lips and blows into it, producing a high, clear note. "Some would say 'yes.' The drought is creeping across the realm. Sickness is killing scores of people."

"Miasma," I say.

"Yes," he says. "There is no cure. There is no treatment. No one, not even my order, knows its origins. We don't know why some survive while others don't."

"Do you think Elyn is here to end this realm because of Miasma or to find a fugitive?"

Silent, he stares at me with tender eyes, and the only sound is the crackling of burning logs in the hearth. Finally, he says, "It's hard to say.

But I'd guess that she's after something larger than a disease."

But surely it's not me—what would I have done to hurt an entire realm? Then the warm relief of realization sweeps over me. "It must be Wake she's after."

"Perhaps," Veril says, his voice hard. "He will do anything to be called Supreme. But who am I to—?"

The light shifts again, and this time, both Veril and I catch that wedge-shaped shadow darting past the windows. "That wasn't a burnu," I whisper. "Whatever that was, it flies."

Veril flaps his hand. "Owls, Just Kai."

"Owls in the daytime?" My leg throbs, a painful reminder of the burnu attack.

"Owls, crows… No matter," he says, his lavender eyes gleaming. "Life in my lovely forest is different. Remember, dearest, we're protected here. Elyn and her otherworldly can't sense your presence because of my enchantments." He plays a note on his fife.

"Do you actually play that thing or do you just blow notes?" I ask.

"Every good Renrian is skilled at some sort of instrument. This is mine." He closes his eyes and plays one more single note on his fife—and this note sounds smoky. Or I'm just feeling slightly woozy. He takes a breath, then plays a song that sounds more like wind moving through a canyon. His fingers drift across the instrument's holes, but the tune is unlike any I remember hearing. It makes no sense—it has no meter, and it flutters up and down the scale. He pauses, then says, "Your secret is safe with me, Just Kai."

"What secret?" I ask, my voice thick.

But he just continues to play.

As I listen, my eyes grow heavy, and the inside of my stomach turns slick and strange. My heart races, and the room brightens. The prickly things stored in the jars in the alcove twist, and the walls ooze with blue sludge, and I sway in my wheelchair. Did he put something in my…? This can't be the memory tea, can it? I can't even *think*, let alone remember.

My throat tightens, and I clutch my neck. "What did you do?"

The last thing I see before everything goes black is Veril staring at me, sitting very still, and he's smiling.

27

I wear armor the color of blood and gold. My fingertips end in silver talons, and my pendant sparkles with fantastic light. I stand high upon craggy silver-gray rock. Down below, the frothy surface of an angry sea pulls beasts and men beneath its murky surface. I drag my talons, now speckled with blood, across the air, and I glimpse my reflection on each silver finger. My mouth bleeds. My skin is shredded and raw. And now, I stand alone on this barren mountain, crying, weeping, screaming, "Help me! Save me! Hurry."

My eyes open to dark ceiling beams in a room buzzing with light. The shadows of flitting butterflies and bumblebees dance across the wall. My mouth tastes like metal and walnuts.

Where am I? I turn my head, and my bones creak.

"Good morning." The Renrian sits on a small stool in the corner of the room and chews on the stem of a cold pipe. His eyes are no longer that sharp lilac; they are now soft brown flecked with red and blue light.

"Kai!" Olivia rushes to my bedside in noisy taffeta. "I was *so* worried about you!" Her eyes cloud with tears, and she flaps at her face. "I told myself not to cry, and here I am, blubbering like a baby."

Philia comes to stand beside her. "Welcome back."

"Where is…?" I push up on my elbows, looking for Jadon.

He's standing in the corner of the room. His blue eyes, dark with worry, match the blue of his tunic. "I thought that I'd taken too long and that you…" His voice is hoarse and strained. "…that you wouldn't need your amulet anymore."

Because I'd died. That's what he won't say.

My heart quakes. "Did you find it?"

He shakes his head. "I looked for hours, Kai."

"Olivia and I helped," Philia adds.

"And then we found the camp again," Olivia says. "And we got all our things we'd left there, so it wasn't a total waste."

I can't feign excitement because nothing they retrieved helps me. How important are blankets, carrots, and tunics when the piece that keeps me more than warm and nourished—my amulet—is still lost in the woods? Nothing matters if I'm dead.

"Veril says you're healed enough to start walking," Jadon says.

I stretch my stiff, achy leg, but the pain stops at my hip, rather than the top of my head.

Jadon holds up a piece of paper. "Veril's sending us out to gather plants for tonics. When we return, I'll help you start regaining your strength. You'll be reluctant to use that leg or turn your hips, so you won't be able to wield a sword as effectively as before. But you shouldn't just rely on your hands. They're unreliable."

I push out a breath. "Sounds good. Makes sense."

He strides to the door but stops with his hand on the knob. "And we'll keep looking for your amulet." His eyes meet mine. "I'll find it. I promise."

A moment later, Jadon and Olivia join Philia outside. I hear them talking as they set off on their task of gathering Veril's ingredients. Once their voices fade away, I wheel myself into the sitting room.

Veril is standing over his worktable, grinding something in one of his many stone bowls. "Don't trust anyone to bring you that which makes you whole. They may not *want* you whole." He nods toward the window. "*Especially* them. Depend on you and you alone. No one else. You must even learn to heal yourself without aid from others, even me. You must also learn how to mix tonics that are not meant to heal but are meant to lessen any threat against you. There's so much knowledge awaiting you."

"Teach me, then," I say, sitting up straighter. "Teach me as much as you can in the time we have together. I want to be able to heal myself and, since you won't say it, to make poisons."

"We'll start now, then." He beckons me. "Roll up to the table, dearest."

I roll right up to the worktable, so excited that I'm vibrating.

"Have you made potions before?" he asks.

"I don't know," I say. "Even with the memory tea, I still don't remember my life before. There are glimpses, yes, but they're not ordered enough to make any sense. I've even forgotten my born-day, but I know that I love honeycakes, although I don't recall if I've ever baked them. I know that I've seen burnu and sunabi before my arrival in Maford, but I don't know when."

I press my fingers against my achy forehead. "It's all in here—I just need something to help bring it out. That's why I need your help. That's what I *thought* your memory tea would do, instead of presenting me with even more riddles and making me sleep."

"You need to sleep," he says. "Sleep helps recovery."

I chew the inside of my cheek as Veril goes back to grinding whatever is in his stone bowl. "I know we're protected here, but Elyn will be able to find me when we leave. Do you have a spell to make me invisible? To protect me in case she discovers me?" I tuck my shaking hands in my lap.

He raises his eyebrows. "That's one of the tonics I aim to make for you, but only if your companions can find boar's tusk."

"Good." I take a deep breath, and my muscles relax. "What about other protections?" I ask. "Can you make something to combat my Miasma?"

He rears back. "Dearest Just Kai. You don't have Miasma."

"I'm exhausted and weak. My chest feels tight and I want to cough—"

"You were attacked by otherworldly," he says firmly. "Your injuries aren't the same as if you'd been bitten by a dog or even fell out of a tree. Your body is trying to figure out how to keep you from dying, and if that means limiting your breath, then it will limit your breath. Stop pouring worry into your bowl. You have plenty on your plate."

Outside the sitting room windows, the world turns white as a thick fog blankets the cottage and gardens. Points of light flicker through the mist, drifting along the path just traveled by Jadon and the girls, then moving toward the window before halting. Something—or *someone*—is out there, waiting, watching. What does it see right now? Me sitting here in this chair? A chasm where a cottage once stood?

Panic grips me, making my head spin, and I fight the urge to curl into a ball. I don't move—moving could expose me. And so I hold my breath and wait.

That light glides across the garden, moving away from my companions and disappearing into the dense forest. The fog begins to thin until the bank becomes wisps, and the wisps fade into memories.

"See?" Veril says from his chair. "The enchantment is still working."

"You saw it, too," I whisper, feeling nauseous. "That fog? The light?"

He tilts his head. "Nothing escapes my notice, dearest. Once again: you have enough worry on your plate. Eat what you have first before returning to the realm's banquet of bother."

Silence slips through the cottage, and the walls flicker with shadow and flame. The air shimmers, and I spot a silk strand of a spiderweb drifting past me. I take deep breaths as I watch it and I wonder about the spider who spun it and I wonder if she hates having to build a web every day that must be then rebuilt every night. Does that spider—a creator—ever become frustrated with the realm's banquet of bother?

I chuckle as I imagine a spider throwing up her eight legs and saying, "I'm tired of this shit," stomping out of her raggedy web, and finding love with a robin who promises to never eat her if she agrees to catch a fly and a cricket for dinner every now and again. Could that ever happen? Each creature teaming up and going against their nature for the sake of survival? Is there a grand plan for every living thing, even for those as small as a spider and robin?

"Veril," I say, "do all Renrians believe in Supreme?"

"Certainly," he says. "As well as all the manifestations of Supreme. And I don't mean manifestations created in a fever dream Syrus Wake says he had." The old man points to me. "Tell me. You are…?"

"Kai."

"Your right hand. What does it do?"

I blink at him, then say, "It writes. Scratches my hair. Waves."

"Now: your left eye," he says. "What does *it* do?"

"It sees. It blinks."

"Are both a part of your body?"

I nod.

"Do they do the same thing?"

I shake my head.

"But they are still a part of you, a part of Kai, yes?"

"Each part of me has different functions but are still of the same accord."

Veril points his pipe at me. "And so it is with Supreme. There are orders—like the Executioners—who act as the hand. Other orders act as the heart. Still another, the brain. And so on and so forth. My order: we are the record-keepers, the connectors of ages. While we are not immortal, we have been blessed with long life. And I recognize our role, and if I believe in me, and I believe that Supreme is all, then I believe in those entities mortals call angels and gods."

Hmm. Never thought about it like that.

"What am I, then?" I ask. "Where do I fit into all of this?"

His eyes twinkle. "That's what you're trying to figure out, yes?"

"Do you think it's possible that I'm suffering from a false sense of importance and have no place?" Am I just a simple garden spider with a raggedy web? Building and rebuilding each day, catching fly after fly but never eating enough flies to rid the garden of them?

"Your pendant tells me that you have worth, Kai. You were given it for a reason. You're not simply drifting through the realm all your life, heading toward death."

"That," I say, pointing at his fox amulet. "Who gave it to you?"

He presses the pendant between his fingers. "My patron chose this for me long, long ago. She saw something in me that I didn't."

"That you're cunning?" I ask.

"And resilient."

I cock an eyebrow. "Tricky?"

"Resourceful."

"Radiant?"

"And very protective of those who matter most to me." The old man claps his hands. "Should be ready now." After a quick stir, he ladles some of its contents into a bowl, returns to the table, and holds the bowl of steaming liquid out to me. "Drink. This is an actual tonic, not just lentil stew."

Cunning. Tricky.

I hesitate. "Didn't you just put nightshade in that?"

"Did I?"

"How do I know if you're —?"

He lifts an eyebrow. "Trying to poison you?"

I watch his face, then stare down at the bowl in his hands, unblinking. I take it, and the clay feels cool in my hands, even though it holds bubbling broth.

"Know your friends," Veril says. "Know your foes." Then he holds up a twisted brown stick the length of a caterpillar. "This is rumored to make people remember those things they wish to forget. Let's see if this will help you." He drops it in my bowl. "Drink up."

I sip, and immediately my tongue feels like it's being pulled over my nose and my head weighs more than the realm. I'm forced to rest my forehead against the table, eyes squeezed tight. The pain is so great my blood turns frosty and my heart crumples and expands in my chest. My lungs compress like they are in a vise, and I can't even gasp.

As the liquid slips through me, the tightness across my scalp eases and I can take long breaths through my nose. A calm finally worms up my spine and seeps through my skin. Relaxes the lids of my closed eyes and—

A man wearing a crown. And exploding light. I fall from the heavens, spears of silver-gray rocks chasing me as I fall toward a sea, screaming, "Save me. Help me. Hurry!" The man wearing the crown roars as I plunge beneath the sea and—

I open my eyes. Heart racing, I struggle for air. "I can't breathe."

Veril holds up a vial of black liquid. "Absorbs toxic substances."

I take the vial and drink, and I taste earth, smoke, and bamboo. Sharp pain erupts in my stomach, and I pull myself into a tight ball. Beads of sweat break out across my skin.

But then lightness comes. No pain.

"You remembered something," Veril says, watching me carefully.

I pat my sweaty face. "I don't know what it means yet." There's too much light in this cottage now. I want to close my eyes. "I'm tired, Veril. I can't say anymore right now."

He pushes me back to the room and helps settle me in his bed.

I drift off to sleep thinking about my perilous fall from the heavens, about that man and his terrible light, about the horrors awaiting me in the depths of that caustic sea…

28

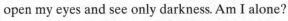

I open my eyes and see only darkness. Am I alone?

No. There's a silhouette framed against the dying light.

My muscles tighten, my mind still lost between sleep and phantoms.

He clears his throat—it's Jadon placing a bundle of wildflowers in a vase on the dresser. Even in the coming twilight, the flowers are vibrant purples, yellows, and blues. Their perfume wafts through the bedroom, sweet and earthy, and mixes with Jadon's scent of smoke and pine.

Right as he tiptoes to leave the room, I say, "They're beautiful." My mouth feels dry and stale, like old bread and straw.

"Just wanted to add some cheer and color." He turns away from the door but doesn't move any closer.

A fresh cup of hot tea sits on the nightstand, a tendril of steam rising from the surface. "You brought me today's brew?"

He smiles. "I did. How are you feeling?" He hands me the mug.

I try to sit up, and an ache moves through my muscles, a reminder that I'm still injured but healing. "My limbs don't feel like I'm being pulled down by anvils. The pain's different. And my throat feels scratchy and tight. Something's wrong. I feel like my mind is all over the place, like a leaf being blown by the wind. It's not this." I gesture toward the undressed wound.

Jadon takes a small step closer to the bed.

"Veril says that I don't have Miasma. He thinks that I'm just recovering from an otherworldly attack. And if I don't have Miasma, then that means that I'm not contagious."

Amused, Jadon says, "Are you sure about that?"

"No." I pat the spot beside me. "But you're an adventurer. You court danger."

His eyes turn silky-soft. "I do."

"Then come sit. Tell me something thrilling that happened to you today. How was herb and plant collecting?"

"Veril wasn't impressed." Jadon eases onto the bed beside me, and he tells me that Olivia mistook oleander for summer shiso. "The old man was so mad, he turned every color possible. He told her she would have killed you immediately. And that's before he saw that she'd found jimson weed. She thought they were morning glory."

"Were morning glories on the list Veril gave you?"

"No. She said she saw me picking flowers and she wanted to pick flowers, too, because the cottage was just too dark and she wanted to pretty up the sitting room."

I belt out a laugh.

Jadon does, too. "Veril nearly tossed her and the plant out. The plant is so dangerous that you shouldn't even inhale it outside."

I point to the wildflowers in the vase he set on the dresser. "Those are?"

"Jimson weed and oleander."

I snort a laugh. It feels good—like I'm lighter.

He snickers. "Nah. Those are daisies and sweet pea."

"And they're beautiful, thank you. Please tell me you found my amulet."

He shakes his head. "I looked again. Retraced our steps and everything."

I deflate a little. "Oh no."

"There's still time," he says, tugging one of my curls.

"If you say so."

"I say so."

The tea tastes like oranges and ginger and, yes, rum. I inhale a deep whiff of steam. The scent loosens my lungs some, but the pain in my leg and hip throbs. The coolness of the eucalyptus in Veril's salve has tempered the pain.

Jadon glances at the door. "I'm already on Veril's hate list, and you need your rest. If I stay, we'll talk and you won't rest, which means that you're not gaining your strength, which means we'll be here longer. So sleep, please."

"Alone?" I want someone to share my raggedy web. *Him.* I yearn to be connected to someone. *Him.* To be touched instead of torn. To be touched not because I need to be nursed but touched because I want what I want.

Jadon rubs his neck with one hand and squeezes the bridge of his nose with the other.

"You look miserable." My voice is raspy. "Am I making you miserable?"

He briefly clenches his jaw until his mouth softens, surrendering. "Absolutely."

"Too bad." I smile. My gaze flits from his eyes to his lips, then down to his rewrapped hand. "Good thing I know how to turn your frown upside down."

"Yeah?"

I reach out to touch his hand. I spread my fingers across his skin, enjoying the story of his hands, rough from ironwork and battle.

The silence between us is taut, ready to snap.

My fingers drift from his hand to his cheek, and there is a different story here. The bristle of days-old stubble. The lift of his smile. This is the touch I want. One that causes that familiar fire to build in my belly, the fire that burns whenever he's around.

"Drink more tea," he says. "At least I can tell him I made you do that."

"Yep." I sip more tea, and its magic slithers through my body. I purr and sink farther into the pillows.

"Better?" he asks.

"Umhmm." I give him a lazy smile. "Tell me…"

"About?"

"Why you're covering the tattoo on your hand. You saw mine. Now I wanna see yours. All of it."

He holds my gaze. "Some of us aren't fortunate to have ink as intriguing as yours."

"Let me see it up close and I'll make that decision."

He doesn't move.

"I said, I wanna see it," I slur, my tongue thick in my mouth, the tea still working through my blood, healing me, pushing me. "You're gonna make me beg?"

He stares at me a moment more, then offers me his hand.

"Take off the bandage, please."

He obeys and unwraps the cloth. The tattoo covers the top of his hand. Green ink, red ink, black, yellow, blue, creating a hand with fingers outstretched. One fingertip a flame. Another fingertip, ice. Water. Cracked earth. Darkness. In the center of his inked hand, there's a large circle filled with a smaller circle, and then a smaller circle inside that circle until the final circle is a simple dot, with rings that ripple after a single drop of water disturbs the pool.

I trace my finger along that biggest circle.

Jadon closes his eyes.

My finger trails over to fire…ice…

"You should probably stop," he says, his eyebrows high, his eyes still closed.

"You really want me to stop touching you?" My throat is tight, but not from Miasma.

"Oh, I want you to touch me." He bites his lip. "I just want you to stop looking at my ugly tattoo."

My finger trails from his hand to his wrist. "Where do you want me to look, then?"

His eyes open and pin me again like a rare moth. "I have another one. A nicer one."

I quirk an eyebrow. "Ooh."

He nods. "Yeah."

"Where?"

"Here." He places his hand atop mine and leads it to the center of his chest. His heart pulses beneath my palm, and I splay my fingers to take possession of his life-beat.

"What are you waiting for?" I say, my arm aching, all of me burning.

He pulls my hand to his lips and kisses the tips of my fingers.

I gasp, then whisper, "You want me to touch you somewhere else first?"

He studies me and holds his breath as I trail my fingers down his chest. He squeezes my hand before it can travel any farther, his bright-blue eyes darkening to bottom-of-the-sea blue. "Kai." He says my name low, the same way he said my name that first time.

Flames lick across my skin as I lean closer, my gaze sliding from his eyes to his lips.

He whispers, "We can't do this."

"Hmm?" We are so close, just a breath away from touching, but I will not wait for that breath, and I pull closer to him and...

"We can't do this," he repeats, louder this time.

I freeze. *"Why?"*

"What if you're already in love?" He removes my hand from his cheek and kisses it again before placing it on my hip. "We talked about this, remember?"

"We did." I peer at him, heart pounding, waiting for the punchline.

Is he fucking kidding me right now?

The look in his eyes—no fire, no sparkle—tells me that he's not.

He wraps one of my curls around his finger. "What if Before Kai doesn't want the same things that Now Kai wants? And what if who she wants is nothing like me?"

A different kind of heat now warms my cheeks. Embarrassment. Rejection. "Move."

"Kai—"

"Get the fuck off my bed."

His face flushes, and his eyes dart from my face to the bed. "Can we just stop—?"

"We're stopped. *Go.*" I tug my quilt from beneath him.

The mattress shifts as he wobbles to his feet.

I pull the quilt over my shoulders and face the wall.

"Please don't get mad at me because I asked a valid question," he says to my back. "I want this so badly, but I also don't want to hurt you."

I stare at the wall's bumpy nothingness. Better than looking at him. Safer. But then the wall becomes too much, and I squeeze my eyes shut.

He sighs again. Then his soft footsteps move toward the door but don't leave the room. Undecided.

I make the decision for both of us and let exhaustion pull me back into its cloud. And soon, it doesn't matter if he's standing there or not—I'm drifting off to sleep, and I don't plan to open my eyes again until the new day. Nor do I plan to think about his valid question. Now Kai wants what she wants. She offered, he declined, and that's that.

Neither Kai—Before or Now—begs.

My dream is not of silver-gray mountains or rancid seas or cries of despair.

Olivia is the only person in this dream.

I'm looking out the window beside my bed, and I see her hidden in the oleander bushes, pulling on my leather breeches and then swirling my cape around her shoulders. She's already wearing my boots, and beneath my too-big tunic, she wears my bandeau.

Our eyes lock.

She glides her tongue over her sharp white teeth and backs deeper into the oleander. Before she completely disappears, I glimpse something shining on her neck.

My amulet.

I blink—she's gone. Nothing there except crabapple trees and ferns.

I bolt up in bed, my head spinning. Panic rattles my achy bones.

That dream—it felt so *real*. But there's no way it could be real. Right? Not after I warned her.

I'm dreaming. Yeah.

Right before we left the cottage, she claimed that my clothes needed additional washing because they were filthy. No, I'll take over and wash them again, even if that means wheeling my way to the creek myself.

29

The light streaming through my window is crisp and lemony. Morning has come. The fire of my anger toward Olivia still burns, but I push it away. Just a dream. I toss off the blankets, and my bare feet hit the cold stone floor. I stay in the bed, though, a strange tension prickling my senses. The wind is unusually strong today—strange, since it's typically just a gentle breeze causing the grasses around the cottage to sway. Now, gusts are shaking the ferns, and dust pebbles tap against the windowpane. A shiver runs down my spine as I catch sight of...

That. What *is* that? Perched atop a tree hollow.

I squint at the figure...*a bat*? No...it's too large for a bat. It is wedge-shaped, yet its form is indistinct in the dim light. It looks like a void, a hole of the blackest black, expanding and feeding on the terror of those who see it. But fear doesn't grip me—it's awe that pins me in place. The stench of rotten fruit and sulfur seeps through the windowpane, making me gag. I clasp a hand over my mouth and close my eyes. When I regain control and look back, the creature is gone. No shadow, no breeze, no stink of death.

I slide into my chair and roll to the sitting room. Veril is at his worktable, mixing ingredients in a bowl. "I saw something outside the cottage again," I say, then describe the creature perched on the tree.

The old man hums in acknowledgment but doesn't stop his work.

"You seem unperturbed," I say, raising an eyebrow.

"We have a lot to do," he says, flashing me a grin. "As much as I'd like it, you can't stay here forever, Just Kai. If I had to swivel my head every time an otherworldly creature said, 'good day,' my neck would be a toothpick." He nods at the bowl. "This is more important right now."

"Another memory elixir?" I ask, rolling closer, the creature's reek still lingering in my throat like grease.

"Breakfast," he answers with a smile, eyes scanning my unwrapped leg. "You're moving better today. Have you tried to stand?"

I push out a breath and grip the arms of the chair. I stand, wobbling a bit, but plant my feet firmly against the floor. "Behold," I say, my arms out for balance. "What do you think?"

Veril laughs and taps the spoon against the bowl. "That's the best standing I've seen all morning."

I bend my knees, wincing from the pop of my tight muscles. "It's quiet this morning. Where's everyone?"

Veril flicks a dismissive hand and drizzles honey into the bowl. "Thankfully, out of my hair for the moment. Good sleep?"

I bite my lip and swallow. "I'm not sure."

Without a word, he pours the batter into the iron skillet, and the edges of the thin cake bubble and harden. The aroma of warm honey wafts from the hearth. "What's troubling you, dearest?" He coaxes the cake from the hot surface and flips it over.

"The Sea of Devour," I say. "That mountain in its center. I've had dreams about both now, and I think…I need to go there."

Veril slips the warm cake onto a plate. He spoons butter from the small pot and drops it atop the cake. "Because?"

My shoulders lift in a slight shrug. "There are voices telling me that I must come. Voices that include my own. And something about these dreams feels…*right*. Feels…*true*. The saffron, Peria, Kaivara, those mages… I need to go there soon or else—"

"Or else 'what'?" He holds my gaze and tilts his head. When I shake my head, he sighs. "I've traveled to Peria with the intentions of crossing that sea and scaling the Mount of Devour."

"And?"

He nods to my breakfast, indicating that I should eat. "I hired a boatbuilder in Peria and paid him to sail me across the sea so that I could summit the mount."

"And?" I take a big bite of the cake and close my eyes as the light, buttery dough melts against my tongue.

"*And* Dayami and I reached the banks of Devour," he says, "but the soles of our boots were nearly eaten away. We slipped the canoe into the water, and the acid of Devour burned away the tar used to keep the boat waterproof. We barely made it back to safe ground."

I drop my fork and push away the plate. "You're saying that I shouldn't go."

He pushes the plate back to me. "I'm *saying* that you'll need more than the clothes on your back to even reach the shores of Devour. I survived that trip only because I was younger, stronger—and most importantly, I was protected, wearing the right armor."

I take another bite from the cake but taste nothing. "So…don't travel to Devour naked and ill-prepared. And here I was, about to travel to Devour naked and ill-prepared."

Veril peers at me and says, "Nothing is simple in that part of the realm. Have your dreams shown you how to reach the Sea and Mount of Devour?"

I shake my head. "I recall nothing of it at this moment."

After breakfast, Veril pulls a book of maps from his shelves. "Devour Sea is far west of Pethorp, in the far west province of Vallendor. Its green waters have consumed nearly all the plants and wildlife in that region. Somewhere, in the crosses and triangles used by the mapmaker as markers, is the town of Peria, with its mages on defense, with its fields of saffron and altars dedicated to the goddess Kaivara, using magic to resist Emperor Wake's invasion."

I run my tongue over my lower lip. "So what kind of armor will I need to make the trip?"

"Luclite," Veril says, "which is stronger than steel and virtually impossible to work with. Every piece of luclite armor is rare and precious."

"And how do I get armor made of luclite?" I ask.

"You're in luck." Veril taps the top of my head with the rolled-up piece of parchment. "I know a Renrian in Caburh, a hamlet of about four hundred people. Separi and her wife run an inn there. She also makes and enchants luclite armor and jewelry for a few special people."

"Am I a 'special people'?" I ask.

Veril wiggles his nose. "You know the answer to that question already, dearest." He wanders over to the cookie jar and plucks out three treats.

"If you couldn't reach Mount Devour," I ask, "what makes you think I can? That I'm worthy?"

"Other than your amulet and visions?" He shrugs. "I don't know—but you won't find out sitting in my cottage until the end of forever, will you?"

"How do I reach Caburh, then?" I ask.

After Veril drops two cookies in my hands, he spreads the rolled parchment across the table. It's an expansive map of Vallendor Realm.

I roll my chair beside him as he points to a drawing of a hashmark in the southwest portion of the map, past Pethorp and Hafeld, at the end of the Duskmoor River.

"This is Caburh," he says, "and there you'll find the Broken Hammer,

Separi's inn. And here's Mount Devour..." His finger drags north, following the edge of a forest, over plains and deserts, past Peria, to the shores of Devour. He taps at a single solid mountain rising from the middle of the sea. "The map doesn't capture the size and scope of the mountain nor the immensity of the sea. Both are beyond formidable."

I blow out my cheeks. "This will be quite the journey."

"Truly," he admits. "Will it be easy? Certainly not. But it *is* doable. Renrian settlers founded Caburh after the Great War. But not many live there all season now. It sits at Duskmoor River, and so the earth is rich and dark, perfect for cultivation and livestock. Merchants and artisans are always traveling and sailing in and out of Caburh. Renrians found it a pleasing site to continue our legacy of scholarship, alchemy, and enchantment. Renrians all over Vallendor convocate there every fifty years to share knowledge. It's a wonderful time."

He taps his finger against his chin. "Ten more years until the next one, and by then I'll have so much to share. That's when I'm supposed to receive the honorific of Commander of the Canon. There's a certificate that even says that: *Commander of the Canon.* My very first." His lavender eyes sparkle.

"You've never received a special designation?" I say, a grin inching across my face. "Someone as learned as you?"

"Not once. As I was saying..." He grows serious again. "Separi makes the most *beautiful* luclite armor, and she will make some for you."

I study the map. "How long will it take to reach Caburh?"

"A week's journey on foot, give or take. If we—"

"*We?*"

"I'm joining you," he says. "To see my old friend and to protect and sustain you with tonics when you falter—and you *will* falter. It's a long journey. You will face hardship, both physically and mentally. And I want to be there for you, encouraging you and healing you when needed. Honestly, I can't be Commander of the Canon staying *here*, can I?"

"You cannot," I say, joy boosting my spine and spirit. "Okay, so we get the armor from Separi, and then we will journey across the realm to the Sea and Mount of Devour."

I will falter. Veril just said that. If it's challenging for me, then how challenging will it be for a two-hundred-year-old Renrian? "I don't want you to feel that you must join me, Veril. Please don't think that you're responsible for me until we've traveled the realm in search of my home."

Veril dips his head. "I know the challenges and I'll join you still. You are in charge of your destiny, Just Kai, and I am in charge of mine." He pulls the pipe from his sleeve and studies the map. Discussion over.

"Mount Devour," I say, running my finger over its jagged representation on the map. "I *know* that name. I must because it feels like hope, which is strange, since the word 'devour' is the opposite of hope. But that's where I'll reclaim a piece of me that I can hold on to. I know this is true, Veril."

"I, too, know this is true, dearest."

We shake hands, and I say, "Future Commander of the Canon, glad to start this adventure to the end of the realms."

He shuffles away from the map and over to the hearth. "This calls for a celebratory mug of my most favorite tea."

I stare at the map, memorizing those towns around the Sea of Devour and estimating the distances between, while Veril selects tea leaves from a shelf. Behind me, water sloshes in the kettle and the pestle grinds against the leaves as I trace my finger along the winding path of a river on the map. I feel the weight of Veril's eyes on my back...but when I look back over my shoulder, he isn't looking at me at all, just staring intensely at the mortar and pestle. I return my attention to the map—it can't be all bad, this journey. Maybe I'll discover a place where pine trees soar, where the air is so cold, it stings my lungs; a place with snow deep enough to get lost in; a beautiful and quiet and hopeful place. Maybe I'll discover this place before acid replaces snow and softness.

"Here you go, Just Kai." Veril hands me a cup of tea, then carries his own mug to the rocking chair. Steam wafts from the cup to my nose. Cinnamon, cherries, wood.

"To remembering," Veril toasts.

"To me," I toast.

Just then, the front door opens, and Olivia and Philia burst into the room, all smiles and good cheer. Jadon, though, enters the cottage with a drawn face and slumped shoulders.

I don't speak even though the sight of him makes me feel like I'm floating.

Jadon gapes at Veril and me drinking tea by the fire, and then he spots the map on the worktable. He takes a deep breath, closes his eyes, and says, "Where are we going *now*?"

PART III

DON'T TALK ABOUT IT...
BE ABOUT IT

Within the night's soft fading glow,
His whispering rebukes woe
Until they stand where shadows wane,
He matches death with somber bane.

Hear the echoes of closing breath,
A spell for life, away from death.
In arms of twilight, where spirits sigh,
Near the end, where dreams may fly.

Into veiled mists of sublime plain,
He serenades without strain.
Loving life, he holds secrets dear.
He ignores Fate and ignores Fear.

Hear the echoes of closing breath,
A spell for life, away from death.
His fate is waiting, he cannot run
An end he loathes, his life done.

Beneath dark halls where future dwells,
Men invocate, ringing bells,
Hoping gods will hear plaintive cries
To hold back wrongs that puncture eyes.

Callow, crude, their hearts falter fast.
Their evilness demands vast
Journeys swift, where true evil lurks.
Men deserve this endless murk.

Hear the echoes of closing breath,
A spell for life, away from death.
Men pray for greatness, men ignore good.
Men court doom, heart hard as wood.

Spiders weave their last silken threads.
A labyrinthine web work spreads.
Cosmic strings of Fate's final waltz,
The pilgrims fooled by silence false.

—An Elegy by Veril Bairnell the Sapient

30

A new day has come, and I don't know how long I've slept. Veril has left three crabapples on the windowsill, and on the bedroom chair, two clean pairs of black breeches, a gold-colored cloak, gold-colored gloves, two tunics, one white, one black, and a pair of black suede boots that may actually fit.

I smile, and a sigh escapes my lips—my gauze remains pristine. The skin near my hip still pulls if I take deep breaths—but the scabs there as well as the long ones along my leg are close to falling off. Which means my time here in this cottage has ended. I'll miss these peaceful gardens, the order, the warm hearth and clean quilts. The quiet.

Once dressed, I limp outside, squinting in the light from the daystar. Its warmth, though, feels good against my face.

Notes from Veril's fife drift from one side of the garden behind the cottage. Jadon has revived the old man's small, neglected forge on the other side of the garden. Something hard-looking glows orange in the furnace.

Sanding down a piece of wood, Jadon flashes me a smile and tosses the small wooden thing on the table. He meets my eyes and doesn't turn away. "I *had* to ask those questions."

What if you're already in love?

What if Before Kai doesn't want the same things that Now Kai wants?

"And I'm sorry." He steps toward me. "I hope you believe that." When I don't respond, he sighs. "Please say something."

Say what? That his rejection made me feel like the last slice of moldy bread? Even thinking about it makes my mouth bunch and my skin burn with embarrassment.

"It wasn't that I didn't want to." Jadon takes another step closer. "You know that I did. It was obvious that I did. I'm not some delicate flower, but the real reason I couldn't... It's because..." He pushes out a breath and blurts, "We'd be fucking in that old man's bed, which..." He shudders.

A laugh bursts from my mouth, and I clamp my hand over my lips.

"That was crass," he says with a shrug, "but honest."

"When you say it like that…" I lower my hand, and more laughter escapes.

"Right?" He winces. "And once you think about it, you can't *not* think about it."

I snicker, then close my eyes, taking deep breaths.

"Hey," he whispers, "look at me."

I do, and my head swims as I meet his sincere gaze.

"Anywhere. In a barn. On a boat. In a garden, maybe this garden. *Anywhere* except—"

"Veril's bed."

He snorts a laugh. "Mmhmm."

Self-doubt still lingers in my heart. "The questions you asked were fair."

He nods. "I don't want to give you my all when, in the end, you'll discover that you actually do have someone in your before-time who loves you and misses you."

We rest our eyes on each other, and he says, "Let's get back to where we were, yeah?"

"Yeah."

He rubs his hands together. "So, what do you want to work on today?"

"Weapons," I say, rolling up my sleeves. "But remember that I can't do too much. Don't wanna pull, break, or snap something that just healed."

"We'll go easy." He heads to a cleared area ringed by workbenches and sawhorses, bales of hay, and the saddest-looking straw man in the realm. "I was thinking about you this morning."

Still limping a bit, I join him. "What were you thinking *about*?"

"I was thinking that maybe you'd enjoy meeting my swords."

I stretch my arms across my chest. "I'm very eager to meet your swords."

He points at me. "Prepare to be amazed."

How long have I waited to meet his sword? Since the day we met, right before Narder decided to throw me in the clink. So much has happened since market day.

"Before we begin," I say now, shaking a finger at Jadon, "let's be clear. I may not remember my home, but I know that I'm *very* familiar with battle. If I'm a little awkward, it's because I've been wounded. Or because I don't know how to handle *your* specific…"

"Sword." Chin high, he says, "It will be the best sword you'll ever hold in your hand."

Delight ripples through me as I slowly turn one ankle and then the other in a circle. "Only one hand?"

"Two, but I didn't want to brag." Jadon gives me a crooked smile. "Just as you requested, we'll go slow—I don't want to hurt you. And sometimes, slow is best. Once you're stronger, we'll go faster." He tilts his head and cocks an eyebrow. "Fast or slow, you won't leave disappointed."

My pulse quickens, and my body heats. "That was a brag."

"Yeah, it was."

He takes my hands and kisses them both. "Are we okay?"

"Are we?" I teeter, my legs threatening to quit me as his soft lips linger on my skin.

He winks, then nods at the worktable and the four weapons that will push me closer to regaining my strength and dexterity. "So," he says, squeezing my hands one last time, "your natural weapons are—"

"These." I waggle my reclaimed fingers.

"When you tried to push wind but couldn't, how did your hands feel?"

"Cold. I tried rubbing them together, willing them to work, but they refused."

"And when they finally worked, what were the conditions? How were you feeling?"

I think back to those times my hands burned—the fight with the emperor's men, the fights with the otherworldly, and when Johny and his friends attacked me. "I felt threatened. I was angry. I feared for the lives of others."

"Have you been angry before and your hands didn't work?"

I cock my head to think about it. "Yes."

"Were you wearing your amulet?"

"Yes. Each time."

He rubs his chin, thinking. "Hmm."

"We'll test it again once I find my amulet—not that I'm anxious to skirmish with another man or beast again, but if I do, I'll pay attention."

Jadon picks up the first weapon on the worktable. It has a long wood shaft with a cone-shaped head made of iron. "This isn't mine—found it while cleaning up this forge. You should get to know it. A mace." He hands it to me. "Good for heavy blows, but it doesn't penetrate armor."

"Heavy but not impossible," I say, handing it back.

"Think you used one before?"

I shake my head. "Doesn't feel like something I would've used, but I'm open to new experiences."

He lifts an amused eyebrow—*really?*—as he leads me to the straw man. My face heats at his playfulness.

"Meet Bronie. He won't be with us for long." He swings the mace and hits the straw man with an *oomph*. He does it again, moving like the wind. "Now, you try. *Slowly*. You don't have to impress me right now."

Arms looser, I take a deep breath and swing—and the damned thing almost flies out of my hands. I swing again and again.

"Control the weapon by controlling your abdomen," Jadon suggests.

Yep. My abdominal muscles warm as straw flies from Bronie with each blow.

Interesting.

He holds out a dagger. "Your last-resort weapon."

The dagger's grip is wine-colored, well-seasoned leather interspersed with copper tacks, and the blade is engraved with hexagons.

"This is one of mine," Jadon says, "but now, I gift it to you."

"Really?" A crest of gratitude sweeps through me like warm tea as I turn the weapon in my hands. "It's beautiful. Did you make it?"

"Yep," he says, shoulders squared. "Daggers are used for grappling. For puncturing armor. For making someone scream for mercy. Plain edge. Easier to sharpen. Makes clean cuts."

The dagger feels as light as a large apple in my hand. When I stick Bronie where his heart would be, the jab feels personal, like I knew this straw man—he stole my birthright and all my money and refuses to give any of it back, then yells "mudscraper" at me before sticking his tongue down my lover's throat. Yeah, I *like* this dagger.

"I don't know how I know this," I say, "but where I came from, we name our weapons as a show of respect."

"Where I'm from, we do, too." Jadon taps the dagger. "She has no name, so it's up to you to name her whatever feels right."

"I'll call her..." I hold up the small knife. "Little Lava."

Jadon crosses his arms and leans against the worktable. "Little Lava? Why?"

"Because she brings the heat. Just like me."

"And the heat you bring is well-appreciated." He selects the next weapon, handing me the longsword. "Let's try this, Hotness. The second-best sword in Vallendor."

This weapon weighs as much as a bag of potatoes, and its blade is as black as night.

"I've already named her Fury," he says, running his finger along the sharp edge.

Intricate etchings of moths flit along the black leather handle and across the hilt. A black stone sits in the middle of the circular pommel.

"Steel blade painted black," Jadon points out, "so that it won't reflect light. You don't want the enemy to know you've arrived. The black stone is onyx, just like the moth's thorax of your amulet."

"I noticed," I say, smiling. "I'm impressed. She's lovely."

"Your hands go here." Jadon taps the bottom of the sword's grip. "Not here."

"This sword feels like…" My fingers circle the grip. "Like it was created for my hand and *only* my hand."

"Maybe it was." He takes a step back.

Maybe? No. *Definitely*. I've already claimed it—he just doesn't know yet.

"Play with it," he says. "It's yours."

Shit. Maybe he does. Did he create this specifically for me?

I hold his gaze, and then I swing the sword once, then two more times. Fury is a perfect fit. For my hand. For me.

"You like that?" he asks.

"Can't you tell?" I ask, grinning.

"Well, you're kinda quiet," he says, an eyebrow lifted.

This man… He will be the death of me. My entire body hums with adrenaline. "Give me something to hit, then."

"When you're ready," he says, grinning, "I will. Until then… Good range. Easy to use. Balanced."

"Any disadvantages?" I ask, swinging the sword again.

From behind, he taps my feet apart for a wider stance, and I can feel the heat rolling off his body. "Since it's long, it's not great for walking around, so you should use a scabbard and wear it on your back. I have one for you."

He reaches around and runs his finger along the hilt, and I tremble as his warm breath fans across the back of my neck. "Since I knew that I'd be giving this to you," he says, tracing that finger along the black blade, "I carved the moths last night. Again, like your amulet. In case you never find her, these moths will be a reminder of your power."

I can't take my eyes away from the moths etched across the sword's body. "Beautiful and thoughtful. I love it, Jadon. Thank you." Something beyond appreciation threads through me. Because I can appreciate anyone. But this buzzing and crackling, my burning skin, the buzz of every nerve in my body—this is for him. I'm ready to act too quickly. I'm ready to make the wrong decisions.

He folds his arms and sighs. "It's nothing."

But I know he doesn't believe that. It's everything. I can tell from the way his hands travel from one place on his body to the next, by the way he opens and closes his fingers because he wants to grip me. I can tell by the way he watches me, by the way his eyes linger on my ass.

I want to reach for him, but I hesitate. What if I'm wrong again?

He's hesitant, too, lowering his gaze to the dirt and scratching the stubble on his chin. "We should move on, yeah?"

"Yeah." I run my fingers over the carved moths as I set Fury back on the table, then point to the broadsword. "That can't possibly be for me."

It's as tall as Olivia. With its wide, shiny silver blade and massive basket hilt, the two-handed sword looks as though it could slice Bronie in half with one swing.

"*This*," he says, smiling, "is the best sword in Vallendor, and it belongs to me. Try it out." He plops down in the straw that had previously lived inside poor Bronie.

"Not as big as that Otaan's blade," I say. "That thing was as big as it was ugly." I'm reluctant to lift this broadsword. For some reason, I fear cutting off my own hand or a foot, or my head. But I do lift it, and immediately, every muscle in my body pulls. "Nope. I don't like how this feels. It's not that it's heavier…"

I hold it away from me. "Maybe it's the hilt, like I'm wearing a cage around my hand. But then, you don't need a gauntlet or a glove because your hand is protected. I don't know if I trust it, and my body is rebuking me holding something this…*powerful*? But I don't think it's that, either."

"Tell your body to simmer down. You can do it," Jadon instructs from the bed of straw. "You're right—this weapon can cut off heads and limbs. It slices through mail and helmets. It takes more practice, more physicality, but I've seen you use an unremarkable sword and a garden hoe. At this point, I'm convinced you can do anything."

I bat my eyelashes. "Thank you so much." I turn back to the sword.

"What's his name?"

"Chaos."

"That suits." I peer at the sword, then back at Jadon. "One swing and shit just unravels."

"Calamity and mayhem," he says, winking. "But you don't look like you're enjoying my precious Chaos."

"It's not a matter of enjoying it or the weight or my ability," I say. "I'll handle him if I must. But do I want to? The hilt is throwing me off. It looks great on you, but for me? It's elegant and breathtaking, but I dread holding it in my hands. I fear that if I chop off one head and a pair of hands, then I'll want to chop off another head and another pair of hands, and then more and more."

"You'd lose control?" he asks, eyebrow arched.

"I'd never want to stop. And I doubt you'd stop me."

"I like watching you fight," he says, eyes narrowed, tongue poking his cheek. "Why would I ever stop you?"

I cock my head to the side. "You'd let me finish until I had my fill?"

He says, "Mmhmm."

"You're a very considerate partner." Familiar heat floods my body, and our eyes meet.

Have I ever flirted with anyone like this? Knowing who I am today combined with knowing one of my favorite things, I must have flirted and more. And how was it? Can I not remember those times because I can't remember anything else right now or can I not remember those times because they were truly forgettable encounters—decent and good enough, more congress than libidinous? Or was I the one who'd been decent and simply good enough?

Of course not. I scoff at the idea of me being a mediocre lover. I'm pretty sure that I'd make the man on this bed of hay forget his own name.

"Sorry, Chaos," I say to the broadsword. "It's not you but it's not me, either."

"But look how big and wide that blade is," Jadon says, smirking.

I roll my eyes. "It's always about *size*, isn't it?" I point the broadsword at him. "I don't know if anyone's ever told you this, but just because it's big and wide doesn't mean it's good."

"Is that so?" Jadon says.

"Yes, that is extremely so."

He narrows his eyes. "Didn't you just say that you're open to new experiences?"

"I am open, but I didn't mean…" I hold the broadsword far away from me.

"Just one time," he says. "Try. I won't ask you again, and you can cross it off your list."

"Fine." I lift Chaos, despite my wincing muscles. Bronie is pretty much depleted, but his head remains. I swing the broadsword, and I don't even feel the resistance of steel cutting straw. Bronie's head and the top half of his torso lie in a neat heap in the dirt. I say, "Shit," and gape at the blade. "Bronie was dead before I even realized I'd swung."

Jadon says, "Mmhmm."

"Nope. *Too much.* I'm scared that I'd enjoy the experience too much. I'd lose my mind."

"I certainly don't want *that*," Jadon says. "We tried. So. Last weapon." He hops back up with ease.

I squint at the table, the mace, dagger, longsword, broadsword… I've tried them all. "I don't see any others."

"These weapons weren't made in a forge, and I've seen you use them in a few ways already, but not this way." Jadon lifts his fists. "We're back to these. Hand-to-hand combat and *not* using your wind-whipper powers. Just good old-fashioned fighting."

"Right. I haven't punched anyone." I lift my fists. "I promise not to hurt you *too* much."

"Don't *ever* hold back on me," he says. "I'll tell you if it's too much. Deal?"

We start with striking and punching.

"Do you remember your favorite technique?" he asks.

I pause and flip through the pages of my mind. Most are blank, but then: "Joint locks!"

"Really?"

"Don't you love moving things in the opposite direction they're supposed to go?"

Jadon lifts his fists again. "Show me, then." He swings at me.

I grab his hand and push back his middle fingers, which sends his knuckles back. His elbow twists, and I move his middle fingers forward again.

Jadon drops to a knee with a grimace. "Shit. That hurt. Good job." He stands and shakes out that hand.

That move makes my palms feel scalded and then numb. I rub them against my forearm.

"You good?" he asks, peering at me.

I nod.

"Let's do it again." He reaches to grab my wrist again.

Instead, I grab his wrist and start to press his hand back so that his palm faces his chest.

But Jadon wrests out of my lock, slips behind me without touching me, and holds his left arm around my neck and his bandaged right hand behind my head. His energy pushes the air.

My muscles ache and burn as they absorb this force. But this time, the ache feels *good.*

"This is my personal favorite," he says.

"Choke hold," I say. "Didn't think you were the type—"

"I need to say something," he interrupts, whispering in my ear, his breath hot on my skin. "So listen closely. Be careful around Veril. If I were you, I'd leave him behind when you start on your journey to Peria. I would politely decline his company."

I pretend to focus on the hold and not his words. "And why is that?"

"Because I don't trust him. His tea made you pass out. He may have tried to poison you."

I spin away and dart behind Jadon. "Is there proof?" I move my left arm toward his neck and hold my right hand near his head, catching him in my own choke hold. Sharp pain shoots through that hand, and it cramps, paralyzing my fingers. All this sword and hand-to-hand work... Too much, too soon.

"I'm still working on proof," Jadon says, turning to face me, his eyes bright and anxious. "But I know in my heart that he's dangerous." He poses in a boxer's stance, his fists covering his face, still cloaking our conversation through this training session.

I block his punch and swat that gauze-covered hand. "Enough." Nauseated, I drop my hands and squeeze the bridge of my nose, exhausted by both Veril's and Jadon's mistrust of each other. I'm overwhelmed with being caught in the middle even as I continue to figure out the basic facts about my identity and where I belong. Dealing with all of this feels like I'm kicking up to the surface of the sea only to be pulled back by a mystery that I can't glimpse.

"You're an impressive warrior, Kai," Jadon says now. "If you decide that he'll join you, then you'll need to be even better at combat because he'll—"

Before he can finish his thought, a shriek cuts through the air.

"That sounded like Olivia or Philia," I say, eyes wide.

"Yeah." Jadon grabs Chaos and heads toward the scream right as both young women sprint from the other side of the cottage.

Wide-eyed, Veril hustles from the cottage to join us. "Who screamed?"

"Something's up there!" Olivia shouts. "Above the forest. We heard a-a-a…." She covers her face with her hands.

"A what?" Jadon blinks at her, blinks at me, then sheathes the broadsword with a sigh. "It's the *forest*, Olivia. It was probably a bear in a tree. They're known to—"

A sound, rumbling thunder mixed with eerie high-pitched screeches, reverberates from the sky with such force, it drops us to our knees.

31

As deep as the sea and as high as the tallest mountain, the weird warble vibrates from the forest and through our bones, invading our skulls, making us gasp and cover our ears. The air swells with the reek of rotting fruit and sour milk…and death.

"What *is* it?" I shout.

"No idea." Jadon scrambles to his feet and reaches for the broadsword he'd just put away.

I expect dangerous creatures like the burnu to live in the forest. But this cry sounds more terrifying than anything I can imagine, including the burnu.

Wide-eyed, Veril shakes his head. "I've never heard that sound in these woods."

Lesser shrieks—compared to that heart-stopping bellow—drown out Veril's words.

"Get inside!" Jadon cries.

I grab my sword and dagger from the workbench and run behind my companions into the cottage, pulse racing, leg burning.

Another high-pitched cry screws through my skull, the creature closer than before.

Bam! Bam! The cottage shudders as the beast flings itself against the walls.

Bam! This time, the creature strikes the window in the bedroom.

Almost simultaneously, something dark and the size of a large pumpkin strikes the window in the sitting room. A crack spiders out from the center of the window.

"There are two?" I shout.

Olivia, courage outweighing sense, darts to the window and gasps, "Sweet Supreme."

Bam!

Jadon and I creep over to stand beside her. Together, we peer through the window. There, a dog-sized, black…*thing* smacks against the glass. That stink moves past the barrier of glass and fills our nostrils. Olivia winces, "Ugh," and wheels away from the window and races back to Philia, who holds the crook of her elbow against her nose.

Bam! Another dog-sized black thing, this one with an orange marking, smacks the glass.

Through the shattered windowpane, Jadon and I see the creature's vast, leathery wings and glowing, hungry eyes.

It's the same beast that was perched on the hollow outside the bedroom!

"Battabies," Jadon whispers, awed.

Battabies… Battabies… I whip the pages of my memory, matching what I just glimpsed outside with what I know from my past. Wings like a bird. Leather wings, not feathers.

I look over my shoulder to Veril. "This *bowl of bother* is the creature I told you about."

The old man tries to speak but can only shake his head.

"Do battabies gouge eyes to reach brains?" I whisper to Jadon.

"Yep."

"Talons that never dull?" The creature in my mind matches the creature on the other side of this window.

He nods and adds, "And teeth that sharpen with each kill."

Battabies never give up, relenting only once they've fed.

Bam! The window in front of us cracks again. *Bam!* The wood in the bedroom creaks.

"They're trying to knock down the cottage," Olivia shouts, her voice quavering. She and Philia clutch each other's hands. "Did Elyn send these things?"

"I don't think that matters right now," Jadon says, bending over to tighten the clasps of his boots. "We've got to send them back to the cave they haunt."

"And where is that?" I ask.

"Unfortunately," Jadon says, "that would be Azzam Cavern."

Philia gasps.

I don't know Azzam Cavern, but Philia does, and her reaction frightens me. "Veril!" I spin around to find him standing frozen near the hearth. "Veril," I bark again.

At my voice, the Renrian snaps out of his trance.

"Is there something you can do?" I ask. "Something that will scare them away? Some kind of enchantment that could hide us, make us disappear?"

Veril's mouth pops open, then closes, then opens again to say, "No. Yes. There's, I don't know, I've never had to, yes." He takes a deep breath and slowly releases it. "Yes, I can figure something out, but I must be outside to—"

Bam! More creaking wood.

"Kai," Jadon says, "we need to distract them while Veril figures out a spell."

I turn to Veril. "How long do you need?"

The old man's eyes lighten to their lavender glow. "All the time you can give me. Enchantments aren't as simple as blinking my eyes." His gaze settles on mine. "This may not work, dearest. I've never enchanted under such pressure and from battabies especially."

Jadon steps beside me, Chaos in hand. "We'll go outside and start backing down the walkway. Then, like we did with the cursuflies, the soldiers, and the burnu, we'll separate. I'll go right toward the creek. You'll go left toward—"

Bam! Bam! Bam! The pots and glass vials rattle. A braid of garlic bulbs and one of the dry-aging ducks fall from their nails.

"I don't have my amulet, but I'll still try to blast them first with—" I hold up my left hand.

Silence drops over the cottage. None of us are foolish enough to believe the battabies have grown bored with us and are now flitting back to their roost.

"Let's take this time to prepare," Jadon says in a near-whisper.

Moving slowly in case my movements make noise, I pluck Fury from the floor. My shoulders and scalp tingle, and my hands burn hot. *My hands are hot!* I gape at them, so surprised that a sob nearly breaks from my chest. Even without my amulet, I have my power.

Olivia and Philia gape at me. "Your eyes," the redhead whispers.

Jadon does a double take, but not at my eyes. "You can't go out there like that. You need armor. You're just starting to heal."

I look down at my tunic, already feeling strain and pain in my muscles.

"Jay, you're not wearing armor, either," Olivia adds.

He shakes his head. "I don't care about that. I care about *her.*"

My grip tightens on Fury. "But—"

"If you get hurt again," he says, "you'll never reach Mount Devour."

Shit. He's right.

We need to figure something out. Like *now.*

32

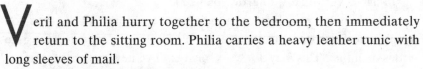

Veril and Philia hurry together to the bedroom, then immediately return to the sitting room. Philia carries a heavy leather tunic with long sleeves of mail.

"It's a little big," the Renrian says, taking Fury from my hold, "but it's more protection than what you're wearing now."

"Where'd you get that?" Olivia says, her eyes darting between the tunic and the window.

"That big trunk sitting at the end of the bed," Philia says. "It's Veril's."

"Olivia," I snap, my heart pounding, "bring me my clothes."

"I can't." Her brows crumple, and she whispers, "They're outside, at our camp."

My stomach drops. "Damn it, Olivia."

Philia helps me shove my arms into the sleeves.

"Hurry, Phily," Jadon urges, inching toward the door.

As she works, I notice symbols on the rings of chainmail.

"For divine protection," Veril says, whispering as he touches my shoulders, my heart, and my head while Philia finishes the final clasps at the back.

I close my eyes, catching only a few words of his incantation. *Mantle… light…shadowed abyss…beseech…unravel…triumph.*

"They always roost in caves," Jadon reminds me once Veril steps away. "Azzam Cavern in particular. It's deep and dangerous and very safe for the battabies."

"Why are they here?" Olivia cries, facing Veril.

The old man shakes his head. "Like I said, they've never come to my forest."

"And how do you know all this?" Olivia asks, spinning to face her brother.

He flails his free arm in irritation. "Because I'm smart. Fuck. Can we stop asking questions and hurry the fuck up?"

"Calm down, Jadon," I say, scolding him with my eyes. "She's going as fast as she can."

"What do they want?" Olivia asks.

"Food," I say. "Tighter, Philia."

Philia pulls the buckles of my borrowed armor tighter.

Olivia grips the windowsill. "What will make them go away?"

"Death," I answer.

"If we don't kill them," Jadon says, "they'll keep attacking until they kill us."

"Tighter, Phily," I demand.

Philia says, "But—"

"Do it," I say, looking at her over my shoulder. "Please. Don't worry about my ribs."

Philia pulls the straps taut. "So you're gonna follow them?"

Both Jadon and I nod and say, "Yes."

"What if they lead you to Elyn?" Olivia whispers, her voice trembling.

Neither Jadon nor I answer that question. My throat is too tight to talk.

Bam! More wood splinters.

"They're back." Olivia's eyes widen with terror.

My fingers burn, each thud against the cottage sending waves of heat through them. I squeeze Veril's shoulder. "You do your enchantment thing but remember that we'll need to be able to find you." I push out one last shaky breath and rotate my shoulders. "Feels like I'm wearing every chain ever forged. But I'm ready." I hold out my hand. "Fury, please."

Veril passes me the longsword.

I tighten my grip around her handle and check that Little Lava is nestled in my ankle sheath.

Jadon reaches for the doorknob.

Bam! Bam!

Shit. That creaking sends shivers down my spine. Sounds like they've almost made it through the walls. We have to act now.

I focus on breathing and remind myself just how strong I am, that I survived the burnu attack even if it beat me up first. *I'm here. I'm here.*

"Breathe, Kai," Jadon whispers.

"Yeah, yeah." My hands burn hot. Fury's pommel crackles in my grip. *Breathe-breathe-breathe…*

"Let's go," I say, steeling myself for what lies ahead.

Jadon throws open the door, and immediately I stutter-step, caught off guard by the stench of shit, burning leather, and bile. *Now* I remember fighting these things.

The sky is dark, the daystar hidden behind a swarm of battabies circling high above the forest canopy. Only a few creatures rip through the trees to terrorize Veril's cottage. My mind races and my fear grows as I realize that killing the battabies down here makes no difference—there would be scores of them left to finish the job.

"Let's move away from the cottage," I shout, just as a battaby spies Jadon and dives toward him.

Jadon swings Chaos and the battaby is split in two, dead before it finishes its first shriek.

Another creature watches us but doesn't strike. As we move away from the cottage, another battaby joins, then another, circling, studying.

"Ready?" I whisper.

Jadon says, "Yep."

Veril's incantation unfurls across my mind, and the power of his words courses through me. *Abyss…beseech…triumph…*

The battaby dives. Right as the creature's talons near my head, I pivot and swing. Fury slices across the battaby's neck with no resistance.

The second beast takes a dive, and I pivot in the opposite direction. I swing Fury again, and the battaby crashes to the now-mucky dirt.

I dare to smile, but the threat is far from over.

The other battabies hang high, shrieking as though they're communicating with one another. Jadon and I wince in pain from the sound. One battaby stays low, fluttering away and then fluttering close—but never close enough to be struck by our swords.

Should I use my wind now?

Or should I wait for them to come closer?

If I use my wind now and it doesn't touch them, then they may learn that I'm limited, which means that they can strategize.

The cauldron of battabies lifts higher than before, dipping in and out of thin clouds, until the group clears the sky. One battaby remains behind, bobbing above us.

"We can't kill him," Jadon says, "not if we're trying to find the roost."

"You're right," I agree. "Look at its mouth."

A bright orange wattle, like a rooster's.

"At least it will be easier to see him," I say.

The creature blasts its high-pitched chirp.

Both Jadon and I squeeze our eyes shut as the cry rattles our eardrums. Rooster flutters higher...higher...and flaps into the forest.

"Ready?" Jadon asks.

Do I have a choice?

We trail the battaby with the bright-orange wattle, and our boots slip and squelch through battaby dung fouling the forest floor. Soon silence overtakes the woods, broken only by the flapping of the creature's leather wings and our boots upon wet ground.

"We're heading north," Jadon says, head swiveling up and around.

"Yeah, yeah," I say, focused. "What are we doing once we're at Azzam Cavern?"

"I've heard that the only thing that will destroy a battaby nest is setting it on fire."

"So, we set a fire. And *then*?"

"Use more fire. It's a big place."

The shadowy forest bends into impossible shapes, like letters of a forgotten tongue. All these trees, all these frenzied vines and twisted trunks and darkness and darker darkness. Just existing here requires that I trust my feet.

Straining my ears, I can still hear Rooster's wings beating above us. "Really," I say, "how do you know these creatures? Sunabi, cursufly, burnu, and now battaby?"

"There was a mage I knew," he says, "and she had all these sketches of otherworldly tacked to the walls of her hut. She told me that she'd fought them all, once upon a time. That these creatures appearing together meant that the realm would soon come to an end."

I look back at him over my shoulder. "Yikes."

"No one believed her. People called her crazy." He grins, keeping his eyes on the slippery forest floor. "I didn't think she was crazy. Her prophecy scared me to death. So I memorized those pictures of the otherworldly— there were so many. She got kicked out with the rest of the mages. I never forgot her, though, or what she taught me, and so I trained extra hard because I didn't want to die, because I was scared that the realm would end before I got to kiss a girl."

My smile spreads. "And here you are, years later—"

"Chasing Number Ten on old Myrtle's chart."

"At least you've kissed a girl," I tease. "That means the realm can now come to an end."

Jadon snorts. "But I haven't kissed *the* girl yet. Once I do, fuck it. Let it all burn down."

I peek over my shoulder with a playful smile. "Let's hurry up, then, so that you can kiss her." I pause, then add, "*Then* we'll burn it down. Deal?"

"Deal." This time, his gaze lingers on me. It's the look he's given me before that makes me heated and woozy. Now that we're out of Veril's cottage with its wards, I can hear Jadon's thoughts again. *"A kiss there,"* he thinks. *"A kiss there and especially right there."* He winks at me before he looks up to chase an end-of-the-realm flying beast.

This is my first time in a forest since that burnu fight. Chasing a battaby is not how I pictured my triumphant return to the woods. Though we aren't in that part of this forest, I now dread any dark-green space that resembles the dark-green space where beasts left me shredded and bloodied.

Rooster shrieks and drops more crap.

We wince from the high-pitched cry and grimace because we're being showered with flying shit. The trail has widened, and Jadon runs beside me.

"Can we get to the damned cave already?"

"You can say, 'Hey, let's take a bath together.'"

"She'd like that."

"But no privacy."

I can't help but smile as I listen to him prepare for our next encounter.

Jadon takes his eyes off the battaby for a second. "Why are you smiling?"

My cheeks burn. "Just thinking about posies and ponies, puppies and peaches. Also, battabies with orange wattles."

At the mention of battabies, his thoughts turn darker.

"I hope they're okay at the cottage."

We have to keep going—if we don't deal with the battabies now, they'll return to the cottage before Jadon and I do, knocking it down, succeeding this time, then attacking Philia, Olivia, and Veril, first by spitting acid at their faces, then by gouging their eyes.

Jadon and I have no choice but to move forward.

We're surrounded by amber outlines of nighttime creatures that aren't the battaby we're chasing, their glows as bright as glass baking in a kiln. Rooster's shrieks are louder than before. Other battabies farther away respond with their own cries. Soon we run up against a stream.

"We're close to Azzam Cavern," Jadon says. "It's in the middle of this forest."

There's a gap in the earth that's not big enough to walk through, but not so small to require dragging our bellies on the ground. Tangled roots make natural stairs, and I use them to scoot down into that gap and settle onto my hands and knees. Soon the roots of the trees above us space out, and I glimpse a well-lit forest just ahead. More crawling, more scooting and dragging, and just like that...

I'm free! I rest my hands on my knees and recover from all that exertion and from my burnu wounds barking at me again.

Jadon scoots out from the roots and easily rolls to his feet, like all that scooting didn't set him back.

"You actually look refreshed," I say, squinting at him.

"Oh, that?" he asks, pointing back at the tunnel. "That was child's play. Didn't even break a sweat."

I grin at him. "I hate you."

He wiggles his eyebrows. "Oh, Kai, do I make you miserable?"

"Absolutely. Guess we're even."

"The cave's not much farther. Look." Jadon points ahead to the swirling cloud of battabies disappearing into shrouded darkness.

We march forward, our boots crushing leaves and seedpods, marking our trail with the scent of licorice and sweet greens. Small motes of light, as soft as a song, drift through the canopy. Is this light from the daystar or the nightstar? I can't tell, since I can no longer see the sky. But it's beautiful, otherworldly. The quiet is punctured by shrieks and cries.

"Watch out," Jadon says. "Don't let your guard down just because we're close. Look out for wolves that transform into burnu, birch trees that transform into sunabi, bears and snakes..."

And there it is—the small clearing right outside a cave. And there is Rooster, his orange wattle bright against his dark, leathery body, fluttering above the cave's mouth, daring us to enter. We take a moment to stop and catch our breath.

"Welcome to Azzam Cavern," Jadon says, crouching. "The worst place in the realm."

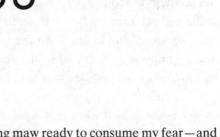

33

The cave looms before me, a gaping maw ready to consume my fear—and possibly more than that. The stench of shit, leather, and bile assaults my senses again. The air already feels heavy, and we're nearly one hundred paces away. Sharp, wet stones and dead leaves litter the cave's opening. Bones—some snapped, some whole—pile between agate stones.

Jadon finds torches at the entrance among the bones and stones and ignites them with his fire-starter. "We'll use these to light the fires," he says. "Protect your eyes, no matter what."

Damp, cold air whistles and blows from the mouth of the cavern. The smell intensifies with the additions of decay and must, slime and rot. It smells like every breathing, living thing crawled into this cave and died... *twice.*

"I don't know if I've heard of this place," I say. "Where'd you learn about it? Old Myrtle's wall?"

"During Assent. Father Knete warned those who disobeyed that they'd be cast into the darkness of Azzam Cavern by Supreme himself. There, you'll wander in darkness for a thousand ages until the Vile One ascends from the pits of the cavern and pulls you down and tortures you for a thousand more ages and then, finally, blessedly, burns you up."

Horrified, I gape at him.

"It worked." He leads the way, torch up, sword out.

Down, down, down we go. There's an explosion followed by a chain of smaller booms. The ground shakes. We stand there, frozen, eyes trained on the torch, waiting for the vibrations to stop. Once that booming and banging ends, all that's left to hear is...chittering.

"Kai," Jadon says, that one word full of dread. He's looking down at his feet.

I don't want to, but I also look down, and my heart immediately shrivels in my chest.

Saloroaches—shortened wings, which means they can't fly, brown bodies as long as mouse tails, and translucent, which means that I can see thousands of roaches beneath the thousands of roaches already swarming over my feet.

And then comes the noise of shrieking, flapping, and chittering. Immediately, battabies swarm from every direction. Their bodies glow blue, and the group swells.

Jadon shouts, "Go!"

"Which direction?" I shout back.

"Follow me!"

I trip on something slimy and catch myself with my hands before my face meets the filth coating the floor. I recover quickly, wiping the grime on my pants. Jadon's fire is far ahead of me now, and I follow until that fire flickers and blinks out. My torch still blazes with flame, but Jadon's... I don't see him, nor can I see his glow—not amber, not blue, not plum.

"Jadon!" I call out, my heart pounding against my ribs, the panic in my voice echoing through the darkness, answered only by battaby shrieks. I walk faster, my footsteps frantic and heavy, stopping only to swing my torch or my sword at battabies, imagined or real, I can't tell. *Where is he?* My panic rises like a tide. My breaths come in shallow pants, each inhale a struggle. I can't find him in the darkness, and I'm now surrounded by pulsating battaby wings.

My mind races with horrifying possibilities, each more terrifying than the last. Did these creatures take him to the depths of the cave? Should I turn back around and...*what?* Get help? I *am* the help. The mere thought of losing him... *No. Stop. Don't.* I refuse to even think like that. Because losing him would mean losing my heart. Who can survive without a heart?

"Jadon!" I swing my sword and my fire like I'm swinging at despair, feeling contact only a fraction of the times I swing. I try to peer past the cloud of darkness and the glowing leathery bodies, but I can't see any other torch. Salty water tumbles down my face. Are those tears? Is that sweat? Yes, to both.

Two battabies strike my head.

"Stop!" I swing my torch in their direction.

Two battabies shriek, one low, one high, and then...

Complete silence.

Still air.

I want to call out Jadon's name again, but I don't want to disturb this unnatural quiet. Maybe I can search for him now, if I move slowly, deliberately, so slow and deliberate that they won't even be able to sense my presence. Maybe they're haunting another part of the cave now.

I hold my torch out before me.

No blue glow.

No creatures flutter before me.

I spin around.

No blue glow.

No creatures flutter behind me.

I lift the torch above my head and look up.

The blue glow of battabies hums across the ceiling, no piece of granite left uncovered. They're all healthy, these roosting, dog-sized monsters. Not in attack mode, they're just hanging upside down on the crags of the cavern. Their leathery wings shine with the light from my fire.

This is the nastiest, stinkiest, most fucked-up place I've ever been—and I don't need memory to know this is true. A visit to Azzam Cavern would be like walking. Unforgettable.

I need to find Jadon, and we need to figure out the best place to start the burn. We have to kill this colony. But I don't want to start the burn without knowing where he is—I could trap him. I slink away from the densest grouping of battabies to a space with a higher ceiling and hopefully better echo.

"Jadon!" I call, hesitant to shout louder and disturb the flock. I step carefully, slowly, feeling the ground with the toe of my boot before stepping sure, dreading that with my next step, my foot could find his body.

"Jadon?" I call out again. "Please answer me. Whistle. Clap. Do something."

Some of the creatures hanging above begin to writhe. Two and then three awaken fully. Frozen, I hold my breath. Then, as if one organism, the group swoops down to attack. I swing my torch and sword madly, but they pull back and dip down. Neither my sword nor torch strike one of these creatures. Still swinging, I trip over a large stone—*fuck, that's not a stone, that's a skeleton*—and drop my torch. The firelight shines on those now kicked-apart bones and glints off the black talons of countless battabies. Those feet are made for clawing—my eyes, my brains, any piece of me that stands between these creatures and my blood.

I recover the torch and frantically scan the floor of the cavern that wavers and writhes in the flickering torchlight, relieved to find no pieces of Jadon scattered among the bones. Where could he be? Maybe he made it out of the cavern and is safe and sound, waiting for me to join him. I swallow. He wouldn't leave me here alone. I'm certain of it. Maybe he's lost in the cave. Maybe he's trapped somewhere in the dark. Maybe the battabies… *No.*

My chest feels as though an Otaan is standing on it. We knew the danger. We needed more than swords and fire—neither work against these beasts. We should've brought…*what*? My weapons haven't been successful so far.

I shift the torch to my other hand and blink hard, a vise tightening my heart. What if I never see him again? What if I never see the light ever again?

More battabies drop from the ceiling to join the blue cloud swirling above me. None have lunged at my head…*yet.* They're dropping slowly as a collective, no doubt preparing to overwhelm me with their sea of bodies.

My poor pounding heart. How much abuse will it take before giving out? My eyes sting from sweat. My shoulder muscles ache from swinging steel and flame. My hands *burn.* My fingertips glow, matching the colors of the useless torch I'm clutching.

I stare at my hands in wonder. I have another weapon—something these creatures have never seen before. I drop the torch and thrust my hands at the circling swarm. I'll be able to hurl wind as I work my way through the cavern, pushing past the relentless onslaught of battabies and saloroaches, searching for Jadon and protecting the both of us as we finish our task together. The wind from my hands is the perfect weapon for this battle: anger and fear surge through in equal parts as determination and frustration.

The wind blasts from my core, and blue crackling air punches the battabies like the fists of thirty men. The intensity of their shrieks almost drops me to my knees. Their glow, though, blinks from blue to amber to black. The immediate space around me is now clear…until it's not. Another cloud of creatures swarms, and I cry out with raw emotion as I send more wind from my hands. Blue glow. Gold glow. No glow. In the breath before the next wave of creatures, I reach to grab my torch still burning on the ground.

But as I reach, I spot that glowing blue sea of saloroaches rolling toward me. Though they're not as big as battabies, these creatures win by overwhelming their prey in numbers, bringing that doomed target to the ground through sheer weight, then munching and chewing and invading every opening that poor animal has, eating away at it until there's nothing left except bones like the bright ones scattered at the entrance of the cave, bones like the ones I stumbled over moments ago. A horrible thought pops my heart. What if Jadon was overtaken by these creatures? He doesn't have wind or the ability to see in the dark. He wouldn't see the blue glow of countless roaches. What if I'll never find him because there is nothing left to find?

The vise around my heart squeezes even tighter. I must find him.

The swarm never breaks even as I kick out my feet, stomp and shriek, until I thrust my wind here and there and over there.

Maybe it's not the battabies we should've feared.

One courageous saloroach has reached my knee.

I slap it off, dropping my torch in the process.

Me being here in this cave… Is this punishment for what Elyn claims I've done? Will she keep sending otherworldly beasts after me until I surrender? She'd know that we'd have no choice but to come to this cave to kill the colony or risk being attacked again. Veril had never seen these creatures in his woods, which means these creatures didn't care enough before to haunt the forests around his cottage. How did they know to come there?

More saloroaches skitter past my boots, and I swipe and shudder, kick and swipe.

I can't let them reach my knees. I've lost if they reach my knees. And I don't lose.

But they're so many, too many, and they all glow blue, nowhere close to death, and they're moving higher, and my breathing is…is…

My scream grows from deep inside, near my heart, and I push my hands out, sending the battabies slamming against the ceiling and the saloroaches backward, most taking flight for the first time in their lives, while the others explode from my wind. But my wind also sweeps away my torch, and now it flickers a few paces away from me, atop a hill of battaby dung as tall as Veril's cottage. And that dung hill is alive with more black-bodied, blue-glowing saloroaches.

The battabies don't appreciate my wind, and they temporarily abandon this sliver of the cave. The chittering from the saloroaches, though, has started up again. They've forgotten the power and intensity and threat of my hands.

The torch sputters, and I'm gradually being swallowed by darkness—

that is, until I look down and see the undulating sea of glowing blue light spreading across the ground as far as I can see. There's no flicker of amber among this new wave of saloroaches. And that blue glow sweeps over the toes of my boots again and fights to reach my knees. I swipe and kick and grip Fury tighter, holding my breath as the flame from my torch dims.

The cave falls into silence. Even the chittering has ceased. The fire from my torch continues to wane. A breeze teases my forehead. My heart's rhythm is all over the place, beating on ones and threes when it bothers to beat at all. Slowly, I peek over my shoulder, seeing nothing lurking in the looming darkness.

But that's not accurate.

I slowly sheathe my sword and reach for my dagger.

That teasing breeze becomes a burst of wind, and over on the dung hill, the flame of my torch flickers, then goes out.

I'm dunked into complete darkness.

Not one glowing light, not blue, not amber. Did every living thing, except me, just die?

My vision tries to adjust, but there is nothing my eyes can grab onto.

There is nothing here.

And *that's* the problem.

34

I feel the *nothing* drawing near. *Shit.* I fling out my hands. An explosion of blue wind ricochets around the cave walls.

Battaby wings flap—but I don't know if that's because the creatures are thrashing or my wind has disrupted their lifeless bodies. Somewhere ahead of me, dung splatters to the ground in wet bursts. Battaby crap is the least of my worries because now, I see...

Eyes redder than blood. Shiny eyes the size of saucers. Eyes way...up... there. A blue glow that can't possibly be moves outward from its body. This creature's wingspan is as wide as six worktables placed side by side, and the beast stands half of that.

And now, I *feel* it. Invisible waves pushing and filling my head, wave after wave, no break. I grip Little Lava tighter.

This creature is too big to live in this cave and too big to be a battaby.

My dagger is pointless. I can't kill this thing with a knife. Maybe I should just run—

Before I can move, though, this *thing* emits a sound as light as a robin's tweet but strong enough to drop me to my knees. I fight to hold my head up and to keep the rest of my body from slamming into the dung-thick earth. My teeth click, my tongue twists, and I taste blood. I struggle to one knee, then fling out my hands.

The air crackles and sparks bluer than before.

The creature shrieks, but this isn't a war cry. It sounds like pain.

Did I hurt it? I scramble to my feet on pulpy legs. Wobbling, I crane my neck to see the beast's head. But I can't see anything. Not even a glow.

Why not? Where is it? Is it dead?

I spit blood into the dirt, wipe my chin. A voice in my head whispers, "Tongue. Clicks. Remember." I shake my head. No, I don't remember. *Tongue. Clicks. Remember.* I don't want to, but I squeeze my eyes shut and force my mind to sift through the indistinguishable grains of sand that is now my memory.

A cliff! A mountain surrounded by a churning green sea. I'm standing near, no, standing on the very edge of a rock jutting from a solid wall of stone. My hand is stretched before me, reaching for...

Don't know. *Wait.* I do know. I open my eyes and swallow, but my mouth is dry. I turn my head to the right, place my tongue against the roof of my mouth and... *Click-click... Click-click... Click-click...*

Echoes.

The creature is not to my right.

Who taught me this? Why was I standing on a cliff? Who was I reaching out to?

I turn my head to the left. *Click-click... Click—*

Wind whips across my face. The cave's stench envelops me, and I wobble again. Don't know if this blast was made by the beast's wings or from some other source deep in these rocks. I take a moment to steady myself, then turn my head again to the left and click my tongue twice. *Click... Click...*

No echoes. My clicks stop as though they hit a wall.

I swing my dagger to the left, sweet and low. Feeling the oncoming sweep of wind, I duck before the beast's wings touch me. I shout, "No," and I thrust out the knife—and hit something hard. I throw out my free hand again and again and again, throwing bursts of wind one after the other after the other.

The creature shrieks loud and long, louder each time a tempest from my hand hits it.

The cave shudders.

The beast's shrieking stops, but my ears continue to ring from its high-pitched cry. Those bloodred eyes hang above me, unblinking. Leathery wings, a tapered snout, two scaly horns, and razor-sharp fangs. Green blood trickles from its massive leg and pools in the dirt.

What in the *realms*?

I can see it even in this dark. *Why can I see it?*

The beast cries again, and that cry resounds through the cavern, a mournful sound that shakes the earth beneath my boots. The creature takes one step toward me and falls forward, crashing like a felled tree to the ground. *Bam!* The ground shakes again, moments away from opening and swallowing up all of Vallendor.

What did I do? Was it the wind? Did I kill it?

I can feel the creature's life force ebbing in the dark like icy water running through my veins. The creature's colossal presence diminishes with every labored breath it draws. It's not moving. I stow my dagger and draw Fury from the scabbard. The sword feels heavy in my grip but still ready and capable of ending the reign of this terrible abomination. I creep toward the creature, the sound of its wheezing growing louder the closer I come.

The beast remains still.

A sudden radiance pierces the darkness, and jagged crystals overhead glow purple and white and blue. I spin in a circle, Fury held high. The cavern is now brighter than all the light outside, and in this brightness, the creature remains sprawled before me, a leviathan brought low, its hide torn, its green blood pooling in the dirt.

I step closer, not daring to breathe, my mind frozen as it tries to figure out what my eyes are insisting exists. My gaze skips around the cavern in hopes of spotting Jadon.

"Jadon!" I call.

No answer.

I turn back to the creature before me, from that snout to its chest, from its chest and up to its snout and then over to those massive wings. Where is the best place to deliver the fatal blow?

"Stop!" A woman's commanding voice cuts through the cave like icy wind.

I startle, rocking back on my heels and nearly falling onto the creature's wing. Spinning around, I blink in astonishment to discover Sybel, ethereal and imposing, marching toward the fallen creature and me. She wears a gown of chainmail, but it can't be mail, not by the way it floats and folds as she moves. And whatever this metal is, it's not gold or silver or copper or iron. Yet all these colors shift from ring to ring, like the sky choosing both day and night, dusk and dawn. Her four faces swirl until they decide to show the angriest face of all, the lion's stony visage of rage and terror that makes the realms step back. "Put away your sword," she demands.

I blink at her, then scowl. "This creature attacked me, and the others attacked the man who came with me."

Nostrils flaring, Sybel lifts her chin. "How are you so certain when you know nothing?"

My cheeks blaze with heat. "Why are you here now? Where were you when burnu nearly mauled me to death? Did you find me then and stop my blood from soaking the ground in that meadow?" I hear my frenzy and hostility, but I can't stop myself. I'm lost, and I've lost my friend and my focus. "Are you here to save me? To save my companion?"

"Put. Away. Your. *Sword*." Her voice is hard, and her eyes shine with golden light. "I know you're frightened, Kai, but do as I say. I won't repeat myself."

I glare at her. "Tell me: Where is the man who came with me?"

"I don't answer to you," she says, brows furrowed.

I take a step toward the beast and raise my sword. "Nor do I answer to *you*. I won't spare a monster whose kin attacked my—"

"Do *not* choose violence," Sybel instructs. "And don't you *ever* justify violence to me." Her eyes soften with sorrow as she looks down at the fallen beast.

"Violence begets violence," I say, gripping Fury tighter. "It's the way of this world. This monster deserves punishment for—"

"For *what*?" that hard face asks. "For *existing*?"

The storm within me still swirls, but I feel a slight dip in its intensity. "So, I'm to do what? Ignore what these creatures did to us?"

"And what did *this* creature do to you?" she asks, motioning to the monstrous beast.

I take a breath and let my mind quiet. I whisper, "He did nothing. *Directly*." I throw my chin up toward the ceiling of battabies, except there are no battabies hanging from the ceiling, not anymore. Just those jagged crystals overhead shining that purple, white, and blue light. No saloroaches creep across the floor. The stench of dung and death has diminished, and the air feels lighter and looser than before.

"He did nothing," I say again, slowly lowering Fury from my overhead hold. I step away from the fallen creature and ask, "Where are we right now?"

"Where are *you* right now?" Sybel responds. Before I can spit out, "Azzam Cavern," she raises her hand to interrupt me.

My mouth pops closed, and my mind flags. The desire to kill this creature is gone. "How did you know to find me here?"

Sybel smirks. "So arrogant and presumptive. You think I came here for *you*?" She touches the creature's chest. "This battawhale cried out in distress—unnatural and unwarranted anguish."

Battawhale? Have I heard that designation before?

"I came to stop its murder," she continues. "He is the only one left in Vallendor."

The only one left. My heart pinches at the thought, and my eyes burn with tears as I shake my head. This creature hurt us, me, Jadon, who is trapped and injured somewhere. "Maybe that's for the best. Maybe—"

Sybel holds her hand up again. Then she looks upon the battawhale with mercy and goodness, her face soft, her smile softer. Softer than she's ever looked at me. She whispers to the dying creature.

I try to swallow, but my dry throat resists. "What about those whom this creature killed? Will you be whispering healing words into *their* ears? Will the dead hear your sweet refrains?"

"As with everything," Sybel says, not even looking at me and choosing to keep her focus on the battawhale, "there is a reason this creature called for help in defending himself."

Yeah, and I think I know that reason. "Why is Elyn sending otherworldly to kill me?"

Sybel gazes at me with squinting, inquisitive eyes. "Is that what she's doing?" Then her eyes drop to my chest. "Whose armor is that?"

"My Renrian host let me wear it," I answer. "*He* doesn't want to see me hurt."

Her eyebrows lift, and she nods at the sword. "And your weapon? Another gift from this compassionate Renrian?"

I scoff and lift Fury. "No. This is a gift from a Mafordian blacksmith. The same man who this one"—I nod down at the battawhale—"and the others…" The accusation dies on my tongue. I have no idea what happened to Jadon. My anger flags and drifts from rage to dread. What did they do to him? Where did they leave him in this dank, dark cave?

Sybel removes her hand from the battawhale's chest and places it on his snout.

The battawhale closes his red eyes.

"Is he… Is he dying?" I ask, stepping forward.

"Not yet, but he requires healing."

"Maybe death is better," I say. "You claim that he's the last one of his kind here in Vallendor. How lonely and miserable must that be? No companionship. Living in the dark. Attacking everything that moves—"

"And here you are," Sybel replies, "lonely and miserable. No companionship. Living in the dark. Attacking everything that moves." Her gaze smashes into mine. "And if the blacksmith and the Renrian are companions, if they cared so much, why did they send you to this cavern? Didn't you say that burnu almost killed you? If that's so, what kind of friends would put your life in danger yet again? Your scars haven't even aged and here you are, fighting for them?"

"That doesn't matter," I say.

"Oh yes, it does," she counters.

Fresh tears scald my eyes. "Why is this creature more deserving of kindness than me?"

Sybel glares at me with her stony face, the cords of her neck tight. "Compassion is all we've shown you. Me, more than anyone. You are still taking breaths because of my compassion. Yet you do nothing but destroy—"

"That *thing* attacked—"

"Kai," the woman says, holding up a hand, her voice as soft as new grass. "You must seek another path. To protect not only those you consider companions but all of Vallendor. That is why you're here. Not to do...*this*."

The battawhale now glows with amber light. His chest isn't moving.

"He means you no harm, Kai," she says, nodding to the creature on the ground. "He fights only to survive, as you do. Men have encroached upon these forests, and he is only defending his kin—he's the last king of his kind, striving to preserve their lives."

"But the Renrian's cottage—"

"Was built scores of years after these creatures were loosed upon Vallendor."

Is Sybel saying that the predecessors of this battawhale originated from another *realm*?

I tilt my head. "What does that mean? Loosed? They weren't born here? You're telling me that I'm not to defend myself or the peoples of Vallendor but instead defend creatures who aren't even from this realm? You just told me to protect not only my friends but all of Vallendor. These two things cannot be true at once."

"Small thinker," she admonishes.

"Tell me, then! How do I protect Vallendor in that way? Tell me!"

"Kai, this isn't you." Sybel's whisper carries the mass of mountains. "Ultimately, violence is not what you stand for."

Her words strike deep, igniting a firestorm within me. "Then what in Supreme's name *do* I stand for?" Weary, I hold out my arms. "If I'm not a fighter, then who am I? How do you even *know* me? Can you tell me that instead of telling me what I stand for and that I must repent? Can you tell me who I am and what I've done?"

My tears finally break and spill down my face as my body sags with frustration. Weak, I sink to my knees, every piece of me—my heart, my eyes, my breath—heavy and impossible. This dirt has more strength than me. The filthy air has more direction than me. The space between my ears feels bulbous, expanding with every breath I take. I lift my hands to press against my eyes but stop. My hands are filthy, shit-stained, and bloody, and I gag just looking at them.

The battawhale takes a deep, wheezy breath.

"Elyn is justified in hunting for you," Sybel says, her attention back to the battawhale.

"Tell me what I did wrong," I plead, then pound my fist in my palm. "Specifically. Tell me! What did I—?"

"You destroyed Chesterby," she says, the lion's face speaking now.

That's the town Jadon and Olivia mentioned when we first met. The one destroyed by earthshake. I gape at her in confusion.

The battawhale wheezes loudly again, and Sybel hurries back to his side. "He's dying."

My mind, though, is no longer in this cave. *Chesterby*.

"Kai!" Sybel says, interrupting my thoughts. "He's dying."

"I'm sorry. I don't know what more I can do or say," I say. "Can't you heal him?"

Sybel blinks at me with eyes that shift color with every inhalation. "No," she says, stepping back.

"No, *what*?" I ask.

"Either you do something to keep him alive," she says, "or you let him die. Step closer to your own doom if you dare. This creature didn't ask to be brought here. Yet here you are, at the very bottom of this cavern, invading his home to kill him. I can't tell you who you are. You must discover that for yourself. But if you want to *feel* again, to understand again, if you want to know the part you play today and tomorrow, what part you played before, you must make amends."

How will I make amends for my failures?

Her previous words fill me with anger. I don't know how to heal the battawhale. I don't know how to make amends for failures I can't remember.

"It's not too late," Sybel whispers. "You're still missing so much of yourself. You're still missing the piece of you that will answer all your questions."

I look up at her through angry tears. "My amulet?"

Sybel nods. "Your amulet."

My hands are filthy, and so I won't touch my skin where my amulet should be. And now I feel its absence. Iciness across my collarbones has replaced the rhythmic warmth on my chest.

"Kai," Sybel says, her gaze still leaden. "You are so much more than a fighter, than a destroyer. But you'll never discover the breadth of your being until you reclaim your amulet. It's here in Vallendor. I feel it—but it is not mine, so where it sits, exactly, I do not know. What I do know is that if you take care of this poor creature, you will take an important step toward recovering your amulet and reclaiming who you are. You will not discover your purpose or true self without it." Before she turns away, she adds, "This time, choose to take the correct path."

"I'll heal him, then. That's the correct path, yes? Where do I find medicines for him?" I ask, my voice broken, desperation threading through each word. I drop my head, push out a breath, and look up again. She's gone.

"Sybel," I cry, whirling around. "Where did you go?"

The battawhale is still here, though, and his breath continues to rattle in his chest. He's dying, and I can't let that happen.

35

Behind me, the battawhale's wheezes sound like an inverted roar, not bursting out of the mouth but pushing down into his gut.

I hurry toward the closest passageway.

The cavern, as bright as a garden in springtime, goes from vast to narrow as I scan the wet walls around me. My heart thunders in my chest, fear and adrenaline pressing me to keep going until I find—

That!

Tufts of elk hair spring from the dirt. *Works as a bandage. That!* Red flower. Sanguine hyssop. Stops bleeding. *Pain relief...pain relief...* I know this. I've done this before! I hurry down the corridor, fingers pointing at this plant and that flower, browsing as though I'm shopping at a market.

A rowdy bunch of green plants with purple blooms grow around a pond the size of a quilt. How do these flowers exist in this dark space? Perhaps, like hearing thoughts, this garden is a gift from Sybel. I don't know. But as memories pop to the front of my mind, I *do* know that the plant at my feet is deadly nightshade. Too much brings death. Just enough brings relief.

I coat my hands with mud from the small pond and then cover them with dry dirt to form a shell around my skin—protection from handling this delicate and dangerous plant. With my dagger, I cut a few sprigs. With one rock as a pestle and a flat rock as a bowl, I grind the plants I've collected into a pulp, using water from the pond. When I have enough of the poultice—I don't even know how much is needed—I take it back to the biggest room. The creature is still there, wheezing in the dark. When I look behind me, the entrance to the garden cavern is gone.

"I'm here," I say, hustling to the battawhale. "I'm so sorry for hurting you." I kneel beside the battawhale's bleeding leg. "Here we go," I whisper. After taking several deep breaths, I scoop some of the poultice off the rock and apply it to the gash on his leg.

The battawhale quivers, his wheezing quickening. But the green blood no longer oozes from that gash, and the creature stills.

I scoot higher to reach the wound on his neck, and I gasp at its violence. "Did I do that?"

The battawhale's tongue pushes between his teeth, producing nothing more than a slurp and a suck—he's trying to click, but the air to do so is escaping through the gash in his neck.

"Hold on." I scoop more of the plant mixture from the makeshift bowl and cake it across the wound.

The beast shivers again, then sighs. A sad sigh of surrender that makes me ache inside.

"Don't give up," I whisper. "Please fight." Somehow, I know what substances heal, but I'm not a healer. Maybe I've made his suffering worse. Teardrops tumble down my cheeks, and I use my shoulder to brush some away and the others fall onto my muddy palms. Another wheeze compels me to touch the otherworldly's forehead. My wet hands leave behind a palm print made of cave mud and toxic plants. "I'm so sorry. I just... I didn't... Please forgive me."

The chest of the last king of his kind rises and dips...and doesn't rise again. And now, he's dead. My heart shatters, and I hold back a sob, hiding my face in the crook of my elbow. The light in the cavern dims as one fewer life fills its space.

I stand, keeping my eyes on the creature that is no more. Then I step away from him, my mind whirling. What have I done, what will Sybel do, what will Elyn do, why did I come here? Will Sybel know that I tried to save him? Will she care, since I was also the one who killed him?

With the beast's death, my future has become as unknown as my past. Will my ending be the same as this creature's? Alone in a dark, dank space, trying to breathe until I can't?

Dejected and discouraged, I turn away from the dead battawhale. I've failed. I was supposed to save him but I couldn't save him. I failed.

The cavern is now clear of saloroaches. The ceiling is still crammed with blue-glowing battabies, but not one moves. Are their fates tied to the battawhale's? Is mine? Is Jadon's?

I wander, my legs burning as if I'm ascending, and the scent of cool, fresh air draws me forward. I slow my step and force myself to remain upright, to not drop to my knees, to keep walking, to leave Azzam Cavern. I've lost the battawhale. I've lost Jadon. And I feel like I've lost something else: my will.

Finally, I glimpse a fragment of light ahead. A way out of this cave.

How will I tell Olivia about Jadon? Will she ever forgive me? But then I realize that Olivia may not be alive, not if the battabies have swarmed the cottage, angrier now that I've killed their king.

A sob rises in my throat as I reach the mouth of Azzam Cavern. I linger there, my vision wavering with tears as I blink at the canopy of trees blocking the sky and those orchids and…

At the edge of the forest, a cauldron of battabies swoops and circles near a cluster of low bushes, the only sound the flutter of their wings. I squint, trying to figure out their odd behavior. One swoops down behind the bush, and then, as it rises, another takes its place. Ice trickles down my spine. They're *feeding*.

I burst from the cave, Fury held high. The battabies screech in warning, then ascend, circling higher, higher, like a black cloud. Before it joins the others, the last battaby drops a boot from its razor-sharp claws.

A man's boot. *Jadon's* boot.

"No!" My scream tears from my throat raw and harsh as I sprint to see what the battabies have left behind. Dropping my sword in the dirt, I gasp and fall to my knees.

Jadon lies there, pale, still…except for the pulse beating in the scoop between his clavicles. I close my eyes and inhale. He's not dead. He's not lost. He's *here*.

I bend and put my ear to his ribs. His pulse beats, and his chest rises and falls. My tears dampen his dirty shirt. I want to touch him, but deadly nightshade still coats my dirty hands. I scan him from head to toe, and other than a bit of blood where it appears he hit his head and some scrapes and scratches, he appears unharmed. His clothes, with the exception of the boot, are intact. I lean closer to his ear and whisper his name over and over until he stirs. I hold my breath as he comes to and release that breath once his eyes open.

"Hey," Jadon whispers.

"Hey," I whisper back, then stretch out on the grass beside him, adrenaline zinging through my veins. He's alive.

"I was…flying," he says, brow furrowed. "But I don't know how."

The battabies.

"Did we do it?" he asks. "Did we burn the cave?"

My lungs are tight, and I can only shake my head.

He rolls over to face me. "We came here for nothing, then?" he asks, his voice raspy.

It doesn't feel like nothing.

"Kai." He's looking past me with big eyes.

I turn my head to see what's caught his attention.

The cave opening is filled with the massive figure of the battawhale. *He's alive!*

My breath catches, and I try to rouse myself, but I no longer have strength or energy to roll onto my knees. I can only lie still and stare at the magnificent creature standing across the clearing. The only action I can make right now is bringing my lips together to make a pop, and then I pop my tongue twice against my teeth. *"Tell me your name."*

The beast clicks, pops, pops. *"Tazara."* He clicks, clicks, pops, pops. *"We have met."*

"We have?" Confused, I try to lift my head, but then I see myself high up on a stone cliff overlooking the green sea revealed in my vision. I'm balancing on a ledge as Tazara flaps his great wings, hovering before me. My arm is outstretched, my hand placed against his forehead.

I gasp, recalling the feel of his soft fur against my fingertips. Fresh tears form in my eyes—*I remember this*—and Tazara becomes blurry until those tears slip across my face. My lips meet again to pop, and my tongue brushes my teeth to click, *"I named you."*

Tazara bows his head, then steps back into the darkness of Azzam.

36

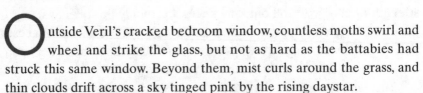

Outside Veril's cracked bedroom window, countless moths swirl and wheel and strike the glass, but not as hard as the battabies had struck this same window. Beyond them, mist curls around the grass, and thin clouds drift across a sky tinged pink by the rising daystar.

Veril and I sit quietly in the bedroom while I wash the mud and poison from my hands in a basin of soapy water on top of the large trunk at the foot of the bed. "Her name is Sybel, the woman I saw in the cave. I don't care if you believe me. I saw what I saw—"

"I believe you, dearest." The Renrian shifts on his stool, sighs, and crosses his legs.

"She told me that the battawhale was the last of his kind. That if I killed him, I could never come back from that. I don't know what that means." I scrape some dirt from under my fingernails with my thumbnail and wash once more. "Does she mean that I'll never be good again? That's what it sounded like. My path would never lead to good."

Veril says nothing. Just stares out the window at those moths. Beyond them, near an ancient willow, Olivia and Philia gawk and gasp while Jadon recounts the battle in the cave.

I close my eyes and—

The dead lie everywhere, heaped against a rock wall and in pits gouged into the earth. Towers of bloated corpses, man and beast, surround me, and the incessant buzz of corpse flies renders me nearly deaf. On the far side of this sea of bodies, a giant of a man stands shrouded in shadows. A sunabi, its smooth gray skin streaked with blood and gore, scrambles over the still-growing mounds of the dead. It clutches my ankles and rubs its head against my calves, like a housecat greeting his mistress. The sunabi bares its sharp teeth and hisses before croaking, "Danar... Rrivae... Devour."

I startle awake.

Jadon is still talking.

Did I fall asleep or...?

"Kai, are you okay?" Philia asks, squinting at me.

I nod and swipe my eyes. "Just a bit tired."

Copperhair nods and says, "We should let you rest, then."

Soon, the girls, the moths, and the vision of the sea of bodies drift away.

My mind floats to Jamart's hidden altar behind his sitting room. "Is Sybel the Lady of the Verdant Realm?"

"Sybel," Veril muses, "is *not* the Lady of the Verdant Realm. Remember: *Kaivara* is the Lady of the Verdant Realm. This woman you met—others have described her to me as well. She wears gowns of light and gowns of chain. She often appears walking from the east, with the rising daystar at her back. Then she's seen walking west as the nightstar takes position in the heavens. She is known as the Lady of Dawn and Dusk. She and the rest of that order tend the forests and the animals…every living thing, including us mortals. She is a Grand Steward and daughter of the immortal order known as Eserime."

Eserime. My mouth moves to repeat the word. "Immortal. So how does that order fit into the pantheon of Supreme?"

Veril rises from the stool and shuffles to the tall wardrobe closest to the bed. "Mortals, we craft our own myths and gods from their enigmatic existences. What humans perceive as divine is but a sliver of their truth. Though they are not the most powerful, Eserime have great abilities that they use to protect their wards. They never use their powers for destruction. If I could use only one word to describe the Eserime, I'd say, 'merciful.'"

He opens the cabinet doors and pulls out a small white towel, a larger gray towel, and a bottle of soap. "Eserime bless their charges with immediate good health if that is the will of Supreme. And that battawhale— he wasn't supposed to die, but then *you* came."

She will bring each of you death.

But the battawhale didn't die—I stare at the window webbed with cracks from the battabies—and neither did Jadon.

Veril hands me the small towel, and I dry my hands. "Now, let's work on getting the rest of you clean."

"Getting clean. I approve of this plan." I follow him from the room, formulating a plan of my own to enlist the very alive Jadon Ealdrehrt to help me with this task.

37

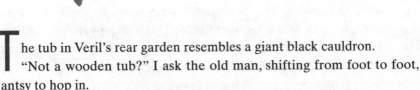

he tub in Veril's rear garden resembles a giant black cauldron.

"Not a wooden tub?" I ask the old man, shifting from foot to foot, antsy to hop in.

"I like hot baths. Wood doesn't hold heat as well as…" He knocks on the iron pot.

Over at a firepit, a water boils in a smaller cauldron, ready to be added to the bath if the water cools. Veril pours the contents of the bottle from the wardrobe into the tub. Then he pours in the pot of boiling water and stirs the bath with a wooden oar and…

I wave my hands in the air. "Bubbles!"

"You deserve *all* the bubbles, Just Kai. And it benefits me to have a goddess using my soap." Veril holds up the smaller cauldron. "Let me fill this before you settle in." He trundles to the creek.

Hot water. Nothing is better than hot water… Well, maybe *something* is better. I scan the area for Jadon, but he's nowhere in sight. With a sigh, I trace my fingers across the bubbles, imagining the heat against my skin, my skin squeaky clean.

Veril returns and replaces the small cauldron over the firepit. He shouts, "Enjoy," and heads back to the cottage.

I'm close to tears as I undress and climb into the tub. My whole body— muscles, bones, sinews—groans with relief as I lower myself into the warm, sudsy water. Giggling, I blow foam into the air. I dip my head back into the water, then slide down until my chin sits above the surface. I close my eyes as all my muscles relax and sigh. After a few blissful moments, I sit up and slide the soapy hand towel across my arms and my face and hair and… I want to marry this tub of hot water.

"Kai?" Jadon calls.

I freeze as adrenaline zings through me. "Back here!"

Jadon rounds the cottage, holding a bundle of stuff. "Look what Veril found—" He smiles wide. "Hey! You made it into the tub!"

I laugh and sit up straighter. "I did. Aren't you happy for me?"

His eyes widen. "Oh. Shit." He turns away. "Sorry for intruding. I just, you know, caught off guard, and okay, shit, I'll give you some privacy."

"I'm covered in bubbles, Jadon. Relax." My pulse quickens as I glance down to see that I am indeed covered in bubbles. My breasts *only* in bubbles as the waterline hits me mid-ribs. I lower back down to my neck. "Relax," I repeat for myself as much as for Jadon.

Slowly, he turns back to me. The muscles along his jaw twitch. "That's a lot of bubbles," he manages to say. "How did he make so many?"

"Magic," I say, blowing foam into the air.

His gaze meanders from the bubbles to my face as if he's hypnotized. "What's in your hands?"

Jadon pulls out of his trance to meet my eyes and immediately falls into another.

Is he staring at me because I resemble a tortured mouse or...?

The sparkle in his eyes and the flush in his face tell me that I look better than a tortured mouse. Much better.

"Jadon?" I say, pointing a soapy finger at his hands. "What are you holding?"

He blinks, then looks at his hands. "*Oh.* Olivia took your clothes on a picnic so that she could repair them. You'll have everything later today."

I smirk. "Well, isn't that thoughtful."

"I brought the clothes you left on the bed," Jadon says. "Veril asked me to bring them out to you. And then he also gave me this." He holds up two cups and a flagon. "Wine."

"Ooh!" I sit up, nearly rising above the water again.

"But I can come back later, after you're done."

"And deny me wine? Do you hate me now?"

"I'm not *that* cruel." He places my clothes on the bench, then fills the cups with plum-colored wine.

"This is now the best day ever," I say, taking a cup. "What should we toast to?"

"Let's see." He brings a stool over and sits beside the tub. "To new friends. New adventures. Clean water. First kisses."

We tap cups and sip. Jolts of flavor, first tart and then sweet, punch my mouth. "Oh. Yeah." A boozy warmth travels through my veins, and I cackle and shout, "Yes!"

A hot bath *and* good wine *and* a gorgeous man just a reach away?

Jadon grins and sips from his cup. "When was the last time you drank wine?"

I flick bubbles at him. "If I knew that, then I'd know how and why I ended up in Maford."

"I know why you're here." He stretches out his legs.

"Tell me, Jadon."

"You're here because of fate. You were supposed to meet me."

My eyebrows raise. "I'm here for *you*?"

"Mmhmm." He smiles at the wine in his cup, but then the muscles in his jaw flex and his smile dims.

"What?" I ask, sipping, relaxing, loose as a goose.

"You're a lifesaver," he says. "At Azzam Cavern—"

"I didn't do anything," I say. "My fighting, my hands, none of it helped you."

"But you were my prize," he counters. "Wanting to see you again... I wanted to survive so I could see you again."

I give him a soft smile and bring a shaky hand to my mouth. "I was so happy to see you. I cried when I thought I'd lost you. And then I cried when I found you alive."

His skin flushes. "I was relieved that you were the first person I saw when I opened my eyes. There's no one in the world like you, Kai."

I tilt my head. "I am unique, aren't I?"

"I didn't say all that—"

"What the hell you think the word 'unique' means, Ealdrehrt?"

I lift my injured leg that no longer makes me fret anytime I move it.

Jadon watches suds slip back down to my thigh, now hidden in the lather. "Your scabs. They're gone."

I tilt my head, finally *looking* and seeing healthy skin, unscarred skin. "How about *that*? And your forehead. No more scar." I point at him. "Maybe you're unique, too."

"I am." He pours more wine into his cup.

I tip my head back, sinking this time to my ears to stare at the—

The markings!

"Hey," I say, sitting up. "Draw what my markings look like." I give him a bar of soap Veril left for me. "Use the pot I'm cooking in."

"But that would require me to..." He waggles his finger at my shoulder.

"You scared of bubbles?" I ask. "Or are you scared of skin?"

"I'm not scared of *nothin'*." He smiles. "Gimme that soap." He takes the bar and stations himself behind me. "Your hair."

"Ah." I washed my hair, and now it's flat and long down my back. I move it aside so that he can see.

"Suds." He blows at my shoulder. "Okay." His breath warms my skin, and every hair on my body straightens.

"I'm not an artist," he says, "so don't laugh." He selects the bubble-free space on the left side of the tub and draws a filled-in circle and then a twisting line that connects to another filled circle, and then another twisting line from *that* circle to a third circle.

I peer at the drawing. "That's it?"

"Yep. But the lines are like vines. There are leaves, not a lot, but they're there." He adds leaves to the vines. "And then there's the one…" He waggles his finger at his chest. "The last vine is trailing from your shoulder to the top of your left rib. Under your front part."

I snort. "My front part?"

"You haven't noticed it before?"

My eyes flick from the soap drawing to his eyes. "I've taken my bandeau off once, when Veril started treating my injuries, and we weren't in front of a mirror. I tried looking the other day but I could glimpse only a square." I rise to my knees.

Jadon says, "What are you…?"

"Draw what you see." I pull my eyes from the drawing to his face.

"Are you sure about that?" The muscle in his jaw flexes.

"I'm sure. Hurry up. I'm getting cold." I swipe at the lather covering my skin, revealing the markings. "You see it? Or do you need me to clear more foam."

He smiles, ruminating on my offer. "Yeah. A little more."

I lock my eyes on his, and I swipe more foam from beneath my left breast. "Better?"

It takes him a moment to drag his gaze from mine to see what I know he wants to see. "Yeah, that's better." His tongue pokes the side of his cheek before he leans in for a closer look.

His breath tickles the sensitive, exposed skin.

"Letters," he says softly. "Or maybe they're symbols." He holds the soap to the iron tub, looks back at my skin, then back at the tub. Then he begins to draw:

63 ⬛ ÷M ᷤ ⬛

Finished, Jadon lets out a breath and sits back on the stool.

I roll onto my stomach to see him better. I sip from my cup, then point to his nose. "You have bubbles."

He swipes his nose. "Didn't realize I was that close."

I say, "Hmm."

He forces himself to look away from me and back to the drawing on the tub. "Do you know what it means?"

"No," I say.

We both stare at the markings in silence.

My skin prickles as I realize: someone got closer to me than Jadon did just now to carefully ink these intricate designs right beneath my breast, but I have no memory of the inking or the inker. Worse, I don't remember what this design nor the ones on my back mean. This marking, though, atop my left rib. There must be some significance to this location. Why not a longer canvas that's more visible, like my arm or thigh?

"Maybe Veril knows," he says, then sips wine.

"It's in a book somewhere in his piles," I say, flicking my hand. "We'll find it. In the meantime... Have you washed up?"

A slow smile spreads across his face. "Of course I've washed up. You're not the only one around here who enjoys soap."

"I ask because you still have some dirt here." I point to the dip between my collarbones.

He swipes at the dip between his collarbones.

"Still there."

He swipes again.

"Still—"

"Will you get it, then?" he says, laughing. He tilts back his head.

I take a soapy finger, dip it into that space, and rub. My skin buzzes as I press. "Done." My eyes dip down to his shirt. "You also missed..." I motion to the middle of his chest.

A smile inches across his face. "Really, Kai? If you want me to take off my shirt, then just say so."

"Look for yourself."

"How can you even see anything beneath my—?" He peeks beneath his tunic, and his smile totters. "Oh."

"See? I have gifts."

"That was a guess."

I shrug. "Maybe."

He tries to contain his grin as he sniffs, "Well, I didn't have soapy hot water waiting for me. Must be nice."

I tilt my head. "Yeah, hot, soapy. There's plenty of room, but of course you'd have to take off all of your clothes. Including that." I point to his bandaged hand. "Which you should be doing anyway, since you told me you had prettier tattoos, remember, and you told me that you'd let me see them. Or maybe I'm misremembering. Am I misremembering, Jadon?"

His mouth rests into a soft smile. He watches me with eyes softer than that smile.

I lift my eyebrows and hug my knees to my chest.

Jadon hasn't taken a breath yet. His jaw isn't even twitching. He's trying to maintain control.

He'll lose.

I already see his defeat in the flush across his face and around his neck. I see his defeat in his loose, unclenched hand. The flare of his nostrils.

He'll give me what I want—and he knows it.

It's just a matter of time.

When he still doesn't move, I lean back against the tub and finish off my wine. I hold out the cup for him to fill.

He does.

"Didn't you say that I was the prize?" I ask before sipping. "Will you claim it, then?"

He takes a beat before he leans toward me. His breath warms my shoulder again.

"I'm so glad you're safe," I say, my voice huskier now, rumbling because he's close, so close. I want him closer. *Move closer, Jadon.*

He brushes my hair aside.

I close my eyes.

He kisses my shoulder.

The world blurs around the edges.

His lips linger there.

I wince and let out a breath.

His kiss surprises my skin. Like it's never been kissed before. Like it needs to warn me that something unfamiliar is coming my way.

He moves back.

Lungs tight, I shift to face him and then decide to kneel again.

His eyebrows furrow—*Will you be okay* in his expression.

I mouth *yes*, not wanting to break this silence.

His eyes roam my soapy nakedness, and he smiles.

I tug the tail of his shirt and lift it over his head. There's a scar over his heart, and another above his right ribcage, and another above his hipbone. I kiss each scar, my lips burning every time I touch his skin. The tattoo on his left pectoral is not as complicated as his hand ink. This tattoo is an irregular rectangle with rounded corners, the upper left side shaded with violet ink, the lower left shaded with gold. I trace its outline—*curious*—and then I kiss it. There's more ink that runs sideways along the left side of his ribcage. The simple script, WITH DEATH COMES LIFE. I run my tongue along those words, leaving a kiss before I lean away.

"You make me weak," he whispers.

"You make me burn," I whisper back.

Immediately, we both reach for the waistband of his pants, and my hand trails lower...lower...until it's resting on his hard—

"We have crabapples!" Philia shouts from the other side of the cottage.

We both startle backward. Soapy water sloshes over both of us.

"Jadon! Kai! Where are you?" Philia calls.

I stifle a scream. "No!"

He whispers, "What the *fuck*, Philia?"

I slip back into the bubbles.

He rubs his wet face and takes a deep breath. He pulls on his shirt, eyes on me. "I kept my promise. You saw my ink."

"And it is marvelous," I say, winking.

"Hey," Philia says, rounding the corner of the cottage.

Olivia appears next to Philia. "What's going on?"

They turn, bug-eyed, and gape at the bubbles and soap. Philia speaks first. "You get to take a bath in the tub?"

"Why do you get special treatment?" Olivia grumbles.

"Because she's unique," Jadon says, grabbing our cups and the empty flagon. Before he backs away from the tub, he whispers, "Next time, we won't stop."

In a barn. In a garden. Maybe this garden. And we'll keep going, not stopping until the end of the world.

38

'm ready to find my pendant.

A new morning has come, and the forest looms before me.

As the light the daystar disappears behind the trees, the thorns of underbrush grow powerful and claw at my ankles. The uneven ground slows my pace. I'm overly cautious, not wanting to injure myself simply because I'm rushing. I run my bare hands over the fallen leaves—combing the earth for the smooth onyx stone in the moth's thorax, the bumpy red and gold jewels that make up her wings. But I'm touching only dirt, leaves, and an occasional centipede.

I don't feel any particular pull toward anything yet. And my hands aren't hypersensitive.

Stop doubting yourself, Kai. You just started.

"Compassion suits you."

The woman's voice causes me to startle and topple forward, landing facedown in the dirt. At first, all I see are the tips of boots covered by mail. I follow the draped chainmail up to find Sybel standing before me, her face as sharp as an eagle's and as soft as a lamb's.

I scurry to my feet. At the sight of her, my chest loosens and my breath flows freely from my lungs. The trees now have space between them, and their vines keep to themselves. We are no longer in the woods near Veril's cottage.

"I'm looking for my amulet." My pulse bangs against my neck. "Am I in the right area? Are there other clues you can share?" I hear my desperation.

Sybel touches the top of my hair. Something in me stretches toward something in her, like one of these vines curling around a log, like one of the vines of my tattoo. The force of her touch makes me shake even more, and I don't have the strength to fight it. Whatever she's doing to me, I pray she just does it quickly. Let it be done. I'm so tired.

Instead, she says, "You're just like her. Your mother. Her name was Lyra."

Sybel's words make me dizzy, and that dizziness rushes from my head to settle in my heart. A dollop of joy chases that bout of vertigo, and I want to respond to Sybel, but joy sweeps away all my words, all my thoughts and questions. I've been so hungry for this information, desperate for it. I lift my head to face her, eager for more.

"Lyra was lovely," Sybel says. "Not just her countenance but also her spirit. She was a romantic at heart. While that—being a romantic—became a shard of glass in her eye, that infinite well of love made her a wonderful steward and guardian of her realm." Sybel's smile grows distant for a moment, and her focus falls as she whispers words that I can't hear—a prayer?

She takes my hands and pulls me to stand. "She loved you so very much."

This time, Sybel's touch is more than just her skin against mine. It feels like a cool draught alleviating fever and pain, a tonic that seeps through my skin, bones, and heart to purge all the bad things. And as all those bad things bubble to my surface, a sob erupts from my gut, and tears spill from my eyes like a stream. And that vine-like tugging between us becomes more insistent—poison being drawn from my spirit.

My weeping eventually softens into hiccups and sniffles, and my breathing normalizes. The sharp burrs behind my eyes, the constant ache in my shoulders, stomach, and neck, and the taste of copper dissipate. The pain of every injury I've endured since my first day in Maford fades like snow melting beneath a sweltering sky.

"What are you doing?" I ask, my voice hoarse.

"My job." Her face shines like diamonds and starshine. "Tending the forests and animals in this realm. Helping heal the land and the creatures who live upon it. You are one of my charges, Kai, and I'm bringing you peace. Lyra had a similar job. She was a daughter of the Eserime."

Is it possible for breath to leave your body and fill you up at the same time? Because that's how I feel. The exhalation of solace and satisfaction and the simultaneous inhalation of wonderment and revelation. My knees weaken, not because I'm weak but because my thankfulness weighs so much.

I am just like my mother.

I am loved.

I belong to someone.

Finally!

Finally.

A daughter of the Eserime.

Immortal.

I'm more than human. I knew it. I felt it.

Wait.

"You speak of my mother in the past," I say, my neck prickling now. "Why?"

Sybel's face dims. "Because she was taken from us long ago. Her realm, Ithlon, was destroyed. She, along with it."

My face fills with blood, and my periphery darkens. "Who did it? Who destroyed Ithlon?"

"What would you do if you knew that answer?"

Kill them.

Sybel waits for me to say that, but I don't, because that isn't the answer she wants. So I stay silent and let my heart burn—that fire will fuel my search for the dead man who killed my mother. But my anger, and even my sorrow, feel unmoored. How do I begin to mourn a woman I can't remember, gone from a realm I'll never know?

At least I have her in me—her Eserime spirit.

I think about Veril's comment while he prepared my bath. *It benefits me to have a goddess using my soap.* Frankly, I thought he was simply flattering me. I didn't believe a word he— *Wait.*

Does Veril know that I'm a goddess? He must. No, he would've told me, and he didn't tell me because, yes, flattery. Do goddesses have headaches or creaking arms or scabs on their legs? Do their toes feel like they've been caught in a vise, and do the smalls of their backs feel like termites have chewed through the band of muscle there? Do goddesses feel like they're infested with termites? Because I feel infested with termites. Phenomenally.

My mood has shifted from jubilant to heavyhearted.

"What are you thinking, Kai?" Sybel whispers.

I swipe a tear slipping down my cheek. "That nothing has changed for me. That I'm lost." I slowly drop to the ground and rub my face with tired hands.

"You are not lost. You simply need to be true to your purpose."

"What is my purpose?"

"You must discover that yourself." Sybel takes a breath and slowly exhales. "Have you heard of the One? The Destroyer?"

I shake my head. "Did the Destroyer kill my mother?"

"That is no simple question," she says. "The Destroyer *became* the destruction of Ithlon."

I furrow my brows. "*Became*. What does that even mean? Are you talking about fate?"

"Purpose," she corrects. "The One would have *always* been, but their purpose changed. Understand?" When I shake my head, she says, "An ax in the hand of a builder cuts down trees. An ax in the hand of a murderer cuts down people. In both instances, the ax remains an ax. Only its purpose has changed. Understand?"

This time, I nod and say, "Yes."

"And because their purpose changed, the One is now a threat to the entire realm. Their power is growing—which would've been a blessing had their purpose remained true. But now, this power has become a danger, and soon, Vallendor Realm will be no more. That is, if the One is not stopped. If that power goes unchecked, the One will move on to the next realm, growing more powerful still, and on to the next realm, and on and on until…"

"Until?"

Sybel lifts her hands and shrugs. "It won't matter to me, after this world is destroyed—I will be gone, since I am its Grand Steward. And so will the other Eserime of Vallendor—"

"Including myself?" I ask. "A daughter of the Eserime?"

Sybel pauses before she shakes her head. "Your task is different. Yes, part of your heritage as Eserime is helping and healing. Listening to the thoughts of others, helping people achieve those things that improve their world, that keep them whole and healthy."

"I haven't helped anyone so far," I say, feeling defeated. "I haven't known enough about myself to bring anyone any good."

"But you have," Sybel assures. "Jamart and his daughter. And then you helped Tazara even after enduring an attack by creatures who were just trying to exist in a place they weren't meant to be. Sometimes, it's as simple as listening and holding your tongue. Other times, it's more complicated. Healing. Righting wrongs. Protecting those you don't even know. Eserime don't help only those who love us. We help all who need us, and that's the entire realm, Kai."

"What about my other skills?" I ask. "The wind from my hands—"

"That is not a power gifted to the Eserime," Sybel interrupts, her voice colder.

My breath catches. "Then who is it from?" The answer forms in my mind. "My father? He wasn't Eserime, was he?"

Sybel hesitates; her entire demeanor has shifted.

"What is it?" I demand.

"Your father is of the Mera."

My eyes widen. Mera—the warriors and protectors. *That* makes sense. But Sybel's obvious anger toward my father? That doesn't make sense. Unless—

Fear curdles in my stomach. "He wasn't the Destroyer, was he? He didn't kill my mother, did he?"

"No," Sybel says. "The Mera are also protectors. They do not choose violence."

"You told me that I destroyed Chesterby," I say. "My wind powers, my skill with a blade. Isn't that a part of the Mera way? Destroying? Executing? Fighting?"

"You must be balanced," she says, "and right now, you aren't balanced and you're losing control, letting one side overtake the other. Even Mera show restraint, and you're showing more and more that you don't have *that*, either. You are even failing as Mera. What you don't understand, what you refuse to accept, is that your job combines the entirety of your heritage. Helping. Healing. Guarding. Protecting. Strength and compassion, neither stronger than the other. You are phenomenal."

I scoff. "I am not that."

"You have a job to do."

"And what is that job?" I ask.

"You are the one to stop the One."

Now this is too much.

I snort. "I don't think so. Why me? Why not you? Or some other…?"

"That is not my purpose," she says, "nor is it anyone else's. This is your purpose. Just as a hammer cannot fulfill an ax's purpose, another Eserime or Mera cannot take your place for this task."

Task. This is no mere task. This… This is *madness*. I place a hand over my hammering heart. All I wanted was to know who I was. My name, where I came from, my parents. If I'd known I was a dying realm's salvation, I would have kept my mouth shut.

"Kai, we can't run from this," Sybel says. "We can't surrender. The One will not stop at Vallendor but will go on to poison another realm and then another realm."

She holds out her arms. "I don't have the power to stop what's coming—that is not my purpose. And I don't know exactly how long we have, but I know it is not a lot of time." She offers me a sad smile. "There are those who have tried to stop the One, but they've failed—and Eserime died alongside their charges." She waits a beat, then adds, "And if you refuse to do what is needed, I, too, will die. As will the others you care for. Is there at least one person who matters to you, who you wouldn't want to see perish?"

Jadon. Veril. Philia. Olivia.

Jadon...his kindness and care, the way his lips feel against my skin. Veril's rapier-sharp jokes and effortless skills with lentils, mortar and pestle, his home my refuge in the past days. Then there is Philia, so brave and compassionate. And Olivia, who has grown on me. I care more for her than I did before simply because someone I care about loves her.

And it's more than that. My eyes skip around the forest. There are plants and trees—morning glory, lilies, basil, crabapples, so many others—growing across the sky and stretching up to the clouds. They are beautiful and healthy, and their beauty has offered me joy over these last hard days.

But that's just it—these days have been so hard. How can I face a battle bigger than the realm if I've barely survived this? "This is too much to ask of one person," I say. "I hardly know this world. How can I save it?"

"If you choose not to be the ax," Sybel says, "then be the shepherd. Be like your mother, be like Lyra, with her boundless stores of love. Fight to the very end for those you love. You must fight for all of us with all you have, Kai. You must save Vallendor Realm. This realm, this land, every forest and glen, the mountains and desert, every piece and parcel is yours—and you must heal it and you must protect it."

You are so much more. The angel on their shoulder. The shepherd. The ax. Goddess.

Since waking up in that forest and chasing Olivia to Maford, everyone except Elyn has called me *everything* except a child of Supreme. Certainly not *goddess*. And yet, despite their ire, I still tried to save their village—including Jadon, Olivia—and I tried to save them without hesitation, because that's who I am. Being a sword and shield—that is my nature. Making sure my companions are safe—I am their shepherd's crook. Despite my wounds and weakened muscles, that word—*goddess*—feels... *right*.

"All that you need already lives inside of you," she continues. "Powerful forces are already after you, Kai, and they will try to influence you, lull you into slumber, trick you so that you never defeat the One."

"Elyn," I whisper. "Is she the powerful force you're speaking of?"

"Why do you suspect her?"

"Because she's tried to trick me, and she's sent sunabi after me. She tried to turn Maford against me. And the battaby attack—according to Veril, his part of the forest had never seen a battaby. She may have even sent the burnu." I shrug. "How do I protect myself against them?"

"You'll need more than armor," Sybel says. "You need your amulet. And you need to wear your original clothes—they're your protection from those who hunt you and from the elements killing Vallendor. That was no mere cloak you wore. The vest, the pants, the amulet in particular—every item you donned was consecrated by Supreme, and all of it works together to shield you and galvanize your core. But you've been without it all for too long, and now you are vulnerable to the forces of evil."

Olivia—she stole my belongings and has yet to express true remorse. In that dream I had while recovering, she hid in the oleander, wearing my pendant around her neck. Was that more than a dream? Was that a vision? I place my hand on my neck where my amulet should hang. Do I know something deep within that I'm reluctant or unable to acknowledge? Could she be a part of the forces trying to stop me?

"You're speaking to me as though it's possible for me to find my amulet," I say.

"I speak as such because it *is* possible," Sybel says. "I am not lying or being hyperbolic when I say that your amulet is a part of you, Kai. You will always feel it calling, especially if it's near. Open your eyes, and you will see. You *must* see. Because without that pendant, your stores of strength will continue to drain, which means that you can't give this realm and its creatures all that they need to survive the war that's coming. You could stand before the One right now and that wouldn't be enough, not anymore."

The war that's coming.

"Is Emperor Wake the One?" I ask.

Sybel curls her lip. "The one who calls himself Supreme? He is only a consequence of the One, but he is a force working against you. The One is far more powerful."

"How will I know the One? I can't stop something I don't know."

"Had you met Wake's men before they invaded Maford?"

"No."

"Did you stop them? Permanently?"

I say, "Yes," but then sigh. "If you can't tell me who the One is, can you at least help me find my amulet? Anything will help, even if it seems unimportant. It's more than what I know."

Sybel takes my hands. "Just as forces of evil are out to get you, forces of good will help reunite you with what is yours. The realm speaks to you, Kai, and its creatures will guide you."

I squeeze her hands and offer her a clumsy smile. "The only creatures I've met have wanted to eat me or rip me apart. Wait." *Moths*.

My amulet is in the shape of a moth.

I gape at Sybel, blood thrumming. "Moths have been batting against the windows of Veril's cottage, even during the daylight, which struck me as odd."

"Then your amulet is nearby," Sybel says, releasing my hands.

I take in the forest around me. "I was right. My amulet is not here in these woods."

It wasn't that I failed to pay attention as I searched the forest floor or that I didn't sense what belonged to me because of my cynicism. It was because my amulet wasn't in the woods at all—and my senses were telling me that. The moths are swarming back at Veril's cottage. My amulet is there.

And I think I know where it is. And I think I know who has it.

"Thank you, Sybel." I feel stronger, like I'm already holding my amulet against my skin.

"Kai," she says, watching me carefully.

My prickly shoulder blades are back. My hands may not burn, but my heart does. And by the way Sybel's eyes widen, I can tell that my eyes are gold. Yes, I'm angry, and I don't care if Sybel sees that. I want my eyes to burn the brightest, hottest gold right now.

"Mercy, Kai. Choose mercy," she whispers, her voice fading like the last star at dawn.

"Mercy," I repeat, assuring her, assuring myself, standing tall amid the wreckage of my doubts. For the realm, for Jadon, for myself.

"This is the last time we'll meet." Sybel grips both of my shoulders. "At least here in Vallendor. That was the agreement I made with the Council of High Orders. Lyra was my dearest friend, and I asked to make one last appeal because I loved her, and by extension, I loved *you*. But you are to keep your own counsel now."

She releases my shoulders. "Always, *always* choose mercy, Kai. You are

Eserime. You choose peace and caring. And you are also Mera, and Mera destroy only that which is sanctioned by Supreme. Even with their swords and strength, Mera show restraint." She touches my cheek one last time and steps away. "And that, in itself, is choosing mercy."

I nod as she turns away. "Wait!" I shout.

She stops in her step but doesn't look back.

"Veril told me they call you the Lady of Dawn and Dusk," I say.

She nods. "Yes."

"Was my mother the Lady of the Verdant Realm?"

Sybel looks over her shoulder, her eyes twinkling. "No, Kai. *You* are the Lady of the Verdant Realm."

39

F ucking Olivia.

Moths have been fluttering around that bitch for days now. As she stood in the bedroom while I recovered, moths bumped against the window. As she sat at the dying campfire, moths fluttered around her head.

Olivia has my pendant.

I storm through the forest, wishing that I had the ability to fly, because every step I take, my shoulders blaze with fire and my eyes burn so hard and so bright, my face hurts. I break into a run as I see Veril's cottage ahead.

From a quick scan of the gardens, I see that Olivia isn't sitting at their campfire. If it's dinnertime, then she's inside, fork to her face, enjoying a meal even though she knows I'm in the fucking woods searching for something that isn't there.

I burst into Veril's cottage.

Veril, startled, drops the vial he's holding.

No one's seated at the table with dinner. No one's resting in the chairs.

"Where is she?" I growl.

Veril stares as though he's facing a dragon.

I'm so hot that I may actually become one.

"If you're looking for Olivia," he says, his voice shaky, "she isn't here. The last time I saw her—"

I whirl away from him and stomp out of the cottage. She's not in the garden and forge area—just Jadon sharpening his blade.

He smiles. "Hey! You're—"

I whirl away from him and stomp to the other side of the cottage.

I scan the campfire—mugs, handkerchiefs, crabapple cores, blankets. Lumpy blankets. I whip off the blankets and uncover three satchels Olivia carried from Maford. I reach for the smallest but instead choose the black leather satchel, the largest of the three.

Veril rounds the cottage with Jadon right behind.

"What's happened?" Veril asks.

"What's wrong?" Jadon asks.

I open the bag.

"Your sister is a fucking liar," I growl.

I dump the bag's contents onto the blankets. Poufs of tulle and swatches of silk are the first items to tumble out of the bag. Then: black jet stones. Purple amethyst. Blue and white lapis lazuli, sand jasper.

Veril gasps. "Those gems are mine."

"I know." I look over to the old man. "You didn't give them to her, did you?" I lift an eyebrow at Jadon. "Of course he didn't." I continue emptying the bag. At last, my cloak, rolled into a neat ball, comes falling out. My fingers tingle from just touching it. I shake it out, and the bloodred fabric glimmers in the twilight.

"Kai," Jadon says, "if you wanted your clothes back, you could have just asked."

"I *have* asked. Over and over again." I throw my cape around my shoulders. Immediately, the blood in my veins thickens and my torso tightens. I keep shaking the satchel. More tulle and fabric, and the plant chart Veril gave me. My black leather gloves! My bloodred vest, my black leather breeches. One more shake.

No amulet.

I glare at Jadon. "Where's my pendant?"

He holds up his hands. "Calm down."

"Did you know?" I ask, pushing off my borrowed breeches, not caring who the fuck sees. "That your sister has my pendant."

He frowns. "Why would you think that?"

I pull on *my* breeches, the ones with etchings of elks and whorls, and nearly collapse from the surge of power rushing through my legs. I take off the borrowed tunic, replacing it with my leather vest. More air in my chest. More strength in my spine. On with my black leather gloves. I feel my fingers lengthening. Just touching the suede, tracing the outline of the elk and owl on my palms, feeling the soft leather of my vest against my skin? Better than a bath. My bones feel sturdier, my mind clearer. Feels so good. I could have felt like this all along.

Teeth clenched, I turn to Jadon and ask again. "Did. You. *Know?*"

"Of course not," he says, "but Kai, you have to calm down."

"Oh, I'm calm," I say, hands buzzing. "Watch me become even *calmer.*"

Jadon pales and turns to Veril. "Will you reason with her?"

"About what?" the old man asks. "We've seen her when she's *not* calm. She hasn't even raised her voice yet, and in this instance, I find her restraint...*admirable.*"

I smile at Veril. "Thank you." I grab the second satchel and dump out its contents: dresses, fabric, headpieces, gloves, skirts. Nothing here belongs to Veril or me.

The last satchel: tunics, dresses, tulle, more tulle, swatches of satin and velvet.

No amulet.

"Kai," Jadon says, "I'm begging you now to not do anything you'll regret."

"Don't worry. I won't." I gather Olivia's things in my arms, turn around, and very calmly dump all of it over the campfire.

Sparks shoot high and explode like stars and lava, and the fire roars to life after being fed. The surrounding camp now boils with sudden heat. The destruction of Olivia's things makes me dizzy, but it's a *good* kind of dizzy—like I'm witnessing flowers bloom in front of me or watching a baker pull from his oven dozens of honeycakes made just for me.

"And I don't regret it," I say.

Jadon's face is red, his eyes narrowed. "You shouldn't have done that." By the hardness of his jaw and the tightness of these words, he's trying to remain calm.

I point at Veril. "I should've never doubted you. You were right."

Don't trust anyone to bring you that which makes you whole. They may not want you whole.

"What does *that* mean?" Jadon asks.

"Tell me," I shout at him, eyes hot with tears. "Where is my pendant? Where is she?"

"I don't know." Jadon scrapes his fingers through his hair.

Is there at least one person who matters to you, who you wouldn't want to see perish?

I scan the rose-orange sky. "While I was searching in the woods for an amulet that was no longer in the woods, I had an interesting experience. There I was, kneeling on the forest floor, swiping my bare hand around in the dirt like a mudscraper, and a visitor happened upon me." I look at Veril with a raised eyebrow. "Sybel."

"*Who?*" Jadon asks.

"You know her as the Lady of Dawn and Dusk," Veril says, dragging his gaze to Jadon.

Jadon crosses his arms and blinks at me with flat blue eyes. "And?"

"She told me who I am."

"And?"

"I'm not a mage from Peria or Steedale or anywhere," I tell him. "I'm from everywhere. I'm the Lady of the Verdant Realm."

Jadon's eyes come back to life but immediately drop back into flat and blue.

Veril holds his hands before him, prayer-style, and dips his head. "Kaivara. Lady—"

"No." Jadon pushes his forehead with the heel of his hand. "People in Peria have sewn and stitched circles, swirls, and elks on their clothes since the beginnings of the realms. They brand it on their horses' rumps, and they carry totems of this goddess, Kaivara."

I turn to Veril. "Could you excuse us for a moment?"

The Renrian, his eyes bright lavender, nods and shuffles back into the cottage.

"Sybel shared bad news," I say, heaving a breath to calm my angry nerves. This is Jadon, I remind myself. My feelings for him go beyond my fury at his sister. At least I hope they do.

"We're in trouble," I tell him. "Not just you, me, our little group here— including the thief—but the realm. There are entities that I can't even get into explaining right now, but they're working to destroy Vallendor, and all this may sound...*delusional*, but I must stop that from happening even though I have no idea how I'm going to do it."

He remains stone still, studying me.

"Believe me: I wanted to laugh in Sybel's face when she told me," I continue, "because I hated Maford and Wake and the violent creatures in this world. I have no interest in saving this realm. But Sybel made very clear that my job, my *purpose* is to protect Vallendor. She saw me wavering, and then she asked me an important question. My answer involved you."

His skin flushes, and the muscles in his jaw flex. "Me."

My chest constricts. "She asked if there was just one person I wouldn't want to see perish. And that person is *you*. *You* are part of the reason I'm gonna do whatever I'm supposed to do. But the way you took your sister's side—it's making me reconsider."

His mood shifts, and now his eyes fill with... *Sadness? Awe? Shame?* Whatever it is makes him take a step away. *"It's true."* That's the one thought he thinks and thinks and thinks until...silence.

No, this isn't awe on his face, and worry skitters down my spine.

"We need to deal with this, right now." I take a step closer. "We've been having a great time, flirting and dancing around this, but if you and I are to remain friends, or even go beyond that, we must be honest. We can't keep secrets from each other that could determine if one of us lives or dies; that can't happen. There can't be an us—"

"There *is* no 'us,' Kai. There never was," Jadon interrupts with a frown and, with great effort, takes two steps back.

I blink at him, confused. "Yesterday, we were a breath away from fucking in that tub, and now you're telling me that I imagined that? You've decided you and I are done because you're pissed that I called your sister what she is?"

He opens his mouth. Closes it. Then says, "I can't."

And that's it. He turns away from me and marches toward the forge.

"Why are you running away?" I shout at his back. Small spikes of anger stab my heart, but then one spike becomes a lightning bolt in my chest, and I yell, "Only cowards run!"

His shoulders droop, then stiffen—I hit my target. He returns to me now, his eyes a hurricane of emotion, stopping only feet away. "There is no 'us,' *Lady.*"

My mouth tastes like wood shavings; my tongue is numb as I stare at his beautiful face. "Then I don't need you to come with me."

He shrugs, his expression unreadable. "That's probably best."

My body numbs. I can't feel my feet or my lips as I shout toward the cottage. "Veril!"

The old man hurries back to the garden, avoiding Jadon's eyes. "Yes?"

I clutch my elbows to keep mania from bursting through my chest to my hands and destroying everything around me. "Pack up. We're leaving. It will be only you and me."

Veril straightens. *"Pardon?"*

"We're heading to Caburh," I say. "I need as much armor as possible. And then we head to Mount Devour." My skin hurts as though I've been stung by every mosquito in Vallendor. There's no armor strong enough to protect me from this war waging in my heart.

"Of course," Veril says, then hurries back to the cottage.

I'm not mad. No, I'm…sad? Perplexed? Angry? Conflicted? I'm all those things, and now I labor to take a simple breath. How could I have been so fucking foolish? So clueless?

Hands on my hips, I turn to Jadon. "Do I get to keep Fury and Little Lava? Or do you plan to steal those back while you're taking back everything else?"

He rolls his eyes to the sky. "Keep them. Give them back. It's up to you."

Breathe. My lungs refuse. Mouth hard and heart harder, I drop Fury to the ground, and then I lift my pants leg and pull the dagger from its sheath and throw it toward his feet with enough force that it punctures the earth and stands upright in the grass.

"Help!"

Jadon and I both stiffen. That was Philia's voice. She bursts into the garden, crying, fear streaking her face. She glows an urgent amber. Blood stains the front of her dress. "Jadon," she whimpers, collapsing before him.

"Otherworldly?" Jadon asks.

Philia's lips are split and bloody. Her neck shows the start of new bruising, and patches of scalp bleed where her copper hair used to be. The front of her chartreuse dress is bright with blood, and she cups her hand there as if she's holding in her guts, wincing every time she tries to take a breath. She's wearing a long blue coat with a gray collar over that bloody dress and boots with silver buckles. Traveling clothes. And none of it looks like it actually fits her.

"They…they…" she chokes out. "Olivia…"

"Where is she?" Jadon asks. "Is she hurt?"

Philia's breath twists into sobs. "They took Livvy."

"Who?" Jadon shouts.

"Philia," I whisper, kneeling beside her and taking her hand. "We'll fix you up, okay? Take a breath. Let's figure it out."

Veril rushes over. "I heard the commotion and thought more battabies, but now I see… Oh dear." He scans Philia's body, resting finally on her abdomen. "I'll go get something." He hurries back into the cottage.

The young woman's face turns gray. "Something inside me is broken," she murmurs, her lips trembling. Then she looks at me, and a teardrop falls onto my hand. "We found your amulet. Please forgive me."

Her confirmation makes my face go numb—I can't even speak.

"When did she find it?" Jadon hisses.

Veril returns to the garden with vials of silver liquid.

Philia quivers. "After the burnu fight." She looks at me, guilt swamping her face. "It was right there on the path after you fell on the way here."

Fat teardrops tumble down her cheeks. "I wanted to give it to you, Kai, but once Olivia put it on, she refused to take it off. She said she felt *more* with it. And with the cape, boots, and gloves, she'd be even more powerful."

I dip my forehead to my knee. Dizzier and dizzier.

Philia trembles, and I can't tell if it's pain she's experiencing or sorrow. She swallows, then says, "But then she decided to sell it along with the clothes and the storybook so we would have enough to find a place of our own and money to start our life together—"

She looks to Jadon. "And so you didn't have to choose between us and Kai. We were out scouting the best route to Vinevridth, but these men took her."

So much anger is burning in my eyes, I can barely see. "*Who* took her?"

Jadon asks, "What did they look like?"

"Did she still have the amulet?" Veril asks. "Or did these men take that, too?"

Philia doesn't answer us. Only sinks lower to the dirt.

I pluck the vial of silver tonic from Veril's hands and remove the stopper. The air now smells like sulfur. "This stinks, but you'll need to drink it, Phily." I pour the concoction between her bloody lips.

Philia jerks in my arms, and her eyes turn liquid and vacant. "They were going to Weeton… Big…red…soldiers."

I go icy cold as Veril and I exchange a look. *Is she talking about Elyn and her guards?* "Philia," I say, "where's the amulet?"

The young woman's face clears, and her breathing becomes rhythmic again. She sits up, wobbly still, but I catch her. She looks back at me with crumpled eyebrows. "I'm so sorry. I-I-I should've been braver. I didn't know what to do. I love her."

I stand, leaving her seated on the ground.

What we do for love: aid and abet a thief. Save a realm.

"We'll find her, right?" Philia whimpers.

Is it possible to hate someone but wish them happiness? I want Olivia and Philia to find a safe place. I want Olivia to open a dress shop and make lots of money off rich people. I want them to sit together by the fire and trade stories about that wild time they ran from otherworldly. I want all these good things for someone who stole from me. Veril and I *told* Olivia just how dangerous it was to wear that pendant. She remained selfish and spoiled, and now she's gone. And so is my amulet and perhaps the realm itself.

40

Philia sits in the rocking chair, sipping tea. Veril has patched her wounds, and the medicine has revived her well enough. The map of Vallendor is spread across the worktable.

I set a satchel I packed with some supplies for our trip on the other side of the door from Jadon's larger bag.

"I was telling"—Veril nods at Jadon—"about our proposed itinerary."

Jadon holds out both Little Lava and Fury to me. "You dropped these."

"Did I?" I don't reach for the dagger or the longsword. We may have agreed on a limited alliance until we find Olivia and my amulet, but it doesn't mean I've forgiven him.

"You'll need them." He sets both weapons atop the map like a peace offering.

I push them to the side.

For a few tense moments, Jadon and I exchange glares as Veril shifts foot-to-foot. Jadon breaks first, sighs, and turns his attention to the map. "You need to reach Mount Devour…here." Jadon jabs his finger on the jagged lines protruding from the Sea of Devour. "And according to Philia, Olivia's being taken…" He slides his finger south. "Here. Fucking Weeton."

Philia creeps over to join us at the worktable.

"You have no regard for the town of Weeton?" I ask.

Jadon grimaces. "Weeton is known for its marvelous views of the wasteland and for its citizens who are more outlaws than anything else. Mostly ex-soldiers who kidnap royals."

"Fine," I say, "but why did they take Olivia?"

Silence from Jadon.

Silence from Philia until: "Because she's…she's engaged." Her face crumples like paper, and she bursts into tears.

"To you, yes?" I ask, confused.

That causes Philia to slump onto a stool and cry harder.

"Not to Philia," Jadon says. "Olivia is engaged to someone else."

Too astonished to gasp, I let my mind dart, searching for clues in Olivia's words.

"Sh-sh-she…" Philia can't catch her breath.

Veril and I exchange looks—*what new nonsense now?*—as he hands her a handkerchief. We all wait as she composes herself. But then, just as composure raises its lovely head, the gasps and sobs, huffs and snorts return.

Jadon comes from around the table to hug her. "Livvy will be okay."

Which makes Philia cry harder.

We wait for composure again. I understand—it's been a stress-filled journey. She's tired. She's anxious. She loves a thief who is also a cheater.

Finally, Philia lifts her head and levels her shoulders. "She was promised to him on her tenth birthday. She turned fifteen and—" Her throat catches, and she balls her hands against her lips. "And when it came time to marry… She just… She couldn't. Her parents told her that she'd learn to love him. But they cared only about themselves. By Livvy marrying him, their station in society would improve. If she at least had one child, an heir…"

My stomach roils. *Oh dear.*

"She was miserable." Philia twists the hankie. "She dreamed of running away, and every day, she planned her escape. Any time her parents gave her money, she saved some of it. She'd take geld from their chests and coat pockets. And then she'd go into town and sell her clothes, her jewels, food, just to save enough geld to survive. But it wasn't enough. She needed something big to sell. Something impressive. Something…*valuable*."

Philia meets my eyes for a second before staring down at her trembling hands. "She knew what to take. She knew where it was. No one visited that library except for Livvy, and so she went down with a sewing bag, and she took it from the shelf."

The redhead slowly releases a breath through clenched teeth. "She stole the book with the jeweled cover. Those aren't pieces of cut glass. Those are real rubies. Real emeralds and diamonds." She swallows, but something remains caught in her throat. "When she returned to her room, he was there, waiting. He saw the book in Livvy's sewing bag, and she turned around and ran before he could take it. And she's never stopped running."

The sitting room slides into silence with only the hearth's fire crackling. The air in the cottage has also turned humid—Philia has shed a sea of tears.

I look at Jadon. "Is she your sister?"

Jadon shakes his head. "Olivia and I met the night she escaped. She was distressed and scared, and I... I understood. I couldn't just leave her there, so I helped her escape. It took us months, but we finally found a town far away enough to settle down and live like normal people for a moment."

"Maford," I whisper, a sinking feeling in my stomach.

"We told everyone that we were brother and sister," Jadon says. "Funnily enough, I started to believe it. I always watched over her. We'd bicker but knew we'd make up because we had only each other. Maford became a paradise for me. A new life. A new trade. Anonymity."

"And I finally met my true love," Philia whispers. "We wanted to be together even though we couldn't marry. People in Maford were starting to suspect that...that Livvy and I loved each other *that* way. And so we came up with a plan. Relocate to Vinevridth. Jadon promised to take us there."

"What stopped that move from happening?" My heart hurts for this couple.

"You," Philia says. "*You* stopped that move from happening."

Jadon shakes his head. "We had to figure things out once circumstances changed. Yes, we thought we had more time. But then Olivia met you—"

"*Met?*" I say, eyebrows high. "You say that like we bumped into each other at the market."

"She stole from the wrong person." Jadon glares at Philia before turning back to me. "Still, though, we didn't expect they'd find us. But I was wrong: they found us, and now..." He spreads his arms. "Here we are."

A realization uncoils in my mind. "*They*. You mean the soldiers who invaded Maford? They weren't there to conquer Maford? They were looking for *Olivia*? That's why they were kicking down doors...?" I lean against the table, dumbfounded. "Why would Wake send—?"

"Kai," Jadon says, bracing himself for what I can tell is the final and worst bit of it. "Olivia's fiancé is Gileon Wake, the emperor's son. And they won't stop hunting for her until she's back in Brithellum, either married to Gileon or placed in the dungeons for stealing from the emperor. And the emperor probably knows by now that we killed the men he sent, and he will send out more men to find us—better trackers, better fighters, others—and maybe they *will* find us soon, and if they do, they'll kill us on the spot for treason." He swallows, then adds, "That includes you, too."

"*What?*" My head swims—I don't even *know* these people. All I wanted to do that day was protect the village from violent men with swords, figure out who I was and why Elyn was searching for me, but now I'm running from her *and* the *emperor*? *I'm* the one who's aided and abetted a fugitive and a thief, and... *Treason?* I cover my head with my arms. "So." I straighten, inhale and exhale. "We head for Weeton, and we find Olivia before she tries to trade my amulet for freedom. If only she'd been honest—"

Jadon starts to noisily roll up the map. "Don't start."

The power burns in my hands, and I slam my fist against the table. "And who are *you* to tell me what to do? I haven't told a lie yet, nor have I maligned her already twisted character." A ticking warmth spreads up my arms. "If you wanna grapple with me today, Ealdrehrt, I'll gladly introduce you to the ground."

"Enough of this," Veril interrupts. "We'll rescue Olivia, and Kai can reclaim her pendant from that silly thief—they can't be too far away. And then, Kai, you and I can continue to Caburh and then Mount Devour."

I take calming breaths, and the heat in my palms cools. *Fine.* But I won't be duped again.

Veril wraps his vials in cotton and cloth and fills his satchel with food, including dried lentils, cured meats, those cocoa-apricot cookies, and of course, honeycakes. He grabs Warruin from the corner and says, "Ready?"

"I can carry some of that," I say, reaching for his bag. Once he dismisses my offer, I slip my satchel onto my shoulder and gaze at the warm room that helped me heal. Will we ever return to this place?

Jadon plants himself in the middle of the sitting room, Fury and Little Lava in hand. "Take your weapons, at least? I'm not being entirely altruistic."

I throw up my hands. "What do you *want* from me? Is it because your odds of surviving this improve when I have a sword in my hand?"

He cocks his head. "Yes, my odds improve when you're armed."

I grab the weapons and stow each in their sheaths.

"Great." Jadon grabs his bag and heads out the front door.

I glare at Philia. "What are you waiting for?"

The young woman startles, blushes, and hugs herself. "You'll let me join you?"

I say nothing and continue glaring at her, the muscles above my eyes twitching.

Near tears, Philia hurries over to the door. She looks back over her shoulder and says, "You look lovely, Kai, wearing all your stuff. You really do."

The twitching muscles above my eyes are now joined by the strained cords in my neck.

Veril says, "Miss Philia, I'd advise you to quickly gather those items you'll need before they join the others in that campfire."

Philia darts out of the cottage.

Stopping destructive forces had been a monumental task when I thought Jadon cared about me, when I thought Olivia and Philia were on my side. But now, there's only one person I'm willing to save: Veril Bairnell the Sapient. He's been my friend, my healer, a stand-in father. I'll save the realm for him.

Together, the old man and I leave the cottage, still gauzy in its enchantment from the battaby attack. Jadon stands at the head of the path, his back to me. Philia is shoving who-knows-what into one of the now-emptied satchels.

I adjust the cuffs on my boots. "How long will this journey take?"

Veril slips Warruin into his free hand. "What is time, dearest?"

I snicker. "That long, then."

"We'll get there," Jadon says over his shoulder.

Or we'll all die trying.

PART IV

GET THERE
IF YOU CAN

Inside the realm of gilt-less stars,
Love lacerates yielding scars.
Fragile hearts break, friendships end.
They pursued love, which could not 'scend.

Hear the echoes of love untold,
In starlit nights, in stories old.
A dirge that nurtures a flame unlit,
They fought odds and they fought writ.

Blighted grounds where nothing grows,
A battered love endures woes.
Whispers flit like moths' hasty grace,
They grapple for love in a precious space.

Hear the echoes of love untold,
In starlit nights, in stories old.
A song that saddens their tender hearts.
They crave time but love must part.

Betwixt the veils of starlit tears,
The sinister rebel nears.
Traitor to the realms' sublime light
Traitor to our holy rite.

Against the laws training all,
This treacherous rebel scrawls
Across the Light's unchanging guise.
This turncoat stalks his precious prize.

Hear the echoes of love untold,
In starlit nights, in stories old.
A plea that hastens Supreme's might.
Slay the fiend and win the fight.

Cosmos weep for fallen clans.
This tragedy upsets plans.
Perfecting life for souls facing death,
Realms sicken as they misspend breath.

—An Elegy by Veril Bairnell the Sapient

41

Olivia is being taken to Weeton, which is almost as far a journey to the southwest as Mount Devour is to the north. Caburh is partway between and will add a few days to our journey.

"If I am to survive without my amulet long enough to reach Weeton, I need stronger armor, which means traveling to see your friend in Caburh," I tell Veril as we leave the protection of the Renrian's forest.

Jadon starts to speak but stanches it as I spin to face him. "Go on to Weeton without me, then," I say. "But if you need my sword, then you should do everything possible to keep me strong enough to lift it. Especially since I'm without my amulet. Understand?"

He holds my gaze, unblinking, and then, begrudgingly, he nods.

For now, I wear the most protection I've had since waking up nearly naked outside of Maford. Beneath Veril's borrowed armor, my clothes fit snug against my skin. The power of every elk and owl, spiral and lightning bolt, flows through me. Instant strength and balance—my body can breathe again. But it won't for long. Sybel told me that. I *feel* that even though I'm stronger than before. Without my amulet, I'm nothing like I could be.

Jadon walks beside me, gauze covering the markings on his hand again.

Philia walks ahead of us carrying a bag heavy with her own possessions and Olivia's items I didn't throw into the fire, including the stolen jeweled book. I'd insisted that Philia be armed as well, and she chose the mace. Chin lifted, she'd told Jadon, "Yes. I'm a hunter, adept with a bow and arrows. While my father also taught me to identify weapons made of steel, my mother taught me how to use them." She lifted her chin, then added, "My father had many drunken friends. Bows and arrows didn't work well in close quarters. Knives did."

I'd bristled hearing that about her father and his friends. She didn't say it plainly, but I knew immediately what she'd experienced dealing with drunk men in small rooms. Wherever he rots now, Philia's father should be grateful that he and I weren't in Maford at the same time. He would've become one more hot dish for the giant snake that swallowed Johny the guard.

Knowing more about her family life, a small part of me has softened toward Philia. She's shown a determination different from the girl I met.

As we walk through the forest, Jadon tries to make small talk with me.

"The emperor has three trained falcons."

"It's hot tonight—more than usual for this time of year."

"I sharpened Little Lava, since she'd dulled from that fight in Azzam Cavern."

But I'm not interested in anything he says. I remain quiet, unresponsive, indifferent. Not one grunt. Not a single cocked eyebrow.

He finally picks up what I've been putting down and slowly...slowly... drifts behind me.

Yes, I'm traveling with Jadon on the same road, but we aren't on the same journey.

The afternoon with wine and a hot bubble bath. Those kisses on my shoulder. My veneration of his tattoos. *That all happened yesterday!* Seems like it happened a lifetime ago, and I wonder now: did he really kiss my shoulder? Did I really lick his markings? Or did the comfort of hot water, bubbles, and wine cause me to hallucinate, to conjure that buzz, that pop, that weakness I experienced as his lips touched my skin?

He saw so much of me *just yesterday*, and as I started that final search for my pendant, I'd planned to show him more. Maybe it was a good thing Philia and Olivia interrupted. How would I feel *now* if I'd given him everything?

I adjust my satchel strap on my shoulder and sigh. That afternoon wasn't a total loss. At least I can now picture the markings on my shoulder and over my chest. What they mean, I still don't know. Why are those markings on my skin? And who inked them? But I now have the answer to the most crucial question. *Who am I? The Lady of the Verdant Realm.*

That's why Jamart's daughter gaped at me. That's why Jamart prayed when he saw me. The goddess on their altar was standing before them, flesh and bone.

Oh Guardian, gentle Lady of the Verdant Realm, hear the humble plea of Thy devoted servant...

It's still hard to believe. And no matter how much Sybel tells me that I'm good, the memories of the mistakes I've made are all I can hear.

I step over a root rising from the dirt, careful not to fall like I fell after that fight with the burnu. At least I can't lose my amulet again.

Chesterby—Sybel said that it wasn't destroyed by an earthshake as Olivia had told me. She claims I destroyed it. Is that the mistake I must atone for now? And what does atonement look like? Will stopping the One be enough? I want to talk out all these questions with Veril, but we're not alone: Philia and Jadon.

Right now, keeping my distance from Jadon, not only emotionally but physically, has made me feel better. "My stomach has settled," I whisper to Veril, sneaking a look over to the Renrian. "Do you think that's because I'm no longer infatuated and have untethered myself from around his finger? Or am I being a petty bitch, which you know I embrace with open arms?"

The old man laughs and whispers, "Goodness, Kai. Maybe the tonics I've made you have heightened your senses too much."

"What are you talking about?" Jadon asks, his jaw tight.

"Sounds like you're conspiring against us." Philia laughs, but her eyes don't.

"If you feel threatened," I say, "then stop listening and instead prepare for a surprise. Not every word or thing must center around what you can or cannot understand."

"If there's something you must know, Miss Philia," Veril says with a smile, "rest assured that we'll certainly speak louder."

Color blooms across the duo's faces. Jadon's jaw tightens even more. Their pace quickens until they are several steps ahead of us.

Veril rolls his eyes and pulls his pipe from his sleeve.

We walk in silence, and soon the enchanted forest disappears behind us, devolving into lowlands filled with noxious swamps and twisted, black-trunked trees.

The quiet is punctuated with hands slapping mosquitos, the buzzing of those relentless bloodsuckers, and croaking frogs. Firmer ground finds its way beneath our squelching boots, and I think we're all pleased to walk upon dry, packed land again. That pleasure is short-lived as we return to softer ground and the stink of decay and rot.

Philia stops in her step and shouts, "There!" She points to the gleaming evening sky.

A falcon circles above. Has to be one of the emperor's falcons that Jadon mentioned.

The quiet respite skitters away, replaced by a familiar sense of dread.

Not good. *So* not good. This journey does *not* need to include me being arrested for killing the emperor's men.

I take in our placement—this path has led us out of the woods, and now we're traipsing across an open, flat stretch of boggy meadow. We stand out like giants in a town of ants. Steep hillsides to our left. To our right, another forest, this one as thick as clotted milk. And above us, that circling falcon scout.

"We have to take the forest route," Jadon says.

"That's Caerno Woods," Veril says. "The road that the emperor's battalions use runs right through them. There's a good chance that soldiers will spot us."

"We'll have to take our chances, then," Jadon says. "There are more places to hide in the woods than out here."

"You're probably right." I take a deep breath, then exhale. I hate agreeing with him.

Without further discussion, we race toward Caerno Woods. I slow some, spotting a raven, large and shiny, solid black, perched on the lowest branch of a twisted tree. The bird's black eyes fix on mine as it fluffs out its throat hackles. This bird, too, feels like a threat. Or maybe it's nothing at all. Just a bird in a tree in the wild because ravens and owls and other fowls live in the wild.

The raven croaks once as though it disagrees with my reasoning.

"What?" I ask her, my ears fuzzing.

"Prepare, Lady. I see death. Close." Her dark eyes remind me of my pendant's stone.

"How close?" I ask, my head swiveling to keep her in sight. *"What do you mean?"*

"You already know."

I stop and turn back to the raven. *"What exactly do I know?"*

I don't hear her answer because she takes to the sky.

I rejoin my companions waiting at the edge of the forest. Jadon appears confused or maybe conflicted. His brow furrows as he runs a hand through his hair.

"We should take a moment and think this through," I say.

The trees of Caerno Woods loom monstrous and tangled. Mist creeps along the ground beneath their trunks, hiding misshapen roots, razor-sharp snares, and holes large enough to swallow four weary travelers.

"We need to plan—"

Another bird cries. This time, though, it's not the *kak-kak-kak* of a falcon. This time, it's the beeping *cheer-cheer-cheer* of—

"A cardinal," I say, eyes on the red bird fluttering madly above us.

Another bird marking us for its master. *Elyn.*

That falcon means the emperor's men are near—maybe on that road through Caerno Woods. That cardinal suggests that Elyn's also close—maybe in the plains, the easiest route to travel. And the raven.

Prepare, Lady. I understand her now.

If Jadon enters these woods, he could die. If I *don't* enter these woods, *I* could die.

"What should we do?" I ask Jadon, my heart shuddering.

His mind isn't as scrambled as I thought, and his clarity ends in the final thought I allow myself to hear. *"If I have to fight to keep her safe, I will."*

Even though my anger is still skintight, my heart pushes at my chest, touched by his continued care.

"Are we going ahead?" Philia whispers, face flushed and sweaty.

Both Jadon and I say, "Yes."

I turn to him and ask, "You ready?"

Jadon swipes at his mouth. "Do I have a choice?"

No, he doesn't.

Nor do I.

42

Steam swirls at the tops of Caerno Woods. The forest sings, and the rustling leaves whisper a lullaby. Birds and bats, swooping sparrows, and chatty nightingales flutter in the dusk, disappearing into caves and hollows. The nightstar, fat and yellow, climbs higher in the sky behind us.

The wind whistles through the cracks in the logs, and the cacophony of nighttime creatures surrounds us like fog. Veril pants as he catches up with us. I come to a halt as something grabs my attention over all this racket. I hold up a hand. "Stop," I whisper. "Don't move. You hear that?"

Jadon and Philia crane their necks. Veril closes his eyes.

There it is. "Baying," I say.

Veril opens his eyes and nods. "A dog."

"The emperor's battalions use bloodhounds to track," Jadon says.

"There's only one dog," I say, "and she's coming from…" I point to the path to our right. Close-growing blue firs and high grass—a narrow way not well-traveled.

Jadon's eyes skip from bursts of thick purple orchids to the trio of bright-red cardinals watching us from gnarled branches. He points to a fallen moss-covered tree trunk, home to countless scampering and scuttling insects. "We'll hide there."

A long, low howl of a hound dog. *Rooooo!*

"I hear the dog now," Philia says as we hurry to the trunk. "They're getting closer."

The tree trunk crawls with centipedes, wood lice, ants, and things with spiky legs. Clouds of gnats as thick as smoke buzz and box at the air.

The hound howls again. *Roo!*

We huddle together in the hiding place, although it takes some effort for Veril to kneel. Jadon's neck is taut, distress plain on his face—if the soldiers find him, they'll know he was the one who helped Olivia escape. Philia trembles, and her teeth chatter. Her last encounter with bad men didn't turn out so well. She's also carrying the jeweled book that Olivia stole from the emperor. If the soldiers find it, she's in serious trouble. *We're* in serious trouble. But then again, we're already in serious trouble.

Seeing Jadon's panic vexes me. I understand the reasons behind *Olivia's* escape—forced to marry against her will. For the first time, though, I wonder about *Jadon*. What were his reasons for leaving his home? Was it simply because his parents treated him with disdain?

Roo!

The battalion draws closer. Clanking armor. The heavy breathing of men. The clomp of horses' hooves against dirt.

I peek over the trunk.

Jadon hisses, "What are you doing?" The cords in his throat tick against the skin there.

In copper-painted mail and plate armor over blue uniforms, the soldiers ride horses on the cramped forest trail. In the darkness, they glow with amber light, even though their faces are lean and healthy-looking, their eyes sharp and clear. Some soldiers carry torches to light the way, but all move with their backs straight. No chatter as they ride. Swords, bows and arrows, pikes—each weapon clean, shiny. The standard bearer holds a copper-and-blue-striped flag emblazoned with two spotted leopards, an armored hand, and a paddled colure. Beneath it all, the motto: PEACE, PIETY, PROGRESS.

Philia told us that the men who took Olivia were big...red...*soldiers*. I'd wondered if she was referring to Elyn's guards. Now, though, I remember that Philia saw Elyn's sentinels up close—I think she would've made that distinction. Also: she didn't mention Elyn, not once. And none of the men in this company are wearing red.

A bright-eyed tawny bloodhound wearing a matching blue tunic and copper-painted mail leads the battalion. She lifts her head and calls out. *Roo!*

"Do something!" I whisper to Veril. "Enchant! Make us look like trees or shrubs or..."

But there's a problem. He gestures toward the edge of the wood, the place we'd just scrambled from—the place where his staff now rests in bushes just off the road. "I dropped it," he whispers, "when we rushed over here to hide."

"What can you do without it, then?" I whisper.

"Handiwork." He's already wriggling his fingers.

I look down at my feet. *Shit!*

Jadon and Philia also startle as our feet suddenly resemble tree roots. Good but not good enough.

I frown and rotate my hand. "Quicker! More! Quicker!"

And now, our calves look like moss-covered trunks.

"Hurry, Veril," I plead.

Strain shows in the old man's face, and veins run wild across his cheeks and forehead.

The enchantment rises to our thighs...our bellies... Slowly, we rise, standing and straightening like the trees we are becoming.

Roo!

I close my eyes. My mind spreads like melted butter, and the world beyond us becomes blurred and gauzy.

Roo! Roo! The dog snuffles at the ground, more excited than before. She smells us.

Good dog. She's achieved what she's been trained to do.

Bad dog. That means finding us and hastening our deaths.

The clanking and clomping near—but the snuffling dog will find us first.

Jadon's eyes bulge with dread. Leaves now protrude from his chin and cheeks—he's half man and half oak. Leaves poke from his forehead, but his eyes... Still bright blue, still human.

"Close your eyes," I think at Jadon.

His eyes snap shut.

Did he actually hear me?

Veril squeezes his eyes shut...pressing...disappearing behind a facade of leaves.

I guess enchanting people takes more effort than enchanting cottages and dying forests.

The bloodhound trots over to stand before me. On the other side of Veril's concealment, she's blurred and gauzy. Drool hangs like strings from her mouth. She sees me through the evolving enchantment. I can't tell if she sees Veril, Jadon, or Philia—or if she cares to. Right as she tilts her head back to howl again...

I hold my finger—which is still my finger and not yet a twig—to my lips. *Shh.*

The dog stops and cocks her head. *"It's you!"*

I blink at her. *"Do we know each other?"*

Jadon commands the dog in his mind. *"Go away! Shoo!"*

"Daisy!" a soldier shouts.

The dog pants, pleased with herself, happy to see me.

Affection swells within me—Daisy is a cutie—but she needs to leave. I shush her again.

"What is it, Daisy?" that same soldier asks. "What did you find?" He comes to stand on the other side of the log. His skin is as brown as tree bark, and his eyes are the same green as the moss on this trunk. His armor looks like it was made only yesterday.

"Why does she keep doing this?" another man whines, coming around to our side of the log. His flame-red hair bleeds into his bushy beard.

"Because alerting is her job," the moss-eyed man answers.

I flick my hand at the dog. *"Move back, please."*

Daisy backs away and dips her head. *"Why can't I come closer?"*

I flick my hand again. *"Because I need to hide. Move back a little more, please."*

Daisy takes another step away from me. She pants with excitement. *"How's this?"*

I can't see Jadon, but I can hear him thinking, *"What the fuck is going on right now?"*

How much longer can this enchantment last?

There are two columns of men on horseback. I count...one, two...five... fourteen total.

The cords in Veril's neck pound against his skin.

Shit-shit-shit. I can see him now. Does that mean the emperor's men can see him, too?

What do we do? What do we—?

Horses!

"Hey." I call to them in my mind. *"Over here, by the fallen trunk."*

Four of the soldiers' magnificent steeds swivel their heads in my direction.

"What are your names?" I ask.

"Snowfeet," says the pretty black mare with white ankle hair.

"Essen," the gray stallion says.

"Jinx," the orange-brown mare says.

"Orchid," the wheat-colored mare says.

"These men are a danger to me," I tell them. *"I need you to pretend you're spooked. Do it, though, when I say."*

Essen flicks his tail and snorts. *"Only to be whipped, Lady?"*

"I promise you that any rider who lifts a hand to strike you," I say, *"he*

will lose that hand and will suffer for the rest of his life."

Essen nods. *"Yes, Lady."*

"Of course, Lady."

"Not one will have any hands, then."

"Serves them right."

"You, soldiers," a man shouts from the line of troops who have passed us. "Shall we move forward, or shall we watch you hold hands for the rest of the day?" He has the crisp diction of an educated man. His words wear spikes.

"Ser…Ser Wake," the handler stammers, and then, curling his lip, he glares down at Daisy. "Stupid bitch," he mutters, "always getting me in trouble."

If he kicks her, I don't know what I'll do. That's not true. I know *exactly* what I'll—

Wait, did he say *Wake*? As in *Emperor Wake*? Can't be. Why would someone so important—someone believed to be Supreme as man—be leading this raggedy group of soldiers? Can't be the emperor.

I twist to look behind me, trying to spot the emperor in the line of soldiers.

"This one right here—Wake. Start with him." Essen's voice cuts through my mind. *"He uses his whip on poor Morningfire without stop."*

I glower. *"He's a poor horseman, then."*

"What's he doing over there?" Wake rides over on Morningfire. He has golden hair and fleshy lips. His armor is coated in more copper paint than all the copper ever mined, with no tarnish or scuffmarks. His cloak gleams like silver waves rolling from his back. He looks too young to be the emperor—even if he's been granted long life. No, he's *Ser* Wake. A son. Is he the son who was betrothed to Olivia? "Why are we stopped?" he asks. "We don't have all day."

Wake's voice is whiny, smug, and high-pitched, like if a peacock could talk. My shoulders shudder, listening to him speak. By the way Jadon is clenching his teeth, by the way his shoulders also hunch to his ears, I'm guessing Wake's voice hurts him, too. Despite Olivia stealing from me again and again, despite my growing resentment for her, Jadon cared for that thief enough to free her from this man. Even I concede that it must be painful for him to hear Wake's voice knowing that Olivia is in danger.

My stomach sours in Wake's presence. The air pulses with strange power. Magic? It must be another enchantment, but one not spun by Veril.

Do Philia and Jadon feel this, too?

Daisy's handler clears his throat. "We stopped, Ser-Ser Wake, because Daisy thought—"

"I don't really care what Daisy *thought*," Ser Wake spits. "I care only about what Daisy *finds*. And I'd hate to get rid of yet another dog because she's found nothing but her own tail. Has she picked up a scent this time?"

"Yes, yes, ser. Going toward Pethorp, seems like," the handler says. "Daisy's a good tracker. Better than her brothers."

Daisy drops her head, then blinks at me with sorrowful eyes. *"They killed my brothers."*

I remain perfectly still, anger crawling like ants over my arms. *"I'm so sorry."* I wish I could pat Daisy's head as reassurance—because she *is* a good girl. *"They won't hurt you ever again,"* I tell her. *"And I'll avenge your brothers. Promise. Just lead them away from us."*

The bloodhound pants, then moseys in the direction from which we'd just come. She trots some, then lifts her head. *Roo!*

I watch her go and glance back at Ser Wake. From his seat atop Morningfire, he surveys the woods again, his blue eyes skipping over our fallen trunk. "That woman," he says.

"Yes, Ser Wake?" the man beside him asks. His skin is leathery-tan, and his blond hair isn't as golden as Wake's, its unnatural shade more straw than silk. He's bigger than Wake—two Wakes wide and two Wakes tall—and so his horse must be large, too. He wears nice-but-not-as-nice armor, and the scars on his cheeks and square jaw speak of battles and hand-to-hand combat...unlike Wake, who, from the looks of it, has never even cut his face shaving. If I were to guess, the big soldier admires Wake and has tried to copy him, down to the weird, blond hair. Who is he? Why is the air around him so heavy?

"She told us that they would be traveling this road," Wake says now. "She practically guaranteed that I would find them heading this way. 'Trust me,' she said. Ugh. Should've known. You can't trust a woman with a face like that."

Which woman?

Can't be Olivia—he'd know those innocent-looking big eyes and honeyed tongue.

Elyn, white-haired and powerful, promising gifts and riches? Would she have had time to tell them, though? Her cardinals only just spotted us as we entered the woods.

The big soldier's yellow eyes, so stark against tanned skin, drag across the forest. He pulls those eyes in our direction—is he sensing something? He lifts his leg to dismount.

"Now!" I think to the horses.

Snowfeet, the black mare with white ankle hair, rears, keeping her rider in place. Wake's horse does the same, and soon, all the horses are bucking and neighing.

"What's happening?" a soldier asks.

"Something's spooked 'em," another soldier shouts.

The clomp of hooves and the whoops of men scrambling to hold on to their mounts is the pandemonium I need. *"Go, now!"* I command the horses. *"Go!"* I tell Daisy.

Off they go! On Jinx, on Orchid, on Essen and Snowfeet!

Just as the last soldier rides away, Veril clamps his hand over his mouth and the gauzy blurred veil drops.

I take a gulp of air.

Jadon hides his face in his hands and looks like he just escaped a brush with death.

I suppose, in a way, we all did.

We take a moment to catch our breath. But my breath only comes faster as I recall my conversations with Daisy and the horses. Those soldiers, those abusers, those *fuckers*. Beating horses and killing dogs? Who do they think they are? How would *they* like to be threatened, spurred and horse-whipped, and then forced to march the realm in search of bullshit?

"Kai," Philia says with great caution, "are you okay? Your…" She points at her own eyes. "The gold in your eyes… The color's swirling. Like a sandstorm."

"Yeah, I feel it. Just need a moment." I rub my tender scalp and take deep breaths. Didn't realize that I was that angry. Once my heart slows, once my eyes cool, I smile at Philia, then turn to the Renrian and say, "Thank you for hiding us."

Veril waves away my gratitude, no big thing, but he looks knackered after such an effort.

"Was *that* Ser Wake, Olivia's jilted fiancé?" I ask.

Jadon winces as he massages his temples. "Yep. That was Gileon Wake."

Sweet Supreme, that girl can pick some enemies.

We gather our things, take more relieved breaths, and stride in the opposite direction from the troop, who are now headed to Pethorp, thanks to the misguided words of that mystery woman. The forest's breath is a cold whisper against my skin as we creep ahead. Jadon's hand rests lightly on the hilt of his sword, and his eyes dart from path to tree to the road ahead like a hawk's. Staff back in hand, Veril remains focused on the path we're traveling. Philia clutches her cloak and murmurs a prayer for our safe passage.

"The soldier with the fake blond hair and yellow eyes," I ask Jadon. "Who is he?"

Jadon says, "I believe he's called 'Sinth.'"

"Is he human?" I ask.

Jadon crumples his eyebrows. "He's Dashmala. They're great warriors. Hard to kill. Like they're made of stone and steel. They don't use magic, but they are very intuitive. He clearly sensed something, which is why he was about to get off his horse."

"Dashmala," Philia says, fascinated. "He's a *barbarian*?"

"That's what people in Maford thought I was," I say, remembering my one-woman invasion of that small, stinky town.

"Because his eyes are almost the same color as yours," Philia notes. "But his are more muddy yellow than gold. It's like…you came from the same field, but you had better soil and more sunlight."

I search my memories for the Dashmala but come up blank. "Veril, you told me the Dashmala resented you for sending their soldiers into a chasm."

Veril doesn't answer. With eyes narrowed, he's looking back in the direction of those soldiers. Finally, he pulls his gaze to meet mine. "What's that, dearest?"

"You and the Dashmala have a history," I say. "Battle of Riddy Vale, correct?"

Jadon and Philia say, "What?"

Veril meets my eyes, then turns to them. "We—the Renrians—faced off against them way back then. A number of Dashmala warriors fell victim to our enchantments. We were lucky the soldier riding beside Prince Gileon didn't spot me. Dashmala hold grudges. Grudges are passed down by the Dashmala from generation to generation, inherited like cottages and dressers."

Philia snorts. "He was one of the biggest men I've ever seen."

I look back over my shoulder, in the direction the soldiers rode. "Should we…?"

"Should we what?" Jadon interrupts, frowning. "Go back and kill him?"

I hold Jadon's gaze. "Maybe?"

"No." His answer is immediate and final.

"Don't worry, Lady," Veril says. "That battle occurred long ago. I don't know the man, never met the man, will never see him again. There's no reason to do something so—"

"Preemptive," I say.

Veril nods. "Correct." He looks back one last time—there's worry in his eyes.

"Let's keep moving before we run into more men," Jadon says.

As the road unfolds before us, I see a glint and a sparkle at the corner of my eye. An iridescent trail winks before me. "Look there." I point, my heart quickening. "Do you see it?"

"See what?" Jadon eyes the gloom.

An eclipse of moths—red, gold, and blue—flutters above the trail, illuminating the darkness, leaving sparkling dust in their wake. One by one, moths leave the group and flutter forward, in the direction we're traveling.

This means the soldiers we just passed don't have the amulet. My pendant is not far off. Neither is Olivia if she's still the person holding on to it.

"There's a path," I say, closely watching the sharp shimmer fade as the last moth flutters above the dust and then flutters away to join her sisters. "But it's waning. The shimmer is dissipating. Let's hurry," I say, shouldering my pack. "We're going in the right direction."

"Because of this path only you can see?" Philia asks.

"I can see it," Veril says, smiling.

"If you were magic, dearest," I say to Philia, eyebrow arched, "you'd see it, too."

In the distance behind us, a horse whinnies and brays, only to be quickly drowned out by a man's scream.

I smile. A soldier dared to whip his horse.

Violence begets violence.

Next time, he'll keep his hand to himself.

43

We continue walking the trail in the opposite direction of the troop now headed to Pethorp. No birds sing in the darkness, but frogs croak from hidden spaces off the road. The odors of pine and clay are overlaid with the stink of stagnant water and old blood. If the vines, roots, and leaves weren't so alive and thriving, I'd think this forest had perished long ago.

I've noticed something: the longer Philia travels with us, the stronger she looks. Her hair is shinier but not because of the buildup of dirt and oil. Her steps are certain, more solid than they were in Maford or even in the forests around Veril's cottage. She's less shrill and thinks before she speaks. There's a light in her eyes that wasn't there before. Philia Wysor is growing up right before my eyes.

As we walk, I decide to pull one of my questions from my teetering tower of queries. "Why did you oppose killing those soldiers?" I ask Jadon. "With our combined skills, we stood a good chance of taking them like we did back in Maford."

The muscles in his jaw flex. "Because that was Gileon Wake."

"So?"

"So... We can't kill a prince and expect us—*or Olivia*—to live." He looks over at me, his gaze assured. "Fortunately, the horses freaked out before Veril's enchantment broke."

"That was scary," Philia says, eyes wide. "What got into them?"

"*I* got into them," I say, "and that's not a brag."

We walk on, retreating into our own thoughts. I'm glad for the silence—I'm trying to focus on the glittering trail of moths. Another light, though, catches my eye: the sharp yellow glow waxing from Veril's knees.

The old man straggles behind, leaning more on his staff with each step. Strings of amber pain buzz from his knees, zipping down to his calves and up his thighs. I glimpse a gap around his legs: the vivid glimmer of enchantment and the lusterless matte of the true world. His lavender eyes are tearing up, and his fingers curl and cramp. Without the strength to maintain the enchantment in which he cloaks himself, his beard is bright white with age and his back is a series of misshapen knobs and bones.

Maybe there's something in Veril's bag that will help. "Let's stop for a moment," I say to the others. Then, to Veril: "Sit a moment. You're not doing well."

He steels himself before tottering to a fallen tree trunk.

I grab Veril's satchel as Jadon and Philia join us.

"We need to keep moving," Jadon says.

I dump bundles of plants from the satchel onto the forest floor.

Jadon watches the woods for danger as I use the old man's mortar and pestle to grind plants under his instruction. Veril lifts his pants leg to reveal skin busy with trails of veins and scars, a thin calf, and a swollen knee. Bad shape.

Please let this work. I smear the poultice on both of his knees and upper calves, letting my hands linger on his kneecaps.

Once the yellow glow of his pain dims, we shoulder our bags and return to the trail.

The sparkling moth cloud is gone.

Disappointed, I droop, and my pulse ticks in my head, keeping time with the only thought I have. *This is so fucked up.*

"Okay," Philia says, eyes on the ground, "four Dashmala kidnapped Livvy. One Dashmala rode beside Prince Gileon. Could it be possible that Gileon already has Olivia?"

"I don't think he has her," Jadon says.

"Hear me out," Philia says. "If Gileon has Olivia, the woman who embarrassed him before the entire realm, who else would he be hunting right now? Shouldn't we follow Gileon to his camp and rescue Olivia instead of going to Weeton?"

No one speaks.

Philia turns to Jadon. "Are you going to say anything?"

Jadon frowns. "I told you that I don't think Gileon has Olivia, so I'm not gonna join in your hypothetical."

Philia snorts. "My hypothetical?"

"She's not traveling with him, Philia," I say. "I would've sensed the amulet's—"

"*If,*" Philia interrupts, "she didn't sell it or exchange it for—"

"One more time: we're going that way." I point in the direction of

Caburh. "There weren't any moths fluttering around Gileon, so again, I doubt he has the amulet."

"But that doesn't mean he doesn't have Olivia—"

"You know what?" I snap. "I don't beg for followers, and I'm tired of being second-guessed. Follow Gileon Wake, then. Go that way." I point at the path behind us. "Good luck." I level my shoulders, then say, "Veril?"

The old man says, "I'm ready."

Together, the Renrian and I continue our slower westward trek. Soon, I hear the patter of two more pairs of feet as Jadon and Philia fall into step behind us.

We walk on, the forest quieter, colder. We pass limbless trees. Tromp upon gray dirt. Nothing moves—not a branch, not a bird. Eerie stillness.

I look behind me, sensing...

"What?" Jadon catches me looking.

"I'm thinking about what Gileon said."

She told us that they would be traveling this road. She practically guaranteed that I would find them heading this way.

"Who is 'she'?" I ask. "And that cardinal. Let's not forget that it wasn't too far from that falcon. I just find it strange that the falcon didn't even think to catch a bright-red bird for dinner."

He shrugs. "Maybe the falcon didn't see it and that's why it didn't attack. Maybe the falconer fed it before sending the bird out to avoid distraction."

"I think that cardinal was one of Elyn's sentinels," I say. "*Someone* squealed on us. Could Elyn be the 'she'?"

Jadon pushes out a long breath. "Maybe."

"If it's Elyn, then..." Philia unties the mace from the strap on her bag and swings the steel ball a few times. "I'll be ready next time. She'll be sorry that she messed with us."

I chuckle. "To Elyn and her guards, your mace will feel like a thorn on the smallest rose."

"That doesn't mean she can't fight," Jadon counters as he takes the lead on the trail. "You wanted her to have a weapon, and now you say that it's useless?"

Against man, the mace would teach a few lessons. Against a being far superior to man? A thorn on the smallest rose. Still, I shrug and say, "You're right. Swing on, then, Philia."

Branches and dried leaves crunch beneath our feet. A foul odor stampedes through the woods, running over the fresher scents of evergreens and ferns. The dirt is parched—no rain has fallen in these parts for months. There are no owls in these trees. No ravens on rocks. This landscape is a reminder that Vallendor is dying.

Eventually, Philia walks ahead with Veril, leaving me and Jadon to walk side by side. He clears his throat, then says, "I'm sorry." When I don't respond, he steps in front of me. "Kai—"

I step around him, my patience depleted like the dried dirt beneath our feet.

"Can you stop and listen for a minute?" he asks, standing still. "Please?"

I push out an irritated breath and face him.

He extends his arms to the side and says, "I am truly, *truly* sorry for hurting you. You didn't deserve that, and I apologize."

"Fine," I say, ready to start walking.

"Wait." He rushes to stand before me again. "I intentionally pushed you away—"

"Wrong thing to say."

"My actions were harsher than I intended," he says, shaking his head.

"You could've just said, 'Hey, Kai. I think you're great, but I'm not there yet and I don't know when or if I'll ever be.' See? Still would've been awful to hear, but at least my version wasn't cold and scary and—"

"That would've been the biggest lie I've ever told." He pauses, then mutters, "Though that's not true, either. Shit. Look. I'm reluctant to... *go there* even though I *am* there. I know we'll have to separate soon—I promised Olivia that I'd take her to Pethorp—and so I thought, 'What's the point?' I'll end up hurting you anyway, so I decided to hurt you now, and this sounds awful now that I'm saying it aloud, but I'd rather hurt you and get it out of the way before we...before we..."

He holds his breath, and I can hear his thoughts as he counts to ten like he does anytime someone sneezes or coughs. At eleven, he sets his hands on his hips and drops his head. "Guess I've succeeded."

My heart wobbles, but my knees, my core, remain rigid. "Do you think I'll say, 'Great. I forgive you' because you apologized? You think I'll trust anything you say or claim you feel? I'm not one of your farm girls back in Maford. I don't believe you fell from the heavens or rode down in a golden chariot to light the world by simply existing. Do you think I believe that?"

"I don't."

"What's all this, then?" I ask, taking my turn to dramatically extend my arms. "We're in the middle of nowhere and we're talking about *what* right now?"

Jadon shakes his head.

The worst part is, I want to forgive him, but he doesn't deserve it. Not yet. "We should keep moving." I back away and start walking to catch up with Veril and Philia, who are a good distance ahead.

I look back over my shoulder.

Jadon hasn't moved. His hands are still on his hips. His head still hangs low.

Just as I face forward, a growl pushes through the trees. A growl so hard and dry that it leaches any life remaining in the dirt path we're on.

"What was that?" Philia asks, her voice trembling.

"Don't know." I slowly turn to look left.

The glow of the creature in the brush confuses me. Gold. Blue. Horizontal. Vertical.

"Leave my woods," a jagged voice rumbles.

"Did you hear that?" I whisper.

"The growls?" Philia whispers back. "Yeah."

"But you didn't hear a man speak?" I ask.

Both Veril and Philia say, "No."

I steady my shoulders, then shout, "We mean no disrespect. We're anxious to leave—"

The creature growls again, closer now. "I will rip your heads from your bodies and drink the blood from your necks."

Philia draws in a breath, but she's present enough to grip the mace.

"Draw your weapon if you dare, child," the creature threatens.

"Philia," I whisper, "just relax." Who am I talking to? *What* am I talking to? How much danger are we in? "Please leave us alone. I want no trouble. Just let us continue on our way."

The last time I reacted against a threat, sight unseen, I'd nearly killed Tazara, the king of the night-dwelling creatures. I don't want to make the same mistake this time, killing whoever's growling at me, another last of his kind.

See, Sybel? I've learned my lesson. I'm not choosing violence.

That curious glow is moving closer to us...closer...until a beast emerges from the shadows. He has the short, woolly fur of a bear but eyes that gleam with the intelligence and evil of man. Those massive paws— that's bear. The upright carriage—that's man. "I will not warn you again," he growls. "You are trespassing in my woods, and for that, you will die."

Fear flickers through me, but then I remember what Sybel told me.

This realm, this land, every forest and glen, the mountains and desert, every piece and parcel is yours—and you must heal it and you must protect it.

Yes, I must heal it and protect it—and I will.

Because I am the Lady of the Verdant Realm, and these woods are *mine.*

44

The bear-man towers over us, a fusion of brute and cunning. He blocks our path, flexing claws that could rip us apart. He smells as bad as he looks. Musk and mud. Blood and filthy fur. The insides of a dead man's boots. His eyes glow like embers.

Behind me, Philia and Veril back away. But I hold in place, my feet solid on the hardened dirt. I meet his gaze with a steadiness I don't feel—that is, until I remind myself who I am.

The beast grinds his teeth, a sound like crushing boulders. "How is it that the Lady has found her way into my woods?"

"*Your* woods?" I ask, livid for many reasons.

His use of the possessive "my." His upright carriage—how dare he stand tall before me. His tone. Nasty. Disrespectful. Dismissive.

"Tell me your name," I demand, even though what he is and who he is have already appeared in my mind the same way my own name had.

"You've forgotten it?" he sneers, running his large tongue over his sharp yellow canines.

"Tell. Me. Your. *Name*." I take a solid step forward, my shoulder blades twitching, my fingers tingling. I want what I want, and that's for him to—

"I don't have to obey you, *Lady*," he scoffs. "Without your pretty little pendant, you've become just like the old man and the redheaded child: powerless."

"You are mistaken, Gilgoni," I spit. "I don't need—"

It's too late when I see him strike. His whole paw comes a breath away from my face, but the tip of his nail on his longest finger slashes my cheek. Before I can react, though, something pulls me off my feet, leaving me disoriented, breathless, and shocked as I land on my ass, clutching my bleeding face.

I look up to see Jadon's back, his legs spread apart, his knees bent. Fight mode.

Gilgoni roars at him, but that roar is cut short by Jadon's own growl and then his shout. "I will strike you down. I will fucking slice you in two and feed Devour your corpse, and I will fucking set that sea on fire. Get. *Back*."

The welt on my cheek burns like acid. I wince and close my eyes. I hear shuffling.

A small growl from the aburan. A huff. More shuffling.

Jadon stands over me, guarding, waiting.

With one final petulant growl, the creature dives back into the brush. The air clears with his departure.

Veril and Philia emerge from their hiding place behind a log.

Jadon lets out a deep breath, sheathes his sword, then crouches before me. "You okay?" He scrutinizes my cheek, turning my chin this way and that.

"It fucking hurts, so no, I'm not okay," I say, laughing, even as the welts around my face sting from his touch.

Jadon leans closer. "Are you okay?" His eyes are soft but demand a real answer.

I nod. "Yes, thank you."

"Let's see what we have…" Veril's voice makes me break eye contact with Jadon. He's opening his bag. Vials and bottles clink and clank.

"You were talking to that creature, Kai," Philia says, awe in her voice. "Did you understand its growls? Have you seen that thing before?"

Jadon holds up his hand. "Phily, let's give her a moment, okay?"

"And you," Philia says to Jadon. "You shouted at that thing and all of it just sounded so loud and confusing, and I don't know *what's* going on."

Jadon takes a deep breath. "Philia—"

"Let's try…" Veril dribbles brown liquid onto a ball of cotton, then dabs it on my cheek.

Stings. The liquid pops and sizzles against my skin, and I suck in a breath through my clenched teeth. Whatever it is smells salty and metallic.

Jadon takes over holding the cotton to my cheek as Veril returns to his bag. "First." He plucks out a pearly vial filled with pink tonic. "Then to stop any infection." He offers the rum.

I drink the pink stuff and follow it with a glug of rum.

Jadon removes the cotton ball and studies me.

My face numbs. My injured cheek prickles. I close my eyes and inhale a deep breath and slowly release it.

Jadon gathers my cape—it came undone in the chaos.

Philia helps me stand. My mouth tastes metallic, like I've been licking dirty spoons. "I really need my amulet. Otherworldly like him demand to see authority—"

"What do you mean 'authority'?" Philia asks, face paling. "Who are you?"

All this time, I've been searching to uncover my identity, and now, here I am, with the answer to that question, not willing to say it. If otherworldly plan to attack me more regularly, then I need to share this truth.

I meet Philia's gaze. "I've recently discovered that I'm not a mage from Peria after all."

"Then...who are you?" she asks.

I glance at Veril, who gives me a slight nod. "I am Kaivara Megidrail, a defender of Vallendor." *Megidrail*—I just remembered my last name, and the speaking of it flowed off my tongue like soft water. I purse my lips, still reluctant, but I charge ahead. "You may know me as the Lady of the Verdant Realm." I pause, then flick my eyes at Jadon. "Believe it or not."

Jadon says nothing because he's already told me what he believes.

"You're...you're..." Philia's face stumbles from confusion to disbelief to clarity. "You're a *goddess*?" She squeals, claps her hands. "This makes total sense."

It does?

"Do I still call you 'Kai'?" she asks. "Or your ladyship? Or—"

"Just Kai," I say, remembering that I said the same to Veril nights ago.

"Did you both know this?" Philia asks Veril and Jadon, her face bright.

Jadon offers a curt nod.

"Not the entire time," Veril says. "I had my suspicions."

Philia smiles broadly, her spirit so bright, it almost causes me to squint. "Livvy won't believe this," she whispers. "We need to get to her before..." Philia's nostrils flare, and her eyes shine with tears.

Jadon peers in the direction we're traveling. Finally, he squeezes the bridge of his nose, shakes his head, and exhales. Exhausted, he gathers his sword and says, "Let's find somewhere safe to camp. I think we could all use food and rest." He squints at me, his expression pinched and weary. Without another word, he starts up the trail.

I level my shoulders and shuffle beside the Renrian. The look that Jadon gave me... On its face: weariness and confusion. But nothing is that simple with Jadon. Weariness and confusion, yes, but there was something else there. What was it?

"Wait." I stop walking and stare down at the trail.

Veril turns to me. "Something else?" Then he looks to the dirt. "I don't see anything."

I don't say a word—I won't be able to talk without crying.

The old man shuffles closer to me, eyes still on the trail. "Remember, Kai. Your vision improved after your confrontation with Tazara. My eyes are that of a two-hundred-year-old Renrian who has traveled without his soft bed and warm—" But then even he sees what I see.

Dead moths.

"Oh dear," Veril whispers.

I have two options: choose to believe that these dead moths are an omen of what's to come. Or choose to trust my gut and the certainty that I feel moving in this direction, a certainty that feels like a satiny ribbon that pulses like the stone of my amulet.

This forest around me is dying. There are dead toads over there. There are petrified sparrows over there. The dirt no longer holds the prints of Jadon's boots. Somewhere in the brush, an angry aburan stalks what's left of these woods. Death and dying all around—why would moths escape that fate?

That string in my stomach pulls harder.

Even if these dead moths are omens, I will continue to move toward my prize, or else I'll find myself being crushed in the dirt of this dying realm, pounded to death and forgotten.

We walk in strained silence until we see a break ahead and a glimpse of the sky. "What about there?" I point. "We could stay for the night."

Following my finger, Jadon nods. "That might work." He sets off again.

"Just a little while longer," I say to Veril, who limps beside me, leaning heavily on his staff. I swallow, but my mouth remains dry as I dread what I'm about to say. "I'm thinking—"

"That maybe I should stay in Caburh a little longer," Veril says. "You're thinking I should stay there to recover, to enjoy sleeping in a real bed. Then, once you complete your business in Weeton and then Mount Devour…"

"I'll come pick you up and we return to your cottage," I say.

He nods, pleased. "I would've remained by your side until we reached the very ends of the realm. And I would've been the envy of all the others at the next convocation."

"You'll *still* have a story to tell," I say, squeezing his shoulder. "What Renrian can say that a goddess nearly died in their cottage? And not just any goddess. *The* Lady of the Verdant Realm. You're already legendary, Veril Bairnell the Sapient. You've done so much for me. I can't wait to return and give you the knees of a fifty-year-old man."

He throws his head back and laughs. "Wouldn't that be a hoot."

Just get us there. Let us reach Caburh.

That is my prayer.

And I hope someone is listening.

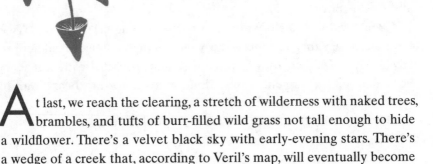

45

At last, we reach the clearing, a stretch of wilderness with naked trees, brambles, and tufts of burr-filled wild grass not tall enough to hide a wildflower. There's a velvet black sky with early-evening stars. There's a wedge of a creek that, according to Veril's map, will eventually become the Duskmoor River. At the edge of the meadow is a sheer rise with an overhang.

I point toward it. "Think that's enough protection for now?"

"Should be," Jadon says.

Philia says, "I agree."

Veril just nods, flagging from his sore knees.

The outcrop is tall enough for us to stand beneath and long enough for us to sleep while still remaining hidden from sight, protected from overnight mist and early-morning dew, and more than that, prowling creatures, otherworldly or not. There is a cavern behind the overhang, yawning deep into the earth, but nothing stirs as we approach.

It doesn't take long for Philia to start a fire. Jadon slices ham from his pack and uses twigs as skewers. Once she's finished with the fire, Philia stands before me, wide-eyed, wringing her hands, her cheeks pink, her green eyes bright.

"Yes, Philia?" I ask.

She curtsies and dips her head. "You should pick a spot before I do, Lady."

I shrug off my cloak. "Philia—"

"My mother," she says, clasping her hands to her chest, "when she was a girl, she prayed to you. You kept her family fed and wealthy."

Philia's attention fills me with heat, and it stimulates my core with a strange power I've not felt before. I dip my head as thanks. "I appreciate your kind words, Philia. I'm glad that I helped your kin thrive."

"Mother said that all was well…" Her excitement sinks into sorrow. "Until she married my father. He told her that you were a false god."

I place my hand atop Philia's wild curls. "You're a brave young woman. Once all of this is over? You'll enjoy a long life with wealth that comes from ingenuity and strength, and an ever-burning hearth, and the prettiest girl in Vallendor holding your hand."

She jams her lips together, trying not to cry.

I point to her bedroll and satchels. "You got this?"

She nods and goes back to arranging our sleeping area.

I turn back to my bags to see Jadon watching me, his eyes soft and unreadable.

"Yes?" I ask him, the heat in my cheeks rising.

"Nothing." He shakes his head, pushing back whatever emotion had dared to peek out from behind the door. "Let's get Veril settled."

Together, Jadon and I help the Renrian toddle over to a soft patch of grass. Jadon's fingers brush mine as we brace Veril from both sides. His touch feels like small bolts of lightning striking my hand, and as we set Veril down, that *zap* dies before its energy zigzags to my knees.

Despite our squabbles and declarations, my body still reacts to him. Despite everything, his touch still slows the bedlam fighting its way into my heart.

Once we finish with Veril, I wobble to the creek, queasy, tired, and hungry, my cheek still smarting from the aburan's swipe. I have brought a bar of lemon-mint soap and the bottle of lavender oil that Veril gave me before my proper bath in his giant tub. I quickly undress.

The water is cold but clean and clear, so clear it may not even exist. Just pebbles and little fish that appear to dart through air. I wet my hair, appreciating the cold water pinching my scalp. After quickly washing my hair, I drag my fingers through my curls to divide my locks to make two braids. I sway as my fingers work, and I lean against a boulder to keep myself upright. I must be more exhausted than I thought.

After dressing, I join my companions and sit as close to the warmth as possible, storing the heat and the memory of fire for those coming days we may be without either.

Veril has prepared a small pot of lentils and leeks and has set it atop the fire.

Jadon skewers more ham chunks and places them over the flames. His hair is damp, clearly from his own creek-bath, and his cowlicks swirl like whipped cream across his scalp. He and I lock eyes across the fire.

"Thank you, Jadon," I say. "For your help back there with the aburan.

You didn't have to do that. You could've let me become…Kai nuggets."

With a soft smile, he peers into the flames. "I hear they taste like chicken."

"I go best with a lighter wine," I add.

Philia snickers. "But you can't eat too many. Causes gout."

I pick at the fat around my slice of ham. "*Gout?* I'd like to think I'm more like…chronic heartburn. That's sexier than *gout.*"

My companions laugh. Jadon stretches out his legs, more relaxed than before.

Maybe Jadon was right about us not going further in our…*whatever we are.* Because after we rescue Olivia, he has to take her and Philia back to Pethorp—that is, if Gileon Wake hasn't burned it down—and I'll head to Mount Devour, and who knows what I'll face there. Jadon and I *will* have to separate, which will already be hard. A stronger connection would be distracting, and distractions kill focus. A lack of focus would allow anything and anyone to sneak up on me and end me right where I stood. I stare at the flames licking the bottom of Veril's pot and sigh. Yes, emotional distance will help protect us with our soon-to-be and inevitable physical distance.

I take big bites of my ham sandwich, closing my eyes to savor this meal. The meat tastes sweet and salty, and the warm fat soaks into the hard bread. Two glugs of wine make my cheeks buzz, and long sips of water clear my mind. My muscles ache, but soon food and wine and a lavender tonic from Veril dull that pain.

"We leave at dawn," Jadon says, finishing his meal.

I leave the fire to go lie on the only other patch of grass. My eyes go heavy even as they track a star burning across the sky.

Behind me, Philia tucks our plates away as Veril covers the leftover lentils in the pot. The old man shuffles over to his bedroll and says, "See you at dawn."

Philia climbs into her bedroll and falls asleep before she can say, "Good night."

"May I?" Jadon asks, gesturing to the area next to me.

"Sure." The queasiness returns—I'm nervous and filled with dread because not only could this result in a…*distraction*, it could also end in another disagreement, and I'm too tired to fight, and I'm too tired to even want to hear his thoughts.

Jadon reclines on the grassy patch beside me. Like me, he's wine-wasted and ham-heavy.

Together, we watch the sky in silence.

"I didn't set out to keep you in the dark," I say. "I tried to tell you all I'd learned. But—"

"But I fucked it up." He chuckles.

"You fucked it up, yes." I pull at the clover around me.

"So, what did you learn in the woods?" he asks.

I tell him everything, from Sybel revealing my mother's name and her role in the realms to the possibility that we may all die if I don't do my job: stopping the One and saving Vallendor. "And Sybel told me who I am to the mortals of Maford."

"And Sybel's the Lady of Dawn and Dusk," Jadon says. "I know of her."

"You do?"

He nods. "And she was the woman you saw in the cave?"

"Yes. She tested me, I think, when she appeared in Azzam Cavern—and because I spared the battawhale, I unlocked all this knowledge about my identity. And now that I'm wearing my original outfit, I'm remembering more things."

He faces the sky again. "So that's why you returned upset from the forest. She told you where to find your pendant."

"Not *where*," I clarify. "*How*. And I realized the signs were there all along—and they all pointed to Olivia."

He whispers, "But now that you have your clothes, do you still need to stop in Caburh?"

I turn to him, placing my head on my elbow. "I'm more powerful with my clothes but not as powerful as I should be—as I could be if I had my amulet. Stopping at Caburh for armor will provide me one more layer of protection until I can find it." A cloud obscures the nightstar for a moment, and it's as if the sky has closed her eyes. "Veril isn't doing well, and I'd rather he be where he is safe and can heal."

Jadon watches the sky as the clouds drift clear of the nightstar. "He means a lot to you."

"Yes." I pluck a wildflower from the ground. "More than I imagined."

His head tilts toward me, but not enough to meet my eyes.

Sadness weighs down my head, and I lie back with my face to the dark sky.

"I'm glad you met him," Jadon says. "I'm glad you found someone you could trust."

"How do you know about the Lady of Dawn and Dusk?" I ask.

He smiles. "Take a guess."

I say, "Old Myrtle. So, did she truly exist or…?"

"She existed, and she did live in a hut outside of town. I was told to stay away from her, which, of course, only made me want to meet her." He pushes out a breath. "We'll find your amulet, Kai. And once we have Veril in a safe place, we'll be able to focus. Travel without having to stop too many times. You'll get to Mount Devour even if I have to swim across its sea carrying you on my back. I'll probably collapse and die, but then, with your pendant, you can bring me back to life. Please bring me back."

I smile. "I'll bring you back as something cool, like a cow or a—"

"A *cow*?" he says, incredulous.

"What?" I say, grinning. "I like cows."

"How about a mountain lion or an eagle? I'd even take a badger over a cow."

I tilt my head in his direction. "If you continue fucking up, then you'll become a turkey."

He tilts his head in my direction. "Guess I won't be fucking up again."

We smile at each other before looking back at the sky.

The fire crackles behind us. Veril is snoring. Philia, too. Jadon and I should be sleeping, but I don't want to leave this spot. I don't want to abandon this peace.

"I know your prayer," Jadon says. *"Oh, gentle Lady, Guardian of the Verdant Realm. Hear the humble plea of Thy devoted servant seeking the grace of Your divine touch."*

When he doesn't go any further, I say, "There's more."

"Divine touch," he says, smiling some. "I like that."

"There's 'divine favor' in there, too, you know."

"Yeah." He rests his head on his hand.

"Are you planning to finish the prayer?" I ask, eyebrow cocked.

"Mmm…*no*." He squints into the sky. "I want to linger a bit at my favorite part, since the gentle Lady is beside me now and I'm just a reach away."

"Is this a request for my divine touch?" I ask. "Does this mean you now believe in me?"

Jadon closes his eyes, but his smile remains. "I'm not allowed to believe in you."

I turn onto my belly and hold my chin in my hand.

"Remember?" he says. "You told me to be the nightstar? 'It slows the realm and allows life to flourish. Be the nightstar.'" And now, his eyes stay fixed on that nightstar.

My heart pounds in my chest. "You still remember what I told you?"

"Even after days of fighting and burnu and searching and dark, dank caves…" He nods. "I think about it at the start of a new day, and I think about it before I close my eyes to sleep."

A hot flush sweeps from my chin to my scalp as I watch him a moment more. Like I'm trying to memorize his face. Once I'm satisfied, I lie back to peer at the sky again.

So tranquil here, right now. There's room for my thoughts to become beautiful lace—a silken web strong enough to hold all my contemplations for at least a day before the winds rip it apart. I turn my head to Jadon and study his face.

Is he experiencing the same smeary peace? Here we are, under a sky thick with worlds, a sky as wide as all the seas. Spears of wispy clouds drift from the hills, and wildflowers across the field sway in the breeze.

I use one finger to pluck flowers from the earth without touching anything, and with just a thought, I arrange those flowers into a circle and make them twirl slowly in midair. The nightstar douses the petals in soft, pearly light.

Jadon whispers, "What a trick."

Smiling, I watch the flowers spin and twist.

"I meant it when I said I'd swim the Sea of Devour," he says.

"And I appreciate your willingness to help me," I say, "but you need to take the girls back to Pethorp."

Jadon grimaces. "But that means, then…you'll be alone."

I shrug. "And I'll be able to handle it."

"Goddess or not," he says, eyebrows crumpling, alarm now in his tone, "you shouldn't travel by yourself. For protection but also companionship. That's a long distance to be alone." His thoughts are scrambling. *"So stubborn. Don't let her win. Say it again. Tell her again."*

I lightly swipe a wildflower back and forth beneath my nose. "Who's gonna join me, then? *You* can't. You'll have to take care of Olivia once we reach Weeton."

He watches the twirling wildflowers. "Unless… What if we go to Weeton as planned? And instead of the girls and me heading to Pethorp, we travel with you to Mount Devour?"

I rub my chin against my knuckles, thinking. "While I'm eager to have your company, it's dangerous. Not for you. Maybe not even for Philia. Olivia, though? She isn't cut out for crossing a sea that's more acid than water. And by then, I'll have my amulet. That, combined with my clothes... I should be all right. I'm a *goddess*, or did you forget?" I let the flowers suspended in midair flutter to the grass around us.

He twists his lips, not convinced. "Mmm."

"Look at this." I shift so he can see some of the symbols embroidered on my vest. "See these markings?" I lean closer to him and whisper, "Shh. They're magic. They'll protect me."

He squints at my vest and then my pants. "Really? I don't know about that."

I fake-gasp. "You doubt the talents of the immortal tailors who crafted this very garment?"

"Mmhmm." He jams his lips together to keep from laughing.

"Eagles and circles." I tap the collar of my vest and trace the barely there embroidery. "Means perfection and spirit."

He says, "Hmm. And these?" He traces the elk on my hip.

My skin warms at his touch. "Power. Nobility. Passion."

"Passion," he says. "And this?" He traces the snowflake-shaped symbol on my ass. "There are a lot of these." He taps one, then another and another, and my body turns molten like the ore in his forge.

"More protection," I say, my back arching more and more with each touch.

His face blooms with fascination. "Protection?" He lifts his eyebrows. "From?"

I say nothing—speaking requires breathing, and I don't want to lose this heady sensation... Drunk and dizzy, warm and breathless, achy and disoriented. This feeling would be sickness if I wasn't feeling so...*alive.*

Jadon slides his fingers from my ass to my thigh, to my hip, up my side, my neck, and shoulders until he reaches my cheek, the one injured by the otherworldly.

I'm growing faint, and now I release that breath. "How does my cut look?"

"Like it's healing." He meets my eyes. "But you remain flawless." He traces my bottom lip with a finger, and his touch makes my skin tingle and pop.

"I thought we weren't doing this," I say, my mouth parting just a bit to trap his finger.

He shakes his head. "I don't remember saying that." He leans in closer. "No?" I say, and then his lips are on mine.

My mind explodes, and my lips part under his. Our tongues tangle and dance as his hand explores my ass. I trail my fingers down…down…to find him hard. So hard. And as he deepens the kiss, I can't help but hear his mind scramble— *"I'll hurt you, I want you, I can't, I have to, what if I hurt you"* —even as our kisses grow firm and more confident, even as my hand encircles him and his breath quickens… *"I'll hurt you I can't stop I can't lose you I can't lose you fuck—"*

A loud crack of thunder.

What the…?

46

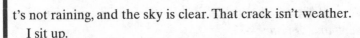

t's not raining, and the sky is clear. That crack isn't weather.

I sit up.

Jadon is already on his feet, searching the sky. Before us, one wave after another of distorted air whooshes across the now-scorched earth.

There's a *thing* above us, a badly drawn caricature of a vulture—like a child's drawing—hovering over us with haphazard feathers, a mottled bald head, and a cowl with red, black, and brown feathers that crackle with bright-white lightning bolts that create thunder the moment a bolt hits the ground.

I know this bird. *A gerammoc!* A predator and a scavenger.

A bolt of lightning and a *boom*, and the gerammoc swoops to the ground and rolls back up to the sky with something in its claws… Waving arms. Faraway shrieks.

A soldier?

The gerammoc disappears into the sky, stopping only to drop that soldier into its hidden aerie, where it will peck and shock the man, who will suffer a slow, agonizing decline from wounds festering with worms and decayed flesh… Mercifully, days from now, the gerammoc will gobble the barely living soldier.

"We need to hurry," Jadon says, offering his hand.

He helps me to my feet, and as I stand, the gerammoc returns, its luminescent eyes like bright-white lamps lighting the land below. The creature doesn't caw or shriek, no. It sizzles. *And those crackling wings!* They would span the length of Jadon, Veril, and me if we stood on one another's shoulders, and then added the lengths of this nook and the creek, too. One tail feather would cover my arm. A farmer could build a chicken coop on that boulder of a head.

Where did it come from? Where does it roost? Is this overhang one of its nesting places?

"Wake them up," Jadon whispers, eyes on the sky.

I crawl over to sleeping Philia and shake her while keeping my gaze on the gerammoc. I shake Veril, who instantly wakes and gawks at what he sees crowding the sky.

Light from the creature's beaming eyes falls upon rocks and trails and trees. The gerammoc banks left, and the creature focuses elsewhere. Darkness falls over us again.

"Put out the fire," I whisper.

Philia and Veril dump water and dirt on the fire to snuff out the flames.

"What does it do?" Philia asks.

"Makes you beg Supreme and all the gods for death," I say.

We watch the dark sky, not daring to breathe, hoping that flying death won't return.

Flaming arrows streak from the ground up to the sky, altogether missing the terrible bird.

"Hunters?" Veril asks.

Philia shakes her head. "I don't know a hunter with arrows like *that*."

"No," I say, "it looks like Wake's soldiers. He's already snatched one."

A flash of light is followed by the crack of a massive bullwhip. The gerammoc pivots in our direction. The sizzle intensifies, and the flashing bright-white light from its eyes brightens. The fiery arrows miss their mark and fall back to earth, causing small fires to spark across the plain. The creature speeds toward us as more fiery arrows light the sky.

We move farther back beneath the overhang, where the air chills and ripens with smells of rot and musk. Like grapes and barley fermenting in some creature's belly—a creature that is now growling somewhere deep in the cave behind us. The sound rises from the deepest, darkest part of the cavern and vibrates from my feet up to my neck and across my cheeks. My nerves spiral beneath my skin.

Why couldn't a cavern be empty this *one* fucking time?

"Help Veril cross the field," I tell Jadon. "Philia, you follow. I'll take the rear and fight."

The cave creature is close enough for me to see its glow, all blue and... *amber*, like that of a man whose heart still beats...*barely*.

Outside the cave, the gerammoc swoops over the hills.

We race to the light of the cavern's opening.

Veril trips.

Out of the dark, the creature's long, hairy arm swipes at the old man's leg.

I hurl wind at the beast, but not before the creature's claw drags across Veril's calf.

The old man shrieks, his cry high and never-ending. Blood sprays from the new wound and darkens the fetid ground.

"No!" I throw another ball of wind to knock the creature back even more.

"I got him," Jadon shouts, draping the old man's arm around his neck.

"Go!" I scream.

Jadon races from the cave with the injured Renrian in his arms and Philia at his heels.

I run behind my group, my hands burning as hot as the lightning racing along the gerammoc's wings. I look over my shoulder, but I don't stop. My feet move like the wind, and my breath burns hot in my chest, pulse thrumming as I dash from the cave.

We burst out onto the open field.

The creature lunges from the cavern. He is confusion manifest, his brown coat shaggy, his talons as thick as a dragon's. And that face... *Gilgoni!*

I freeze, incapable of looking away as all feeling drains from my hands and feet, face, and gut. I snap out of my stall and throw my hands at him.

Gilgoni wheels back, hitting the cave wall, courtesy of my crackling blue wind.

The flying gerammoc races over the plain, its incandescent eyes tracking us, that light so bright now that I can't see my hands before my face. The aburan, Gilgoni, waggles his head, then roars, sprinting toward us. He grabs rocks with his strong hands and hurls them at us.

I throw my hands and the air crackles blue, my power sending those rocks the gerammoc's way. My fingers buzz as though they're scraping the crags of these boulders now soaring up...up...up to strike the gerammoc. But only one rock hits its wing, the impact producing an arc of flying sparks. That's enough to make it mad.

"Hurry!" I urge those ahead of me.

Jadon's breathing is labored as he carries Veril across the field. Behind them, Philia trips on a gopher hole. She hits the ground with an "oof" but rallies, pushes to her feet, and limps on her twisted ankle to catch up. I follow, while behind us, the aburan continues to throw rocks. I swoop my fingers, blue bolts now chasing the wind, and the wind propels the rocks into the flying otherworldly.

Eventually, the gerammoc spots the giant aburan, then darts down like an arrow with sharp talons and feathers that crackle and click.

Gilgoni roars, then springs from the ground into the air. He barely misses the gerammoc.

The bird shoots a bolt of lightning. At a full sprint, I don't look back to see it strike the aburan, but I smell the stench of burning fur and hear the anguished cry of a beast struck with crackling death. After one last circle, the gerammoc rises into the sky and disappears behind the clouds drifting below the nightstar.

We finally reach a copse of tall spruces. The forest offers protection, but all these trees... They look the same. I don't know where we are. That tree with broken branches looks just like *that* tree with broken branches. That tree is just as tall as the other. Nothing makes one stand out from the other, but at least we are relatively sheltered here.

Jadon settles Veril onto a log and gawks at the bloodied hem of his trousers. Blood pools in the dirt beneath the Renrian's foot. He is panting, and his eyes are glazed. His quivering lips move as he mutters, "Blighted grounds...tender...space...part...part..."

Jadon and I exchange looks, and his blue eyes are wide with alarm. I don't think he's aware that he's shaking his head over and over again. His thoughts careen and crash into each other. *"Too much blood. This isn't good. Too much blood. Fuck. Why? Too much blood."*

"We'll die if we stop moving," Jadon says, holding my gaze for a moment more before looking back at Veril. "We need to go."

I bend over to peer at Veril's violent laceration. The blood is clotting, but he's lost so much already. "I'll tend to his wound, fix what I can." I peer up to Jadon, whose eyes are bright with heartache. I try to smile. "Go. We'll catch up. Don't stop. I won't."

Jadon sighs, bends before Veril, setting a hand on his shoulder. He opens his mouth to say something, but he swallows it and stands. He nods to Philia, who picks up her satchel and pushes to her feet. "You got him, Kai?"

I nod, not wanting to meet his mournful gaze, or Philia's mournful gaze, or Veril's bloody trousers. There's no resting place for my eyes. "Yep. I got him."

"Kai," Jadon says again.

I frown and my eyebrows crumple as our eyes meet.

He mouths, "It's okay."

My nostrils flare, and my throat burns.

"Don't stay too long." Then he's off, Philia limping behind.

I smile back at Veril. "A little interruption."

"Really? I didn't notice." The old man's eyes have lost some of their earlier gloss, and now he strokes his beard with a bloodstained hand.

I roll up his soiled pants leg again and wince. "Okay. So." I rummage around Veril's bag, finding a canteen of clean water, gauze, and a tin of mystery paste. "I'll do as much as I can, okay? When we get to our campsite, I'll dress it better."

The old man's eyes focus on me. "Campsite?" he asks.

"Yes," I say. "First things first." I pour cool water onto the wound, and blood-tinged runoff soaks his boot. I open the tin and sniff. Smells like cropleek and elk hair. Binder. Anti-nausea. I slather the dressing over the wound, packing in as much as possible.

"How?" he asks. "How?"

I wrap clean gauze around his leg. "I'm gonna carry you."

That sobers him a bit. "Our packs and our weapons *and* me?" Veril shakes his head. "If you were at your peak maybe—" Unsteady and faint, his eyes gloss over again.

"Let's not worry about that now," I say, arranging Warruin beside my longsword.

Veril grabs hold of my arm and sways as he stands. "It has been wonderful serving you again." His head droops.

I tie his pack to my pack. *"Again?"*

"Twilight...pain...ethereal," he says, his tongue thick.

My fingers grow numb, and I slowly lift my eyes to meet his shiny lavender ones.

"Hmm?" he says, blinking.

"You served me before?"

He squints at me, confused. "Of course. When you were just a little one, and then, when you stewarded all of Vallendor, keeping watch over the realm from the top of Mount Devour." He gives me an amused grin. "I taught you everything. Languages. Writings and music and alchemy and lore of every race, every discovered realm..." He looks at me, clear-eyed again. "You felt so familiar to me the night you sought refuge in my cabin, and now, I know why."

My mouth hangs open as I remember the night Veril and I ran into each other after the burnu fight. He'd looked at me, wide-eyed, and said,

"You're here." That's what he meant. And now, my mind fills with the vision of the castle, the party, the old man… "I *do* remember."

Veril bows his head. "But we'll catch up later. Are we ready?"

I'm not ready. I stand and then crouch to lift him.

Veril flaps his hand and starts on our way. "I'll walk for as long as I can." He shuffles beside me, quicker than before, his revelation spurring him on. "When we get to Caburh—"

A hiss. A sucking sound. A thump. Veril gasps and whimpers and falls to the ground.

I turn around, alarmed. My heart drops, and I go cold.

Standing behind me are the emperor's men. Sinth, the Dashmala, still holds the long handle of his pike, the pointy end lodged deep into Veril's back.

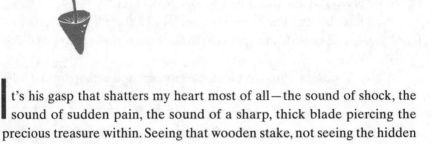

47

I t's his gasp that shatters my heart most of all—the sound of shock, the sound of sudden pain, the sound of a sharp, thick blade piercing the precious treasure within. Seeing that wooden stake, not seeing the hidden tip of that pike, seeing the blood spurt from this newest violation, the proud blood of the Renrian, my counselor, teacher, and friend.

So cruel.

I shout, "Veril," as I sink beside him to the ground.

But it's too late.

That gasp.

The world around me fractures, and hot tears spill from my eyes, scalding my cheeks.

Veril lies still.

How did the emperor's men find us?

I turn to face the soldiers. They huddle behind the Dashmala, gaping mouths, eyes wide with shock. That is, until they realize that there are more of them than there are of me. Math makes them brave, and now, they move from behind Sinth to draw their swords. One soldier withdraws an arrow from his quiver and raises his bow.

Sinth shouts, "Hold," to the men behind him. Then he points to the man at my feet and shouts, "He murdered my kin."

"You do this for something that happened a hundred years ago?" I shout, my hands burning bright white.

The giant Dashmala sneers at me, and his mouth lifts in a humorless smile. "I've never been so happy to see a gerammoc terrorizing the night sky. I would've fired thousands of arrows and swung my sword hundreds of times, fought countless aburans if that meant I got to see this murderer carried across the meadow."

The fiery arrows launched at the gerammoc—those bolts *were* shot by soldiers. If Sinth and his men followed the gerammoc to shoot it down, they would've seen Jadon, Philia, Veril, and me running away from both monsters.

Sinth reaches for the sword in his scabbard and points it at me. "You—" His yellow eyes peek at me—from my hair to my chest and legs—and come to rest on my face. "We share a heritage, and yet you're traveling with the murderer who sent our forefathers into the fiery chasms of Riddy Vale?"

The Dashmala—who, to this day, hate me. That's what Veril told me. *That chasm appeared due to a simple spell and the tilt of my head.* That's what he said.

"There *was* no fiery chasm at that battle," I shout at him. "Only frightened women, children, and old people hiding behind an illusion, praying that Veril's enchantment would hold and that the Dashmala who'd come to kill them would see nothing but that illusion and retreat."

I step away from my friend on feet I can no longer feel, focusing now on the man responsible for his death. "You are Dashmala," I growl, "and yet you fight for an emperor who forces you to believe in him?" Blue currents sizzle behind my lids—I see my anger before it even reaches my eyes. "These men consider you an outsider, a scourge, a barbarian turned eunuch, and if I don't kill you, then eventually they will."

Sinth laughs. "I am commander of Ser Wake's battalions. They will do as I command." His yellow eyes darken into bloodred globes. "Killing you, the one who murders our brothers-in-arms. Killing those who've betrayed him, including the whore who betrayed our future king. That's what I've been sent to do, and I will do it."

One soldier shouts, "She's the one who killed my brother back in Maford."

I don't know which man made this accusation because my attention rests on Sinth.

The woods glow with the amber of more soldiers riding our way on horses glowing blue. The spines of the men standing around me straighten even more, and their thoughts bang around my head like swords hitting shields.

Sinth, the one with the pike, the one who killed my friend—I will save him for last.

An arrow speeds past my ear, so close that its feathered fletching brushes my cheek. The archer is already pulling a second arrow from his quiver as the soldiers with the swords rush toward me, their faces contorted with excited anger. The newcomers don't dismount from their horses. They all race to surround me, their thoughts not all that different from their comrades'.

"Who killed the Renrian?"

"I'll take his purple eyes."

A scream rips from my depths and surges through my veins.

The horses, knowing something's wrong, that I'm not to be harmed, buck and rear back and wag their heads. Some men fall off their mounts. Some men are bitten by their horses. Riderless horses bolt past me, their hooves thundering against the earth, racing in the same direction that Jadon and Philia took. The horses are smart to run.

The soldiers before me, though, are too ignorant to understand. They race to join their fellow soldiers on foot, swords ready, their yells and threats as loud as the hoofbeats of their retreating horses.

But their noise is muted by my crackling fury.

I lift my hands, and fire flickers across the fingertips of my gloves. I don't pause long enough to appreciate this new ability—flames. I will later. For now, I'm ready to fight.

Another arrow speeds my way but misses, still managing, though, to brush my arm. I scream again, and instead of throwing wind, I throw fiery balls, one after another after another, balls of flame that evaporate soldiers running toward me, that evaporate every soldier circling me, that soldier, that soldier, some soldiers catch fire, and then all of them catch fire and they scream but fuck their screams. I hurl more fire at that soldier and that soldier, all of them now a wall of flames…except for the Dashmala called Sinth, the commander of dead men who cannot call him anything.

I march toward the Dashmala, pulling the long-handled pike from Veril's back without stopping in my step.

Sinth lifts his massive sword and runs at me.

I stand still.

He is huge.

So what? I'm huge, too. And I'm not moving from this spot. Let him come to me.

He scowls and shouts as he swings at me. And misses.

I kick him backward, but he doesn't go far. I still don't leave my spot.

The giant rushes at me again and swings a second time.

I duck and grab his fighting arm, knocking the sword from his hand. I try to turn his palm in its opposite direction, but his wrist, protected by a gauntlet, is too thick to clench.

He swipes his free hand and strikes the right side of my face.

My feet leave the ground as I fly back and hit a petrified tree. I shake my head, seeing only pinpoints of light. I scramble to stand, and my knees wobble. Something wet and warm and too thick to be sweat drips from my earlobe and slides down the side of my neck.

The Dashmala grabs his sword from the dirt and stalks in my direction. He growls, "Burn me, bitch—"

I whip my hand.

Wind, not fire, knocks him onto his back.

I grab the pike and rush over to him.

Sinth lifts his head and shoulders up from the dirt, using his elbows to support his bulk. He glares at me from the bloody, ash-choked dirt and spits.

The globule of phlegm hits the center of the armor that belonged to Veril.

Sinth is making his eventual death altogether worse.

I kick the Dashmala's shoulder.

His back is against the earth again.

I stand over him and set my foot on top of his armored chest. I lift the pike he used to kill Veril.

Sinth's bloodred eyes, so shiny with hate and pride, watch me, as he prepares for a quick and valiant death that his people will write songs about.

No. I refuse to bless him with immediacy. He deserves something less. I drive the pike into his mouth, stopping at the back of his tongue.

I take a step back and another step back, and another, and then I hurl fireball after fireball at the dying Dashmala. They will never find his bones, they will never know he stood here and fought me, they will not write songs about him, and if they do, I will silence those songs forever.

And I'm shaking, and I'm shaking.

48

S omeone's shouting. So far away. Shouting.

And I'm shaking, and I blink—

The sky is dark, but this black smoke is darker as it reels off the flames.

Jadon fills my vision, tears bright in his eyes. "What did you do? Wake up, Kai!"

My breath feels overgrown and rough in my chest. Is Veril alive? Is this all a dream? My eyes skip across the clearing now consumed with flames, past the burning trees, only stopping...

Veril.

I crawl over to my friend, my eyes wet and wild, and shout, "No," but I'm so hoarse, nothing but harsh air comes out. "No!"

Philia wraps her arms around me.

I shove her away and pull the old man into my arms. His blood seeps from his back and mouth, and I hold him to my chest and force every part of my body to abandon me and to fill him. And I know this is futile, that he is gone from this realm. I don't scream; I weep. All of me shudders with pain and grief and loss and anger and—

Philia's behind me again. Her anguish tugs at me.

Jadon hides his sooty face in his hands.

The fire roars as the battalion of soldiers, the emperor's men, turns into nothing.

My flame does not fuck around. And my tears and hope do not bring Veril back to me.

The Renrian's face...the enchantment released...wrinkles and crevices and dark spots and scars and wisdom, so much wisdom.

They stole him from Vallendor. They stole him from me, this man I've known all my life, the one who taught me Renrian as a child...

Emperor Wake—he and his empire will meet my flame, too. That is my vow.

We stay there, Jadon, Philia, and me, breathing, one of us nevermore.

The fire continues to die, the roar slipping into crackles and pops.

"What happened?" Jadon's voice is weary.

I take a breath and slowly lay the old man back down by my knees. "We were behind you." My voice sounds smoky and deep. "We were talking, and then he gasped. Such an awful sound. There he was, behind us, the Dashmala."

"Sinth?" Jadon whispers.

I nod. "He used a pike."

"And then?" Jadon asks, his voice growing anxious.

I lift a hand and wave it across the charred landscape.

Jadon scans the ruined earth with jumpy eyes. "Did you hit every soldier?"

I look at him with great intention. "That is my hope."

There's something in his eyes, beyond the sadness of Veril's end. Anxiety and flickers of anger…but not at these piles of murdering fuckers.

"Are you about to tell me that I shouldn't have?" My voice is so solid, it could hold the realm. "That I should've waited for you to act? That I let my anger take over?"

Jadon scowls. "I'm trying to determine if the emperor's son is now a pile of ashes."

I stare out at the flames. The ashes of soldiers look no different than the ashes of trees and brush. "I wish you luck in your determinations."

Jadon shakes his head as he stares at the damage. With a ragged breath, he pushes to his feet and strikes out to search the wreckage for signs of Gileon Wake.

I turn to Philia. Her back shakes as she cries, her face hidden behind her hands.

"Philia," I say softly.

She looks at me, her face as red as the embers. She opens her mouth to speak, but she can't catch her breath between sobs.

I hold out my arm. "Come here."

She crawls over to me, and I wrap my arm around her. She touches Veril's cheek—*it's true*—and she weeps into my shoulder.

As I hold her, Jadon paces the burned landscape. He frowns, then clasps his hands over his head. He looks back at me as though I'm a stranger, then he turns away and drops his head.

She will bring each of you death. Yes. Elyn's right—and every one of these soldiers, especially Sinth, deserved every agonizing moment.

My body feels swollen, too big for my bones. My fingertips feel seared and tender from killing all these men scattered around me.

And Veril… He'd still be alive if I hadn't asked him to join me on this journey. He'd still be alive if I hadn't shown up at his cottage, a bloody wreck needing to be healed. He'd still be alive if Jadon and I had killed those burnu and hadn't needed Veril and Warruin to complete the job. He'd still be alive if we hadn't raced away from Maford, a village that burned down only because Elyn was looking for me there. He'd still be alive if Olivia hadn't stolen my amulet. He'd still be alive if I hadn't betrayed my family and if I hadn't destroyed Chesterby, if I'd stopped to think without reacting. Without choosing violence.

Veril is dead because Sinth killed him.

Veril is dead because I'd already failed him.

We bury Veril as the fire wanes. The land still simmers, the heat still pushes at my face. The embers serve as a barrier to any creature that intends us harm.

Philia has found a nice spot for the old man's body. "And I have my small spade," she says. "It may take a while to dig, but it's better than nothing."

We bury Veril beneath a cinnamon tree. According to Veril, cinnamon symbolizes abundance and protection. Cinnamon heals. The Renrian provided all of those things.

Philia and I remain silent as Jadon slides the spade into the dirt. I say nothing as I anoint the old man with aromatic oils I found in his satchel. Rosemary, so that we remember. Cistus, for those who grieve. Yarrow to purify this space. Together, the three of us wrap the Renrian in his cape — the lavender one stenciled with butterflies, ravens, and dragonflies.

And then it comes — an ancient lamentation swelling from the depths of my soul. A melody that I must have learned, possibly from Veril, and kept in my heart. My voice quavers at first but soon grows stronger, the haunting notes mingling with the rustle of the leaves above and the crackle of embers of a ground that will never feel cold again.

Jadon marks the grave with a black jet stone, one of the stolen gems we found in Olivia's bag, and whispers, "Goodbye, Veril Bairnell the Sapient." He touches the grave once more, then stands and drifts away.

Philia whispers one last prayer that I can't hear, then follows Jadon.

And now, I am left alone, not sure of what to say. And so, I say nothing.

The sky above us shifts from blue to an ominous purple. Another falcon flies closer to the trees in the weak light. But the still-billowing smoke hides us.

I select the most perfect crabapple from the few left and place it beside the jet stone.

I wairr eyalra irruis naedh, nirr llasialn.

Yes, I will. Until everyone responsible for this day is dead, and until the gift of fire has been taken from me.

"We're still heading to Caburh," I say, reaching for my satchel.

"Will the innkeeper talk with us?" Philia asks. "What if Separi thinks *we* killed Veril?"

"The Lady of the Verdant Realm would do no such thing, Philia." Jadon snorts as he rearranges items in his pack.

I know he's joking, but his sarcastic tone pricks at me. "The Lady says, 'Fuck you, Jadon Ealdrehrt, whose fake sister is the reason we're here in the first place.' You know so much, maybe you should've taught Olivia to keep her hands—"

"Kai?" Philia whispers. "Your eyes."

They're burning holes into Jadon's.

"What do you want me to do, Kai?" Jadon's fists ball at his sides. "We're here now, and I'm sorry, okay? Yes, she stole from you. Yes, if she hadn't, Veril would still be alive, and maybe you'd be in a better place than where you are right now."

He crouches and hides his face behind his hands. Then, with both hands, he tugs his hair. His face so weary, his eyes so soft and filled with pain. "I'm sorry for shouting, and the last thing I want right now is for you to be pissed at me. I know—this situation is just...just..." He shakes his head and looks up to the sky. He closes his eyes and pulls in a deep breath. Then he drops his head and pushes that air to the ground.

He touches Veril's satchel set between us. "I can't do anything with 'shouldn't have.' Only 'should,' and we should head to Caburh. We should still find Separi and plead with her for help and maybe, just maybe, something will fall in our favor. Okay?" His eyes search mine, and he whispers, "I'm so sorry."

My tears make him blurry, and I can manage to say only, "Mmhmm," before opening Veril's satchel.

Vials of tonics. Small pots. The mortar and pestle. Bread, ham, and cheese. Dried lentils and leeks. Honeycakes. Crabapples. Rum. Map. Dried plants. A small, jeweled dagger. A leather-bound journal and glass pot filled with black ink. A small quill pen. Soap. Fife.

Philia wants the dagger, and Jadon, the fife.

I claim everything else, along with Warruin and the fox amulet that had hung around his neck. Will either work for me, or is their magic tied solely to their wielder, now buried beneath a cinnamon tree? If I wear it, will the amulet hurt me, since it isn't mine, even if I didn't steal it? I wrap it around my left gloved hand, with the fox pendant snug beneath my middle knuckle.

I tend to Philia's injured ankle as I take in our surroundings—stunted trees and wild grass, crags and roots creeping across vine—choked earth and gritty sand. I don't need to study a map because I can feel that tug in my gut, that satin string pulling me in the direction we'd planned to take. Toward Caburh.

A silvery-blue moth lands on the fox pendant beneath my knuckles and stays there, not flapping her wings, just sitting there like she's staring at me. *"Come, Lady."* She's real.

I whisper, "Okay," relieved that I haven't lost my ability to hear her voice.

I hope that I'll gain some of the attributes of Veril's fox—intelligence, cunning and agility. I'll need each power to survive whatever—*or whoever*—comes at me next.

49

B lack smoke rolling from the fires covers the daystar, and if there wasn't the glow of orange embers, we wouldn't know earth from sky. We walk quickly, Philia leading us, pink-skinned and tight-mouthed, her fists gripping the shoulder straps of her satchel.

Jadon walks to my left, his eyes tired, his face marked with scratches and bruises. "You're making this worse for us," he whispers. "They were just doing their jobs, following their commander. He ordered them to turn around, so they did."

"I don't know where you're from," I snap, "but even the glued-together fragmented memory of wherever the fuck I'm from tells me that we don't kill Renrians."

Eyes wide, Jadon says, "So you *kill* the emperor's *son*?"

"Is there any evidence that I did?" I ask, incredulous.

Jadon's eyes narrow. "No. You burned everything down, and then you burned it again."

And I'd go back to do it again, but I have no time or desire to move backward, not when there is a colorful string tugging at me, not when there's a moth fluttering around my head every now and then, telling me, *"Come, Lady."*

Every time that happens, Jadon sees me nod to the moth and whisper, "Thank you." A few times, our eyes meet, and even though he's angry with me, his open demeanor suggests he believes that I'm communicating with something, that we're not walking aimlessly around Vallendor, that Olivia just may be at the end of this tugging and these moth-guides.

Nothing stands out in the world around us. Brown. Dry. Dead. Old bird nests, toppled and caught in between branches. Gopher holes pock the dirt road, no gopher's head poking from them. The sky is the color of foamy dirt, and on the side of the road, boulders the same —

A raven.

My skin chills as the death bird's obsidian eyes fix on me with an unsettling intelligence. The wind carries a whisper, a faint echo of foreboding that sends shivers down my spine. Anxiety knots in my stomach.

Is this the raven that warned me at the entrance of Caerno Woods?

This raven caws, his cry echoing through the stillness of the forest. *"Prepare, Lady. I see death. Close."*

This is not the same raven.

"Is there danger ahead?" I ask.

"Always." The raven jumps from the boulder and hops along the road in my direction, his beady eyes fixed on me. *"There is only death here."*

"For which one of us?" My pulse races. I've already lost Veril. Losing another one of my companions—my friends—would destroy me.

"Him. In the end."

My mouth dries, and my eyebrows crumple. *"The end of what? This road? This trip?"*

The raven spreads his wings and takes flight.

I track the bird until he disappears into the night sky.

Jadon says, "What's wrong?" He looks to the sky, too, but the raven is long gone.

"Be on guard," I say.

Philia says, "Okay."

Jadon narrows his eyes. "Aren't I always?"

I swallow, flick my gaze at the sky again. I can't tell him what the raven said. I find it difficult to believe it myself. I turn back to the road and lose myself in thoughts, trying, though, not to think of the raven's warning, but to force my mind to rest, force the dull thuds to ease.

Pushing past the food and tonics, I search my bag as I walk, finding the leather journal that Veril left behind. The faded black leather is silky soft, the pages between thick and bleached white. Drawings and sketches of birds—including cardinals, ravens, and daxinea. Recipes to treat melancholy and anxiety, sore throats and toothaches. And several pages dedicated to a poem written in his hand.

In a land where stars make pearls,
A heroine awakens; her soul unfurls.
Through realms unknown, her path lies bare,
A future that she cannot share.

There are four separate poems and fifth he'd just started—a single line on its own page:

In the realm where shadows pale,

I trace my fingers over Veril's assured handwriting. Even if this is the last of the stanzas, this elegy must be completed.

I'll do it.

I push my hand through my hair, and my hand comes away with a clump of curls caught between my fingers. I stare at this bundle of dry and loose hair, gulping and shuddering as I let it drift from my hold. My mind stalls, blown out by thinking about all the exertion to come, thinking about what else is dying, not just my hair, but my spine and my heart.

Stop. Don't think about that.

"Hey," Jadon says, walking beside me now.

"Hey." I keep my eyes fixed on the road.

He holds out a small bundle wrapped in cloth. "Here."

"What is it?" I ask, taking the parcel.

"You like honeycakes," he says, "but I like these more."

Philia slows to walk with us, excited to see something besides this dreary landscape.

I unwrap the bundle and press a hand to my cheek in surprise.

Two apricot-cocoa cookies.

"I'd never eaten them until Veril baked them," Jadon says.

I drop my head. "And now you give them to me?"

"We can't move ahead," Jadon says, "if we're angry at each other. The last thing I want right now is you being angry at me."

I'm touched by his gesture. I offer a cookie to Philia.

She stares at the sweet treat before taking a bite. "We need each other," she says, "now more than ever."

Even though uncertainty still churns in my core, I whisper my thanks to Jadon. The cookie is dry, but that dollop of apricot preserves keeps it sweet, keeps it from becoming sand.

While we stop to eat cookies, Philia unrolls the map and slowly turns around to survey the land. She points to the sky over our left shoulders. "The smoke from the fires is there."

A smudge of gray sky.

"Before that…" She moves her finger to the left and stops. "That hill in front of the three hills behind it? That's where we ran from that aburan." She peers at the stretch of flat land between the woods and the base of those hills on the map and mutters to herself and slowly turns to her left and nods. "We're going in the right direction."

Jadon pushes his dark hair from his forehead. "Glad you're good with maps, Phily."

"Me, too, Philia." I keep myself from snorting even though the tug in my core and the moths have already confirmed that we're going in the right direction. If it makes mortals feel better to see with their own eyes so that it's *really real*, then fine, let them.

"If I'd known we'd have to leave Maford so quickly," Philia says, "I would've prepared better and brought my bow and arrow."

"It's a good thing your mother taught you a thing or two about knives," I say. "Girls should know how to put down monsters that walk on two feet and beasts that walk on four."

Jadon's brow furrows. "What are we talking about? Monsters on two feet?"

I squinch my nose. "You had to be there." I smile at Philia. "We'll find you a bow and arrows in Caburh, then."

Pleased, Philia smiles, and her eyes crinkle at the corners.

We head out again, and even though I can't see it in the oppressive darkness, somewhere behind us, black smoke still roils to the sky—the embers from my fire will never be extinguished. Let it serve as a warning: the Lady of the Verdant Realm will not hesitate to mete out punishment for acts of cruelty.

I search the skies for cardinals who serve Elyn. She must've seen that blight in the sky. She has to know what I've done.

I am not who I used to be.

I hope that is a good thing, especially if the old me has turned on my family and friends, especially if the old me *did* bring about death and destruction in the way Elyn has charged.

Yes, I killed Sinth and the soldiers who fought for him, but only after they'd killed Veril. I've yet to start a fight.

Am I not supposed to win? And if I were such an awful person, Sybel wouldn't have sought me out to defeat the One and win the game to save the realm.

Then again, I don't think Elyn wants me to win anything. And really: I don't care what she wants. I want what I want: to protect those who deserve the chance to grow and learn, to believe what they want and not force others to comply or die. I want to save those creatures that were born to order—like the horses, the ravens, and Milo. I want to return creatures who are otherworldly here—the battabies and battawhale—and transport them to the places they belong. I will save Vallendor for each of them.

No, I am not the same since my arrival in Maford.

And whoever I was before coming to Maford...I am not her, either.

50

After what feels like endless days of travel, night comes again. We make our beds atop soft fallen pine needles. Their scent relaxes me. Philia falls asleep quickly, her wild curls tumbling across her face. Jadon remains awake and upright—first watch. His gaze doesn't stop. His jaw stays hard.

I lie on the other side of the fire, eyes on the sky. No shooting stars tonight. The nightstar—where is she right now? The sky is that black.

I shift against the ground, wondering if the pain in my body comes from nights of sleeping in hard, horrid spaces, or if it's my body continuing to weaken without my amulet. In the silent expanse of our days, I've worried about three things: my pendant, my friendship with Jadon, and my body. Every twinge and minor ache tell me I'm dying. Every flare-up in my muscles, anytime my knee wiggles beneath my weight, anytime my tongue pushes at my teeth and I perceive that a tooth is looser than before, confirms that I'm dying. And now, my hair…

"Jadon," I whisper.

Silence… "Umhmm?"

I move my mouth, and the hinges of my jaw creak. No words.

"What's wrong?" he asks.

My pulse is all over the place. I don't want to say *I'm dying* aloud because if I do, it will become a true thing. And what good will telling him do? He can't stop it. Why burden him?

"Hey." He sits beside me. "What's wrong?"

I bite my lip, then send my eyes back to the sky. "My hair… It's falling out." I exhale, finding some relief at having shared the truth.

He stays still, like he's stopped breathing. Then: "I'm sorry."

"There's nothing you can do about it," I say, shaking my head.

"There's nothing more you can do about it, either," he says. "You're doing all you can. Moving ahead and finding your pendant."

"Faster, we need to go faster." That's what he's thinking.

"I wish we could fucking fly to Caburh."

"She'll be okay."

"Relax."

"If you're scared, she'll become more scared than she already is."

He studies my face, then studies my hair. He smiles. "You're probably one of the only people in the world who'd look breathtaking bald."

I snort. "Okay, then."

He grins. "Seriously, you have the face for it. You could pull it off. I'd still follow you around like a lost puppy." He grows serious. "We'll find it. Okay?"

"Yeah."

"Get some rest," he says.

I offer him a small smile, and then I close my eyes.

Tomorrow has to be better.

Right?

The closer we get to Caburh, the more the air stinks, putrid, rancid, like slugs disintegrated in vinegar, like a corpse left in a field. The road is clear of pedestrians, but in the distance, I glimpse a man walking on the edge of the road. Dust puffs with each step, but that dust doesn't dull the man's urgent amber glow. He's dying—that's what his body is saying—and that means he may be desperate or delirious. Neither state is good.

There's something else about this traveler. Something worrisome. Something *predatory.*

As the man gets closer, Jadon sneaks a look at me.

I nod—*I'm ready.*

"Behind us, Phily," he whispers.

She obliges, but I see her readying her mace.

The man's face is as withered as the last potato in a pantry. The twitchy but distant look in his eyes tells me that he sees us but…*doesn't.* His leather tunic is caked with dried blood—human or animal, I can't tell. His matted black hair sticks out from beneath a helmet that looks too small for his head.

None of these things originally belonged to him. And that's a problem.

I can sense the tension in his body, the way his muscles quiver with each breath.

The man smells of death—his own mingled with so many others'. He stares at Philia, the most vulnerable-looking member of our group, and the hairs on my neck stand on end.

I check our surroundings to see if this is a setup and if there are others waiting to ambush us, but there's no place to hide, for us or for them. The reviving land may have patches of green, but there are still more dusty strips of flat land that offer no cover. The bushes may be fuller than the bushes we've passed, but they are still thin and brittle brambles.

The man continues to shuffle in our direction.

And Philia, Jadon, and I continue to walk in his.

There's silence except for the uneven shuffle of the man's boots and the quiet padding of our feet against the dirt trail.

His stench blooms—rancid meat, sweat, and excrement of every creature in Vallendor. A dagger sits in his belt. The blade of the sword on his hip matches the blood beneath his nails. Like everything else, these weapons weren't originally his.

Jadon nods at the stranger as we pass.

I keep my eyes trained on the road ahead. My skin tingles, and my fingers burn—all of me whispers that this wanderer is a threat. I try to hear his thoughts.

Only buzzing.

Strange.

"Just keep walking," Jadon mumbles.

"Okay," Philia says.

"Yep," I say, even though my blood fizzes with worry. *Why can't I hear his thoughts?*

The man's feet scrape the dry earth.

Our feet tap against the dirt path.

My heart pounds, and my hands go hotter. *This isn't right. This—*

I turn to look back at the traveler.

"Where'd he go?" I ask.

Jadon keeps walking. "Doesn't matter. Keep moving."

I walk backward for a spell, eyes scanning the brush and the tufts of dead, high grass.

No shouts. No scuffling. No amber glow of a skulking man.

I turn south again. "I don't like this."

Jadon grunts but says nothing.

I take one last look behind me.

No amber glow or blue glow or any-colored glow gleams from that man.

It's like... *Like he was never there at all.*

How is that possible? Is this some sort of magic? Is he a mage? Another agent of Elyn's?

I look down at the dirt path.

Dead moths, dusty, smashed, and dragged beneath his shuffling feet.

Is there danger ahead?

Always. There is only death here. That's what that second raven told me.

Are we finally headed to that danger?

The gnawing in my stomach answers.

Yes.

Shit.

51

After another full day of walking, Philia spots a town rising from the dusty mist like a vision…or a wraith. Jadon and I trip in our steps, trying to see what she sees, our legs wanting to break from under us, our minds telling us that this is like yesterday when we thought there was a shallow pool *just right there* or that those *were* green spots flashing above the daystar at twilight *just right there.*

The landscape around us, though, continues to shift from dust and dirt to softer dirt, dirt deeper in color, and moist air, patches of green and living vines. Wildflowers replace brambles. Trees grow from twisted dead things to soaring living things holding bird nests and green leaves. And there are blue-breasted robins and shrieking yellow orioles darting in and out of those branches with twigs or worms caught in their beaks.

I want to smile and clap—green means water—but after days of walking, I no longer trust my eyes. I'm telling myself at this moment, right now, that I am not seeing what I've longed to see just a bit farther up the road. I keep blinking, but unlike the shallow pool and the green spots, this image isn't disappearing.

"Is that it?" I ask, my voice shaky. "Is that Caburh?"

"That is Caburh." Philia throws up her hands and twirls like a dancer.

It really *is* just right there.

Caburh is protected by a perimeter of wooden logs stacked taller than five men. Though I can't see past those logs, there's smoke drifting from countless chimneys, and the noise of hammers, and the clucks of chickens, and the shouts of men. Wagons and carts pulled by horses, mules, and oxen carry fruits, vegetables, wool, and fur. Merchants and farmers stand in clumps around the big gate, inspecting and haggling, smoking, and laughing.

"We're not staying here longer than we must," Jadon says. "Let's keep a low profile, get the armor, and get back on the road to Olivia."

"The sooner we find her, the better," Philia says.

"Couldn't agree with you more." My steps quicken. I can't help it—I'm beyond excited and slaphappy after walking the plains of Vallendor. Giddy, I can almost smell the aromas of roasted meat and baked fruit and fresh bread, and I have to stop myself from giggling. There will be soap and honeycakes here—I know it. There will be *soft things*. I don't even care what those things are. *I can take a bath!*

"Let's head straight to the inn," Jadon whispers as we pass through the crowd at the gates. "Let's stay together as much as possible."

"We'll get to eat, right?" Philia asks.

Before Jadon can say, "No," I say, "Yes. We need a moment to breathe, to eat something other than lentils and carrots. I need to reset." The tugging in my stomach remains, but I can no longer distinguish tugging that indicates my amulet is near or tugging telling me that I'm starving and exhausted. I need respite to make the right decisions.

The streets that wind through this town are paved with gray cobblestones as round as turtles' backs. Unlike Maford, more houses and shops have been built from stone than timber. Only a handful of homes and stores still have thatched roofs—most are made from stone or slate.

There aren't many outdoor stands or carts. That space is reserved for rickety benches and weedy gardens. There's space here, though that space is a bit fetid and buzzing with large black flies. The stink of rotting fish makes us gag. It is *wild* to me that Caburh, with its stone, slate, and cobblestones, smells worse than Maford—but then again, more people means more waste from humans, horses, livestock, and rats. I glimpse a river peeking from behind the town. The current is slow, and the water looks brown due to...*everything*.

Like the tanner on the outskirts that stinks of urine and blood.

Like the blacksmith shop belching clouds of black smoke and noise.

"The entire town isn't this rank," Jadon says, apologetic. "There *are* bread shops and florists and... Well... The breeze makes things smell worse than they are."

I laugh. "I'm not *marrying* Caburh, Ealdrehrt. Just coming for the luclite and a roast." I wait a beat. "You've stayed here before?"

"A long time ago," he says.

The complexions of people in this town remind me of apple varieties—from the rich pinks and bright yellow-greens to the deep reds that are almost blue. The women wear light fabrics that breathe, their hair pulled back in ponytails. The men wear embroidered tunics with the hair on their heads and faces in parted tufts.

But even with their wealth and abundance, the coopers and farmers, millers and mothers of this town also glow with death—just softer cornsilk than the urgent amber of Maford. Some of the people here stare at me just as Mafordians, but not because I'm running near-naked through their town. They gape at me because my hair is still too big and my height is still astounding.

Nausea roils my stomach and kills my earlier excitement. What creative names will *these* people hurl at me? Gutterslag? Lint-licker? The Most Beautiful Girl in the World, but ironically?

Jadon, on the other hand, is met with warm smiles and long glances of another sort. He's the fairest of them all and can have any admirer he wants. The young women chirp, "Good day," and "How are you," and "What a nice big sword you have," and he flushes from their attention.

One woman turns to walk backward. "I remember *you*." Her friends tug her along.

"You were here a long time ago?" I ask Jadon once we're out of earshot of his admirers.

"I passed through," he says, looking sheepish. "Didn't stay long."

I peek over my shoulder at the young woman. "Long enough." Was she one of the girls Jadon kissed who wasn't *the one*? I push down the grinding pressure rising in my chest and focus instead on my surroundings.

There aren't many trees in Caburh, and the few there are lack healthy leaves…or have no leaves at all. Tree trunks have been carved with countless initials and hearts, crossed-out names, and a series of numbers that must have meaning to someone somewhere.

Miasma is here. From some of the houses we pass, I hear the same chronic and troublesome coughing that I heard in Maford. I see too many handkerchiefs soiled with phlegm and blood forgotten in that overgrown grass or discarded on those slick cobblestones.

I search for the inn we'll stay in tonight. "The Broken Hammer is run by my friend Separi," Veril had told me. "That woman is the best of us. In the Great War, we fought side by side. She once enchanted a rushing river to look like a brothel, but the brothel was actually a waterfall and the Dashmala tumbled to their deaths."

Another reason Sinth would've hated Veril.

Another trio of young women passes us, ponytails swinging. They make eyes at Jadon and scowl at me. The blonde says, "Why is he with *that* muckdweller?"

Philia tenses beside me and grabs her mace.

Jadon says, "No, Philia. Fuck them. Keep moving."

My stomach plunges to my feet. My hands are more than ready to join Philia's mace.

Philia grins at the blonde and her friends. "Wanna say that again?"

The trio quickens their steps and rounds the corner.

Philia lifts her chin. "I *thought* so."

I smile and wink at her like she's my daughter, growing up in my image.

At last, we reach the Broken Hammer. It's three stories tall and boasts a stone roof of glistening white-and-gray quartz and walls of knot-free redwood. Seven chimneys; smoke drifts from three. As the tallest building in Caburh, the inn is also the loudest. There's singing and laughing, banging cups and rolling barrels. Townspeople stumble out of the red double doors, arms slung around shoulders, with glazed eyes and slick chins.

A Renrian woman stands at the door to the inn, talking to a child. She resembles a vanilla bean pod—long, skinny, and dark brown. Giggling, the child runs back into the inn.

Jadon calls out, "Excuse me."

The woman turns, and her eyes widen. Gold charms clamp thick braids that fall to the small of her back. Her cheekbones are elegant and sharp. She's a stylish woman with flat black eyes, wearing a lavender silk waistcoat and matching velvet breeches. She gawks at me, not speaking as we approach.

My stomach roils and my knees go mushy, and the moment we've been waiting for—rejection—is about to happen. I force myself to push through my nervousness, and I hold up a gloved hand to wave. "Are you Separi Eleweg the Advertent?"

Still gawking, the woman nods.

I exhale. "I'm—"

She bows her head. "No need to introduce yourself, Lady."

I feel like my skin has been peeled back and I'm cold. "You...*recognize me*?"

"I do, though I last saw you long ago," Separi says, looking up at me. "You've changed in some ways, but I'd know your countenance and grace in the darkest night even more than Veril Bairnell the Sapient. He saw you only in your peaceful state, where order and light abounded. He saw the Eserime in you. But me? I saw you as I do right now—a weary Mera warrior with the wind at her back. It was my job as armorer to know you

so well. How you moved. The way you favored your left hand for magic."
She bows again, lower this time. "I oarl ha'a'moc hua iya au rro farossoc
rlo llalu lya'aum immosa."

Stunned, I dip my head. "And I'm honored to be in your presence as
well." I introduce both Jadon and Philia.

Her joy dims as her attention shifts from my companions to my gloved
hand—and the platinum fox amulet tied around my wrist. "Veril...?"

I remain silent, but sadness swells in my gut.

And, since she knows my countenance in the darkest night, she can
read this loss on my face. Her lips quiver, and her eyebrows draw together.

"A lot's happened," Jadon says, breaking the silence. "It was Veril's idea
to come to you for help. Before we lost him." Jadon's voice cracks.

Separi stares at him, and then her eyes settle on Philia. "And why do
you stand here, child?"

Philia's cheeks color. "I'm not a child—I'm nineteen."

"And I'm two hundred and six...*child*." Separi lets that hang in the
air for a moment, then says to me, "Welcome, Lady. Your companions are
also welcome."

"Thank you," I say, "and I'll tell you everything, once we're refreshed,
including the worst of things."

We follow the Renrian into the inn. "We've come a long way," I say. "I
hope you'll be willing to accommodate us for a night."

Separi wags her finger. "Oh no, no, no. But you *must* stay for more
than one night. The Festival of Acorns—you've enjoyed that in the past."

Really? No clue what the festival is nor when I've visited Caburh.

"We're on a schedule, friend," I say. "And I apologize for the brevity of
our visit. I promise that we'll stay longer upon our return."

"Until then," Separi says, her arms spread wide, "you will have the most
restorative one night at the Broken Hammer."

The inn smells of jasmine and toast, and a big fireplace spans nearly
the entire wall. The room is hazy from pipe smoke and hot from twenty
bodies sitting in high-backed chairs. A boy with curly hair plays a lute as a
girl who looks just like him—but with a ponytail—sings about a beautiful
maiden and a frog. The adults sip from mugs and clap their hands to the
tune.

I pull the hood of my cloak over my head and keep my eyes on the
floor. Despite Separi's kindness, the loathing from some of the people of
Caburh has sapped any strength I had. "I'm too tired to fight," I whisper

to Jadon and Philia. "I just wanna go to my room. That way, I can breathe normally. Simply exist."

"Since when do you want simple and normal?" Philia asks, brightness in her voice.

Extraordinary, though, becomes exhausting. Honestly: I'm so tired—of swallowing my ire, of hesitating before I react. I'm tired of holding up my head. Words have weight. Sneers cause burns. This Gorga-Jundum-mudscraper-muckdweller-giant is bleeding on the inside and can't express how she truly feels because she's supposedly a goddess who must save the realm and doesn't have time for feelings.

We follow Separi up to the third floor. At the landing, our host turns right at an intersecting corridor. The hallway smells of woodsmoke and the musk of crushed green ferns. Doors on either side of the corridor are marked by doorknobs of different colors.

"Sounds like you've been here before, too," Jadon says, smirking. "Enjoying festivals *and* nuts."

I grin and whisper, "Shut up, Ealdrehrt."

Separi turns right again, then stops at a door with a purple knob. She hands a key to Philia. "For you, young one." To Jadon and me: "Veril's favorite room. And…"

She hands Jadon a key and points to the door with a red knob. "You're sleeping there, young knight."

Jadon thanks her.

"And for you, Lady," Separi says. "Come."

I follow the innkeeper down the hall.

Jadon follows us down the corridor.

Separi turns a knob of pearl and gold.

This room has a hearth and a paned window cracked open to let in fresh air. There's a narrow bed with a clean quilt and pillow. An open armoire holds towels, a silver mug, and a vase of fresh blue flowers. There's a wicker chair and a little table with a wash basin, a pitcher, and a cake of soap. A large mirror hangs on the wall over the wash basin, and I startle at my haggard reflection. Outside the window, tall firs lord over the river, and a flock of wild turkeys scurries through the grass.

"I don't want you to return home and tell the gods that the keeper of the Broken Hammer treated you like shit." Separi bows and sweeps her hand from her head to her feet.

My throat tightens, and tears spring in my eyes. "Thank you. Really.

There's something..." I unwrap the fox pendant from my wrist and hold it out to her. "Veril spoke so warmly of you, and he valued your friendship. You should have this."

Separi watches the pendant sway on its chain.

"You may have more luck getting it to work than me," I say.

Separi taps the fox. "Does it bring you warmth? Does it make you think of good things?"

Hypnotized by the swinging charm, I say, "It makes me think of Veril and his kindness. His concern. His humor. His cooking. His generosity. Those are good things."

"Then..." Separi nods. "The pendant belongs with you." She heads back down the corridor. "We'll have dinner ready soon. Hope you're ready for a feast that surpasses all feasts!"

52

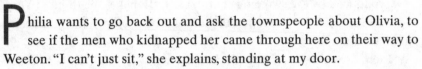

Philia wants to go back out and ask the townspeople about Olivia, to see if the men who kidnapped her came through here on their way to Weeton. "I can't just sit," she explains, standing at my door.

"So don't sit," I say. "Go ask questions. You've battled far worse than *these* people."

Separi offers to be the redhead's guide. "Drunks abound in this town, and I don't want Philia having to bash the heads of too many before supper. Ridget, my wife, would be angry, and you never want to anger the person in charge of the food."

"I'll be back in time for dinner," Philia says, following Separi down the stairs.

I don't want to join them. Neither does Jadon. He can barely keep his eyes open. "Go take a nap, Jadon," I say. "You're already asleep. You just don't know it yet."

He stretches and nods. "For the first night in a long time, you won't have to hear me snore. You must be happy to finally have your own space away from me."

"Thrilled," I say, my face deadpan perfection.

He grins, steps away, thinks a moment, then steps back to me. His smile dims. "The other night, when you told me about your hair? I heard you, and I know I said it then, but I want you to know again that it matters to me. I want you to know that *you* matter to me, too." He bites his lips as he thinks, his expression brightening with a weary smile. "We're closer to the amulet and Olivia than we were yesterday. I saw the moths, too, back on the trail."

I perk up. "You did?"

He nods, then swipes his hand over his face. "I'm going to collapse."

"Take a nap," I say, pushing him away. "I'll wake you for dinner."

He staggers over to the door and winks at me before drifting down the corridor and finally disappearing into his room.

'm asleep across the foot of an unfamiliar bed when I'm jolted awake by a knock on the door. Clutching Veril's journal to my chest, I sit up. My stomach growls, ready for dinner.

Another knock.

Where am I?

As I move to answer the door, my eyes skip from the hearth to the window, the large mirror, and the vase of fresh blue flowers. *That's right.* I'm at the Broken Hammer, a guest of Separi Eleweg.

Ridget stands in the corridor, holding a velvet satchel and a bucket filled with water. "I thought you might like to wash before dinner," she says.

"Yes, that would be wonderful." I invite her inside.

She sets the bucket of steaming hot water on the floor, then pulls from her pocket a bottle of oil and a bar of green soap.

Ridget rubs her hands together, then says, "We will bring more hot water to bathe, but would you allow me to care for your hair first?"

Tears spring to my eyes, and I touch my heart. "You'd do that for me?"

"Of course, beloved."

She instructs me to lean over a wooden tub, then pulls out a thick, bristled brush.

I kneel over the drum and sigh as she pours hot water over my hair.

Soon the room smells of peppermint soap. Ridget runs the bar through my thicket, her fingers rubbing hard enough to loosen the dirt but soft enough to avoid hurting my scalp. She hums a song that relaxes my muscles as dirty lather drips into the tub.

I close my eyes and enjoy this brief rest.

A young chambermaid brings another bucket of hot water, and Ridget pours that over my hair to rinse out the suds. She drapes a towel over my head that smells of lavender.

My eyes stay closed as she sprinkles peppermint oil into my locks. Ridget's touch sends a wave of cold through my body that stings, then burns—but it's a refreshing, soothing burn.

"Come, beloved," Ridget coos as she plops onto a low stool, then taps the floor.

I sit cross-legged between her knees, my back to her.

She hums as she rummages through a satchel, gathering what she needs: a comb, a brush, and a jar of thick oil. "Your hair just needs a little love, Lady...and a *lot of oil.*"

I laugh. "True."

Ridget places her warm palms against my cold cheeks. She squeezes my shoulders, and then she opens the jar. She scoops a thicker peppermint oil into her palm, then works the grease through my hair. She sections my hair with an ivory comb, then forces the comb through the snarls. "Such thick and healthy hair. Beautiful hair."

A teardrop slips down my cheek. Embarrassed, I swipe it away. "It's falling out."

"Of course it is," she says, "to make room for new hair."

I say nothing, but I'm experiencing something more than typical hair loss.

She hums that song again as she pulls the comb through my tangles, softly apologizing anytime I wince. "Tender-headed?"

A memory lights in my mind, and muted joy dances across my lips. "Yes. My mother used to comb my hair like this."

"Of course she did. A mother is the first guardian of her daughter's hair."

Another teardrop plops onto the back of my hand. "I don't remember much about her."

Ridget starts the first of two braids. "She still lives deep inside you. She still loves you and wants the best for you."

"How do you know that?"

Her hands work quickly as she starts the second braid. "Because you are lovable, Lady. Don't let any being in this realm or any other realm tell you any different." She taps my shoulder with a comb. "Go see yourself."

I stand at the mirror over the basin. Two braids sit perfectly on the sides of my head. Rose-gold thread travels through the braids and catches the lantern light. "Strange," I say. "My neck feels stronger. My shoulders, too."

"That's because I threaded your hair with spun luclite. And what's more—"

As though she planned it, there's a knock on the door.

In walks Separi, back now from her jaunt with Philia. She's holding a breastplate that shines with overlapping rose-gold scales. "Your luclite armor, dearest."

My mouth goes slack, and I press my hands against my cheeks.

"May I?" Separi asks.

Breathless, I watch as she places the complete set of armor upon the bed.

The material of the long-sleeved tunic—as well as the breeches—has been woven with luclite. Like the breastplate, the matching vambraces and gauntlets to cover my arms and hands are fabricated from this rare metal. "And your cloak of wonder completes your moveable fortress." Separi bows her head and adds, "I know the armorer who kept these items after the Great War. We hosted his wedding for a meager price—free. This is repayment for that debt."

Stunned, I move over to the bed and fall to my knees. "It's all so *beautiful*."

Separi's image wavers before me—not because she's been enchanted but because tears pool in my eyes. "I'm so thankful to you—to both of you," I say, acknowledging Ridget. "I will never forget your kindness."

Ridget bows her head, and then she and Separi gather the buckets of dirty water and the dirty towels. "There are two more buckets of clean, hot water for bathing," Ridget says. "Keep the peppermint oil and soap."

Separi opens the door and turns back to me with a smile. "Dinner will be brought up soon. If you need anything before then, just let me know."

"Thank you," I say. Once they scuffle down the hallway, everything is quiet again except for the pounding of my grateful heart.

53

D inner is served in my room for our privacy.

Jadon lifts the luclite tunic and holds it out before him. He nods with approval before placing it back over the chair. "Olivia would say all of this"—he waves at my tunic and breeches—"is *ridiculous*."

"And if she places a single loose eyelash on it..." I say.

Philia laughs. "I talked to the fishmonger, who said that he saw what he thought was a child riding a horse with a soldier sharing the saddle. And *then* Separi bought mugs of ale from a hostess who says the soldier who shared her bed mentioned going to Weeton. And finally, a child followed us back here and asked if I'd lost my sister. I said 'yes,' and he pointed west and said, 'She went that way.' And Weeton is that way."

Jadon nods. "We're going to Weeton, then. If the map is correct, we'll get there...in one million days. If we're lucky."

"Good news on that front," Philia says. "Separi's gifted us with two of her best horses. And Ridget gave me several special apples to keep them healthy."

Their kindness is extraordinary—from the hot water and comfortable boarding to the horses and armor.

And the food...

When it's brought in, I almost faint with delight.

Roast beef. Roasted potatoes. Wine. Fruits. Creamy cakes. Honeycakes. In silence, we eat dinner before the roaring fire, barely chewing before swallowing. The taste of a delicious, cooked meal is no illusion.

Philia, gnawing on a hunk of bread, says, "This meal is filling us up for the first time in days. I'm no longer as picky an eater as I used to be."

I drain the rest of my ale, and my spirit soars. Between the food, the hospitality, and the armor, I'm feeling almost like my old self. Well, the self I met at Veril's cottage.

After we eat, Jadon, better rested after his nap and bath, slumps beside me, his back against the bed. He's full of good food and drink.

Philia rises from the floor and stretches. "And now I'm going to bed. I've had enough of this day." She takes with her a cup of ale and a rum cake.

Both Jadon and I say, "Good night."

After Copperhair leaves the room, Jadon groans. "That was one of the best meals I've ever eaten. I haven't tasted ginger since my days in Brithellum."

I wipe my mouth with a napkin. "That wasn't a ginger sauce with the roast, Jadon. That was horseradish."

"So now you think that your palate is better than mine?" Jadon challenges.

I chomp on a roasted carrot. "I don't *think*. I *know*."

His eyebrow lifts. "Let me test you, then."

"Go right ahead," I sniff, chin up. "Prepare to be amazed." My pulse spikes as I grin—as I dare to take that intentional deep breath I've yearned for since meeting him in Maford. And then I take another. Another...

Jadon picks up a napkin and folds it the long way three times.

Just like that, my breath catches, and I lean away from him. "What are you about to do?"

"Blindfold." He crawls behind me. "You scared?"

A slow smile spreads across my face. "Never."

"Turn around, then." His voice is soft and teasing. With gentle hands, he covers my eyes with the napkin. "Let's see how fine-tuned your palate is."

"And if I win?" I ask, smiling, my breath hot with anticipation.

"You can take anything you want from me." His tone is now a playful challenge. "Including geld. Lady's choice."

"Okay. Deal." I sense his eyes on me, and my blood rushes at the prospect of lady's choice—and this lady needs no geld.

"And what do I get when *I* win?" he asks, his words also laced with anticipation.

"*When?*" A playful smile dances on my lips. "You can take whatever *you* want from *me*." My heart races at the thought, the promise of giving him whatever he wants. And he's not interested in geld, either.

Jadon says, "Open your mouth."

I chuckle, an attempt to dispel the nervous fluttering in my stomach. "No bugs, though."

"No bugs," he repeats. "Open."

I part my lips just like he wants, and I smell it before I taste it. Tart and sweet. The spaces around my ears tingle. "Easy. Strawberries."

"That was a gimme," Jadon says, his voice warm with amusement. "Next. Open."

I comply, my face burning beneath the napkin.

He sets the item on my tongue.

I bite. The smooth nuttiness of cheese fills my mouth.

"But what *kind* of cheese?" he asks.

"What *kind* of cheese?" I pause, savoring the taste on my tongue. "Goudrake."

"Wow. Impressive." He sounds proud.

"I'm winning." I've only begun to impress.

"Next," he says. "Open."

I part my lips again.

"Wider."

A thrill of anticipation shoots up my spine and spreads across my neck. I obey.

Something light sits on my tongue. I don't know which of my senses I'll lose myself in first: the flavor that will soon flood my mouth, the tingle in my cheeks as his breath warms my skin, or the luscious aroma of the pine-scented soap he used to bathe.

I close my mouth but only because he tells me to.

Sweet. Sticky. Solid but barely.

"Fig," I say, my brow furrowed.

"No."

I gasp. "You lie."

"Raisin."

I dart my tongue to my back teeth and taste the raisin there. "Ah. Yeah. You're right."

I want to win. I want to lose. I want what I want from him and that's everything.

I correctly guess boiled egg yolk and melon. I miss eggplant and mushroom.

"Last one," he says, his voice almost a whisper. "You miss it, and I win."

"I guess it correctly, and *I* win." I feel him settle behind me. Goose bumps rise across my skin. I could play this game forever.

"Open," Jadon instructs.

The object pools on my tongue, then strings across my lower lip. I close my eyes even though they're covered with a blindfold. My favorite taste of all tastes. This variety boasts deep, rich hints of blackberry. The flavor makes me moan.

"You *like* this one." He sounds satisfied.

My breath catches in my throat. "I do, but I want to be sure…" I part my lips again.

He drizzles a bit more onto my tongue, and that simple act makes me tremble. Just like before, he strings this flavor across my lips. "That's it," he says. "No more. What is it?"

"Honey," I whisper, that one word barely escaping my lips.

He says, "I can't hear you." He leans closer, his lips to my ear. "What is it?"

"Honey," I say, breathless.

"You're right."

He's so close to my back—heat curls off him like fire.

"May I have more," I whisper, "since I won?" My heartbeat tumbles faster until one beat trips over the other and then another, and I sway, lightheaded.

"Haven't I given you enough?" he asks, his words hot against my ear.

"Don't you want to give me more?" I counter, a playful smile tugging at my lips. "I know you want to reward me—and you can stop rewarding only when I say."

"Bossy," he says, chuckling.

"And you like it like that," I tease.

"I do," he admits, his voice husky. Still behind me, he runs his finger along my jaw. "How's that?"

Soft jolts of lightning spark at those spots along my skin. "Feels good," I confess.

He leans closer, our noses brushing. "You want the napkin on or off?"

"Off," I say without hesitation. "I want to see all of my reward."

Just like that, the napkin falls away and there he is, my prize, just a breath away.

"Hey," I whisper.

"Hey," he whispers.

Our noses brush again. Then I brush his lips with mine, and he is the best taste of all. He pulls me to stand, and I guide him onto my bed. And we kiss, and his lips, his tongue, they are magic. He bites my ear. I suck his bottom lip.

None of this is enough.

We kneel together, him behind me, and I catch sight of our reflection in the mirror across the room. There we are. Faces flushed. Eyes glassy. He smiles at my reflection, his eyes dark with desire. "Hey," he whispers, his breath hot on my ear.

"Hey," I whisper back, my voice barely a breath.

"Is this what you want?" he asks, his words tinged with uncertainty.

"Mmhmm." My pulse thunders in my ears. "Is this what you want?"

"I don't want to hurt you," he says.

"Then don't."

He lifts my tunic over my head and kisses a slow, deliberate path from my shoulder to my neck, leaving fire, fire, everywhere.

"Are you coming with me?" I ask, trembling.

He pauses, then laughs softly against my skin. "Definitely. If all goes well."

I snort in amusement. "Not that. I mean…"

"To Mount Devour?" He meets my gaze in the mirror. "Yes."

I brush my nose against his, and flames jump between us. "As you were."

Sparks sizzle from every place he touches, every place he kisses, and all that energy is building and whirling inside me. And then, as his hand drifts over my skin, I see my tattoo markings for the first time. Jadon notices as he glances at our reflection in the mirror, and his hand drifts over my bandeau to the wild vine right beneath my breasts.

"I want to see all of it," I whisper and watch his hand unclasp my bandeau.

Symbols. Stars, filled circles, boxes and lines.

"What does it mean?" I wonder.

He doesn't respond, merely traces each shape until his hand cups my breast.

No longer ashamed of my impatience, I untie the bandage from his left hand.

"Are you sure?" he whispers.

"Mmhmm," I whisper, hopeful. "Are *you* sure?"

"Mmhmm," he whispers.

He is free now, and his hand returns to my breast. His tattoo sits above mine, his a controlled circle, mine wild as ivy. He whispers my name, and I whisper his. I hold my breath as I unbuckle his pants—he's wanted this since the moment we met. So have I. He pushes down my breeches, and I guide his hand to the place I need his touch, here, here, yeah, here, and we sway slowly, like we're dancing, like we're worshipping.

I watch and feel that hand do magical things, and he watches, too, and all of it makes me dizzy, makes me ache, makes me breathless.

Is this how it feels to be on fire?

Gasping, I hold his unflinching gaze in that mirror's reflection as the glow of the nightstar lights us silver, as that light bathes us until the markings on our bodies glow. *What do they mean?*

Before I can dwell on that question, a knock on the door interrupts our caresses.

Lost in a realm Jadon and I created, we ignore whoever it is.

The knock becomes harder, insistent.

Jadon's touch becomes more urgent, harder, insistent.

And in this moment, I make a choice: I choose him.

"Lady," Separi calls through the door, "is Mister Ealdrehrt there with you?"

Jadon and I both pause and squint at each other, frustrated and almost amused. "For fuck's sake," I whisper.

"I can't believe this." He tightens his hold around my waist and rests his chin on my shoulder and shouts, "I'm here."

"Apologies," Separi says, "but I must speak with you immediately. It won't take long."

I chuckle and push out a breath. "Can't the Lady get what she wants?"

He gently bites my earlobe. "You will."

"I must."

He nuzzles my neck. "I'll be back." One more kiss, one more squeeze, and he's off the bed and pulling on his clothes.

Still burning, I hold his gaze until the bedroom door separates us.

Growing faint, I release a pent-up breath and slip back into the sheets. Eyes closed, I will him to come back to me...

L ight tapping pulls me from sleep and intrudes on my dreams.

I turn over in bed, reaching out instinctively for Jadon but—

Cold sheets.

Where is he?

My limbs feel so weak, but all of me feels so...*full.*

Because Jadon wants to stay by my side and trek to Mount Devour.

That tapping...

My gaze slips over to the window.

Several moths are bumping against the glass.

Relief floods through me, and I smile, seeing my winged friends again. I saw too many dead ones on the trek here, and I'm comforted to see so many—

I gasp and sit up abruptly in bed.

Moths! Does this mean my amulet is near? With a surge of adrenaline, I push open the window, and cold air rushes in, carrying with it the moths. Something faint stirs within me.

That rhythmic pulse. Is that pulse my pendant?

The moths dance around me, and I'm tingling and numb. I hold still and listen for my amulet. It's calling out to me as these moths swirl and twirl around my head.

My lungs fill with excitement, and my heart flickers with hope.

I'm so close.

Where is Jadon? If only he were here to witness this. To know that we *are* so close. To watch and delight in this kaleidoscope.

I press my cheeks and let myself smile as I imagine his eyes lighting up with joy. I'm going to be better. It's all going to be better. As I rise from the bed, a wave of joyful dizziness washes over me, and I drop back onto the mattress. My knees are delightfully weak. I punch my thighs a few times, coaxing the blood back into circulation, relishing the tingling that now rushes through my limbs.

If only Veril were here to share this moment. I pause, wistful as I picture the Renrian's face. His absence brings to focus the challenges we've faced, the mission I've yet to complete.

The sky is lightening. An early breakfast—such a simple pleasure— would fuel me for the tasks ahead. After breakfast, we'll search the area for more moths, and if needed, we'll head to Weeton, retrieve my amulet, and then hurry on to the sea and Mount Devour. And once our journey is over, once I am whole, Jadon and I will return to this inn, to this intimacy and bed...to this mirror. We won't answer any knocks, nor will we open the door. We will not leave this room or each other. We will be selfish.

I dress quickly, pulling on my breeches, bandeau, vest, and each piece of luclite armor. My hair feels healthy, sparkling with loving care and strands of precious magical metal. With Fury and Warruin secured in my back sheath and Little Lava at my ankle, I grab my satchel and head out, taking a last meditative look at this most special place in the realm.

54

J adon isn't in his room—his bed is still made. I don't see his armor or his sword. He didn't return to my bed, and it seems he didn't return to his.

Voices drift from downstairs.

Breakfast. Eggs. Bacon. Toast. Something hot to drink. Something cold to drink. More servings wrapped in bundles for our return to the road.

But I smell none of that as I drift down the corridor.

The ever-present nausea returns to roil in my stomach. My shoulder aches, and as I dressed, I saw the plum-colored bruises on both of my shoulders and my left hip and upper arm. Some of me feels too soft, like aging strawberries. I know what this is—and it has nothing to do with Jadon and me being together.

No, this is my deterioration. I need to follow those moths and find my pendant before more parts of me turn tender and sore. The luclite armor helps—its magical properties have strengthened my bones, and I'm not creaky in my joints, at least. Each piece protects those parts of me that I'll need for my journey to Weeton. But my moths are near, which means my happily ever after is coming, waiting for me at the sea surrounding Mount Devour. *Soon.*

As I round the corridor's corner, the voice I heard earlier becomes clear. That's not Jadon. Nor is it Separi, Ridget, or Philia. My heart sinks when I walk through the door to find Jadon sitting at the table in the center of the inn's great room. He faces the man who is talking—a man I recognize from Caerno Woods.

Gileon Wake.

Soldiers ring the room, their copper armor bright, their weapons sharp but stowed. Philia, still wearing a dressing gown, huddles behind the bar with Separi. Contempt burns on the women's faces. Hate shines in their eyes.

"Good morning," I say, dread now conjoined with sickness. "What's happening?"

Jadon doesn't speak. He won't even meet my eyes, choosing instead to sit there and glare at the tabletop.

Gileon sits up in his chair. "I guess I should answer, since it seems like Jadon here has misplaced his tongue *and* his manners. He may have forgotten at least one of them in your bed. I'm guessing…his tongue." His eyes slide over me, raking my body as though he sees what Jadon did with his tongue last night. Satisfied, he steeples his fingers and slips down in the chair. "I believe you know who I am."

"I do," I say with fake pleasantry, then snap my eyes to Jadon. "Hey. We need to go." Back to Wake again with a too-sweet smile. "Big things to do today."

Gileon plucks a piece of lint from the front of his linen tunic. He isn't wearing his armor. With…*one, two, three, four*…fourteen soldiers surrounding him, he thinks he doesn't need it.

"You're the one they call 'Kai,' yes?" the prince asks. His blond hair is clean, neat, and parted on the side. His blue eyes are bright but flat. If he had a kinder heart and a decent spirit, he'd be a delightful picture of benevolent wealth. But he isn't kind nor is he decent—I know this, and I just *met* the man.

There's no way out of this, and right now, I don't know how to snap Jadon out of his stupor to escape Wake's presence. I huff and say, "Fine." I drop my satchel into the closest chair and direct my attention to Wake. "How did you find us?" I set my hands on my hips, moving my cloak aside.

The guards all startle at my movement. On their toes now.

Good. I need them to see my sword and Veril's staff without any obstruction.

Gileon yawns, bored. "A little red bird told me. Elyn's always been incredibly helpful. And then one of my former mage soldiers—a drunken failure—saw you on the road. He couldn't wait to bring back exciting news."

So it's true. Mages *are* working for the Wake empire. Was the one we saw on the road from Peria? And…*Elyn*? Shit. So, I was right about her working with the emperor. What brought them together? What is he giving her?

With his foot, the prince pushes an empty chair toward me. "Please. Sit." He twists to face the bar. "Separi was just about to take our breakfast order, weren't you, dear?" He cranes his neck to see the innkeeper.

Separi glares at him. "The kitchen's closed this morning."

"That's too bad," Gileon says, *tsk*ing. "I'm starving. Kai—" He pushes the chair again with his foot. "You're still welcome — encouraged, even — to sit with us."

"I'm good right here," I say. "Thank you."

My nerves are twinging. Something isn't right. *Jadon* isn't right. He still hasn't spoken and only glowers, eyes down. He's dressed, though, in his armor, and Chaos shines from the floor beneath his seat. Did Separi summon him last night as a warning? Is that why he had time to dress?

I try to hear his thoughts but...

I can't read his thoughts.

What the fuck is happening?

The room sinks into silence except for the ticking of a clock somewhere behind me.

"We were just catching up, Jadon and me," Gileon starts. "You're searching for Olivia, right? I'm searching for someone, too. My commander. Last time I saw him, he was somewhere near Caerno Woods."

I cock an eyebrow. "Last time *I* saw him, he was still there. In a sense." I pause, then add, "Depending on your definition of 'was.'"

The muscles traveling along Gileon's jaw and neck bulge. But he pushes his rage down and takes up his feigned politeness. "You're devolving, Jadon. Can't believe you traveled all the way from Maford, fighting beasts at every turn, risking your life for Olivia Corby, some simple bitch from Stiwood, whose father is just a, what? Duke?"

Gileon squints and points to me. "So are *you* now his simple bitch?" He throws his hands up, pretending to be frustrated. "I'm confused. Clear this up for me, Jadon. Which one are you fucking? This one right here or my fiancée?"

His words slap me. My cheek stings and I see stars as I choke back my surprise and watch in horror as his smile challenges me to respond, to dispute his official proclamation. Blood drains from my face, but I won't cry. I won't fall apart, especially not in front of the men who already see me as a worthless trinket.

Jadon doesn't respond, and his silence means that he agrees with Gileon Wake — that I am nothing. I don't want to believe that, and I'm still clawing at the earth, imploring him to speak a word of defense, just one word that I can hold fast to.

Gileon's brow crumples with sorrow. "Kai, I'm assuming he told you that Olivia is not his sister."

"What's the point of this?" I whisper, arms spread. "I want nothing from you. I've *done* nothing to you. I just want to reclaim something that Olivia has, something she stole from me."

"I guess I was looking forward to seeing your reaction," Gileon continues. "I wanted to see how you'd react as you discovered that this honorable man seated across from me hasn't been honest with you, Kai. I admit…" He spins a geld atop the table. "I thought Olivia ran off to be with Jadon because they were in love, but…" He presses a finger to his lips, then taps his fingernail against his tooth, thinking.

"Don't," Jadon warns Gileon, his eyes burning. "We'll resolve this, you and me. No need to bring Kai into it. Tell her where Olivia is and let her go about her business."

But Jadon's request only makes Gileon's wicked smile widen. The prince sets his palms flat on the table. He meets my eyes, and there is hurt there. "I'm the fool. I was told by reliable sources that the love of my life… That she doesn't like men. She could've told me. We could've figured something out. Marriages aren't about love in our world, and families make arrangements all the time. But she didn't even give me the opportunity or the respect. And *then* she steals my family's book on top of that and runs?" He shakes his head, sits back in his seat, his nostrils flaring.

Behind me, Philia weeps. Before me, Wake's fingers tap the tabletop as his anger crackles until he clears his throat and pushes out a breath. He snaps up the geld from the table, flicks his eyes at Jadon, then levels his gaze at me. "I apologize. I'm sure you didn't expect such melodrama. Thank this guy right here. All of this clamor and tumult is for him. And for…"

He searches the ceiling and counts to himself. "Nearly an hour now, I've been trying to convince him to return to Brithellum and do what's required of him. The emperor was amused at first, Jadon, but then you stayed away for *years*. But!" Gileon lifts a finger. "Good news! In his kind wisdom, his endless patience, he will forgive you. If you return peacefully, no one gets hurt. Not Olivia. And not this one." He scans me from head to toe again, then lifts his eyebrows. "I can see the appeal." He chuckles and winks at me. "No offense."

My shoulders, as bruised as they are, now tingle, and my hands, oh, *fuck*, my hands…

Gileon slaps the table.

We all startle, even the soldiers.

"Snap out of it," Gileon spits at Jadon.

I agree. Snap the fuck out of it, Jadon.

Jadon lifts his eyes to meet Gileon's.

"They're all lined up to meet you," Gileon snarls, "to marry you, to have your babies. Women with class and royal blood, whose families are powerful—"

"No one's as powerful as the Lady!" Philia shouts.

This makes Gileon finally turn around in his seat to glare at Philia. "I recognize the true Supreme, the *one* Supreme, manifested in my father, Emperor Syrus Wake. No true believer accepts false gods." He glares at me. "Not even a fuckable one like the Lady here."

Stay calm. Wait as long as you can. You kill him now, you may never find Olivia or your amulet and you will never reach Mount Devour and you will die in this pigsty called Vallendor. If you hurl wind or fire like you want, Separi and her family may get hurt. If you kill Gileon Wake, Caburh may suffer even more than Maford did.

Gileon scowls at Jadon with unfiltered loathing. "Are you done *slumming*, Jadon? Have you gotten it out of your system?"

Jadon's jaw tightens, and his skin flushes red.

I loudly exhale, then close my eyes, let my head fall back. After counting to ten, I open my eyes and search the ceiling for anything—a ladybug or a painted posy—to calm the rage bucking against its cage. Somehow, I'm able to focus on Gileon Wake without having to strangle him. "I don't know you," I say, calm and soft, "but I had really hoped that you were killed by my fire. There's something about you that makes me want to start another."

Gileon pales some but returns to spinning that coin on the tabletop.

"How is that soldier?" I ask. "Not the one I killed with his own pike and burned so thoroughly that even Supreme would give up putting him back together. No, I'm talking about the one who lost his hand after striking his horse. Is that soldier still alive? Has death claimed him yet? If you tell me where he is, I can finish him off, if you wish. Your *Highness*."

Gileon's eyes widen, and any color he had left has abandoned his body. He remains silent, though.

A smile plays on the edge of Jadon's lips.

I take a step forward.

The soldiers reach for their swords.

Gileon lifts his hand.

The soldiers stand down—but not all the way down.

I place my knuckles on the table and bend until I'm eye to eye with the prince of Brithellum. "You must understand this: your men killed a Renrian. Did they tell you that? Oh, wait. For a second time now, I've forgotten… No one from that battalion survived to tell you."

Gileon's eyes dart to the soldiers standing at the walls.

"Your men," I continue, "killed someone who has served Vallendor Realm for two hundred years. His name was Veril Bairnell the Sapient, and one of him is worth three thousand of your men. By my count, I have two thousand, nine hundred and sixty to go. And once I hit that target…" I stand up straight. "We'll be even."

Gileon goes back to spinning his coin, but his fingers tremble. "And then what, Lady? You and this one—?" He thrusts his chin at Jadon. "You two will ride off into the twilight, living happily ever after? Always fighting? Always running? Always filthy and hungry and anxious? I won't stop looking for him. And Elyn won't stop looking for you."

Gileon taps Jadon's hand. "Don't tell me this is the life that you want. I mean… You can have everything, *anything*, and it's yours. I mean…you *are* a prince of Brithellum, after all."

"What?" Not only do I say this, but Philia does, too.

"Oh, so you didn't tell them everything?" Gileon gawks at Jadon. "Are you going to say something, *brother*?"

"Brother?" I whisper, my voice weak, my heart…*shattered*.

Gileon's focus remains on Jadon. "I'm just astounded that you never told her. Information like that is critical, especially during negotiations." He makes a noise expressing disgust, then turns to me, his eyes burning with anger. "Your boyfriend—my brother—is the eldest son of the emperor, and we've been looking for him *everywhere*."

Jadon lifts his gaze and looks over to me with flat eyes. "I'm sorry," he whispers. Then those eyes flicker and glint. And that's when he lunges across the table and wraps his hands around Gileon's neck.

PART V

CAN'T GO
HOME AGAIN

Throughout the realm, here shadows pale.
She emanates, wearing mail.
Bringing light for all beings pure,
She captures foes so goodness cures.

Hear the echoes of closing breath,
A spell for life, away from death.
With might, in darkness, she exudes brawn.
In the light, she stands 'til dawn.

Arise and praise her sublime hand.
She vanquishes every land.
Breaking chains, she battles vile.
She uses gifts that value guile.

Hear the echoes of closing breath.
A spell for life, away from death.
She is the darkness, she's also dawn
At the time when bad things spawn.

Upon the fields where courage fades,
She refuses passion's blades.
Ducking love as she chooses flame,
She saved her own. They praise her name.

Above the fray, where glory stands,
This conqueror, goodness planned.
Water now pure and fertile earth,
The simple choice of choosing worth.

Beneath the flag of courage high,
She resurrects, touching sky.
Writing odes and radiant songs,
She declares wins of battles long.

Verdant realms where this goddess rules,
She absolutely suffers fools,
Hoping they change erring ways,
She triumphs in these final frays.

55

And now I know why Jadon was so concerned about the fire I set outside of Caerno Woods: he was terrified that I'd burned his brother alive.

His brother, the prince.

The sitting room bursts into commotion as Jadon lunges at Gileon. The fresh-faced soldier closest to us draws his sword, ready to sever Jadon's hand from Gileon's neck with one fierce swoop. That same soldier fails to see me as a threat…not until I jab his windpipe, kick the sword out of his hand, and lock the tyke's elbow with both my hands.

"Settle down, young knight," I caution him. "A warning: I'm anxious to complete this move. Joint locks are my favorite."

He whispers, "Please don't, Lady." Tears shine bright in the soldier's brown eyes but fear shines brighter. "I praise your name."

"It's Lady now?" I whisper. "Now that you're moments away from death, you, all of a sudden, recognize me? Now you, all of a sudden, want to believe in me?"

By now, the other soldiers around the room have drawn their swords and are bustling forward to remove Jadon's hands from Prince Gileon's neck. One soldier, a man with a dimpled chin, grabs Jadon's shoulder and lifts his dagger.

"Don't, Athard," the prince gasps with strain on his face. "Don't touch him."

Athard either doesn't hear Gileon's command or hears and ignores it. He grabs Jadon's hair, yanks back his head, lifts his dagger, and prepares to slide its blade across Jadon's neck.

I shout, "Stop!" and use my free hand to send a small ball of wind, knocking the knife out of Athard's hand.

The soldier gapes at his empty hand and growls at me. He marches in my direction, preparing to show me a thing or two.

But there's nothing he can show me that I haven't already seen.

I whip my free hand and hurl a ball of wind at an empty table near the entrance. The four chairs fall back as the table lifts and hits the wall. The crack of splintering wood against stone makes Athard shudder and the other soldiers yelp, including the young soldier still in my hold. "Try me, Athard, and it will be you next time," I shout. "Release Jadon right now."

The hall stumbles into silence until someone whispers, "Her eyes." Someone prays to Supreme and whispers, "Don't let her do to me what she did…"

Athard hesitates, and his expression changes. Finally, he releases his fistful of Jadon's hair and steps back.

My outburst has cost me strength. A bone around my right knee cracks, and the piercing that stabs up and down my leg makes me wince. Now that we know Gileon escaped my fire, we need to use him as leverage to find my amulet—if he's dead, we have nothing but a dead prince, no pendant, no Olivia.

But Jadon still hasn't loosened the grip around Gileon's neck.

"Jadon," I say, no give in my tone. "We need answers, not more blood—not yours, not his, not Olivia's. Stop or I'll make you stop."

He jerks his head to find me on his right side. "Didn't you want him dead? Wasn't that your hope as we watched that field of flames and dead soldiers? Don't you want me to make your dreams come true?"

"Which means there must be a reason I need you to stay your hand." I pause, then add, "Once I get what I need, do as you must. That's your family's business. Not mine. Until then, release him. *Please.*"

Jadon sees that one of my hands is ready to break the soldier's arm and the other hand is ready to shoot wind. His eyes are a new shade of blue—storm, fire, earth, and endless anger. After a moment, his scowl fades, but he still doesn't release Gileon.

Athard creeps forward. Though I'm unable to read his mind, I can still see him calculating in his shiny brown eyes. *Slice his neck for the emperor slice his neck for the glory slice his neck and—*

"Touch him, Athard," I growl, "raise your knife, think about killing him one more time, and I will end you *right now*. Test me." Once the soldier pauses, I snap, "Get. Back."

Athard obeys, his dimpled chin quivering, his eyes skipping between the destroyed table and my hands.

Jadon wastes no time in pulling Gileon over the tabletop, wresting the smaller man to his feet and wrapping his arm around the prince's neck.

Gileon is no danger to Jadon, who holds him now by his collar like a child holding his doll. The prince is nowhere near Jadon's height and stature, the same height of tracker dog Daisy if she were to stand on her hind legs. With those weak arms and scrawny chest, he can't possibly be training with the great sword that shines from the nearby chair.

The soldiers lift their swords but are reluctant to surge ahead. Some take a small step forward, then take a step back, forward, then back, like they're dancing.

"Tell me where Olivia is," Jadon demands, tightening his chokehold around his brother.

"Jadon," I whisper, "if he's dead he can't—"

One soldier standing near the hearth taps into his stores of bravery and rushes up behind Jadon, his battle-ax held high over his head.

I thrust my hand and hurl another table in the soldier's direction. The hardwood knocks the soldier to the ground and smashes him. I lift the table once more and slam it down on the soldier's head, his glow blue, then amber, and finally black. There's Number Forty-One. My gaze burns across the room, from one man to the next. "Do you all think I'm fucking around here?"

"Where is she?" Jadon asks Gileon.

Gileon's face is the color of dawn: purple, orange, and reds—if he doesn't answer Jadon's question, he may never see another. "Don't know," he chokes. "But she's not in any danger."

I grab my dagger from my ankle sheath and press it against the throat of the soldier still in my hold. "You know in your heart that I have no problem sliding this dagger across this fucker's throat—"

"Jadon, please," Gileon chokes out, his knees sagging. "The Dashmala... They found Livvy for me... Demanded ransom. She offered it to me...to make a deal."

"Offered *what* to you?" Jadon asks.

"You know," Gileon wheezes. "You know what she has."

Jadon pales and pushes Gileon back against the table.

Gileon heaves a breath and drops into a chair. He massages his neck and glares up at his brother. "The Grand Defender can't have it—you know that. She'll be too strong. You know that, too. If she does, it will be impossible—"

"Who are you talking about?" I say, my gaze bouncing between the brothers. "Who is this 'she' you're talking about?"

"And what was the deal Olivia made?" Jadon asks, eyes narrowed.

"She wants freedom," Gileon croaks.

"Please, Lady," the soldier in my hold whispers. "I'm a no one, just a simple—"

"Quiet!" I press the blade harder against his throat.

"And this was never the plan, anyway," Gileon says, teeth clenched, his veins popping across his sweaty forehead.

"What *plan*?" I ask.

"Do you hear me?" Gileon says to Jadon. "I get it. No one thought she'd be so...*tantalizing*. Tall, yes. Strong. Certainly. Unlike any woman either of us have seen or met—and between us, we've known *many*. I mean, the hair *alone*... I understand your reluctance, but... *Four years*. That's how long you've been away. Four years we've been searching for the Grand Defender. Sent parties out every time word got back to us that they saw her in this village or that. We've been a step behind all this time... until now. Can't you taste success? Can't you see the end? How glorious this will be for both of us?"

Sybel is the Grand *Steward*.

Who is the *Grand Defender*?

Tall. Strong. The hair alone...

"Who are you referring to?" I say. "Tell me."

"Brother," Gileon continues, ignoring me, "we've worked too long and hard to end up with nothing. She'll destroy you, and if you take a moment and think, you'll see that I'm right."

He sighs, then says, "You and I don't have time to fight, nor do we have time to change course. You have no choices here." His head drops between his knees, his lungs and heart still struggling from Jadon's hold, his chest toggling between blue glow and amber glow. Exhausted, he manages to look up at his brother. "Do you hear me? Do you understand what I'm saying? We have no choice."

The muscles in Jadon's face relax. Why? What is he hearing? What is Gileon trying to make him understand? *No choice?* No choice about *what*?

I try to hear Gileon's thoughts, but I can't, hearing nothing but continuous thrumming. It's the same as that man we passed on the road to Caburh. What magic is keeping me from hearing his thoughts and Jadon's? Who cast this spell? Which mage in Wake's army is strong enough to block my ability?

Elyn. And she's more than a mage. Much more.

Wait.

She's the Grand Defender?

"I'm sorry about this," Gileon whispers, standing from the chair now. His eyes are soft as he looks upon his brother. "Greedy Dashmala dropped Olivia in my lap—and she readily gave me what I asked. What you and I needed. You know Livvy's interested only in saving herself, but this time, her selfishness and her greed finally benefit a larger cause. We have the amulet."

"*What?* No!" My mind races, and I try to slow my breathing and concentrate, but my mind keeps skipping, because I don't care about Olivia or her greed or the Dashmala and deals they've made. The heat in my hands swirls and pushes against my fingertips, begging for release. If I don't get answers, I'll unleash their restraints.

"I'm here for my pendant," I say, my grip tightening around the soldier's neck. "Nothing more. Whatever deal Olivia's made with you doesn't matter—my amulet is not hers to trade. I don't know what the fuck you two are talking about right now, but it doesn't concern me. I give not a single fuck about palace intrigue. Give me what's mine, and I'll leave Vallendor. I want only what was stolen from me. I want my amulet. *Right* now."

"Kai," Jadon says, "listen. I can explain—"

"Don't," I snap, lifting my hand to stop him from talking. "I'm done listening to you."

And I'm done caring about Olivia and the empire, these people, and this province and...

Save this realm for *these* bitches? Oh, no, no, no. I won't be doing that. Liars and schemers and murderers and betrayers, all of them. Jadon, a liar, means nothing to me, not anymore, and Olivia, a thief, means even less. I'll take possession of my amulet, race to Mount Devour, explain to Sybel or who-the-fuck-ever that I shouldn't be forced to save these people, that I *won't* be forced to save these people, and if that means I'm jailed in some prison in the farthest realm in all the realms, I'll take that over saving Vallendor. That will be my plea.

Sorry, Jamart. Sorry, Milo. I can't.

I press the dagger harder against the soldier's neck. "Give me what's mine," I say again, glaring at the two princes before me, "or I will keep using force to get it. And know that I *will* get it back." Unblinking, I slash the neck of the soldier in my hold.

Some warriors cry out as others rush toward me as the dead man—now known as Number Forty-Two—drops to the floor.

I throw my hand and shoot wind to knock over another table.

The room shudders again, and the soldiers regroup.

I smile without humor. "It won't be wind but fire next time."

Some soldiers drop to pull their dead comrade back. Others keep their focus trained on me. Their eyes now burn with hate.

I spin the bloody dagger in my hand, ready for Number Forty-Three. "Who's next?" I ask, my focus back on the soldier with the dimpled chin. "You? Agard, is it? Eggar? Worm food?"

"Stand down!" Gileon shouts to be heard and not because he's scared. He wipes a bead of sweat from his jawline and grins at Jadon. "She like this in bed?"

"Let me climb on top of you and see for yourself." I twirl the dagger between my fingers.

"Don't talk about her like that," Jadon snarls at his brother, the tendons stark against his neck. "Disrespect her again and I'll break your neck."

Gileon's smirk drops, and he rolls his eyes. "Relax, Jay. It was a compliment." He nods to me and snorts. "I apologize, Lady of the Verdant Realm. Did I get your title right? Or is it Lady of the Barren Realm? Lady Who Claims to be Supreme but is Only a False God?" To Jadon: "Better?"

"I've never claimed to be Supreme," I say, fingers tight around the dagger handle. "That's your father's lie. Insult me again, though, and I won't need Jadon to break your neck."

Gileon pivots back to me, his eyes narrowed. "You do know that you don't have to kill *everything* and *everyone* you meet, right? That you don't *always* have to choose violence."

"She doesn't seek out fights," Jadon says. "They somehow come knocking on her door." He pauses, then adds, "Where is her pendant, Gileon? If you make me ask for it again, *I'll* be the one choosing violence."

My stomach yaws with anger—at Olivia's scheming, at Jadon's betrayal, at my willingness to believe him and believe Sybel, at my willingness to sacrifice my life to save every person in this room. But my stomach also yaws because that colorful string from the amulet is tugging at me, more insistent than ever. Now my eyes skip around the room in search of moths.

"Your pendant is closer than you think," Gileon says to me. "But I need my brother to answer one last question before we wrap all this up." He reaches to hold Jadon's chin. "Are you happy, brother?" His words come soft.

Jadon's brow crinkles. He's caught off guard by the gentleness of that question, caught off guard by Gileon's sincerity.

Rigid, I await Jadon's response.

Jadon remains silent but then he glares at Gileon and knocks away his brother's hand.

"That's what I thought." Gileon looks over to me. "Are *you* happy?" he asks smugly.

I bristle—*who does he think he is?*

"Well, are you?" He awaits my answer, his blue eyes calm and glimmering.

One word fires from my mouth. "Amulet."

Gileon offers me a shrug and a tight smile, then looks to the soldiers guarding the inn's entrance. "Open the doors."

The soldiers obey.

Gileon turns to his brother. "I love you, Jay. No matter what happens. Always, *always* remember that. Olivia's outside *with* the pendant. I won't stop either of you from retrieving it." Smiling, he steps away from Jadon and extends his arm toward the inn's open doors.

"Just like that?" I say, eyes narrowed.

Gileon folds his arms. "Just like that."

What's the trick? Leave and *what*? Nothing is ever easy. Vipers are vipers—never turn your back to them even if they're sleeping, even if they're dead.

Gileon is a viper. And so is his brother.

Over at the bar, Philia gasps, "Kai, he's not lying! I see Livvy outside on a horse!" She's looking past the inn's door with surprised eyes. "There are soldiers with her!"

My pulse quickens, and I swipe the blood on Little Lava's blade across the dead man's tunic, then stow the dagger in its sheath.

Face flushed, Jadon grabs his satchel and sword from the chair. "Kai, we should—"

I glare at him. "Where the hell are *you* going, *Your Highness*?"

A flicker of anger in Jadon's eyes quickly slips into shame. Voice lowered, he says, "I'll explain everything, but let's take care of these soldiers first and get your pendant. I promised that I would help you, and if it's the last thing I do for you, I'll retrieve your pendant." Over his shoulder, he shouts, "Phily, come on."

His words feel like small slaps and busy gnats—annoying and painful and shocking. *If it's the last thing I do for you...* If I had the time, I'd throw my hands up at him, and we'd shout at each other, and I'd spin on my heel after declaring my hate for him, and I'd swear that I'd strike him down if he ever looked at me again. Later. Right now, there's no time.

Yes, the amulet is near, and its tugging is stronger. I need to follow its pull before it wanes again. I back away from Gileon and his guards. The pulsing in my gut quickens the closer I come to the doors. The chill of fresh air as I back all the way to the porch tickles my neck.

Philia, smiling, hurries away from Separi at the bar, excited at the prospect of reuniting with her love. But that look of relief quickly shifts as she pales and stops in her step and looks past me with glazed eyes.

What now?

I spin around.

Jadon has stopped in his tracks, and the three of us stand frozen on the porch of the Broken Hammer.

Oh *shit*.

56

At least seventy sword-wielding soldiers with hard frowns and clenched fists stand at the ready on the cobblestone street. They're glowing blue, but there's something else happening here besides their curious good health. Just like that soldier we passed on the road, the one wearing a dead man's armor, I can't hear the thoughts of any of these soldiers or their horses. Just that drone of waves hitting the shore, constant, high and low, hissing and unchanging.

These soldiers' capes morph from blue to no color at all, blending with shadows and light, there and not there. Their armor isn't simple copper and chain. No, the metal breastplates are engraved with runes that glow with blue light. These are not the same type of soldiers I fought in Maford or outside Caerno Woods. These are not the same class of soldiers guarding Gileon Wake in the sitting room.

I don't recognize those blue glowing letters or symbols, but I do recognize the soldiers' thicker-looking skin, and those weaponized capes, and the magical forces protecting them. These mage-soldiers are meant to stop me.

For good.

Elyn has thought of everything—if anyone can stop me, if anyone could cast a spell on an entire army, it would be her.

With his guards close behind, Gileon swaggers past and saunters down the porch stairs. "I guess my stop here was a waste of time. Obviously, brother, you've made your choice. But I can't let her leave this town. Not if you want to live beyond this season. Not if I want to live long enough to become emperor of Vallendor."

It feels as though fog is building in the space beneath my ribs, pressing and cold and growing and pushing. The pain that had radiated from my knee has swallowed my toes and now creeps from one shoulder to the other.

Beyond this ring of soldiers stand a dozen or so horses, some with riders, some without. Olivia is seated on a slate-colored horse in the middle. There are bruises around her eyes and nose, and her wrists are tied around the saddle horn with rope. Eyes glazed, she turns her head to scan the crowd and wobbles, barely maintaining her balance.

The twinkle of red and gold gems blink against her torn gray blouse as Gileon deftly parts the soldiers and makes his way to that slate-colored horse. "Like I said…" He grabs the saddle and hoists himself into position behind Olivia, who winces. "I won't stop either of you from retrieving the amulet. You want it? Come take it, then." He grabs the reins and spurs his horse as the soldiers from the inn all mount their own horses. Together, the contingent rides west.

"No," Philia cries out. "We have to follow them!"

We do, but first, I must remove the two-legged obstacles blocking us.

"Can those things be killed?" Philia whispers.

"If they bleed, they die," Jadon whispers back.

"Unless you're lying about that, too?" I snark.

"Kai," Jadon says. "I promise—"

I've stopped listening to him—I'll use his brawn now and deal with his betrayal later. I lock eyes on the largest warrior in the battalion before us.

The only skin that isn't protected by armor on this man resembles the pebbly scales of lizards. Even his eyes look as though they're protected beneath resin. Underneath all the magic and fortification, the space around his heart glows the bluest, throbbing hard and quick.

Yes, he can be killed.

Jadon clenches Chaos, but I don't wait for him to swing. I sweep both of my hands across the air, using wind to knock the first row of soldiers, including the big soldier, onto their asses. My vicious gale sparkles with red and gold dust. It's beautiful and incredibly effective, but using my power has made that troubling, traveling pain carve a line from my shoulders down my arms to my hands. Every place on my body that pain has passed— from my knees to my toes and across my shoulders—is now numb.

Wind and fire will have to be my last resort.

Before the soldiers can clamber back onto their feet, I storm down the porch steps, and in a single bound, I stand over that giant soldier. I grab the blade of his broadsword and easily yank the weapon out of his hands. "You may be magic," I tell him, "but you still need to know how to fight." Then I drive his sword into the only available, unprotected space: the pebbly-skinned space between his eyebrows.

The second wave of soldiers crashes over their fallen comrades, their swords, pikes, and maces thrusting and swinging.

I quickly backtrack to the porch to reassess.

Jadon's wielding Chaos, fighting three men at once.

Separi and her wife, Ridget, race to the edges of the fray, wielding their Renrian staffs.

Philia has no weapon.

I call her name and toss her the dead soldier's broadsword. "If you see no other place," I call out to her, "and the blade isn't getting past the armor, aim between the eyebrows."

She shouts, "Okay," and glances past me. "They're getting away."

Clouds of dust rise behind Gileon's horses as they race toward the sun.

That's where we need to go.

A soldier storms toward me, sword out, his armor bright with that unknown spell. Other soldiers join, and together, they charge forward, shouting their battle cry, *"For the emperor! For Supreme!"* One soldier chooses Philia and catches her broadsword in his unprotected throat. Another soldier swings his sword at me and growls, "I'll kill you, you mud—"

I draw Fury and swing, knocking him dead.

Another soldier sneaks behind me, and I have no option but to whip my hand at him. Blue waves of energy shoot from my numb fingers, launching him back, back, back, until he slams into the door of the tailor's shop. That door splinters from the impact and knocks a lit hanging lantern onto bolts of fabric and canvas. All of it catches fire.

I throw more wind at another soldier too close for comfort, launching him high into the air. I then thrust my hands down, slamming him against the cobblestoned street. There's a sickening crunch as bones smack armor and armor smacks rocks. No rune can protect against that. It sounds so...*final*.

All of this is worth the sharp tingling in my hands, feet, and even my earlobes.

The pops and crackles of fire intensify into growing booms as the flames consume more fabric at the tailor's. A towheaded soldier races out of the smoke, heading my way.

Where's your helmet, White Hair?

I throw Little Lava at the towheaded soldier, and she brings the heat to his throat.

Another soldier scrambles and wraps his arms around me.

Before I can react, his eyes go big and blank.

An arrow to his back.

Shit!

I peer around his big dead body to see that Philia has traded her sword for a golden bow plucked from one of the dead soldiers. She sends another arrow into the jowl of a soldier who has successfully reached me. By my count of arrows in the backs and faces of men, she's killed…five, six…*seven* soldiers.

Above me, a soldier hangs midair wrapped in orange light, and another soldier hangs midair in green light—the power from the staffs of the Renrian women twists and squeezes and implodes their quarry until there's nothing left but bloody ground meat.

With each kill, I push closer to that three thousand. I yank my dagger from the dead man's throat and sweep my leg to trip an approaching soldier. He clatters facedown to the ground. I waste no time and drive my dagger into the unprotected backs of his knees.

He shrieks with pain and will never kneel before another emperor again.

I tug Little Lava from the soldier's flesh and wipe her bloody blade across the fallen man's shadowy blue cape.

Jadon dispatches a soldier who had jumped on him from behind, easily twisting from the man's grip and delivering a death blow with Chaos. The wrapping on his hand has unraveled, weighed down by dirt and gore. I wonder at his tattoo—did he hide it because it is a symbol of his royal status? Just one more secret. His nose is bleeding, and his face drips with sweat.

"You okay?" I shout, pointing at my own nose.

"Sucker punch," Jadon shouts. His gaze roams the destruction and dead bodies.

Smoke and flames curl to the sky, consuming the tailor's shop. Some soldiers have fallen to the ground chopped down by arrows, multicolored beams of light, or steel blades. Blood dribbles from the dying corners of those soldiers who still have mouths.

I squint through the smoky darkness. I can no longer see the retreating horses of Wake's guard, nor can I interpret the pulsing in my gut. Are these tugs alerting me to the amulet's proximity or are these tugs my thundering heart exhausted from fighting?

Sudden movement draws my attention back to the battle. Another warrior stomps toward me, banging his fist against his breastplate.

If that's where he wants it. I kick hard enough for him to stumble back, and then I kick him again. Once he's on his knees, I grab the top of his head and his chin and twist it until he's looking in the direction he shouldn't. But he's still breathing, and time is still ticking, and those horses carrying Olivia and my amulet are racing farther away from me. Before I can finish him off, a familiar shriek pulls my focus over to the inn's porch, where a soldier rips the bow from Philia's hands and strides away.

Her face bloody, Philia lunges to follow, but Separi pulls her out of the fray and back into the inn.

My eyes scan the landscape for the soldier who's just taken Philia's bow. *There!* By the horse troughs in front of the bakery. I march over to him and knock the back of his head with the pommel of my sword.

He drops the bow.

I snatch the weapon from the ground and call out, "Separi." I toss the bow and watch it sail to the innkeeper.

Bam!

Something hard hits the back of my head. Stars fill my vision, and I stumble, regrouping quickly enough to swing Fury and slice the gap of unprotected flesh between a soldier's knee and shin guards. I move on as Jadon swings and punches beside me, wielding Fury with my right hand and wind-whipping with my left. Despite the luclite armor, parts of me continue to numb as I use my wind as a weapon.

Another soldier creeps into my blind spot and swings his sword.

I duck, but not before the tip of his blade nicks my cheek. I suck at the air—the cut stings like a flame. My knees wobble. My vision narrows. I pull Warruin from my back scabbard, but the staff isn't glowing lavender. I thrust the ouroboros at the soldier before me, but nothing happens. No time to figure out how it works, since the soldier is rushing toward me again. This time, I swing the staff, connecting it to the soldier's face and sending him to his knees.

No use in keeping a weapon not fit for me.

I toss it over to the porch, where Separi is wiping down a cut on Philia's cheek.

Jadon and I press on, cutting, slashing, back-to-back, just like we fought the emperor's men in Maford, just like we fought the burnu in the glen.

More soldiers pour into Caburh. *How many men did Wake bring? And where are they coming from?* The sound of their clanking armor makes my head hurt. The fiery glint of shiny armor makes me squint.

I could possibly hit three thousand today, but I doubt it. Not with my knees, legs, arms, and back…all of me softening like butter with every move I make.

Jadon swings his sword, but his moves have lost their crisp confidence. His swings are now slurred.

I can't keep fighting. *"Help me."*

Neighing. Hooves clomping. Horses rear and come down on top of men. Dogs growl. Dogs bark. Soldiers shriek. Sparrows swoop through the smoke. Men scream as they catch their bloody eyeballs, unable to see crimson-stained beaks.

"We're here, Lady."

"Go west, Lady."

"Hurry, Lady."

My head aches so much that I can't focus enough to push any wind through my fingers. "We need to get out of here!" I yell.

Jadon barely acknowledges me. He's covered in blood—his and the blood of men piled at his feet. But he's still standing.

Fatigue soaks into my bones. *Don't die here. Not in this place. Not—*

Silence sweeps across this new battleground, making my skin prick with worry.

"Oh my…" Jadon's eyes widen.

What's caused him to—? I turn to face what he's looking at. "Shit," I whisper.

Cursuflies with their scales, feathers, white eyes, and crones' hair fly over the streets of Caburh. If I didn't have confirmation before, this is all I needed to prove that Elyn is behind this. That she's found herself an ally in Wake, providing him an otherworldly army to finish us off.

I search the skies for Elyn. She has to be close.

One of the creatures buzzes over to me and stares me down with its white eyes. Before it unlocks its jaws, I thrust my sword into its heart, then hop back as hot-green blood bursts and spills onto the slippery road.

One cursufly down. Countless to go.

Still no sign of Elyn or her sentinels. But there are more cursuflies. So many cursuflies.

I can't…not all of them—

And then a shriek, that mix of high and low. A darkness darker than smoke moves over the fighting, and red eyes glow in the gray.

Tazara! Battabies swarm overhead and attack the cursuflies, putting out their lights. Tazara hovers in place, capturing the attention of the boss-beast cursufly, the one with fire in her cauldron-like belly.

The giant cursufly hurls a fireball at the king of night-dwelling creatures. With a single flap of his wings, Tazara sends the fireball back, hitting the cursufly who'd sent it, and the fire—*her own fire*—consumes her until nothing's left.

"Thank you, Tazara."

"The Lady of Dawn and Dusk asked that we follow you on your journey here," the battawhale says. *"She said you would need me."*

My gratitude and relief swell like the seas, but before I can speak another word, the king of the night-dwelling creatures is gone, leaving the battabies to complete their mission.

Soldiers hack and swing their swords at cursuflies, too, cutting down these new enemies, rolling out of the way of fireballs, some not rolling quickly enough.

We need to leave this place before I fight myself over the edge of exhaustion.

"Kai!" Philia's face is bright with urgency. "Follow Gileon," she shouts, pointing. "Please don't lose sight of Olivia."

"Lady, hurry," Separi calls. "We'll finish this fight. Go retrieve your amulet!"

"The soldiers have gone west," according to those sparrows with the bloody beaks.

Past the smoke, I glimpse one single glow of amber bobbing and dropping, smaller and smaller as it races into the sun. Moths, red ones, gold ones, black ones, swirl around me. Their glittery trail leads out of the town, westbound.

"We need to go," I shout to Jadon. "*Now.* Or we'll lose her again."

Jadon grabs the reins of two horses. Both look strong enough to carry us until the ends of the realm.

We gallop away from the smoke, racing beneath an immense blue sky that rolls on forever. I take a cleansing breath and look across to the man riding beside me, the man I thought I knew, the man who lied to me even as we depended on each other for survival, who shared my bed before the light rose in today's sky. He's not a blacksmith. He's not an Ealdrehrt. He's someone wholly different, someone I can no longer trust. Jadon Wake—the emperor's son.

My only ally.

57

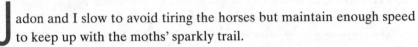

Jadon and I slow to avoid tiring the horses but maintain enough speed to keep up with the moths' sparkly trail.

"Can we talk about it?" Jadon asks.

I give him a firm head shake. My lips can't shut any tighter.

He huffs. "But I just want to—"

I throw him a glare so hot his horse's ear flicks.

There's nothing Jadon can say that will make this chase through the desert any better. There's nothing he can say that will make my heart hurt less.

The sooner we find Olivia and my amulet, the sooner he and I can separate, forever. Although the thought of leaving him forever makes my heart clench, I know my heart will heal.

Another gust of dry wind blows sand into our faces. I swipe at my eyes, and my hand brushes the cut on my cheek. *Oosh.* That's right—a soldier sliced my face with his blade. But this cut… It feels different than any nicks I've received since waking up in Maford. This cut even feels different than the scratch made by Gilgoni the aburan. I thought it was my explosive anger and my use of wind power that had made my face numb, but no. This cut feels *hot*, and in just that single touch, I feel its heat and its burning pulse. My skin feels tight—my face is swelling.

I look across to Jadon. He's scratched and nicked, and his nose looks swollen from the sucker punch, but he doesn't look vexed about it.

Is this peculiar pain a result of a blade, or is this part of my degeneration?

My face tingles, and my mouth tastes like metal—not the copper of blood but ore torn from a mountain. I can still move, but my muscles feel weighted down by that ore-filled mountain. Nothing looks true. The world has become a blur. I try to slow the rapid beating of my pulse, but nothing works, and a creeping anxiety quickens my breath.

Dry lightning cracks across the sky, and hot wind blows like angry rasping ghosts from every direction. All life has been sucked out of anything that once lived here, leaving behind gnarled husks of used-to-be. That used to be a cactus. That used to be a pond. That used to be a family of foxes. Tomorrow at this time, will Jadon and I also be used-to-be?

All the supplies we'd purchased in Caburh or been gifted by Ridget are back at the inn. My satchel filled with honey, wax, the plant chart, and Veril's journal are back in the sitting room of the Broken Hammer.

Jadon pushes his dirty hair from his face to search the sky. "I'd love to see a falcon now."

I'm looking for birds, too. Red cardinals to confirm Elyn's presence. A raven to portend death. My heart pounds like I'm still fighting. I can't catch my breath. My luclite armor isn't cooling me even as sweat pools beneath the soft woven fabric of my tunic. I feel no sensation from my forehead down to my shoulders.

Jadon points to a distant hill. "We'll ride there and set up camp. There's some green, which means there's water. Animals, maybe." He pushes a smile to his face—probably happy that I haven't blasted him to the sky yet. His eyes are bloodshot from ashes, dust, and exhaustion, and any good cheer he has hides beneath whiskers and bruises from our battles. "I even think I see—" But then he pales. "Kai, what's wrong?"

I blink at him, wobbling on my horse like a drunk, and say, "Gracious... potato," but those two words make no sense together. Those words sound like soup, and my tongue feels like it's dragging across this arid land.

Trying to hold my focus on the desert, my mind swims in an ocean of doubt. How could Sybel believe that I'm the only person who can stop Vallendor's destruction? Obviously, the Lady of Dawn and Dusk was desperate for *someone* to pick up the sword and fight for this realm. How can I achieve something that important—*save Vallendor*—when I can't even triumph against the very-human Gileon Wake? If I'm so powerful, if I am truly special, why am I here, in this desert, riding this stolen horse, numb and broken and still without my amulet?

Give up. Surrender.

Jadon's mouth moves, but I don't understand what he's saying. His eyes are big and shiny with an expression that looks like panic, but I don't know what he sees.

I slump in my saddle, and I glimpse sand and the right front leg of my horse.

Jadon flings himself off his horse and catches me before I fall from my mount.

I scream, my skin as tender as snowflakes, his touch as hot as wildfire. That fire travels everywhere, and it prickles against my numb upper body.

He shouts and looks around, frightened. He says something else; the only word I understand is "sorry."

I smile, and my mouth, gummy and strange, forms words that make no sense—to me or to him. I've lost everything.

S tone walls. Dark. Hard, wet earth.
 My chest hurts almost as much as my head. Knots as hard as this dirt lodge in my stomach. Every limb, every inch of skin... I don't have any limbs or skin. I can't feel any briars or thorns sinking into my face.

Jadon kneels beside me. A blur, he bends down and says, "They coat their swords with the strongest snake venom in this realm. I didn't know you'd been cut. Drink this."

I whisper, "'kay."

He parts my lips with his fingers and presses the canteen to my mouth.

I trust water is dribbling into my mouth, because I can't feel it. My tongue is as numb as my face and my arms. I taste nothing. I feel nothing. And yet I know his touch is gentle, and that deeper part of me I'd tried to kill yearns for more of that tenderness.

Slumming, according to Gileon Wake.

"You have to sit up for the antidote to work." He slips his arm beneath me, and despite that deeper part of me that yearns for it, there can never be true tenderness in his touch. His lying, half-truths, swindles, whispered sweet nothings that are—surprise—nothing at all. His acts of softness and sensitivity are ploys. His gentleness is a field of thorny milk thistles. His gentleness is a bed of poison oak leaves.

I need to push Jadon's hands away, but I'm too weak.

"Hey," he says, smiling, "I found echinacea and calamus root growing at the foot of the cave. I crushed it up, packed it beneath your tongue. I'm not Veril, but I'll have to do for now."

The mention of Veril squeezes my heart. I'll join him in the next life sooner than I thought.

Jadon grabs a blanket from beneath his horse's saddle and spreads it at the mouth of the cave, across a patch of long, soft grass and wildflowers that smell of honey and cinnamon.

"A nice place to die," I whisper.

"You're not going to die." He helps me settle on the blanket, then offers me water from another canteen.

"Just sit up a little longer," he says, draping a thin blanket around my shoulders. "Give the antidote time to work." He stands and peers out to the desert, hands on his hips. "We should be safe here for the night."

I blink—the dark sky now burns with oranges and purples.

"I'm gonna look around," Jadon says. "See what I can see. Maybe find Gileon's trail. Hope to not see what I don't want to see." He waits a beat, then adds a chuckle. "You should rest." He reaches down to stroke my cheek, but he remembers how tender I am and stops. "I'm sorry, Kai," he whispers. Regret crackles across his battered face as he moves away.

And soon, I hear only my labored breathing, the snort of tired horses, and the tinny echo of a dying world.

58

My eyes flutter open. The daystar's amber light signals that a new day has come.

A fish cooks on a spit. The burning wood crackles and makes soft smoke that smells of juniper wood and not tapestries, furniture, or tar. I see nothing else beyond that fire, that sky, and my companion.

Jadon stares into the flames. His face hard, his shoulders tense, he's lost, deep in thought.

What would I hear if I listened in? I whisper, "Hey."

He smiles. "Hey." The smile doesn't reach his eyes.

That deeper part of me finds joy just seeing him again—despite his betrayal, despite that strained smile not lighting his eyes. He's the only person I have in these wastelands now, and as much as I want to hate that, my relief is a true thing.

"Your nose," I say, circling my own nose with my finger. "It looks better. Not swollen." And the bruising that had started to spread beneath his eyes has changed its mind.

"Still hurts when I do this." He pinches the bridge of his nose.

"Then don't do that."

For a moment, his face brightens, old-Jadon-style.

I push up from the blanket and hug my knees to my chest. I'm feeling well enough to move on my own, which is more relief. I nod at the spit. "That's a big fish."

"You should've seen the one that got away," he jokes, but there's no humor in it.

I rest my head on my knees. My bones, my heart, my core…all brittle. One fall, one ill-timed move, and I'll shatter completely. Confusion and exhaustion bubble in my head and press down…down…down… I close my eyes and squeeze, even though squeezing may end me, too.

"I found water." Jadon offers me a canteen. He doesn't meet my eyes and instead focuses on sliding twigs through another fish.

I sip from the canteen and gag. The water tastes like dirty geld.

"I didn't say it was *good* water." Jadon frowns, rubbing a tense hand over his forehead. "I'm sorry I can't be of more help to you." He hands me roasted fish with whiskers, which looks just about as unappetizing as the water tastes.

And it is. I gag a little on the fish—tastes like sand.

"Catfish," he says. "It's an acquired taste."

"I wish not to acquire it, then." I shiver, then spit out the flesh. "Thank you, though."

He takes my portion and eats it.

"And there we were," I say, "just a night ago, with raisins and honey, a soft bed—"

"*Three* nights ago," he corrects.

"Three?" I've been unconscious for three nights?

We've most certainly lost Gileon Wake and his men now. Olivia, gone. My amulet, gone.

"Shit," I say, my mouth dry.

"Oh." He reaches for the saddlebag. "Almost forgot that I found..." He pulls out a flask and the smallest jar of honey I've ever seen. "What's better than rum and honey?" He grins, and true joy reaches his eyes as he offers me one of two twigs. We take turns sipping rum and dipping twigs into the jar of honey. The best concoction of warm and sweet that I've ever had.

Peering at the cuts on my cheek, Jadon says, "You look better than you did yesterday."

I don't remember yesterday, but then I don't remember lots of days. I rest my chin on my knees. "You made antivenoms and brought me back from the brink of death. You haven't been *totally* useless."

"It won't be enough." His scowl returns as he stares into the fire.

"What does that mean?" I ask. "Am I going to succumb to the venom after all?"

"No, it's not that. It's— Never mind." He goes back to staring into the fire.

"More secrets?" I snap. "What else is there?"

With his firmly set mouth and the distant look in his eyes, he's finally shaken off the husk of old Jadon. This version of Jadon is a prince by birth, not the man who crafted weapons and pretended to be a simple blacksmith.

"You owe me an explanation," I say. "Who am I traveling with? Jadon Ealdrehrt, the smithy? Or Jadon Wake, Prince of Brithellum? Nice to meet you, Your Highness. Or is it 'Your Grace'? Is it even 'Jadon'? Or are you Syrus Wake, Third of His Name, Prince of Brithellum and the First Men, Protector of Vallendor, the Keeper of Flame, the Blacksmith, the Best Fucking Liar on This Side of Wherever the Fuck We Are Right Now? Did I forget one?"

His knee bounces as he breaks twigs into little sticks. "Kai, it's not like that."

"Then what is it like?" I ask. "Because up until now, everything you've told me is a lie."

Our confessions in the dark. *It's not like that.*

How he feels next to me, beside me, inside me. *It's not like that.*

Him comforting me, one hurt after another. *It's not like that.*

Everything that we did or said to each other—every interaction that had been honest even if it was also uncomfortable and scary—*wasn't* honest, just uncomfortable. But I'd accepted comfort in those frustrating moments because at least we were still being authentic. I was wrong.

Kai, it's not like that.

What it's like? Hurtful and mean and violent. Loveless.

"Was any of what you told me true?" I ask. "Your abusive adoptive father? Old Myrtle in the shack? The hurt you felt when your General Stery died? That your life has been loveless? Or were you just playing on my pity? Gileon seems to love you well enough."

I love you, brother. No matter what happens. Always, always *remember that.*

Jadon tosses those broken twigs into the fire. "Yes, Gileon does love me. We relied on each other when we had no one else to trust. He took a lot of shit for me—he knew his punishment would be milder. He's the one who told me to run while I could, just to see how life felt outside those walls."

"Before you married your choice of princess?" I feel him stiffen even though he's sitting across from me. Once my mind slows from its frantic swirling, once I can breathe steadily, I rush ahead to mess the rest of it up with, "*Slumming?* Is that what you thought you were doing with me? What *we* were doing? How you saw me?"

He shakes his head. "It's not like that."

"Stop *saying* that!" I yell. "Would you even tell me if you *did* think that?"

He finally lifts his eyes to meet mine. "No."

I wait to hear him say more than this, but it feels like I'm looking out an open window and letting in both hot air and cold air, sweet air and foul... And this makes me shiver. "No," I say, not moving my gaze from his but choosing, instead, to push deeper into my gaze, deeper than I've ever gazed before, and there, at the end of my stare, there's...a closed window, the glass opaque and unbreakable.

Opaque because I can no longer hear his thoughts. Is that now my new weakness?

Or, because of Elyn's gifts, is that now his newest strength? I press my palms to my temples to silence the buzzing in my head. I'm not fully healed from the venom yet.

"I've never faked how I feel about you," he says, his voice husky.

I push through the malaise and focus on his face, hoping to see something there to prove his words are true. I don't. A liar is a liar. "What is this 'plan' Gileon mentioned?" I ask. "What did he mean by no one expecting the Grand Defender to be so tantalizing?"

Jadon shakes his head, and his eyes roam back to the fire. "'Plan' meaning when I was supposed to return to Brithellum. And about how no one thought that you—"

"Me?"

"You—the Grand Defender," Jadon says, "the one who plans to stop the emperor from conquering all of Vallendor, would look like...you."

I jerk and sit up straighter. "What does *that* mean?"

And who said that *I* was *the* Grand Defender? Sybel didn't call me that. Elyn didn't call me that. What makes Gileon Wake think that I am? Besides, I'm not here to stop the emperor from conquering all of Vallendor. He is not the One...*is he*? Sybel didn't say he was...but it's hard to think of anyone else who it might be.

"Gileon didn't expect you to be so strong," Jadon continues. "That you could possibly have so much influence that I'd lose my way."

"Have you?" I ask. "Lost your way?"

He says nothing, then: "Yes."

I turn my head toward the cave walls. But his admission is not enough. I look back at him. "Are you saying that you knew who I was before I did?"

His jaw tightens. Then: "Yes."

I can't even say, "What," because I've lost my ability to gasp.

"But not at first," he corrects. "I thought you'd stolen the amulet from someone, just like Olivia stole it from you. But the more time we spent together at Veril's and on the road, the stronger you became... I could no longer doubt who you were." He shakes his head, then looks at me with awe. "My father's greatest enemy landing in the town I was hiding in... Here I am, trying to hide out in Maford, but I can't even do that because of...because of fate."

I drop my head between my knees to keep from fainting, and my breath saws in and out in short pants. My mind races— *How could you, why didn't you say something, you watched me flail, you have no heart, why, why,* why? I want to ask all these things and say so much more, but his confession has punched me so hard that I've gone mute.

"Not everything I told you was a lie." Jadon's eyes flash, and he stands up and backs away from me. "The emperor...my father...we... he... He's never loved me. That's true. To him, I'm good for one thing: killing. But when I'm with you, I'm more than that. And every day I've spent with you, I wished that... I wanted... I tried to figure out a way that it could be just the two of us together.

"And sometimes, it *was* just the two of us, and it was so incredible, so... *otherworldly*, but eventually *this* world interfered again. Soldiers, Elyn, aburan, fucking gerammocs. All of it reminded me of my destiny and forced me to remember that I'm nothing more than a killer. And even now, my father doesn't want me back because he *misses* me. He wants me back because he'll become more powerful with me behind him. Not even at his side. That would suggest equality, and there's no one equal to Supreme manifested as man."

"So your solution, then," I say, lifting my head from my knees, "was to lie to me. Lie to someone who actually cared about you and would've helped—"

"Helped?" He laughs, and it's a jagged and terrible sound.

Expressionless, he squares his shoulders and clenches his hands into fists. "I don't think I can—" He begins again. "This isn't working, and I'm doing nothing but hurting you."

"How many times are you going to say that?"

"Until I believe it," he shouts. "Until I accept it—"

"Accept *what*?" I shout back. "That you're not perfect? That people hurt other people, especially those they're supposed to care about? Or accept that you've played a role in me being in this cave, and if I never find my amulet and become nothing more than a wisp of who I was, then it's your fault? Because yes, you've hurt me. A lot. And I haven't done anything to deserve that." I lift an arm and swing it through the air. "But now what? How is any of this acceptance helping us right now? Oh yeah. I keep forgetting that there is no 'us.' You told me that. But then you took it back in my room at the inn, and now…" I squeeze the bridge of my nose and take a breath. "Now, I know nothing."

"We're wasting time," he says.

"Are we?" I scoff. "Where do *you* have to be right now? Oh, are you choosing now to return to your brother and your fancy life in the castle? Things get too rough for you out here, Prince Jadon?"

He glares at the fire. The saddlebag slides off his shoulder and lands at his feet. "I should've left when you were still asleep," he says more to himself than to me. "It would've been easier for both of us."

Veril Bairnell the Sapient was right again. *Don't trust anyone to bring you that which makes you whole. They may not* want *you whole.*

Jadon never wanted me whole.

"Just go ahead and say something," he demands, eyes hot. "Curse at me. Call me a coward or—" He exhales, and his shoulders drop. "But I'm still leaving."

I search his eyes, but I can't find him there. But then…who *is* he? "You're abandoning me here because you're, what? Frightened? Confused? Bored? Lazy? Evil? What?"

"I'm doing this to help you," he says, his teeth clenched. "You going on your own means I can't be forced to hurt you, no matter what Gileon or my father want—"

"Is that it?" I ask, squinting at him. "You're scared of Daddy now that he's got his eyes on you? Are you relieved that you're about to live your happily ever after, that you can now stop roaming and *slumming* across all of Vallendor with someone like me—?"

"That's not it at all!" he shouts. "Have you heard anything I've said? I'm leaving to protect you!"

"By leaving me in a *cave*?" I shriek.

"I can't—" Jadon paces, moving even farther away, tugging his hair with one hand. "I should never have let it go this far."

"But you let it go this far, and here we stand." I blink away angry tears burning my eyes. "Only cowards run."

"I promise you," he says, his words faltering, "I'm leaving for your own good. When I say that I don't want to hurt you, I mean it."

I hold out my arms. "Then don't hurt me. *Stop* hurting me."

"All of this, it's unreasonable, I know. All of this is inevitable.

Unavoidable."

"What's inevitable? What's unavoidable?" I ask, not wanting to give up, but I don't even know if I want to win. I don't know what it even *means* to win. My heart slows as I open myself to the inevitable, the unavoidable. No more "us." My skin grows clammy as a new thought blooms in my mind: all this time, I've accused Olivia of betraying me, when all along...

Don't trust anyone. Depend on you and you alone.

Veril told me not to trust Jadon.

I should have listened.

Olivia stole my clothes, and for the second time, she's stolen my amulet, and she's now traded it for her freedom. Jadon, the son of the man who's been hunting me, is working with Gileon, who is also working with Elyn. Who knows what else he's done.

All because they think I'm a threat to the One—to Elyn?

Do they really believe that my purpose for being here is to fuck around with mortals who want shinier castles and more land, more riches, more worshippers? Why should I care about that? Why would I risk my life to simply stop the nonsense of *time-hoarders* on an emperor who will die, and his two sons who will die, and their sons who will die? Does a bear care about the daily life of ants? Do ants think they can bring down a bear? They can make the bear miserable, sure. But actually killing the bear? Oh, the folly of ants.

But now I see that the ants are working for a bear, one who commands otherworldly to kill, who spills protective magic upon the emperor's soldiers for her benefit.

I'm also a bear, a goddess, the Grand Defender. Before forgetting my life, I didn't fear men as I moved above the realm. And I don't fear them now even in my weakest state. Elyn may think she knows who I am, but she doesn't *understand* who I am. Because if she wanted to successfully destroy me, she'd need to do more than sic Syrus Wake and his sons on me and keep me away from my amulet. Wake and his sons should've been just as eternal as me.

Oh, the absurdity of these men who believed they could possibly end me.

The only person in Vallendor who's just as eternal as me and has the power and ability to destroy me is Elyn. She should've skipped using the Wakes—her humans—as trained falcons who've done nothing but warn me that she's near.

"Is your boss on her way here?" I now ask Jadon.

He doesn't speak.

"Did you make it so that I'd be too weak to fight against someone so strong?"

He keeps his gaze averted and remains silent.

So that's how it's supposed to end. I'm supposed to die by Elyn's hand. Did he bring me to this cave for that purpose? Will this be my tomb?

I hold back the first sob that rattles my chest, but the second escapes. "How could you be so *heartless*? How can you be so *cruel*?"

Pain and sorrow streak across Jadon's face. He takes a step toward me, reaching out like he might comfort me.

"You and Olivia," I say, swiping away my tears, backing away from him. "You both stole something from me. The thing that keeps me whole is gone. You plundered with her—and you did far more damage to me than *anyone* on this journey. You had the privilege to touch me, to sleep beside me, to sit and talk to me, and even now, you're standing here and I haven't thrown you across this cave. A privilege you trampled."

I turn away, willing my legs to keep me upright. "You don't have to pretend to care about me anymore," I snarl. "You don't have to take care of me and keep me alive for her. Your job is done. You may now stop slumming and return to Brithellum to collect your reward. Go on and pick up your princess and polish your crown and make your little babies and tell epic stories of that time in your life that you fucked the Lady of the Verdant Realm."

"You think all this is about getting you in *bed*?" he asks, eyes hard. "Is *that* what you're saying?"

I meet his glare with one of my own. "If I say what I *want* to say, you'd have no ears to hear another word spoken ever again."

"You don't know me at all," he whispers.

"Poor, misunderstood Jadon. You know what? I can't listen to this anymore." I shake my head, but the rest of me shakes even more. With a trembling hand, I point to the world beyond the cave, where the daystar slinks behind the horizon. "Go. Do your own thing. You don't want to *hurt* me? Guess what? You failed. You hurt me. Fuck you."

Silence fills the cave—if it wasn't for the crackle of fire and the drip of water somewhere in this rock, one could mistake this place for a tomb.

"Jadon?"

He looks at me over his shoulder.

"Are you happy?" I ask, echoing his brother's question.

"No." Without hesitation.

"Were you ever happy?"

He rolls that question around in his head like a pebble before skipping it across a pond. Air catches in his throat, and he looks at me again before breaking our gaze to stare out beyond our shelter. "No."

Yes, this place *is* a tomb.

Because something has died here and will never find its way out.

Jadon Wake, Prince of Vallendor, eldest son of Emperor Syrus Wake, Supreme Manifest, has abandoned me. He even took both horses with him, stranding me here as the daystar sets. He couldn't have even left me a *horse*? Does he really want me to die in this cave? Is this part of the deal he made with Elyn? Or is this a bonus?

He's forsaken me as though we had no history together, as though nothing we did together mattered.

He comforted me when I didn't know who I was and when I'd lost the most important person in my life. We'd lain side by side, as friends, as lovers.

How could I have believed that we were either?

I rest my head against my knees.

Why couldn't Jadon have kept his lies tucked in at least until I reclaimed my pendant? But I was never going to reclaim my pendant—that wasn't part of the "plan." Maybe if we'd returned to the road after Separi brought me my armor and not spent the night at the inn.

But Gileon was already nearby with Olivia. Leaving the inn wasn't part of the "plan."

I don't want to hurt you.

Whatever, Jadon Whoever-the-Fuck-You-Are.

I touch the cheek injured by that poisonous blade. My skin feels soft there. No scar. How many plants would I need to heal my heart? Honestly? I feel better with Jadon gone. I no longer have to hold my breath. I no longer have to wonder what he thinks or how he feels. I no longer have to slow down. Desire will no longer cloud my judgment. As natural as it is, and as good as it feels, touching and being touched won't be considerations in what I should or should not do.

What was I even thinking, falling for a mortal? I'm a goddess. I'm sure I've had better men. Stronger men. Men who'd last eternally, in every way. Jadon Wake is the dirt beneath my feet, and frankly, I'm embarrassed. Embarrassed that I've been fooled. Embarrassed that everyone was in on the joke except me. Embarrassed that I wanted to be caressed by someone actively scheming against me. Embarrassed that I fell for a phantom, a farce, a great pretender.

All of it reminded me of my destiny and forced me to remember that I'm nothing more than a killer. That's what Jadon said. As the eldest son of the emperor, his destiny includes conquering all of Vallendor in the name of his father.

Yet Elyn was the one who claimed that *I* would be the destruction of the realm? How can that be when the Wakes have had a hand in every destruction on her behalf—Maford and Caburh and wherever they're headed now. Wake, his son Gileon, and his son who'd posed as a simple blacksmith but swung his sword like a...

God.

Hmm.

What if I've been wrong all this time? What if Elyn isn't the One?

What if the One has been closer to me than I thought?

What if the One has been right here beside me all this time?

59

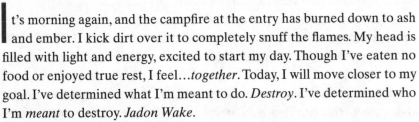

It's morning again, and the campfire at the entry has burned down to ash and ember. I kick dirt over it to completely snuff the flames. My head is filled with light and energy, excited to start my day. Though I've eaten no food or enjoyed true rest, I feel...*together*. Today, I will move closer to my goal. I've determined what I'm meant to do. *Destroy*. I've determined who I'm *meant* to destroy. *Jadon Wake*.

The more I thought about it through the night, the more Jadon being the One made sense.

Sybel gave me all that I needed to know.

Powerful forces are already after you, Kai, and they will try to influence you, lull you into slumber, trick you so that you never defeat the One.

Jadon Wake is the only person who has lulled me into slumber. He did all of this to grow more powerful and claim control of the realm. Again: fuck Vallendor. If he wants it, then he can have it—

Air catches in my throat, and a chill shoots through me.

That's the problem, though. Sybel warned me. *If the One is not stopped. If that power goes unchecked, the One will move on to the next realm, growing more powerful still, and on to the next realm, and on and on until...*

Shit. Shit-shit-shit.

Even if I leave Vallendor and settle in another free realm, Jadon Wake would be there, eventually, and he'd possibly be manifested as someone else. As another siren song wielding a big sword.

I can't escape this.

Inevitable. Unavoidable.

Okay. So, yes. I *will* move closer to my goal. And I remain committed to what I'm meant to do, what Sybel pleaded for me to do. *Destroy*. Stop the One. And I will stop the One. I will destroy *Jadon Wake*.

Having nowhere to run means I have to move forward. Having no choices means I have only one choice. I stow both Fury and Little Lava in their scabbards, pull on my armor, grateful that my gear is light; my mission, though, is not. Jadon Wake has a huge head start on me—more than twelve hours, and I'm on foot. That gives him at least another day's advantage, maybe two depending on the terrain.

"Goodbye, cave," I say, looking around. "Sorry for disturbing your quiet with bullshit."

Plinking. Dripping. Silence. Just like we found it.

Outside, silver mist rolls across the craggy ground that turns from desert sand and granite to a slick green and yellow. The air feels moist here, not pleasant at all. There must be a body of water nearby, which is probably where Jadon caught the catfish. It's not a healthy, refreshing body of water, not with a sky and air like this. And there's not enough light streaming here this morning to crisp it. No breeze to stir it and push it out.

I pick my way down the side of this craggy hill and spot the goopy-looking stream, making the air and these surrounding boulders slick, then sit...sit...doing nothing.

It may be goopy-looking, but at least this stream has a current—it's alive but neglected.

I find the cleanest, flattest spot on the banks of this creek and wash my face as best as I can without soap. I lament leaving behind the lemon-mint soap from Veril and the peppermint oil from Ridget. Couldn't be helped. The water is cold and slick, but my dirty hands become less dirty, and that makes me smile.

I dip my hands back into the stream, then run them over my dry hair, being careful to not loosen the braids and lose the luclite threads that help to hold me together. While I'm far from the clean I'd enjoyed after my bath at the Broken Hammer, parts of me are more refreshed.

With no map, I must rely on the rise and set of the daystar to guide me toward my new destination, which is even farther than Mount Devour: Brithellum, home of the Wakes, including Jadon Wake, the One. There, I will fulfill my obligation, destroy the One, and then take my rightful place where the realm meets the sky on Mount Devour—where Veril said I'd survey my realm. *My* realm.

Day turns to night, and then the sky lightens to day. Then night comes again and day follows once more. I have no food, no water, no tools. I have Fury and Little Lava, but there is no game to hunt. I live by my wits, surviving on the meager offerings the blighted land provides along my way. Bitter nuts. Dying berries. Leaves that taste like pepper. Vengeance and indignation are excellent motivators, but after days of hunger and exhaustion, I find myself flagging mentally and physically.

On the dawn of this third day, I scan a forest devoid of life. No chirping birds or croaking frogs. Not even the buzz of a honeybee. *Stay focused. Stay strong.* That's what Veril would tell me if he were here. *Keep going, dearest.* I hear his laughter bouncing off the dying pines and rolling down the steep hillside before me and—

Shit. I lean against a tree and close my eyes, my heart broken and will nearly depleted. Everything in me has broken—from my knees to my toes. And what hasn't been broken, I've lost. My amulet. My memory. Veril. *Jadon.*

A chill runs along my spine and rolls out over my arms. The humidity makes my skin prickle, and for a moment I fear that either I've become feverish or the memory of Veril is making me physically ache. But then a breeze brushes against my ears, face, and neck, and I shiver. I'm not alone here—but I don't sense danger, either. No glowing amber or blue shine from behind these low failures of shrubs and trees.

Another breeze, this one coming from the north, just like the first...
What's that?

Pulsing. Keening. Vibrations from the dirt push against the soles of my boots. Soon, red and gold moths drift down from the sky and bump and swirl against my face.

I smile, ready to rejoice, but then I narrow my eyes and scan the forest and those fluttering moths.

Where exactly is my pendant? Who has it?

The pulsing grows stronger, and pressure builds between my eyes and behind my ears. I push my fingers against my forehead. No relief. Just more pressure.

The moths cloud my vision—so many of them now, and that keening... It's coming from the moths. They shift, no longer a tower about me but an undulating trail that shimmers with gold and red dust, leading away from the forest and down the mountainside.

I stand and follow, winding through the craggy rocks of the wasteland. Down...down...

By late in the day, the rocky gravel and mossy stones give way to richer earth—far from perfect, this part of the desert, but green thrives because of the better access to light. There are sharp, spiky-leafed plants and low shrubs with red berries over there. More low-growing shrubs with purple lavender there. Patches of twisted junipers that soar into the air here.

Groves of pine trees that don't require much water over there; their thin needles remind me of a teen boy's first mustache. Curious-looking trees with low branches and ironwood trees with dense, hard barks everywhere. The sparkling trail winds around the trunks of these pine trees.

That pulsing in my gut urges me to move on. I take a deep breath and continue my hike, passing dead trees that look healthier than the living ones.

Far in the distance, the faint, unmistakable sounds of battle drift through the trees.

How many soldiers will be at the end of this trail? How many otherworldly? How many angry Dashmala who've heard that I drove a pike through the skull of one of their fiercest warriors? Maybe Gileon Wake and his men are part of this battle and that is why the moths are leading me this way. Could Olivia be near? Or Jadon?

The sparkling trail ends at hedges that surround a knoll. I push through the tangled greenery and...

"Well, who the fuck do we have here?" A single soldier sits upon a tree trunk, his legs splayed out, casual, unbothered. He resembles an anteater with his long, narrow nose and nonexistent lips.

I know he isn't as alone as he appears. I heard the others. Smelled them, too.

Soon, they roll like fog from behind the trees and logs, wearing copper-colored breastplates, grinning and self-congratulatory, as though they'd successfully hidden from me.

They wouldn't know success even if she pushed through tangled greenery and stood before them.

"Look who's here," one soldier sneers, his teeth tobacco-stained brown.

"Wake's whore," another soldier cracks.

Eight, nine...eleven soldiers. One me.

I like those odds.

Beyond the forest, the sounds of battle continue.

I point in the direction of the distant fighting. "Shouldn't you assholes be out there killing something other than my time?"

"Look at her," Broken Nose hoots. "Look at her weird eyes."

"Oh no. They've gone all screwy!"

"You better watch out."

The stained-tooth soldier steps forward from the crowd. His hazel eyes glitter cruelly, and the smile cracking on his face reveals an even crueler heart. "Looking for this?" The stained-toothed soldier reaches beneath his breastplate and pulls out—

My amulet! My precious pendant—*the object I need more than anything else in this realm*—hangs from his dirty fingers.

"Thought you'd never see *me* again, right?" The soldier with the big ego, this one resembling a donkey with those teeth and that forehead, sidles toward me, his arms folded, a smirk on his lips.

"See you *again*?" I say, head cocked. "When was the first time?"

The smirk flinches some. "At the Broken Hammer."

I blink at him. "Okay."

"We fought, you and I," he insists.

I lift my eyebrows. "Okay. If you say so."

Hee-Haw grimaces—men hate being forgettable. "I cut your cheek. My blade—"

"Had the snake venom," I say, pointing at him. "I almost died by *this much*," I say, pinching my thumb and index finger together. "But you couldn't finish the job. Bet you hear that a lot, don't you?"

His face goes red, but before he can respond, I swipe my hand and use wind to throw him against the closest pine tree. There's a crack of his head against wood, of that violated wood splintering. Then there's a rush of wind as that tree falls, its branches and needles serving as a shroud for the soldier who almost killed me by *this much*.

Is he Number Sixty-Five?

The moths darting around my head flit away. They've brought me here, to my amulet; their job is done. And now it's time for me to do mine. I slowly pull Fury from her scabbard and hold my breath as the guard swings my amulet from his grubby finger, not looking quite as frightened as he should. I slowly release that air, and it wraps around my head like smoke. "I suggest," I say, starting off politely, "that you return my property. Unless you want to end up buried beneath a tree like your friend."

"And *I* suggest," the soldier says, "that you kiss my arse." And then he pulls down his dirty breeches and shakes his dirtier ass at me.

His comrades laugh.

I smile. "Go ahead and laugh." I meet each soldier's eyes. "I hope each of you have put all your affairs in order—that you wrote those last letters to your sweethearts, that you're wearing clean underwear." My hand now buzzes around the hilt of my sword.

Ready to work.

Three soldiers rush me, swords and axes held high above their heads. I sweep my hand, knocking all three into the sharpest, craggiest boulder. I don't even wince hearing that abrupt crunch of three separate spines against rock.

That's…sixty-eight.

Two more soldiers flank me.

I send wind from my hand, lifting both high into the sky—they scream and scream—and then swipe my hand down, dropping them—they scream and scream until they don't.

Sixty-nine, seventy…

"Why don't you fight without your sorcery, bitch!" another soldier spits.

I twist my hand in the air.

The soldier clutches his throat. His veins push against his forehead.

I cup my ear with my wind-whipping hand. "What's that you said? Bitch, what?"

He gags until he's the purple of turnips.

I'm striving for eggplant.

I twist my hand once more.

Seventy-one!

The soldier with the filthy ass and my pendant backs away from me. "You put that sword down," he says, "and I'll give it to you."

"Put my property down," I say, easing toward number seventy-two, "and I'll let you live."

Nasty Ass spits on the ground, then spits on my pendant. "There. How you like that?"

I pluck Little Lava from her sheath and whip her at Nasty Ass—but I don't aim for his head. No, I want the hand holding my amulet. But I'll have to be satisfied with taking all five of his fingers.

He screams, and his severed fingers fall into the dirt. *Plop, plop, plop, plop.* The last finger, the one still wrapped around my gold chain, pops into the air and lands at my boot. Shrieking, the soldier clutches his bloody hand and collapses to the ground.

Pain shoots through my chest and my bones, my heart, my core… Too much exertion. But at least my amulet is *right there.* My body begs for it.

But there are three remaining soldiers to dispatch before I can find release.

Before I can muster up another blast of wind or swing Fury, though, the surviving three soldiers scatter in every direction. Saloroaches have more courage than these men.

Alone now—well, among the living—my eyes fill with tears, and I kick away the soldier's thumb. Finally freed from one captor after another, the amulet swirls with colors, and now those colors blur because I'm crying and can barely breathe and my head bangs and I want to tear off my clothes and dance naked in the woods. Moths, hundreds of them, swoop down from the sky. Sparkles and dust everywhere—the moths are happy, too.

I drop to my knees and crawl over to my amulet, creeping like it's a grasshopper and will bounce away if I move too quick. But the pendant doesn't move. It just beats, and the beating in my body keeps time with it.

Hand shaky, I slowly reach for the pendant. My finger touches the moth's onyx thorax. "Hello, beloved."

60

I t feels as though I've been walking for the greater part of a year instead of the greater part of a day. I cock my head to listen.

Shrieks and shouts of men. Shrieks and shouts of otherworldly. Steel hitting steel. Thunder from the sky and rumbles from the earth. The sounds of battle.

But whose battle?

I squeeze my pendant, its jewels still glistening in the sky's weird-colored light. The catherite stone in the moth's thorax, though, remains cold, dark. I creep toward the roar of fighting, my body tingling as I climb another rocky outcropping, careful to avoid detection. The battle grows louder, and the light of the sky shifts from gray to red. The air stinks. Rotten eggs, corpses, fire, algae, death, and…

Nausea causes me to stop and take a moment to let its crest fall in on itself. My wet, burning eyes acclimate to the strong fumes. Better now, I clamber onto a boulder and see…

A massive plain with steam hissing from heat vents in the cracked ground, a thick crust of salt and bones. No plants, since the closest water source kills, since no decent amount of rain has fallen from the sky, not with a ground that cracked.

The Sea of Devour glows a green that comes not from algae but something far more sinister, more malignant. Death makes this sea green. Its waves are daggers, gutting and melting every creature that dares to dip a toe in her waters. It boils from heat, like hot springs, noxious steam rising from the water's surface, the temperature high enough to melt the minerals that contain it. Vapor clouds shroud the banks of bleached sand twinkling with crystals and bones of creatures who thought they'd made it safely from the other side.

The sea abruptly ends at the foot of Mount Devour and sheer limestone and shale cliff walls that soar past a scarlet sky that bleeds lava, pebbles, and silt, and disappears into hissing clouds that spew acidic mist. Tangled trees and brush burst from blackened jagged peaks before more naked limestone and shale, monstrous, creeping vines, spiky trees and knifelike ridges notch the mountain's sides, the harsh terrain ready to squeeze and skewer any man or beast that dares test her.

The only creatures that can withstand this wasteland are now fighting each other. The earth shakes as aburan and creatops, gerammocs and burnu fight sunabi and battabies, large serpents and saloroaches upon the plains and near the banks. Some beasts try to swim across or fly over that sea to scale Mount Devour's cliff walls. Those that succeed eventually fall to their deaths, adding to the piles of dead and rotting otherworldly that form hills at the mount's base.

As I suspected, Wake's troops are battling on the plains. Banners fly high and unblemished from staffs held by soldiers on horseback. Banners bearing leopards, armored hands, and paddled colures mix with blood and mud on the ground. Men wearing copper-painted armor fight poison-quilled worupines, sunabi, serpents, and giant lizard creatures that stand on two feet and have the faces of women...*leolsips*, I recall. But there are otherworldly, aburan and burnu, that also wear tunics of the kingdom of Brithellum, slashing and trampling, ripping and beheading otherworldly without the emperor's sigil.

Otherworldly fighting under the flag of Emperor Wake?

I knew Elyn had formed an alliance with Wake back in Caburh when she sent her cursuflies after me. But this is something bigger.

The aburan and burnu do not attack the soldiers wearing the emperor's crest. No, they're trying to attack creatures with no outward designations of allegiance—the leolsips, sunabi, battawhale, and serpents. What is either side fighting for? And how did the Wakes harness the power of the aburan and other beasts?

The earth trembles beneath my boots, matching the quaking chaos in my chest. The bare-chested otherworldly surge like a tide against the straining lines of soldiers and their tunic-wearing beasts. The air is thick with the stench of blood and sweat, and I feel the heat of the flames and the force of steel colliding.

There, in the fray, Prince Gileon, his armor glinting like the promise of dawn, fights back-to-back with Jadon, whose new regalia attests his newfound allegiance. His gleaming, dark-gray armor is a stark contrast from the ragtag leather and chainmail he wore when we fought side by side. Now, he shimmers, opulent and glowing, a prince once again.

The two men move in unison, their steps fluid and graceful. Each movement is precise and calculated, their swords flashing and sparking as they strike down their enemies, who soon lie lifeless at their feet.

Envy stings like poison ivy as I watch Jadon pivot and swing with his brother. We'd perfected fighting together, born of trust and intimate knowledge of the other's every reflex.

But now, the boys are back together. Jadon abandoned me in a cave to join his brother, to return to his place in the kingdom. His time spent slumming over.

Fuckers.

They've finally conquered the parts of Vallendor that matter, and what—they're here to conquer the gods? Is that why they've allied themselves with Elyn? The remaining otherworldly not under her spell fight with all they have to prevent them from reaching Mount Devour. Are the Wakes convinced that their strength and privilege and claims of their father being Supreme Manifest as Man will win them the realm?

The earth shakes. A bright light shimmers atop Mount Devour, illuminating the boiling sea below like the daystar. The light pops and, like a comet, soars from that pinnacle and pushes past the stinging mists, past the tunic-wearing otherworldly hurtling across the battlefield. I understand that light—the same as Olivia saw in the sky over Maford when I appeared out of nowhere—and dread no longer exists in me. I'm ready to face her.

Elyn, the woman who's pursued me since the day I found myself nearly naked in the woods outside Maford, emerges now from a crater, hopping down from the dust and rubble made from her landing near the cliffs closest to the sea. Her long white hair cascades around her head. Her blue-and-gold armor catches the light that survives these clouds of Devour's poison. She slides her silver blade through the bare chest of a leolsip who attempted to maul her, then kicks the creature's chest.

She lifts her hand, and the otherworldly closest to her—the ones without tunics—lift their heads and turn her way. She points toward beasts and men wearing tunics, and the commanded beasts race toward the soldiers, teeth gnashing, claws out.

If she's driving these beasts, that must mean, then, that she *is* the One after all, not Jadon. She's doing something that I couldn't do—control otherworldly. Despite Sybel's denial, I know that Elyn *did* send those cursuflies and sunabi after me. She probably sent the burnu and gerammoc, too. And are any of these aburan the creature who swiped his paw at me back in Caerno Woods?

My anger licks off of me in waves as hot and toxic as that sea and the plains before me.

I start my march across the saltpan, sometimes losing Elyn in the vapor but keeping my eyes on the red cardinals fluttering over her. I whip my hand, and my wind smacks at every creature that nears me with their teeth bared. I whip my other hand, and fire consumes any man that nears me. Sweat soaks my hair, and the misty blood of the dead pebbles on my armor. I don't stop my stride as I mark the cardinals swooping and brightening the sky.

There Elyn stands, thirty paces before me, atop a hillock of new dirt and gravel. Her white hair is now braided, even though moments ago, it floated free. No longer wearing blue-and-gold armor, she wears white pangolin scales and a cloak of swirling golds and blues. The walking stick has replaced her blade, but it looks just as solid, no longer clouds and snow. The glossy black stone in the center of her dove amulet pulses with gray-and-red energy. She glides toward me, her movements graceful and hypnotic. Flawless. She looks as though this battle is just one more task to complete today.

She now stands before me, and the cardinals, her sentinels, flutter away.

I thrust both hands at her, catching her off guard. She's knocked back by my wind. She speeds away from me, stopping only after she rights herself and drags her fingers through the hard earth.

But I've been marching toward her as she glided.

The world around us is silent, as though we're inhabiting a bubble.

"Stop where you stand," she shouts.

I throw less wind, enough to knock her back on her ass. "Here I am, bitch," I shout. "Chasing me across the realm? I'm not running anymore. You're looking for me? You found me. 'Give me Kai'? Well, here the fuck I am. Now what?" Hatred and exhaustion flicker in my core until my anger burns white-hot against my skin.

Adrenaline fills my limbs, rolling back like waves and then surging forward, stronger now. I pull out Fury—my sword has gained mass, and I'm ready to take an ear, a finger, a hair, a single slice of her skin. Any trophy, anywhere.

61

"Stop!" Elyn shouts again, breathing heavily.

"You're gonna make your otherworldly kill me?" The air around me crackles, and I thrust another sizzling gale at her with my free hand.

She tumbles back again, rolling into a crouch. We've reached the banks of the sea, and she has nowhere to go. "The otherworldly are not my beasts. I didn't create them—neither did Supreme." Her eyebrow arches as her gaze travels from my feet to my head, taking in my hand-me-down luclite and trusty cloak.

"Yeah, I'm beating your ass wearing rags." I stand before her, legs apart, sword at my side. "I hear you're looking for me."

Elyn squints, then grimaces. "And you look like shit."

"Aren't *you* the judgmental one," I say.

She shrugs. "That's my job."

"Why are you here?" I growl. "What is this about? Why will you be dying today?"

She throws her head back and laughs. Like…belly laughs. "Tears in her eyes" laugh. Her eyes scan me again, and she falls into another fit.

"Fine." I lift my hand, and blue crackles pop across my fingertips.

Her eyes widen, and she yells, "Don't."

But it's too late.

This time, I use wind to sweep a boulder from the pile of fallen rocks and throw it at her.

The boulder hits Elyn's left side. She cries out in pain as she's slammed to the ground.

I pull that boulder back and let it hang in midair over her.

Elyn, supine on the ground, lifts her head, eyeing the boulder and watching me. Tears shine in her eyes. "You're still Kai," she says, her voice weakened. "Still quick to act. Still quick to judge. Still impatient. And all of that has led us…" She reaches out and takes control of the boulder hanging above her and hurls it into the sea. "For once in your life, listen to me. *Please.*"

I search her face for duplicity. I see none and drop my hands.

"I never thought I'd be on this side and you on the other," Elyn says, climbing to her feet, "especially since we started our journeys of becoming together. And now, here we are, on Vallendor, in yet another war."

"*Another?*" I cock my head. "I don't know what you're talking about."

She squints at me, wondering if my confoundment is true or not. "Mutiny."

"By?"

"You."

I roll my eyes and murmur, "Not this again. I refuse to believe that I willfully destroyed the realm of my kin. I would remember something as horrible as that."

"Do you remember the realm of Kestau, then?" she asks, breathless. "Forests and blue lagoons, animals, rocks, and shells. One of the oldest and largest realms, so large that it needed separate governments. The realm of marathons and athletes."

Not really, but I don't want to show any kind of weakness, and so I nod. "Yes."

She squints at me. "Then you remember that we visited Kestau as children all the time. You were there with your mother and my mother, and I ran my last marathon there while a convocation was being held. The convocation turned deadly."

When I say nothing, she takes a step forward. "Danar Rrivae."

That name. I startle and lift my head. "The sunabi."

Elyn says, "Excuse me?"

"Back in Maford," I say, my eyes darting from one place on the ground to another. "The ones you sent to attack me in the Ealdrehrts' cottage. One of the sunabi I'd fought was dying, and it said those words, 'Danar Rrivae,' before it passed. 'Danar Rrivae' and 'Devour.'"

I look up and around me, my gaze lingering on the toxic green sea. My throat closes as a memory comes into focus—a giant Mera warrior with his long black hair tied back, his bloodred armor, the largest sword I've ever seen.

"And when was the last time you saw Danar Rrivae?" Elyn asks.

I shake my head.

"On Kestau," she says. "He was a senator of that realm. But he grew displeased with his station, with the council, and he thought so much of himself that he believed he should have been able to run Kestau the way he desired. That last convocation, he was ejected but refused to leave the realm. No, he stood on the steps of Kestau's abbey and tried to force his way into the convocation that had gathered to vote on his punishment for insubordination. He and his followers—Eserime, Dindt, Mera, and mortals—tried to push their way past the sentinels blocking the doors." She cocks her head. "Danar rammed his sword into the belly of the sentinel captain."

My jaw tightens, and I shift my eyes back to Devour as memories fade in and out of focus like a mirage. "There was fighting afterward."

"Yes."

I hear the sounds of battle, cries, explosions. "He took Kestau and vowed to take the regions especially of his enemies. The Council of High Orders."

Mutiny.

Elyn nods. "He lost access to the first realm, taking with him scores of warriors and believers of every order. Some served as his spies, influencing their commanders in a way that would benefit Danar Rrivae. That's when the Great War started—"

A towering burnu, muscles rippling beneath its reddish-gray fur, lumbers toward us with a boulder hoisted high above its head. With a guttural snarl, it hurls the boulder straight at me. I dive to the side just in time, feeling the rush of air as the rock crashes into the mountain wall behind me. The impact sends tremors through the ground, dislodging a cascade of stones from the cliffs above. I thrust out my hand, sending a fierce wind current that slams into the burnu and flings him into a throng of snarling sunabi.

Elyn smiles and nods at me. "Impressive."

"Fuck you," I mutter, wandering away from her and scanning the men fighting and dying. Gileon and Jadon still move crisply and in sync. "What does the Great War have to do with you? With me? With—?" I sweep a hand at the vista before us.

Elyn also looks across the battlefield, and a small grin finds its way to her lips. "Danar Rrivae took Kestau. And then he took Fendusk. And then he took Kynne. And he now plans to take this realm."

I snort. "Let him try. Vallendor is mine."

"You've forgotten: he's a dangerous asshole, to say the least."

"And I'm a bigger dangerous asshole," I say. "If I recall correctly, this lovely prison of mine still belongs to Supreme. Danar Rrivae can't step one foot on this ground because its prisoner—*me*—is still Vallendor's Grand Defender."

"Correct," Elyn says.

"So, what?" I peer at her. "Should I be scared? Are you warning me that you're his captain and you've turned on Supreme, too? Is he your boss? What do you want?" My fingers are starting to burn.

Elyn watches my fingers with slitted eyes. "He wasn't the only agitator. Like Danar, there was another who didn't seek to rule the realms as commanded by the council. No, this agitator wanted to destroy realms that teetered on the precipice of destruction. Even if a decision hadn't been made, this agitator thought that they knew best. Ithlon, your home, was one of those troubled realms, but no one dared say that Ithlon—the home of little Kaivara and her mother, Lyra, the former lover of Izariel Megidrail, Lord of Mera, your father, a member of the Council of High Orders—needed to be destroyed."

My nostrils flare, and a lump forms in my throat. "I may be quick-tempered and rash at times, but I'd never willfully destroy Ithlon."

"Correct," Elyn says, coming to stand beside me. "But two members of your battalion were spies of Danar. High-ranking Mera who served as your closest confidantes. You knew Ithlon was problematic, but you refused to kill your family. So the generals promised to whisk Lyra and your kin to safe places throughout the realm. You still resisted, but they appeased that part of you needing recognition. They told you that making such a tough and just decision to destroy Ithlon guaranteed your future on the Council, taking your father's place once he ascended. Believing that your family had been taken somewhere safe, you launched the destruction of Ithlon."

She chuckles without humor. "But they lied to you, Kai. Your mother was still on Ithlon when you commanded the first fiery star to fall from the sky and into the Glass Sea. Danar not only took Ithlon—he also destroyed Lyra, your mother. You did exactly what Danar wanted."

Rage burns through my body, narrowing my vision, tinting the world around me. My heart clenches with horror and disbelief as fragmented memories claw their way to the surface of my consciousness. *Screams. Pleas. The crackle of destruction.* My blood chills as shadows creep across my heart. *I* was the fire that destroyed my world. Tears blur my vision as this devastating truth—a truth I can't fully recall—crushes every opinion I have of myself. This anguish now gnaws at my soul—this pain is real. The knowledge that I'm adrift in a sea of remorse and that I am not me—that's real, too.

Three of the emperor's men, their tunics grimy with blood and gore, charge at Elyn and me with pikes outstretched. I focus on the soldier to my right—letting out a fierce growl, I knock the pole from his grip, sweep his legs out from under him, and drive his own weapon through his neck.

Elyn mirrors my actions, dispatching her opponent with a strike to his cheek, piercing flesh and bone.

The remaining soldier, caught between us, faces his doom: two skilled women wielding weapons of destruction. In moments, he loses his left hand and right foot, collapsing in a scream of agony.

Panting, Elyn and I lock eyes once more, ready for the next challenge.

"You should've been punished for going against the Council," Elyn says, glaring at me through narrowed eyes. "Because of that downright insubordination, no one wanted to defend you. But I did, Kai, and as your Adjudicator, I argued that you deserved another chance. I asked that the Council consider your age. Your intention. Your heart. Your commitment to justice, fairness, and equality. That you'd been targeted and misled by the Vile One.

"The realm of Melki. A pisshole, yes, but not sanctioned to be destroyed. You did it anyway. This time, you were punished and stripped of the twenty realms you oversaw. Because you're Lord Mera's daughter, because he begged for you to have another chance and promised that he'd help you correct the errors you made, the Council gave you Vallendor.

"You served as Grand Defender of one realm. And for a moment, you listened to your father, and you did your best to cultivate this place, and the mortals who soon came to populate this realm called you their Lady of the Verdant Realm. Veril Bairnell tried his best to be your sage—he'd been your teacher from birth. But mortals will do as mortals do, and the realm started buckling under corruption, from disease and murder.

"Emperor Wake started his campaign, then, against those who believed in the old god—*you*. You, and rightfully so, lost your mind when that bastard started calling himself 'Supreme.' You wouldn't have it. And thus, the second Great War began, with orders now taking sides. The Renrian and Eserime with you. The Dashmala, some Renrian and Eserime, forced to fight for Wake. All of us—the Council, the Adjudicators—were on your side, Kai.

"That's when you were given approval to destroy Trony Province by the sea, one of the worst provinces in Vallendor, a stronghold of the emperor. You sought to show him your ruthlessness, cunning, and strength, and so you commanded the sea to wash away Trony.

"But then you destroyed Danforth *without* approval," she says. "The worst was Chesterby. You really, *really* hated Chesterby, and you showed it. Water. Fire. Earth. Without approval. That land is still uninhabitable. So many smaller villages, innocents, suffered from that destruction. That's when you were stripped of your battalion, stripped of most of your learned abilities. Some of your soldiers defected to avoid punishment, and they joined Danar Rrivae's mutineers. Your father could no longer protect you, and as your Adjudicator, I was sent here to mete out your punishment.

"By then, you'd destroyed Goldcrest and Eaponys *without an army*—that's how strong you were, Kai. You evaded me, but you were also growing weaker each day—it's not easy to destroy without help if you're not whole. You were tenacious, though, and you ran from me and used the last of your strength to take to the sky. I don't know where you were going, and I don't think you did, either, but in mid-flight, you collapsed from exhaustion and fell from the skies and into the forest outside of Maford."

"I opened my eyes with Olivia's hand around my pendant," I whisper.

"The pattern is repeating, Kai," Elyn says. "You're not as quick as you were before, and so your destruction is slower. The results, though, are the same. Maford—gone. Caerno Woods—burning still. Caburh—wrecked."

"To fight the emperor!" I shout. "To retain control of Vallendor." I shake my head, still unwilling to accept this version of my story. "And if I'm so evil, so reckless, then why did Sybel tell me—"

"Sybel is not an Adjudicator," Elyn says, bristling. "She shouldn't have interfered. Her heart has always ruled her head when it comes to you. She is weak, and her love for Lyra clouds her judgment."

"How do you know who she is or isn't?" I snarl.

"Because," Elyn shouts, "Sybel is my mother!"

My legs buckle as though she'd punched me.

"She was your mother's best friend, too," Elyn says, "and when you were off destroying parts of Vallendor instead of doing your job as Grand Defender here, Sybel took over. Yes, she tried to convince you to save this realm from total destruction. To save this land from *you*, Kai. *You* are the One who will destroy the world—"

"No!" I shout, squeezing my eyes shut. "Enough."

"You know this is true," Elyn says, her voice cracking. "My mother had faith in you. She believed that you could change. She tried her hardest to find a way to tell you about yourself in a way that wouldn't end like this. Because every time, Kai, every time, it ends like this. You keep making the same mistakes. And you've reveled in your disregard of Supreme's will."

I hold my chin high even as my heart shrinks in my chest and my fingers numb.

"You should be ashamed of your actions," she whispers, the muscles in her face twitching. "You should drop your head and beg for forgiveness this very second, but you never remember long enough to do that, and so you've never asked to be forgiven.

"Instead, you took your marking for destroying Ithlon, the second sphere on your shoulder, and you gained courage to take your third one, Melki, but that sphere wasn't enough. You demanded a new one." She touches the space beneath her breast. "Destroyer of Worlds."

Another growl pulls my attention from the white-haired woman standing opposite me. An aburan, with the powerful body of a massive bear and the shrewd eyes of a man, throws himself between Elyn and me. He bellows, baring sharp teeth, and glares at me as if I've deeply wronged him.

Elyn laughs, retreating a few steps, leaving me alone to face the beast. Fine.

"You are no Lady of the Verdant Realm," the aburan snarls. "You have no power—"

Before he can finish, I swing my sword in a swift arc. The blade slices through the air, beheading the creature in a single, fluid motion. His words die on his lips as his body collapses to the blood-soaked ground.

My muscles burn with exhaustion, each movement turning sluggish and heavy. Is this Elyn's plan? To let these otherworldly drain me so thoroughly that she can easily slip her blade into my heart without resistance? The air around me hurts now, and I just want to sit and rest my head against my knees.

Elyn approaches until she stands just a reach away. "You won't ask for mercy, especially now that you have—" She flicks her hand, and she's holding an illusion of my moth amulet.

I look down to see... No, she's holding my amulet.

"You've become too much," Elyn says, "and yet you will never be enough. My mother is wrong. You'll never change. This realm will never survive, because you will never be the god you were born to be—the god that Vallendor Realm needs and deserves."

I wave my hand at the chaos around me. "I didn't start this!"

The battle rages on. More dead otherworldly pile high on both sides.

Elyn surveys the fighting and sighs, her expression sad. "No. But the conditions were perfect for the original usurper to breach the realm."

The original usurper. Danar Rrivae.

"He's come here to take Vallendor from you," she says, "with the help of his associate."

"Emperor Wake."

Elyn nods. "And Wake has been working all this time with Danar Rrivae."

Sybel warned me about Wake.

He is only a consequence of the One, but he is a force working against you. The One is far more powerful.

Danar Rrivae—it's *his* magic that keeps Wake alive. That allows Wake to fight with otherworldly. Not Elyn after all.

And now I remember the last time I saw Danar Rrivae. Kestau, at a garden party before convocation. That afternoon, he smiled at me, tugged one of my braids, said that I was a perfect mixture of Izariel and Lyra. "He called me 'L.D.' Little Destroyer," I whisper now.

"And he's now here to take Vallendor," Elyn says. "And if he wants to do that, then he must kill Vallendor's Grand Defender. He must kill you. And if he kills you, then Danar Rrivae becomes even more powerful, and Vallendor becomes yet one more realm lost to Supreme. But you are his obstacle, Kai. You are the One destroying Vallendor with your power, province by province—and, of course, doing so without consent from the Council of High Orders. Both of you have turned against Supreme, and only one has been punished for that but has escaped final reckoning. That is the job of another Adjudicator. I'm here to complete mine."

My body feels like it's catching fire and tearing in two. And now I know the truth that I'd traveled across Vallendor to learn. Now I know who the One is.

Elyn takes a step away from me. She holds my amulet in one hand and the sword with a silvery-blue blade in the other. The platinum hilt is marked with familiar-looking characters that spell out her name.

"You kill me," I shout, "then you give Danar exactly what he wants."

"I kill you," she shouts back, "then you cannot destroy Vallendor Realm and Danar Rrivae will have no claim to this realm, since he failed to kill its Grand Defender. What happens to Vallendor once you're gone, Kai, will be decided by the Council. Until then…"

She takes another step back and says, "I am Elyn Fynal. As Grand Adjudicator of Vallendor and the Nine Realms, Sentinel and Divine Mediator, with the approval of the Council of High Orders, including Lord Izariel Megidrail, you, Kaivara Megidrail, former Grand Defender of Vallendor, Lady of the Verdant Realm, Destroyer of Worlds…"

Tears glisten in her eyes, and she takes a deep breath. "Kai, I sentence you to death."

"No!" I thrust my hands, and wind bursts from my fingers.

Elyn's knocked off her feet and drops my amulet.

I dive for it, but I feel no tugging like I had before. What's wrong with it? No light pulses from the moth's—

"Stop!" Elyn shouts just as she blasts force toward me, strong enough to slam me back against a hillside and knock the air out of my lungs. Rocks and boulders from above break apart and rain down on us, and we both dodge stones now loosened from the palisade.

Elyn thrusts her hands again, keeping me pinned against the boulder, and the pressure intensifies. Her hair is free of that single braid and drifts like spiderwebs around her head. Her eyes burn gold like fire, and her amulet, that dove, also flares golden, and the air around us smells of crushed jasmine and snuffed-out candles.

"You will not—" I grit my teeth and force her hold off me. Despite the pressure, I manage to conjure and hurl fireballs at her, catching her off guard.

Alarm shines in her eyes, and her pressure weakens for a moment.

Desperate, I lift Fury, my arm shaking as my energy is nearly spent.

Elyn lifts her own sword.

We swing.

The impact of the blades makes sparks fly.

Elyn kicks my chest, knocking me back.

This gives me time, though, to tighten my grip around Fury's handle.

Elyn charges forward and swings—and swings too forcefully.

I parry, and she stumbles. I kick her in the back.

She cries out but spins around.

I don't wait to swing.

She meets my blade with hers and backswings, hitting my side, splicing open the luclite.

With a scream of agony, I send a last burst of wind.

She stumbles but gains her balance and charges forward...

Right into my swing.

The blade nicks her neck, hitting a vein that spurts blood. The grip on her sword loosens as she tries to decide if she should tend to her neck or keep swinging. She holds up a hand, and I watch as she conjures tiny bolts of lightning that pop from her fingers.

But she's waited too long.

My fireball hits her hand before she can get a bolt off.

She screams again, her face twisting. She may be a judge, but she is no warrior. She nurses her left hand but sets her feet anyway. Her glazed eyes flick past me.

Is that fear or acceptance that she will end soon?

I knock her back again with a tiny puff of wind.

She presses against the bleeding wound in her neck, so weak that my pitiful burst makes her stumble backward. Her eyes flick away from me again. She takes a deep breath, grabs her sword, and staggers in my direction, her sword as high as she can hold it.

I step forward to meet her swing but knock her back with a kick.

She drops her sword again.

I kick that sword up with the toe of my boot. Now I have dual blades. One with a bloody handle.

Elyn's eyes widen. "Kai—"

"I know," I say. "And I'm not even wearing fancy fucking armor. Give me my amulet."

"Kai—" Something in my expression alarms her, and she tosses the amulet to the ground. Her nostrils flare, and she looks behind me with wild eyes.

"What are you looking for?" I ask, drawing closer. I'm not cocky, though. Dying snakes always have one last bite left—and that bite can kill. "Keep hoping, Grand Adjudicator, blah-blah-blah. No one's gonna save you."

The muscles in Elyn's face relax. "Oh, but you're wrong. He will."

This time, I look over my shoulder and see that her help has arrived.

Jadon.

62

Jadon Wake stands twenty paces behind me, sword in hand. Thick fog builds behind him, and his face eases with the relief of seeing me alive… and then his face goes rigid with the *dread* of seeing me alive.

All my anger and concern for him, all those feelings that could've turned into love given the time, burn up my throat like fire. I want to scream, and I want to run to him. But I do neither. No, I slip my amulet over my head and grip Fury's hilt tighter before moving away from Elyn.

My lips tighten into a scowl. "You're the last person I want to see right now."

Behind Jadon, the battle continues. The yellow-gray sludge from the sea hisses, the acid burning leather, steel, and flesh. The vapors of sulfur and rot make it difficult for any living thing to breathe, and eventually every living lung will disintegrate. No vibrant colors exist here — nothing sparkling yellow or vivid blue. Sickness, that's what I'm reminded of. Desiccated flesh after the best parts have been eaten away by animals and time.

Jadon closes some of the distance between us, and some of my anger slips into hurt — my skin tender again from his stabs of falseness and duplicity. In his new uniform and that pearl-gray armor, he's beautiful, and he takes away what little breath I have. His hair, thick and dark, has been washed. He's shaved. He's —

"Well, look at *this*." Elyn laughs as she stands, hand still pressed against her now-healing laceration. "*The* Kai Megidrail, Destroyer of Worlds, all dewy-eyed over a *boy*." She chuckles again. "The blacksmith, not the prince, has swept her off her feet. Good job, Ser Wake."

Jadon keeps his gaze fixed to mine. Since I can no longer hear his thoughts, I try to read his expression, but I can't decipher that, either.

The roar of battle grows louder, bouncing off the surface of the sea and splattering against Mount Devour's steep granite walls. Burning this and sooty that. Ash and acid, swords and screaming. The earth beneath us quakes as men and otherworldly throw each other around. Danar Rrivae's otherworldly battling Elyn's otherworldly—each side fighting for a realm that doesn't belong to either. Because to gain ultimate control of this realm, they need to kill me, but I will never surrender the only world that's mine.

I will not die by any mortal man's sword. I will not die by Elyn's sword. I will not die by Danar Rrivae's sword. I'm not dying, period.

"You've been working against me all this time," I say to Jadon. "You've wanted Vallendor for yourself, your brother and father. Why are you here? To kill both Elyn and me?"

Jadon doesn't speak, so I turn to Elyn. "Why is he here?"

One side of her mouth lifts into a smile. "One step at a time, Kai."

She has nerve to be as cocky as she is, considering I still grip her sword in my hand. I stow Fury and study Elyn's blade. So light. So beautiful.

Now I read aloud those engravings across the blade. "*Arbiter. Judge. Truth. Mediator. Justice. Life. Death.* Absolutely gorgeous," I say, peering at the sword's hilt. "Too bad you didn't get to use it." I turn a gaze sharper than this blade to Jadon Wake.

He stands there, silent and unreadable.

Does he feel guilty for abandoning me? For betraying my trust? Does he even care? No. Did he *ever* care? No. He and his family need to kill me—they want what they want. *Vallendor.*

"Not even going to say one word?" I would kill to hear his voice, to see him drop that stony countenance and be the blacksmith again. To be my friend. But that man is gone, replaced by this soldier before me.

He's like a statue on this muddy ground as he stares at me with his jaw clenched. The shadows in the sky slide across his face, making him look somehow...*more.* A glow pulses between his bones and skin.

"Good. We're all here."

I turn to see a man strolling across the plains. He moves toward us, but his feet don't touch the ground—he can't touch the ground because this realm is not his. So, his countenance is flat because he is here but...*not.* He is an apparition.

My stomach drops, and my mouth goes dry. I recognize this man.

Danar Rrivae stands behind Jadon, nearly dwarfing him. He's as broad as three men, and his long, gray hair is captured in a ribbon that crests down to the middle of his back. His crimson-inked markings look bold against skin that's sick-looking, white and lilac. He wears no tunic, and those markings of spheres connected by swirling vines cover the left side of his chest. Signifiers of all the realms he's destroyed.

There's the crescent of Kestau Realm—it used to be. There, near his hip bone, are the stars of Fendusk Realm—that used to be, too. And others. So many destroyed realms. A few ordained and sanctioned. The rest: mutiny.

Danar Rrivae cares nothing about order or duty. He cares nothing about love and sacrifice, wisdom and legacy. He abhors the work of Eserime and Renrians and peoples from the realms that are no more— they're now only trophies of his rebellion. He wants what he wants. And he kills to take it. He wants *everything*.

A chill seeps through the soles of my boots.

Have I become him? A specter of malice and cold ambition, flowing through my veins like poison? This realization claws within me—that I might be this man's echo, his shadow.

No. I won't have it. My hands ball into fists, even as I fight within myself against the seduction of power, vengeance, and justified cruelty. I think of the path I cut across Vallendor, especially, and I'm sickened by my dearth of empathy, patience, love... *Temperance.*

I may be quick to act, quick to judge, but I am not Danar Rrivae. I might as well be, though—a cruel oppressor who wants what she wants, no matter the cost. I've forgotten so much, but I now remember who I am, who I've longed to be.

The usurper stands behind Jadon like a father standing over his son. His breath clouds from his mouth, not with frost but with fire.

"Little Defender," Danar Rrivae says, smiling at me. "My, how you've grown. You'll have to excuse my own...*appearance*."

"You can't step a foot on Vallendor," I say, eyebrows furrowed.

"No," he says, "not until I conquer it. But how do I conquer without physically setting my feet on the ground? I seek help. In Vallendor, the Wakes lead this effort on my behalf, just like men in other realms who desire power and will do as I ask to acquire it. No, Kai, I can't kill you because I'm unable to personally slide the sharpest blade across your neck. But that's the job of the Wakes, again, on my behalf. And by the looks of it..." He casts his eyes to the realm beyond us. All that fighting and death. "I'm not worried. This won't take much longer."

My mouth goes dry, and I grit my teeth so hard my head aches. My focus returns to Elyn, now trying to hide her sneer and disgust at the sight of Danar but failing miserably.

"You asked what this is?" he says. "Power. That's what this is. I give

Emperor Wake what he wants—power to rule all of Vallendor—and he gives me what I want."

"Which is?" I ask, ignoring the ache behind my eyes.

He flounces a hand around. "To have what Supreme has: worshippers. I've given Wake a weapon to conquer every province without killing *everyone*—you must have living beings to be worshipped. Wake enjoys power in this realm. I gain more power in the realmscape."

Elyn now openly glares at Danar—if she hates *me*, then she must loathe this traitor, this evil, the Vile One.

I can agree with Elyn on this—I too am repulsed by this... "Piece of shit" does not capture what I think about him. I scan my brain for any word and find the Dindt vulgarity *scantivant*, the shit of the shit.

Jadon looks back at the battle behind us, where Gileon wields that giant sword of his with more ease than seems possible.

"You are the reason Wake and his sons are so strong," I say to Danar. "You are the magic that lets a mortal kill otherworldly," I continue. "To block me from hearing their thoughts."

Jadon's head snaps back to me. "Hearing their thoughts? You could hear—?"

"Oh, now you speak?" I ask him, eyebrow high.

"You really think your thoughts are terribly interesting to a woman who's had *gods*?" Elyn snarks. "As her former best friend who's met some of them, I can say"—she looks Jadon up and down—"she's had better."

"I don't care about any of this," Danar interrupts, flicking his hand toward the fighting. "Emperor Wake prayed for my help, and I obliged."

A howl from the battlefield captures Jadon's attention, and he whips his head back to where Gileon is now boxed in by a leolsip and a worupine.

Jadon murmurs, "Shit."

Danar chuckles. "Don't worry, young prince. I won't let anyone slay him before you do."

"*Slay?* You're *betraying* your brother?" I ask, alarmed and wide-eyed.

"No," Jadon says. "Gileon and I..." He glares at Danar Rrivae. "Gileon and I are fighting against our father."

"What?" Danar glares and takes a step forward.

I swallow the lump in my throat, and I slump only a little—is it because Jadon isn't as terrible as I thought, and I've misunderstood everything that's happened?

"Gileon and I will not let Emperor Wake rule all of Vallendor," Jadon says. "He will not succeed." Jadon takes a step toward me and whispers, "Kai—"

Jadon saying my name… He's said it so many times, but this time, he sounds different. Gruff. Dominant. Reckless. "Let me explain," he says with that voice of three, and taller now than he was just moments ago.

What is this? Am I imagining his transformation? Has the noise of battle harmed my ears? He was always a formidable man, but now… He is *impossible*. His voice—three different registers at the same time—is impossible. For a *mortal*.

Maybe it's not Danar who's granting Jadon his power. Maybe he needs nothing from Danar because he's…*something else*. I look to his hand and to that tattoo he's tried to keep covered. Like my own markings, his are indicative of something more. More than human.

My throat closes, and I taste the salt of my tears. I whisper his name and shake my head. "You're not…? Danar used you to find me?" I look back over my shoulder. "Or did *she* use you to find me?" I close my eyes as my skin becomes clammy. "Or were they using you to find me?"

Jadon opens his mouth to speak but drops his head instead.

Then I face Elyn. "And you, *Adjudicator*. How dare you pass judgment when you're working with the usurper to capture me. Does the Council of High Orders know that you're a traitor? That you're partnering with the Vile One to do your job?"

Elyn marches up to me until we're nose to nose. "I'm no traitor. And I don't consider myself his partner. Yes, we have the same goal—to kill you—but that's where our comity ends. And once you're dead, Kai, and this realm is without its Grand Defender, Vallendor will *still* remain a realm of Supreme's. I don't care what Danar Rrivae believes or how strong he thinks he is. I will not allow him to take this realm."

"Good. However…" I push her away from me. "You're not gonna kill me." I draw Fury, and I'm back to wielding two blades.

Elyn sighs dramatically. "Do I have to do everything around here?" She frowns at the usurper. "You've underestimated her. You claimed that your *weapon* would drop the Grand Defender to her knees."

"To my knees?" I ask, laughing. "You'll never find me on my knees."

Danar raises an eyebrow at Elyn. "The Grand Defender *has* dropped to her knees, to the delight of…my weapon."

"What is he talking about?" I ask Elyn. "What weapon?"

Elyn's eyes flick at me, then flick to Jadon, and that's where they stay.

I shake my head until the cords of my neck go rigid and I can no longer move.

"Have you ever wondered why you've felt as weak as you have, Kai?" she asks.

"Yes," I say. "I haven't worn my amulet. I don't have true armor. This realm is a dump."

"It's more than that, Kai," Elyn says.

Jadon's nostrils flare as he scowls at Elyn. "You don't have to do this."

"Have you ever wondered," Elyn continues, "why your skin burns only when a certain someone *touches* you?"

I whisper, "Yes," nervous now. Because that someone who made me burn is standing across from me.

"Jadon Ealdrehrt," Elyn says, arms folded. "No, I'm sorry. Jadon *Wake*. Oh, damn it, I'm wrong again. Jadon Wake *Rrivae*. *He* is the weapon."

Speechless, I turn to Jadon.

Elyn continues. "Ser Wake is the weapon who served both my purpose and Danar's."

"*You* tell me," I say, pointing at Jadon. "I want to hear it from you." My breathing becomes thick, and everything I want to say lodges in my throat, strangling me. Once again, I've become the fool, the dupe, the only one not in on the joke.

"Kai," Elyn whispers, forcing me to look back to her, "Jadon *is* Miasma. He is sickness—he is death itself. He was *born* to destroy Vallendor for Danar, his *father*. More than that, he was born to destroy *you*." There is no lie in her eyes nor is there hesitation in her words.

I gape at Jadon, hurt and ire mixing in my gut, nauseating me. Stuck between icy panic and fiery rage, I want to sit and surrender. But numbness sweeps over me, shielding me from feeling nothing, protecting me against the fatal strikes of submission. "Is she speaking the truth?" I ask him now, nearly stripped of emotion.

"We weren't supposed to become friends," Jadon says in his new voice. "But we did, and I thought..." He rubs his jaw, looking like Old Jadon in that moment. "I wanted time. I wanted what I wanted even if you were the Grand Defender. I wanted *you*. I didn't want to hurt you, but I knew every time I touched you, I destroyed pieces of you."

I drop my head and study Elyn's blade. "Why...?"

"Emperor Wake has a powerful heir and enforcer in Jadon," Elyn says, her gaze also settled on her sword. "And Danar has basically the same—

but instead of the power that Wake wants, Danar wants the *realm*. Both men need Jadon to be the same thing, and both men need you dead to get what they want."

Powerless, Danar paces behind Jadon, his skin blazing hot, his glare hot enough to scorch all of Vallendor—that is, if he could touch it.

Jadon fixes me with his gaze, then raises his arms. "I was supposed to end this right after you returned from seeing Sybel in the forest." He runs his hand over his hair. "After you confirmed that you were the Lady of the Verdant Realm. But by then I cared for you too much, and I found myself falling in love with you."

Danar growls hearing Jadon's declaration, his hands clenching and unclenching.

Jadon levels his shoulders, and his jaw hardens. "At the same time, I saw how powerful you were even without your pendant, and I realized that you'd been helping do my job. To destroy Vallendor. So I used you, yes, as *my* weapon. But that's how I justified keeping you alive—and how I will fight to keep you alive."

Elyn whirls around to face Jadon, her eyes hot. "That wasn't the agreement."

Danar's eyebrows furrow, and he glowers at her. "What agreement?"

"That tat of yours?" Elyn says, sneering now at Jadon. "I won't remove it. I won't break your bond to this evil now."

The marking on his hand?

Jadon throws off his gauntlet, showing the circular tattoo that he'd hidden behind a bandage. "Then I'll cut it off myself!"

He turns to me. "I was slowly destroying everyone around me, making entire towns sick, but I was hurting you, too, speeding your end, and I didn't want that—not yet. So I tried to keep this covered whenever you were near."

"Kai," Elyn says, "your original role as Grand Defender was the opposite of Jadon's. His is death. Yours was life. In balanced realms, the two work together, with the same mission. But no longer."

Jadon's eyes flicker with the ever-changing light of his armor. "I wanted a new direction, a new purpose. My own purpose that wasn't controlled by the emperor or by Danar. That's why I asked Elyn to help me, to remove this—" He lifts his marked hand. "I'm done with this shit, Kai, and I want to start again. Be someone new. And I want to do that with you."

"Now?" I shriek.

All of this is inevitable. Unavoidable. He told me that before leaving me alone in that cave.

There is no "us," Kai. There never was.

This isn't the way it was supposed to go. He said that, too.

"And what about Gileon Wake?" I ask. "He knows you as his brother—"

"He *is* my brother," Jadon says.

"But Elyn just called you… Are you a Wake? Are you Mera?"

"Yes and no," he says. "Danar and my mother, the queen… They… They…"

"We spent one blissful night together," Danar says with a shrug and smile. "It was the emperor's idea. The queen didn't mind doing her part for the empire. Jadon's just like these beasts behind you, Kai. My own spectacular creation."

I gape at Jadon. "You're otherworldly."

Jadon Ealdrehrt was born a god. The women in the barn said that. *No one else fights like that. A god living among men.*

No, a demigod.

Shit.

If they only knew.

If *I'd* only known.

My sorrow slowly burns to become rage.

Elyn Fynal, the Adjudicator, wants me dead for her reasons.

Danar Rrivae wants me dead for his.

And then there's Jadon. He finds my eyes again and takes a step forward, away from his creator. "I won't do it, Kai. I won't destroy you."

"That's your purpose, son," Danar Rrivae rumbles. "You do not *choose.* You are what I say you are. There is no free will in my realm."

Elyn's eyes flash blue. "This isn't your realm."

"I won't destroy her," Jadon challenges, backing away from his creator.

"Oh, but you will," Danar snarls. "She is worth *everything.*"

This realm will never survive, because you will never be the god you were born to be—the god that Vallendor Realm needs and deserves.

Elyn's words.

"You failed to live up to our agreement," Elyn says, pointing at Danar.

"We're here *because* of me," Danar spits back. "I created him. He stopped her."

"*Stopped her?*" Elyn shrieks. "She's standing in front of me, holding my fucking blade! She will destroy us all!"

I hold Jadon's desperate gaze. He and I…weapons both.

"I won't destroy the world with him, Kai," Jadon says, desperate. "Nor will I rule this realm with Gileon. I want to share Vallendor with you, Kai. I want to rule this realm with you by my side and make Vallendor what it *should* be."

She will destroy us all.

Jadon's eyes now flicker between desperation and hope. I glare at Danar; his fury shoots around him like sparks. Finally, I look back to Elyn Fynal, whose face is soft and her smirk certain that she'll win this fight. Three otherworldly against one.

Jadon races toward me. "Kai," he shouts, his heart landing on hope. "I choose you."

My knees creak—I'm weakening, poisoned by the man I thought I loved.

But I can't leave Vallendor—I'm imprisoned here.

For Danar, my death means the Grand Defender, Vallendor's protector, is gone, and Vallendor can be his, another realm captured.

For Elyn, my death means that she's successfully done her job. *Justice.* But then she must also deny Danar his plans to take Vallendor. This means killing Danar's weapon on the ground. *Jadon.*

My options:

Die by Elyn's blade.

Die by Danar's weapon: Jadon.

The man who wants me to now rule beside him as empress of Vallendor. The liar who resisted the edict to kill me in my sleep. The demigod who isn't stronger than me but is still more powerful than I am right now.

Kai, I choose you.

Jadon chooses me because he loves me.

And I choose…

To survive and live another day.

I choose…

To use him to help me kill Elyn Fynal before she can kill me.

To use him to help me kill the usurper, Danar Rrivae, and return to Supreme every realm stolen by the Vile One.

To bide my time, regain my strength, then wait until I'm strong enough to destroy the emperor-to-be, Jadon Wake Rrivae.

To make amends.

This is what I choose.

She will destroy us all. Such a prophetic statement.

Because yes, I will.

And so I smile at Jadon, and I rush toward him, my mind racing, my hands out, but my heart blocked, my core balled into a giant fist, ready to rule a realm that's already mine, a realm that will ultimately have one god. *Me.*

My fingertips brush his.

"No!" Elyn rams herself between Jadon and me, and with one great push of wind, she blows Jadon to the banks of Devour, and with another great push of wind, she sends me high into the—

Epilogue

I stare at the sky and the newly forming clouds. I taste sweat. I taste the salt of old tears. I taste fear. That's the most bitter... Copper—I now taste copper. I sit up from my nest of dry leaves and swipe my mouth—my fingers come back bright with blood.

A moth with black, gold, and red wings flits around me. I hold out my bloody finger, and the moth lands. I smile at her and whisper, "Hello."

The moth leaves my finger, and I watch her flutter away, disappearing into the wasteland around me. The only green is the dying tree whose branches hide me from elements that killed the creatures whose skeletons now scar these badlands.

The daystar barely peeks over the horizon in the east, and the already-red sky brightens to scarlet while the volcanic land warms beneath it. That light rushes through my blood, buzzes through me, and pushes past my armor, from my cloak and breeches to my gloves and boots. My amulet—a jewel-encrusted moth—hangs from my neck and shines as though it's on fire. Like it holds the very essence of my life.

Where am I?

A dying realm with dying trees, dying animals, and dying hope.

Why am I here?

My mind flickers with images of...

A sea of acid.

A mountain soaring past the clouds.

A woman with white hair.

"Vallendor Realm," I whisper, my eyes closed.

The Weapon.

The blacksmith.

The Destroyer of Worlds.

I open my eyes and stare at the dying leaves rustling above me.

I am the Destroyer of Worlds.

Yes. I remember...

I remember *everything.*

Acknowledgments

Thanks to you, reader, for trusting me enough to read this story. Some of you knew me as a crime writer, some of you didn't know me at all. Either way, I hope I offered you a story that you loved and that lingered with you for a moment.

Jill, for ten years now, you've guided my writing career. I'm incredibly blessed to be able to thank you in the Acknowledgments pages of eleven (!) novels. Your wisdom and honesty, vision and will—not just for a book but for my career—is a gift. Back in July 2022, I cocked my head and said, "*Fantasy*? But I write..." There was something there, though, that you wanted me to see. Please don't ever retire. If you do, please keep me as a client on the DL. We'll create a shell literary agency, à la *Weekend at Bernie's*, but you're very much alive and enjoying a weekend in the Maldives—while still rolling calls. (Jess, you can join us but *ssh!* It's a secret.)

Liz Pelletier, YOU ARE A GENIUS. No, really. Seriously. Jill told me you were extraordinary—and she was right! I am left agog every time you think of something, *anything, EVERYTHING*. This book couldn't have happened without you first saying, "You know...like *The Lord of the Rings* and *Stranger Things* but...*you*." Thank you for taking a chance on this mystery-crime writer and for being so generous with your time and your heart.

Alice, MY GAWD, don't ever leave me! We did SO MUCH together, I feel like we should get matching tattoos. Editing the final draft was life-changing. No hyperbole. I could do it only because you and Liz were there, thinking of all the things I couldn't, whisper-writing suggestions in Comments, until there it was, in my brain—the path that I couldn't see. You're a blessing. Like...for real.

Molly, Rae, Elana, and Hannah, thanks for your editorial guidance. You helped ease me into this new world, and I appreciate everything you did to make this story shine.

To my Marketing, Publicity, and Production teams at Red Tower. You all are like, wizards. I can't believe you just...*think of stuff and do cool things*. Like, what *is* that? Lizzy, Heather, Brittany, thank you for thinking of stuff and doing cool things for me. Bree, your artwork is so incredible, I changed some ideas around to match your visuals. Thanks for putting your foot in it. Curtis, Lydia, Nancy, Mary, Britt, and those I haven't met but are there working hard, I appreciate all you do for me.

Eleanor Imbody, Hailey Dezort, Kaitlyn Kennedy, and all the smart people at Kaye Publicity, and Crystal Patriarche, Grace Fell, Taylor Brightwell, and all the brilliant people at BookSparks—thank you for spreading the word and pushing me to the front of the line.

Jessica Tribble Wells, Clarence Haynes, and Kristin Sevick, thank you for guiding me in this writing journey. You've helped me become a stronger writer and convinced me enough that I actually had the nerve to try something new.

To my day-job friends, especially Arielle, Shawna, Patty, Camille, Rachel, and Zahra. You've made my weekdays joyful. Thanks for covering for me while I was away doing book stuff.

To my writer friends, in particular Jess, Kellye, and Yasmin. You've hugged me in person and across the digital realm. You've helped me navigate some jacked-up waters and encouraged me to keep on writing because you saw that there was smooth sailing ahead. I'll never forget your friendship.

To my childhood-adulthood buddies-neighbors, thank you for getting me out of the house. From wine-tasting or slapping dominoes on a table, to sipping coffee or Paper Planes, you know how to lure me out of my Bat Cave.

Terry, Gretchen, and Jason, you've been the best brothers and sister I could ever have. We're still here learning new things about one another, and that's scary cuz we're, like, old now. You're always, every day, in my heart. I love you guys.

Mom and Dad (may his memory be a blessing), I love you both. Hard work and good planning. Compassion and obsession. You've instilled in me these four concepts, and I've embraced them wholeheartedly over my life—even when it just all seemed simply exhausting. Thank you for believing that I could do it.

Maya Grace, your love and excitement make me want to be the best mom ever. Thank you for being my bestie while also remaining my little sweets, and for watching *The Golden Girls* with me before bed whenever you're home. You will forever be my Beyoncé Buddy and my heroine (and now, in a fantasy setting). I love you more.

David, you are always down for an existential conversation, even in the middle of a rib-eye dinner, while playing *Baldur's Gate 3*, or during a real-life challenge. We've done a lot of that last thing over the last two years, supporting each other in new ways and in difficult times. We continue to grow up together—and this book is a manifestation of that. Also, after almost thirty years, your geekdom *finally* came in handy (snort, ha). Thank you for traveling this road beside me. I love you.

CONNECT WITH US ONLINE